TODAY'S BEST MAINE FICTION

Other books by Wesley McNair

The Faces of Americans in 1853

The Town of No

Twelve Journeys in Maine

My Brother Running

The Quotable Moose: A Contemporary Maine Reader (editor)

The Dissonant Heart

Talking in the Dark

Fire

Mapping the Heart: Reflections on Place and Poetry

The Maine Poets (editor)

A Place on Water (co-author)

The Ghosts of You and Me

A Place Called Maine (editor)

TODAY'S BEST
MAINE
FICTION

Edited by Wesley McNair

Down East

Cover painting:
"Solo Boat VH" © by Connie Hayes, *www.conniehayes.com*

Printed on acid-free paper by Versa Press, Inc., East Peoria, Illinois

5   4   3   2   1

ISBN 978-0-89272-781-0

BOOKS·MAGAZINE·ONLINE
www.downeast.com

The Library of Congress has cataloged the hardcover edition as follows:

Contemporary Maine fiction : an anthology of short stories /
edited by Wesley McNair.
        p. cm.
    ISBN 0-89272-693-8 (trade hardcover : acid-free paper)
    1. Short stories, American--Maine. 2. Maine--Social life and customs--Fiction.
I. McNair, Wesley.
    PS548.M2C66 2005
    813'.01089741'090511--dc22
                                                                    2005009464

For my fellow storytellers
Bob Kimber and Bill Roorbach

Contents

Introduction

This anthology, which gathers short stories by fourteen fiction writers of Maine, would not have been possible just a few years ago. But in the recent past something remarkable has taken place: one by one, several highly gifted writers have moved to the state to make their home here, including Richard Ford, Richard Russo, Debra Spark, Ellen Cooney, Bill Roorbach, and Lily King. Moreover, native writers such as Lewis Robinson and Jim Nichols have emerged with debut collections of their short stories, enriching the state's production of fiction even further.

Not, mind you, that Maine needed to apologize for its lineup of fiction writers before the newcomers appeared. There were plenty of good writers living and working here—the literary celebrities Stephen King and Carolyn Chute, for instance, and well-known authors like Susan Kenney, Monica Wood, Elaine Ford, and Cathie Pelletier. Still, the new arrivals have added their own luster to the state's literary offering, making it undeniable that Maine fiction has fully come of age.

A central purpose of *Today's Best Maine Fiction* is to celebrate the unusual depth and diversity of fiction that all of the writers named above, and various others who are not named, have brought us. As Maine's unique geography and people are constant presences throughout this collection, the anthology also pays tribute to the influence the state has had on the vision of its authors, whether they are recent residents or long-standing ones. Finally, this book celebrates storytelling, so richly on display in these fourteen wonderful short stories, each a striking example of the storyteller's art.

Wesley McNair
Mercer, Maine
July 2005

Monica Wood

Ernie's Ark

Ernie was an angry man. He felt his anger as something apart from him, like an urn of water balanced on his head, a precarious weight that affected his gait, the set of his shoulders, his willingness to move through a crowd. He was angry at the melon-faced CEO from New York City who had forced a strike in a paper mill all the way up in Maine—a decision made, Ernie was sure, in that fancy restaurant atop the World Trade Center where Ernie had taken his wife, Marie, for their forty-fifth wedding anniversary last winter, another season, another life. Every Thursday as he stood in line at Manpower Services to wait for his unemployment check he thought of that jelly-assed CEO—Henry John McCoy, with his parted blond hair—yucking it up at a table laid out in bleached linen and phony silver, figuring out all the ways he could cut a man off at the knees three weeks before retirement.

Oh, yes, he was angry. At the deadbeats and no-accounts who stood in line with him: the Davis boy, who couldn't look a man in the eye; the Shelton girl, with hair dyed so bright you could light a match on her ponytail. There were others in line—millwrights and tinsmiths and machine tenders whose years and labor had added up to a puff of air—but he couldn't bear to look at them, so he reserved his livid stare for the people in line who least resembled himself.

He was angry at the kids from Broad Street who cut through his yard on their dirt bikes day after day, leaving moats of mud through the flowery back lawn Marie had sprinkled a season ago with

Meadow-in-a-Can. He was angry with the police department, who didn't give a hoot about Marie's wrecked grass. He'd even tried city hall, where an overpaid blowhard, whose uncle had worked beside Ernie nineteen years ago on the Number Five, had all but laughed in his face.

When he arrived at the hospital after collecting his weekly check, Marie was being bathed by a teenage orderly. He had seen his wife in all manner of undress over the years, yet it filled him with shame to observe the yellow hospital sponge applied to her diminishing body by a uniformed kid who was younger than their only grandchild. He went to the lobby to wait, picking up a newspaper from among the litter of magazines.

It was some sort of city weekly, filled with mean political cartoons and smug picture captions fashioned to embarrass the president, but it had a separate section on the arts, Marie's favorite subject. She had dozens of coffee-table books stowed in her sewing room, and their house was filled with framed prints of strange objects—melted watches and spent shoelaces and sad, deserted diners—that he never liked but had nonetheless come to think of as old friends. He had never known her to miss a community concert or an exhibit at the library where she had worked three days a week since she was eighteen; every Sunday of their married life, Ernie had brought in the paper, laid it on the kitchen table, and fished out the arts section to put next to Marie's coffee cup.

The weekly was printed on dirty newsprint—paper from out of state, he surmised. He scanned the cheap, see-through pages, fixing on an announcement for an installation competition, whatever that was. The winning entry would be displayed to the public at the college. Pictured was last year's winner, a tangle of pipes and sheet metal that looked as if somebody had hauled a miniature version of the Number Five machine out of the mill, twisted it into a thousand ugly pieces, then left it to weather through five hundred hailstorms. Not that it would matter now if somebody did. *The Burden of Life*, this installation was called, by an artist who most likely hadn't yet moved

out of his parents' house. He thought Marie would like it, though—
she had always been a woman who understood people's intentions—
so he removed the picture with his jackknife and tucked it into his
shirt pocket. Then he faltered his way back up the hall and into her
room, where she was sitting up, weak and clean.

"What's the latest?" she asked him.

He sat down on her bleach-smelling bed. She herself smelled of
lilac. "McCoy's threatening to fold up shop."

"Sell it, you mean?" She blinked at him. "Sell the mill?"

"That's the rumor."

She put her fragile, ghostly hand on his. "It's been eight months,
Ernie. How long can a strike last?" She was thinking, of course, of his
pension held hostage, the bills she was racking up.

"We'll be all right," he said. The word *we* always calmed him. He
showed her the clipping. "Can you feature this?"

She smiled. *"The Burden of Life"*?

"He should've called it The Burden of My Big Head."

She laughed, and he was glad, and his day took the tiniest turn.
"Philistine," she said. "You always were such a philistine, Ernie."
She often referred to him in the past tense, as if he were the one
departing.

That night, after the long drive home, he hung the clipping on
the refrigerator before taking Pumpkin Pie, Marie's doddering
Yorkshire terrier, for its evening walk. He often waited until nightfall
for this walk, so mortified was he to drag this silly-name pushbroom
of an animal at the end of a thin red leash. The dog walked with prissy
little steps on pinkish feet that resembled ballerina slippers. He had
observed so many men just like himself over the years, men in retirement walking wee, quivery dogs over the streets of their neighborhood, a wrinkled plastic bag in their free hand; they might as well
have been holding a sign above their heads: Widower.

The night was eerie and silent. FOR SALE signs had popped up even
in this neighborhood of old people. This small, good place, once
drenched with ordinary hopes and decent money, was beginning to

13

furl like an autumn leaf. At the foot of the downhill slope of Randall Street, Ernie could see the belching smokestacks of Atlantic Pulp & Paper, the dove-gray plume curling up from the valley, an upward, omnipresent cloud rising like a smoke signal, an offering to God. Cancer Valley, a news reporter once called the city of Abbott Falls, but they needed the steam, the smoke, the rising cloud, the heaps and heaps of wood stacked in the railyard, even the smell—the smell of money, Ernie called it—they needed it. He thought of the son of a bitch working his very spot, this very night, wiping the greasy heat from his forehead; he wondered which of life's cruelties had converged upon this man to impel him to cross a picket line, step over a man with a dying wife, and steal his job. Did he, too, have a dying wife? Eight months ago, watching the first of them marching in there under police guard, he could not have mustered a human feeling for the stranger hooking up chlorine cars or running pipe in the bleachery. Ernie's own circumstances, his own livelihood, seemed to melt farther into dream every day. Every few weeks there was word of negotiation—another fancy-restaurant meeting between McCoy's boys and the national union—but Ernie held little hope of recovering the bulk of his pension. That, too, felt like knowledge found in a dream.

As he turned up his front walk, he caught the kids from Broad Street crashing again through his property, this time roaring away so fast he could hear a faint shudder from the backyard trees. "Sonsabitches!" he hollered, shaking his fist like the mean old man in the movies. He stampeded into the backyard, where Marie's two apple trees, brittle and untrained, sprouted from the earth in such rootlike twists that they seemed to have been planted upside down. He scanned the weedy lawn, dotted with exhausted clumps of Marie's wildflowers and the first of the fallen leaves, and saw blowdown everywhere, spindly parts of branches scattered like bodies on a battlefield. Planted when their son was born, the trees had never yielded a single decent apple, and now they were being systematically mutilated by a pack of ill-bred boys. He picked up a branch and a few sticks, and by the time he reached his kitchen he was weeping, pounding his fist on the table, cursing a God who would let a woman like Marie, a big-boned girl who was sweetness itself, wither beneath the death-white sheets of Western Maine General, thirty-eight miles from home.

He sat in the kitchen deep into evening. The dog curled up on Marie's chair and snored. Ernie remembered Marie's laughter from the afternoon and tried to harness it, hear it anew, make it last. The sticks lay sprawled and messy on the table in front of him, their leaves stalled halfway between greenery and dust. All of a sudden—and, oh, it was sweet!—Ernie had an artistic inspiration. He stood up with the shock of it, for he was not an artistic man. The sticks, put together at just the right angle, resembled the hull of a boat. He turned them one way, then another, admiring his idea, wishing Marie were here to witness it.

Snapping on the floodlights, he jaunted into the backyard to collect the remaining sticks, hauling them into the house a bouquet at a time. He took the clipping down from the fridge and studied the photograph, trying to get a sense of scale and size. Gathering the sticks, he descended the stairs to the cellar, where he spent most of the night twining sticks and branches with electrical wire. The dog sat at attention, its wet eyes fixed on Ernie's work. By morning the installation was finished. It was the most beautiful thing Ernie had ever seen.

The college was only four blocks from the hospital, but Ernie had trouble navigating the maze of one-way roads on campus, and found the art department only by following the directions of a frightening girl whose tender lips had been pierced with small gold rings. By the time he entered the lavender art office, he was sweating, hugging his beautiful boat to his chest.

"Excuse me?" said a young man at the desk. This one had a hoop through each eyebrow.

"My installation," Ernie said, placing it on the desk. "For the competition." He presented the newspaper clipping like an admission ticket.

"Uh, I don't think so."

"Am I early?" Ernie asked, feeling foolish. The deadline was six weeks away; he hadn't the foggiest idea how these things were supposed to go.

"This isn't an installation," the boy said, flickering his gaze over the boat. "It's—well, I don't know what it is, but it's not an installation."

"It's a boat," Ernie said. "A boat filled with leaves."

"Are you in Elderhostel?" the boy asked. "They're upstairs, fifth floor."

"I want to enter the contest," Ernie said. And by God, he did; he had never won so much as a cake raffle in his life, and didn't like one bit the pileup of things he appeared to be losing.

"I like your boat," said a girl stacking books in a corner. "But he's right, it's not an installation." She spread her arms and smiled. "Installations are big."

Ernie turned to face her, a freckled redhead. She reminded him of his granddaughter, who was somewhere in Alaska sharing her medicine cabinet with an unemployed guitar player. "Let me see," the girl said, plucking the clipping from his hand. "Oh, okay. You're talking about the Corthell Competition. This is more of a professional thing."

"Professional?"

"I myself wouldn't *dream* of entering, okay?" offered the boy, who rocked backed in his chair, arms folded like a CEO's. "All the entries come through this office, and most of them are awesome. Museum quality." He made a small, self-congratulating gesture with his hand. "We see the entries even before the judges do."

"One of my professors won last year," the girl said, pointing out the window. "See?"

Ernie looked. There it was, huge in real life—nearly as big as the actual Number Five, in fact, a heap of junk flung without a thought into the middle of a campus lawn. It did indeed look like a Burden.

"You couldn't tell from the picture," Ernie said, reddening. "In the picture it looked like some sort of tabletop size. Something you might put on top of your TV."

The girl smiled. Ernie could gather her whole face without stumbling over a single gold hoop. He took this as a good sign, and asked, "Let's say I did make something of size. How would I get it over here? Do you do pickups, something of that nature?"

She laughed, but not unkindly. "You don't actually build it unless you win. What you do is write up a proposal with some sketches. Then, if you win, you build it right here, on-site." She shrugged. "The *process* is the whole entire idea of the installation, okay? The whole entire community learns from witnessing the *process*."

In this office, where *process* was clearly the most important word in the English language, not counting *okay*, Ernie felt suddenly small. "Is that so," he said, wondering who learned what from the heap of tin Professor Life-Burden had processed onto the lawn.

"Oh, wait, one year a guy *did* build off-site," said the boy, ever eager to correct the world's misperceptions. "Remember that guy?"

"Yeah," the girl said. She turned to Ernie brightly. "One year a guy put his whole installation together at his studio and sent photographs. He didn't win, but the winner got pneumonia or something and couldn't follow through, and this guy was runner-up, so he trucked it here in a U-Haul."

"It was a totem," the boy said solemnly. "With a whole mess of wire things sticking out of it."

"I was a freshman," the girl said by way of an explanation Ernie couldn't begin to fathom. He missed Marie intensely, as if she were already gone.

Ernie peered through the window, hunting for the totem.

"Kappa Delts trashed it last Homecoming," the girl said. "Those animals have no respect for art." She handed back the clipping. "So, anyway, that really wasn't so stupid after all, what you said."

"Well," said the boy, "good luck, okay?"

As Ernie bumbled out the door, the girl called after him, "It's a cute boat, though. I like it."

At the hospital he set the boat on Marie's windowsill, explaining his morning. "Oh, Ernie," Marie crooned. "You old—you old surprise, you."

"They wouldn't take it," he said. "It's not big enough. You have to write the thing up, and make sketches and whatnot."

"So why don't you?"

"Why don't I what?"

"Make sketches and whatnot."

"Hah! I'd make it for real. Nobody does anything real anymore. I'd pack it into the back of my truck and haul it there myself. A guy did that once."

"Then make it for real."

"I don't have enough branches."

"Then use something else."

"I just might."

"Then do it." She was smiling madly now, fully engaged in their old, intimate arguing, and her eyes made bright blue sparks from her papery face. He knew her well, he realized, and saw what she was thinking: Ernie, there is some life left after everything seems to be gone. Really, there is. And that he could see this, just a little, and that she could see him seeing it, buoyed him. He thought he might even detect some pink fading into her cheeks.

He stayed through lunch, and was set to stay for supper until Marie remembered her dog and made him go home. As he turned from her bed, she said, "Wait. I want my ark." She lifted her finger to the windowsill, where the boat glistened in the filmy city light. And he saw that she was right: it was an ark, high and round and jammed with hope. He placed it in her arms and left it there, hoping it might sweeten her dreams.

When he reached his driveway he found fresh tire tracks, rutted by an afternoon rain, running in a rude diagonal from the back of the house across the front yard. He sat in the truck for a few minutes, counting the seconds of his rage, watching the dog's jangly shadow in the dining-room window. He counted to two hundred, checked his watch, then hauled himself out to fetch the dog. He set the dog on the seat next to him—in a different life it would have been a Doberman named Rex—and gave it a kiss on its wiry head. "That's from her," he said, and then drove straight to the lumberyard.

Ernie figured that Noah himself was a man of the soil and probably didn't know spit about boatbuilding. In fact, Ernie's experience in general—forty years of tending machinery, fixing industrial pipe the size of tree trunks, assembling Christmas toys for his son, remodeling bathrooms, building bird boxes and planters and finally, attached dramatically to the side of the house, a sunporch to please Marie—probably had Noah's beat in about a dozen ways. He figured he had the will and enough good tools to make a stab at a decent ark, and he was right: in a week's time he'd completed most of a hull beneath a makeshift staging that covered most of the ground between Marie's sunporch and his neighbor's fence. It was not a hull he would care to float, but he thought of it as a decent artistic representation of a hull; and even more important, it was big enough to qualify as an installation, if he had the guidelines right. He covered the hull with the bargain-priced tongue-and-groove boards he picked up at the lumberyard, leftover four-footers with lots of knots. Every day he worked from sunup to noon, then drove to the hospital to report his progress. Marie listened with her head inclined, her whispery hair tucked behind her ears. She still asked about the strike, but he had little news on that score, staying clean away from the union hall and the picket lines. He had even stopped getting the paper.

Often he turned on the floodlights in the evenings and worked in the cold till midnight or one. Working in the open air, without the iron skull of the mill over his head, made him feel like a newly sprung prisoner. He let the dog patter around and around the growing apparition, and sometimes he even chuckled at the animal's apparent capacity for wonder. The hateful boys from Broad Street loitered with their bikes at the back of the yard, and as the thing grew in size they more often than not opted for the long way around.

At eleven o'clock in the morning on the second day of the second week, a youngish man pulled up in a city car. He ambled down the walk and into the side yard, a clipboard and notebook clutched under one arm. The dog cowered at the base of one of the trees, its dime-sized eyes blackened with fear.

"You Mr. Ernest Whitten?" the man asked Ernie.

Ernie put down his hammer and climbed down from the deck by way of a gangplank that he had constructed in a late-night fit of creativity.

"I'm Dan Little, from the city," the man said, extending his hand.

"Well," Ernie said, astonished. He pumped the man's hand. "It's about time." He looked at the bike tracks, which had healed over for the most part, dried into faint, innocent-looking scars after a string of fine sunny days. "Not that it matters now," Ernie said. "They don't even come through much anymore."

Mr. Little consulted his notebook. "I don't follow," he said.

"Aren't you here about those hoodlums tearing up my wife's yard?"

"I'm from code enforcement."

"Pardon?"

Mr. Little squinted up at the ark. "You need a building permit for this, Mr. Whitten. Plus the city has a twenty-foot setback requirement for any new buildings."

Ernie twisted his face into disbelief, an expression that felt uncomfortably familiar; lately the entire world confused him. "The lot's only fifty feet wide as it is," he protested.

"I realize that, Mr. Whitten." Mr. Little shrugged apologetically. "I'm afraid you're going to have to take it down."

Ernie tipped back his cap to scratch his head. "It isn't a building. It's an installation."

"Say what?"

"An installation. I'm hauling it up to the college when I'm done. Figure I'll have to rent a flatbed or something. It's a little bigger than I counted on."

Mr. Little began to look nervous. "I'm sorry, Mr. Whitten, I still don't follow." He kept glancing back at the car.

"It's an ark," Ernie said, enunciating, although he could see how the ark might be mistaken for a building at this stage. Especially if you weren't really looking, which this man clearly wasn't. "It's an ark," Ernie repeated.

Mr. Little's face took a heavy downward turn. "You're not zoned for arks," he sighed, writing something on the official-pink papers attached to his clipboard.

Ernie glanced at the car. In the driver's seat had appeared a pony-sized yellow Labrador retriever, its quivering nose faced dead forward as if it were planning to set that sucker into gear and take off into the wild blue yonder. "That your dog?" Ernie asked.

Mr. Little nodded.

"Nice dog," Ernie said.

"This one's yours, I take it?" Mr. Little pointed at Marie's dog, who had scuttled out from the tree and hidden behind Ernie's pants leg.

"My wife's," Ernie told him. "She's in the hospital."

"I'm sorry to hear that," Mr. Little said. "I'm sure she'll be on the mend in no time."

"Doesn't look like it," Ernie said, wondering why he didn't just storm the hospital gates, do something sweeping and biblical, stomp through those clean corridors and defy doctor's orders and pick her up with his bare hands and bring her home.

Mr. Little scooched down and made clicky sounds at Marie's dog, who nosed out from behind Ernie's leg to investigate. "What's his name?" he asked.

"It's, well, it's Pumpkin Pie. My wife named him."

"That's Junie," Mr. Little said, nudging his chin toward the car. "I got her the day I signed my divorce papers. She's a helluva lot more faithful than my wife ever was."

"I never had problems like that," Ernie said.

Mr. Little got to his feet and shook his head at Ernie's ark. "Listen, about this, this . . ."

"Ark," Ernie said.

"You're going to have to do something, Mr. Whitten. At the very least, you'll have to go down to city hall, get a building permit, and then follow the regulations. Just don't tell them it's a boat. Call it a storage shed or something."

Ernie tipped back his cap again. "I don't suppose it's regulation to cart your dog all over kingdom come on city time."

"Usually she sleeps in the back," Mr. Little said sheepishly.

"I'll tell you what," Ernie said. "You leave my ark alone and I'll keep shut about the dog."

Mr. Little looked sad. "Listen," he said, "people can do what they want as far as I care. But you've got neighbors out here complaining about the floodlights and the noise."

Ernie looked around, half-expecting to see the dirt-bike gang sniggering behind their fists someplace out back. But all he saw were FOR SALE signs yellowing from disuse, and the sagging rooftops of his neighbors' houses, their shades drawn against the sulphurous smell of betrayal.

Mr. Little ripped a sheet off his clipboard and handed it to Ernie. "Look, just consider this a real friendly warning, would you? And just for the record, I hate my job, but I've got bills piling up like everybody else."

Ernie watched him amble back to the car, say something to the dog, who gave her master a walloping with her broad pink tongue. He watched them go, remembering now that he'd seen Mr. Little before, somewhere in the mill—the bleachery maybe, or strolling in the dim recesses near the Number Eight, his face flushed and shiny under his yellow hard hat, clipboard at the ready. Now here he was, trying to stagger his way through the meanwhile, harassing senior citizens on behalf of the city. His dog probably provided him with the only scrap of self-respect he could ferret out in a typical day.

Ernie ran a hand over the rough surface of his ark, remembering that Noah's undertaking had been a result of God's despair. God was sorry he'd messed with any of it, the birds of the air and beasts of the forest and, especially, the two-legged creatures who insisted on lying and cheating and killing their own brothers. Still, God had found one man, one man and his family, worth saving, and therefore had deemed a pair of everything else worth saving, too. "Come on, dog," he said. "We're going to get your mother."

As happened so often, in so many small, miraculous ways during their forty-five years together, Marie had outthought him. When he got to her room she was fully dressed, her overnight bag perched primly next to her on the bone-white bed, the ark cradled into her lap and tipped on its side. "Ernie," she said, stretching her arms straight out. "Take me home."

He bore her home at twenty-five miles an hour, aware of how every pock in the road rose up to meet her fragile, flesh-wanting spine. He eased her out of the car and carried her over their threshold. He filled all the bird feeders along the sunporch, then took her out to survey the ark. These were her two requests.

By morning she looked better. The weather—the warmest fall on record—held. He propped her on a chaise lounge on the sunporch in the brand-new flannel robe their son's wife had sent from California, then wrapped her in a blanket, so that she looked like a benevolent pod person from a solar system ruled by warmth and decency. The dog nestled in her lap, eyes half-closed in ecstasy.

He propped her there so she could watch him work—her third request. And work he did, feeling the way he had when they were first dating and he would remove his shirt to burrow elaborately into the tangled guts of his forest-green 1950 Pontiac. He forgot that he was building the ark for the contest, and how much he wanted to win, and his rage fell like dead leaves from his body as he felt the watchful, sunshiney presence of Marie. He moved one of Marie's feeders to the deck of the ark because she wanted him to know the tame and chittery company of chickadees. The sun shone and shone; the yard did not succumb to the dun colors of fall; the tracks left by the dirt bikes resembled nothing more ominous than the faintest prints left by dancing birds. Ernie unloaded some more lumber, a stack of roofing shingles, a small door. He had three weeks till deadline, and in this strange, blessed season, he meant to make it.

Marie got better. She sat up, padded around the house a little, ate real food. Several times a day he caught a sharp squeak floating down from the sunporch as she conversed with one of her girlfriends, or with her sister down from Bangor, or with the visiting nurse. He would look up, see her translucent white hand raised toward him— *It's nothing, Ernie, just go back to whatever you were doing*—and recognize the sound after the fact as a strand of her old laughter, high and ecstatic and small-town, like her old self.

"It happens," the nurse told him when he waylaid her on the front walk. "They get a burst of energy toward the end sometimes."

He didn't like this nurse, the way she called Marie "they." He

23

thought of adding her to the list of people and things he'd grown so accustomed to railing against, but because his rage was gone, there was no place to put her. He returned to the ark, climbed onto the deck, and began to nail the last shingles to the shallow pitch of the roof. Marie's voice floated out again, and he looked up again, and her hand rose again, and he nodded again, hoping she could see his smiling, his damp collar, the handsome knot of his forearm. He was wearing the clothes he wore to work back when he was working, a grass-colored gabardine shirt and pants—his greens, Marie called them. In some awful way he recognized this as one of the happiest times of his life; he was brimming with industry and connected to nothing but this one woman, this one patch of earth.

When it was time for Marie's lunch, he climbed down from the deck and wiped his hands on his work pants. Mr. Little was standing a few feet away, a camera raised to his face.

"What's this?" Ernie asked.

Mr. Little lowered the camera. "For our records."

Ernie thought on this for a moment. "I'm willing to venture there's nothing like this in your records."

"Not so far," Mr. Little said. He ducked once, twice, as a pair of chickadees flitted over his head. "Your wife is home, I see."

Ernie glanced over at the sunporch, where Marie lay heavily swaddled on her chaise lounge, watching them curiously. He waved at her, and waited many moments as she struggled to free her hand from the blankets and wave back.

"As long as you've got that camera," Ernie said, "I wonder if you wouldn't do us a favor."

"I'm going to have to fine you, Mr. Whitten. I'm sorry."

"I need a picture of my ark," Ernie said. "Would you do us that favor? All you have to do is snap one extra."

Mr. Little looked around uncertainly. "Sure, all right."

"I'm sending it in to a contest."

"I bet you win."

Ernie nodded. "That's the plan."

Mr. Little helped Ernie dismantle the staging, such as it was, and soon the ark stood alone in the sun, as round and full-skirted as a giant hen nestled on the grass. The chickadees, momentarily spooked by the rattle of staging, were back again. Two of them. A pair, Ernie hoped. "Could I borrow your dog?" he asked Mr. Little, whose eyebrows shot up in a question. "Just for a minute," Ernie explained. "For the picture. We get my wife's dog over here and bingo, I got animals two by two. Two birds, two dogs. What else would God need?"

Mr. Little whistled at the city car and out jumped Junie, thundering through the open window, her back end waggling back and forth with her tail. Marie was up now, too, hobbling down the porch stairs, Pumpkin Pie trotting ahead of her, beelining toward Junie's yellow tail. As the dogs sniffed each other, Ernie loped across the grass to help Marie navigate the bumpy spots. "Didn't come to me before now," he told her, "but these dogs are just the ticket." He gentled her over the uneven grass and introduced her to Mr. Little. "This fellow's donated his dog to the occasion."

Marie held hard to Ernie's arm. She offered her free hand to the pink-tongued Junie and cooed at her. Mr. Little seemed pleased, and didn't hesitate a second when Ernie asked him to lead the dogs up the plank and order them to sit. They did. Then Ernie gathered Marie into his arms—she weighed nothing, his big-boned girl all gone to feathers—and struggled up the plank, next to the dogs. He set Marie on her feet and snugged his arm around her. "Wait till the birds light," he cautioned. Mr. Little waited, then lifted the camera. Everybody smiled.

In the wintry months that followed, Ernie consoled himself with the thought that his ark did not win because he had misunderstood the guidelines, or that he had neglected to name his ark, or that he had no experience putting into words that which could not be put into words. He liked to imagine the panel of judges frowning in confusion over his written material and then halting in awe at the snapshot—holding it up, their faces all riveted at once. He liked especially to imagine the youngsters in the art office, the redheaded girl and the boy with rings, their lives just beginning. Perhaps they felt a brief shudder, a silvery glimpse of the rest of their lives as they removed the snapshot from the envelope. Perhaps they took enough time to see it all—birds lighting on a gunwale, dogs posed on a plank, and a man and woman standing in front of a little door, she in her bathrobe and he in his greens, waiting for rain.

Cathie Pelletier

The Music of Angels

"Her eardrums exploded," Grammy Willa said. "She was on an airplane headed for Las Vegas." It was the part of her story where Grammy Willa always paused, waiting for the visual horror to settle down in the minds of her listeners. Outside, wind rocked the porch swing and a thin spray of rain ran down the big kitchen window. Sarah was staring out at the little pile of sunflower seeds she'd left on the back porch. She had brought the seeds from home, a nice handful stuffed into a plastic sandwich bag. As usual, a chickadee was the first to discover the stash, and now others were coming to eat, along with some goldfinches.

Chuck had been listening with great interest to his mother's story. Now that the pause had finally arrived, he took another bite of his chicken sandwich. Lucinda, as usual, was all ears. Everyone knew that Lucinda was now Grammy Willa's favorite daughter-in-law.

"Sarah, sweetie, eat your cake," Lucinda said. She pushed the plate so that it touched against Sarah's hand.

"Five chickadees," said Sarah, moving her hand away. Lucinda shot a pleading little look at Chuck.

"Sarah, you answer when Lucinda talks to you," Chuck said. "She might not be your real mother, but that don't mean you can ignore her."

Grammy Willa cleared her throat dramatically. The pause was officially over.

"She went ahead, against her poor mother's wishes, and flew out there to marry that man she met at Loring Air Force Base, the kind who deals cards all day for a living."

Grammy Willa was known as one of the best storytellers in town. Sarah knew of many days when the tiny kitchen stayed full of visiting women, all sipping from cups with teabag strings dangling over the sides, munching on doughnuts or marshmallow squares, the small driveway out front bulging with cars and pickups of all color and make. People in Mattagash often remarked that Grammy Willa's house looked like there was a wake going on, nonstop.

"And somewhere over the Great Lakes," Grammy Willa continued, her voice now lowered, "she tried to blow her nose, and that's when her eardrums blew up. She was my cousin's daughter."

"And she stayed deaf?" Lucinda asked. She had sloshed a bit of coffee onto her saucer and was now dabbing at it with a paper napkin. Grammy Willa reached for the dishrag, then motioned to Lucinda to let her have the saucer.

"Right up to the day she died, she couldn't so much as hear a dog bark," said Grammy Willa. She wiped the saucer clean, and then gave it back. "But that's what you get for listening to your heart and not your head."

Sarah turned away from the window then and looked at Grammy Willa.

"How could she listen to her head if she was deaf?" Sarah asked. She saw her father smile, then give Lucinda that special little look he'd been giving her ever since they got married. Grammy Willa patted Sarah's hand, which was her polite way of saying, *Shut up, please, I'm talking.*

"That card dealer left her in some rat-loving hotel room," Grammy Willa said. "And you know yourself it'd be tough enough for a young Mattagash girl to survive in Las Vegas *with* eardrums. But how in the world can you cross them busy streets, or go for job interviews, or ask directions from city people without your drums? It finally got to her. The next thing we heard back here in town, a cleaning lady found her in her bed, just like she was asleep." She shook her head then, slowly, the forlorn kind of shake that always came when Grammy Willa wanted to point out life's utter wastefulness. The shake could be over a sandwich, half-eaten and yet thrown into a trash can. Or someone running a water sprinkler all day just so their grass could drink. Or the slow decline of a good friend tucked away in a nursing home. Waste was waste in Grammy's book.

Lucinda raised her eyebrows into a question. "How?" her eyebrows were asking.

"Sleeping pills," Grammy Willa answered. She looked protectively at Sarah. "I wish you'd quit feeding them birds, honey. They carry all kinds of diseases."

"Seven chickadees," said Sarah. "And four goldfinches. Where do you suppose they come from?"

"God only knows," said Grammy Willa. "I've seen butterflies light on dog doo-doo. Things that fly around carry germs."

Sarah stared out into the rain, her eyes rising and falling with the arrival and departure of each chickadee.

"Well," said Lucinda. She needed more coffee to finish her cake, and held out her empty cup when Grammy Willa motioned with the coffeepot. "I guess there's a moral in *that* story."

"Yeah," said Chuck. "Don't blow your nose over the Great Lakes."

"Oh, Daddy," Sarah said. "You're so silly." She finished the last bite of cake and pushed her plate up next to her glass of milk. Then she got up and went to the screen door that led out to the back porch.

"Where you going?" Grammy Willa asked. "Don't you want some more cake?"

"I want to hear their wings," said Sarah. "The chickadees aren't afraid of me." She pushed open the screen door and stepped outside. She heard it shut behind her. She had always been able to tell when the adults had things they wished to say to each other, always knew when her being present stopped them from doing so. She stayed close to the door, where the others wouldn't see her, as she waited for more chickadees.

"Speaking of not hearing," Lucinda said then. "Donna pretends she can't hear me every time she calls our house for Sarah. I got to yell at the top of my lungs to make her hear what I'm saying."

Sarah moved just close enough to the window that she could see inside the house. There was her father, head bowed over his cake as Grammy Willa and Lucinda were girlfriends together. At least that's what Grammy called it. I feel more like Lucinda's girlfriend than her mother-in-law, Grammy was always telling the women who gathered in her small kitchen for gossip and food.

Sarah felt a kind of power in eavesdropping like this. She watched as Lucinda helped herself to another bite of birthday cake.

"Donna hears just fine," Chuck said. "She just don't hear certain people, and it's by choice."

"Well, she heard the judge, didn't she?" asked Lucinda. Sarah saw Grammy Willa wink, then nod approvingly. "The day he give us custody of Sarah, she heard that all right. Even that judge knew Donna is too immature to be a good mother."

"And she sure hears the jukebox pretty good down at the tavern," Grammy Willa said. She and Lucinda were now on a roll. "Mildred says she's down there most nights dancing up a storm."

"And Mildred says she goes home with just about anyone," Lucinda said.

"Lucinda, watch what you're saying." This was when Chuck usually frowned at his new wife. It was one of Sarah's favorite times. The truth was that Lucinda was in her fourth month of being a stepmother, and she was still forgetting what most parents know firsthand: little pitchers have big ears.

"Sorry," said Lucinda. She waved a hand feebly in front of her face. "I slip up sometimes."

Chuck cleared his throat then, his usual signal to Lucinda to end all talk of Donna. Sarah wished this was something she, too, could do. She saw her father now pushing back his chair. Sarah knew he would come looking for her, wondering if she'd heard, looking deep into her eyes, judging her face, as if that would tell them. As if she weren't so clever she could hide everything from them, even how her heart felt. She stepped away from the window.

"Where is she?" she heard her father ask.

Sarah opened the door then and stepped back inside. Lucinda looked up and smiled. Grammy Willa began cutting another slice of cake.

"Sit yourself down and leave those dirty birds alone," she said to Sarah.

"They aren't dirty, they're beautiful," Sarah said. She sat again in her chair at the table. Earlier, she had managed to blow out all ten candles and was told by Grammy Willa, with the smug certainty her grandmother had about most subjects, that she would get her wish.

"Maybe you're gonna be some kind of scientist when you grow up," Chuck said to Sarah, who was now poking at a burned candle with her fork. A few white cake crumbs clung to the stiff hairs of his big, bushy mustache, which moved like a little roller brush above his upper lip.

"Wipe your mouth, Chuck honey," Lucinda whispered. Then she looked at Sarah. "Maybe you'll be one of them people who study birds," she said.

"Ornithologist," said Sarah. She hoped everyone would finally notice how stupid Lucinda really was. But no one seemed to hear. They just smiled that vague smile they keep for kids, when kids say something clever. And then they go back talking about adult things. Sarah turned and looked out at the pile of sunflower seeds.

"How many birds do you see, sweetheart?" Lucinda asked.

"Thirteen," said Sarah, but it wasn't true. There were only seven. She just said it to be spiteful.

Grammy Willa stood and began scraping cake crumbs from one plate to another. Then, she reached into the big pocket of her apron and pulled out a small package. She handed it to Sarah, who quickly tore away the paper. It was a pewter pin, a little bird sitting on a twig.

"It'll look so cute on your sweater," Grammy Willa said.

"I'll take some of that extra cake home with us," said Lucinda.

"Not for me," said Chuck. "Until I get my cholesterol down, I'm up Shit Creek."

"Chuck!" Lucinda scolded. But she smiled anyway. She was always smiling at Chuck, and he was always smiling back.

"It's a bluebird," said Sarah, twirling the birthday pin in her fingers.

"I SAID SHE'S STILL ASLEEP, DONNA. YOU'LL HAVE TO CALL LATER!" It was Lucinda, shouting into the receiver again. Up in her bedroom, Sarah opened her eyes and lay there, listening. Rain had begun a slow patter outside, and now soft little drops of water were landing on the window, clinging there. Sarah could see nothing but the leaves of the yellow birch, wet leaves, green with spring. Behind the leaves, in patches, the sky was a fuzzy gray.

"I SAID TO CALL BACK LATER!" The receiver slammed down into its cradle, and Sarah could hear the little crystals jangling on the lamp above the telephone. The lamp had arrived with Lucinda, one of the many items unpacked from numerous cardboard boxes, all relics from Lucinda's life before she married Chuck. And now, Lucinda's things were in all the spaces where Donna's had been. But Sarah liked the lamp anyway. Lead-crystal diamond shapes dangled like earrings all around the shade. Sometimes, when Sarah passed the lamp in a great hurry, music followed her, as though it had been played just for her.

"THAT CRAZY WOMAN'S GONNA BE THE DEATH OF ME!"

"Stop shouting," Sarah heard her father say. "You're not even on the telephone."

"She's got me so I don't know if I'm coming or going," Lucinda said. And then the lamp played its music again, and Sarah knew that Lucinda was *going*, that she and Chuck had walked past the lamp, had taken their conversation into the kitchen.

Sarah rolled over on her side and looked at the clock. It was almost nine-thirty. Time to get up, even if it was Saturday. On her nightstand sat the little porcelain clown, her birthday gift from Chuck and Lucinda. And three birthday cards, standing prettily, pictures of bows and flowers and rabbits. She'd gotten nine cards in all, from relatives and her best girlfriends. Donna's card had asked *What Is a Daughter?*, and then had gone on to answer that a daughter is someone who is there when you need to laugh, or to cry, or just to talk. *A daughter's laughter is the music of angels.* "It's the kind of card you send to someone much older," Lucinda had told Grammy Willa on the phone. Sarah had heard her, although she pretended to be brushing her teeth. She had let the water run, and then tiptoed to the top of the stairs to listen. "That daughter being a friend business ain't the kind of thing you say to a ten-year-old. And she signed it Love, Donna. Ain't that the worst you ever heard?" Without hearing Grammy Willa's voice, without even seeing her face, Sarah knew that her grandmother was shaking her head at the waste of it all. It was common knowledge that Grammy Willa and Lucinda agreed about everything. Grammy told anyone who listened that Lucinda was a mother-in-law's dream come true, and that she was the best thing to ever happen to Chuck Fennelson. "The Lord sent her," Grammy Willa liked to say. Grammy Willa might consider Lucinda a godsend, but Sarah wished God would send her stepmother someplace else. Lucinda was nice enough, and she tried real hard. But she wasn't Donna. "I ain't gonna try to re-place Donna in your life, sweetie," Lucinda declared, sitting on the edge of Sarah's bed, the same afternoon Chuck had proposed. "God knows, I couldn't be Donna even if I tried. But I can be a real good substitute mother." Sarah wouldn't mind Lucinda, really, if she were some other kid's mother. It's just that she already had a mother, she al-ready had Donna. And now Lucinda was more or less getting in the way of Chuck and Donna ever finding love again. Yet, it was true that in her newly found independence, Donna preferred for Sarah to call her by her first name. "I'm only sixteen years older than you," Donna had said. "I feel more like your big sister sometimes."

Sarah leafed through the blouses in her closet until she found the blue one with the long sleeves. Blue was her favorite color, especially on rainy days when all the blue seemed to have seeped out of the sky. She chose her black sweatpants, and Nikes, and then swept her long hair back and tied it there. She had Donna's hair, no doubt about it. At times, when Lucinda was sitting on the sofa, Sarah could see the little tan bald spot growing like a mushroom on the top of her stepmother's head. "All the girls in my family are thin-haired," Lucinda mentioned once to Grammy Willa. "We hardly ever have to clean our hairbrush, or scoop big globs out of the shower. Mary, Queen of Scots, was real thin-haired, too. There's a lot of advantages to being thin-haired, especially in the heat of summer." But Sarah was glad she had hair thick as Donna's each time she spied the little threadbare patch on Lucinda's head. "Old baldy," is what Donna called Lucinda. And once, right to Lucinda's face, Donna had said, "Now you go on home with this here American symbol, Sarah." And then she had winked. Sarah had smiled all the way home, but she pretended not to know what Donna meant when Lucinda questioned her about it.

At the breakfast table Sarah waited as Lucinda made pancakes on the grill she had bought herself for her own birthday. "With your daddy's permission, of course," she told Sarah. "It's just that men don't know what a woman needs in the kitchen." Sarah remembered the Christmas that Chuck bought Donna a mixer, and Donna had opened the back door and tossed it out into the snow, box and all. "You ain't the man from Sears," Donna said. "You're my husband, and I expect a more romantic gift than a kitchen appliance." But then she had burst into laughter. And she had gone out into the snowy yard in her red housecoat and fluffy slippers to bring the mixer back inside. "Just making a point for next Christmas," Donna had whispered to Sarah. All three of them laughed a lot about that incident, and Chuck told everyone that Donna was a real firecracker and that's why he'd married her in the first place. But the very next Christmas, when Chuck bought them mother and daughter necklaces, Donna was already moved out and into her own place. And she was dating Mr. Simms, who coached Little League at Sarah's grammar school, and was always in a hurry. "Don't that man wear anything but sweatpants?" Grammy Willa had asked Sarah. After Mr. Simms there was Richie Pinkham's father, who worked in the woods but never paid Richie's mother a penny in child support. At least Richie told Sarah that was so. "He's spending all his money on your mom," Richie said. And then, on the playground, he'd pulled Sarah aside and whispered something to her. "Every other weekend, when I stay with my dad," Richie whispered, "I hear him and your mom doing it." Sarah told Donna about the child support thing, but she never said anything about what Richie heard. "Well, that's what you get for dating in a small town," Donna noted, when Sarah had asked if it was true about the money. "Let that be a lesson to you, kid. Get yourself out of here and move to a city the minute you're old enough. You might get mugged, but at least you're the first one to know it. If you was to get mugged here in Mattagash, you might not even be the last one to know."

Sarah ate her pancakes and listened while Lucinda gave her a quick rundown of things she needed at Blanche's grocery.

"Only get a loaf of bread if it's fresh, okay?" Lucinda reminded her, and Sarah nodded. "And whatever you do, pedal on the side of the road so that cars are always coming toward you. That way you can see them."

"I always do," said Sarah. Lucinda liked to remind her of things she had learned a long time ago, from Donna.

"And whatever you do, don't talk—"

"To strangers," said Sarah. "Lucinda, there ain't any strangers in Mattagash."

"Someday there might be," Lucinda said, "and I want you ready for them."

Sarah pedaled on past Blanche's grocery. She had crumpled the list Lucinda had given her and tossed it into the kitchen wastebasket. Lucinda was on the phone to Grammy Willa and hadn't noticed. She had merely waved a quick good-bye to Sarah.

"No later than an hour," Lucinda whispered, and Sarah had nodded. Then, outside, she pulled her tote bag out from under the back porch steps, strapped it on the rack of her bike, and pedaled away. She had been planning this getaway since even before her birthday.

When she got to Donna's house trailer, Sarah knocked lightly on the door. She didn't want to do this. It felt strange to be knocking on her own mother's door. But it was one of Donna's new rules. When there was no answer, Sarah let herself in. Donna was asleep on the living room sofa, flat on her stomach, the Siamese cat curled up at her side. Sarah knew it was Donna because she could see pink socks sticking out from under a pale blue sheet. Only Donna would wear pink socks. The radio was playing music from the classical station they'd just started up, at the college in Watertown. That's where Donna had been taking her Continuing Education classes. When Sarah sat down on the sofa she heard Donna growl softly in her sleep, and then mutter something. Sarah smiled. Donna was famous for growling in her sleep. That's one of the earliest memories Sarah had of her mother, the memories of waking at night when she was just a tiny girl and thinking that some puppy dog must be hurt somewhere. Hit by a car. Hungry, maybe. One night, she had followed the sound to her mother's bedroom door, then into the room where Donna was sleeping, and then right up to Donna's mouth. There it was, the little growl, soft, painful almost. "I snore maybe, but I don't growl," Donna always defended herself. "It's like sleeping with Lassie," Chuck would tell Sarah, and Donna would throw a pillow at him. But Chuck didn't tease about Donna anymore, not since Lucinda had come into the picture. And for the past year, whenever Sarah woke up in the black midst of night, she never heard the little growls she used to hear. Sometimes, she heard the cut-crystal lamp downstairs, if the window fan was on and the little diamond shapes were blowing about. Other times, she heard muted voices coming from her father's room, Lucinda and Chuck talking, or the television turned on to David Letterman. Sometimes, she even heard them doing it, the bed thumping against the wall, and Lucinda making weird little squeaking sounds, like a mouse. But she never heard the pitiful, painful growls that used to come out of Donna's mouth while she was dreaming, while she was aching for a life somewhere else, even while she slept. That's what she had told Sarah. "I'm in pain all the time I'm in this house, this life. I know you don't understand now, but someday you will."

Donna tossed back the blue sheet and flopped over onto her back. Sarah saw that she still had her makeup on from the night before. A layer of mascara grew like a black crescent moon beneath each eye. "I went over there one day," Grammy Willa had whispered to Lucinda, when she thought Sarah couldn't hear from the back porch swing. "Here it was almost noon, and Donna was still in her pajamas. She looked exactly like a raccoon, what with her mascara still on from the night before."

The Siamese cat lifted itself up and stretched, its mouth yawning. It walked over Donna's stomach and came to purr against Sarah's arm, then to meow. Sarah put it down on the floor and it followed her out into the kitchen, waited while she opened a pouch of cat food and filled the plastic water bowl.

"What a hungry kitty," Sarah whispered. She knelt and stroked the arching back.

Outside it had begun to rain again and Sarah frowned to see it. Lucinda would be antsy, watching the road for her now, unless she thought Sarah had stopped at Marilee's to look at the new kittens. The truth was that she didn't have permission to visit Donna alone. And she'd been told so by her father. Under no circumstances was she to end up at Lot #15 in the Mattagash Trailer Park. But there she was. It had hurt her, the first time she ever sent Donna a card, for Mother's Day, to write that new address down. It seemed so foreign. *Lot #15, Mattagash Trailer Park, Mattagash, Maine.* It was a strange feeling to have Donna live someplace else. It was like tearing away a piece of a puzzle, and leaving it forever incomplete. And now, all the pieces of the puzzle were scattered. The big family picture on the bookshelf in the living room, the one of Chuck and Donna and Sarah all happily entwined, had been replaced by Lucinda and Chuck's wedding picture. And now even Lucinda's parents, people Sarah didn't know, people long dead, were staring out from the bookshelf with round, blank eyes bulging out of somber faces. They gave Sarah the willies, but at least Lucinda hadn't thrown the family picture away. She had given it to Sarah. "For your own home someday," Lucinda had told her. "But this *is* my home," Sarah reminded everyone, who just sighed, even Grammy Willa, and said she was going through a stage.

A cracking boom of thunder and the cat fled from its dish, down the rickety hallway. Sarah heard Donna growling herself awake in the living room. She filled the teakettle with some water and plugged it in. Then she found the bottle of aspirin that Donna always kept on the windowsill over the sink. She dropped three into her shirt pocket and then sifted two teaspoons of instant coffee into a cup. The spoon clinked loudly as it stirred hot water over the thin coffee grounds.

"What elf is in my kitchen?" Donna asked, groggy. "It better be getting me coffee, like a good elf should." Sarah smiled. Outside, a genuine storm had begun. A sheet of rain was beating its way up the tarred entrance of the trailer park, toward Donna's gravel drive.

"How'd you know it was me?" Sarah asked. Donna was now sitting up on the sofa.

"You're the only one who feeds the cat," she said. "Did the mail come? I'm expecting my grades for this semester." Sarah put the little white tablets in Donna's palm, and then handed her the coffee. "I think I made the dean's list," Donna added.

"That's great," said Sarah, but she didn't mean it. She was hoping that Continuing Education would be such a mistake for Donna that she'd change her mind about everything. And Chuck would take her back. All of Mattagash knew about the broken heart Chuck Fennelson wore on his sleeve until the divorce was final, and even then he tried to get Donna back, turning up in her yard one night with a gun, which he held to his own head and threatened to pull the trigger. "Go ahead," was all Donna had said. And then she took her cat inside her trailer, closed the door, and flicked out the porch light. At least that's what Grammy Willa had told Lucinda. "Have you ever heard of anything so cruel?" Grammy had wanted to know. But Donna had seen it differently. "If you don't give someone an audience, they can't put on a show," Donna said. When Chuck Fennelson quit drinking everyone said it was because Lucinda had come into his life. But Sarah knew the truth, just as Donna did. Chuck quit drinking so that he could raise his daughter, with or without Lucinda. "I gotta get my shit together," he had staggered into Sarah's room one night to say. "Your mother ain't ever gonna love me again." And then he broke down and cried. That was the night he slept on the floor by Sarah's bed, all night long, his hand reaching up to hold Sarah's own hand.

"This here yours?" Sarah asked, and pointed to a textbook on the coffee table. *Introductory Biology* was the title. Donna nodded and sipped more coffee.

"They know you're here?" she asked. Her brown hair was splayed about her shoulders, thick and full as a perm job, but it was all natural. Sarah didn't answer. The cat was back again, rubbing against her leg, so she scooped it up into her lap and buried her face in its fur.

"Shit," said Donna. She looked out the window at the spring rain beating against the trailer. "You know I'll get the blame for this," she said. "If a bomb was to go off in Paris, France, I'd be the first one Willa and Lucinda would point their fingers at."

"I brought some clothes this time," Sarah said suddenly. "I think if we was to ask Daddy, he'd let me live with you."

Donna said nothing for a time. She seemed to be listening to the rain, and then she seemed to be just staring out at the tarred Mattagash road. The cat jumped down from Sarah's lap and began to rub its narrow body against Donna's leg, as if to remind her where she was. At least Donna turned to look at Sarah then, but Sarah couldn't tell what her mother was thinking anymore. How could she? She had never even *imagined* that Donna would move out of their cute little house one day to live at a place called Lot #15, as if cattle lived there. She had never imagined that a day would come when she would need permission to visit her mother, much less enter her home without knocking. Permission was for going to the bathroom at school, or getting excused from gym class. So how could Sarah ever again think she knew Donna's mind? "That woman don't know her own mind," Grammy Willa told Chuck. "And that's what's wrong with her. I knew right from the start that she was too young to get married, but no one talked to their sons back then. Nowadays you got ministers talking about condoms in church, but back then no one said anything about birth control. We just kept our fingers crossed if we had sons, and we kept our toes crossed too, if we had daughters. Donna was just too young for marriage and motherhood, and that's all there is to it."

But that wasn't all there was, and Sarah wished she could tell Grammy Willa just that. That wasn't all there was to it. Now there was Sarah.

"Honey, I'm gonna try to say this again," said Donna, and Sarah reached down to stroke the cat's back, pretending not to listen. Her eyes were burning, wishing she'd let them cry. "Having you was the best thing that ever happened to me," Donna said, "and never mind what Grammy Willa thinks. But the next best thing was leaving your daddy and going off to school. I don't hate him, Sarah. He's a real nice man, and he's doing all he can to raise you right. But I don't love him." She waited. The rain was now doing a fierce drumming on the metallic roof of the trailer. The phone rang several times, and then all was quiet.

"But I'm not Daddy," Sarah said. "So why can't I live with you?"

"Because I'm not ready yet," said Donna. "I didn't know it at the time, but that judge was right. I'm not ready to be a good parent, and your daddy is. What I gotta do now is get me that college degree. And I feel pretty sure that you're gonna understand all this when you're older."

Donna found a cigarette in a crumpled pack in her purse and lit it up. As she blew a long trail of gray smoke from between her lips, Sarah thought about growing up, about growing older, growing toward that sudden knowledge that everything was okay. Donna made it sound like life was a storm until one day the sun comes out and shines on everything.

"Smoking's bad for you," said Sarah. "Don't they teach you that in college?"

Donna smiled, and then patted the sofa next to her. Sarah came and plopped down, put her feet up on the coffee table.

"Lucinda let you do that at home?" Donna asked.

"Thanks for the birthday card," said Sarah.

"I got you something," said Donna. "It's on my dresser, all wrapped up pretty."

The first thing Sarah noticed in the bedroom was that the bed hadn't been slept in. Donna's rocking chair, one she had redone herself by watching Homer Formsby, sat in the corner. A man's shirt was hanging from the chair's back, and Sarah saw a half-filled pack of Marlboros on the nightstand. Donna smoked Winstons. The birthday package was a heavy box, not too big, and wrapped in what looked like Christmas paper. Sarah carried the box back to the living room.

"It's kind of heavy," she said. She plopped back down on the sofa, next to her mother.

"Open it," said Donna. "And if you're wondering about the Christmas paper, it's because I believe in recycling."

"Sure you do," said Sarah.

Inside the box she found a pair of binoculars and a field guide called *Birds East of the Rockies.*

"Oh neat!" said Sarah. She'd been interested in birds ever since her class trip to the bird refuge near Quebec City. "Gram gave me an old pair of binoculars, but they ain't very good."

"Aren't," said Donna. "Don't they teach you anything in grammar school?" She wrapped an arm around Sarah's neck, pulled Sarah's head up next to her own. "I love you, kiddo," Donna said. "Even if you *are* bonkers."

"Why are you listening to that music?" Sarah asked. She had leveled the binoculars on the radio dial, then adjusted them in order to read the numbers. "You don't even like classical music, do you?" She turned the binoculars toward the storm then, catching a gray wall of rain in her sights.

"I like it now," said Donna. "In Music Fundamentals we been learning all about Mozart and Beethoven. We been listening to music by all them great composers and it kind of grows on you. They got funny names, like Concerto No. 5, or Symphony No. 26, or even Opus 53. There's more to the world than rock 'n' roll. That's my new motto."

Donna blew the last puff of cigarette smoke into a dramatic arc before she stubbed the cigarette out. Sarah followed the stream of smoke with her binoculars, but it was too hazy to pick up clearly, indefinable, too much like the reason Donna gave as to why she had to leave Chuck. Maybe pain was like a gray smoke, wavering, disappearing into cracks and crevices where it was difficult to find, much less deal with.

"If you'd let me live with you," said Sarah, "I'd be here for when you want to laugh, or cry, or just talk."

Donna laughed a big hearty laugh. "Listen to you," she said. "You sound like a tape recording or something."

"But that's what the card said," Sarah protested. "A daughter's laughter is the music of angels."

"What card?" Donna asked.

"The birthday card you sent me," said Sarah. "Didn't you even read it?"

"Oh," said Donna. "Sure I read it, but I forgot. I bought it a long time ago."

The phone rang again, this time a long continuous drone that threatened to never end. Finally, Donna said, "I'm gonna have to answer it."

Sarah said nothing, her binoculars aimed out the window of the trailer, looking at the rain, looking at the narrow tarred road that led out of Mattagash, looking for answers out there in the storm. There were some things, Sarah felt quite certain, that you needed to know *before* you grew up, before everything was so nicely understood.

"Whose shirt is that hanging on your rocking chair?" she finally asked. She turned the binoculars on Donna, who was nothing more than a blurry mass of beautiful brown hair and bright yellow pajamas. The yellow was like the eye of a daisy, which is really just a whole bunch of little flowers. Sarah had learned that in science class. "The daisy appears to be a single flower with white petals," her teacher had said. "But it's really a group of many very tiny flowers." And that's what Donna was, too. "I'm really a lot of people," Donna said. "But you only see me as one, as your mother." What Sarah remembered most about the daisies she had picked in her lifetime was how all the little yellow bits scattered to the winds when you broke the flower apart. *Loves me. Loves me not.*

"There are some things I don't have to answer," Donna said, slowly. The phone was still bleating away in the background. "Even as your mother, there are some things that are private, mine all alone, and that's one of them. Now, I am gonna have to answer that phone. You want me to say you're here, or not?"

Sarah turned the binoculars away again, back out into the sheets of rain covering Mattagash. She shook her head.

"How you gonna get home in this rain?" Donna asked.

"You're gonna drive me as far as Blanche's grocery," said Sarah. She would get the loaf of bread, if it was fresh, and hoped that she could remember the other items on the list she had thrown away. But Sarah had an excellent memory, even Grammy Willa was quick to note. Behind the binoculars, her eyes had teared up full, as they'd wanted to do all afternoon. It was the birthday blues, no doubt about it.

A big rush of wind came up suddenly and shook Donna's seashell chimes, which were hanging by the front door. Sarah tried to find the wind with her new binoculars, tried to focus in on that force of nature that could cause so much commotion and noise without ever being seen, the way love could. There was nothing there but rain, and the shaky movement of grass and shrubs bowing in that invisible breath, bending, breaking. There was nothing there but the fragile sound of seashells clicking with a sad, wistful music, playing Mozart maybe. Donna went to the phone and answered it. Sarah could hear a distant voice talking on the other end of the line, ghostly words coming from a thin narrow wire, from the home she now shared with a woman she barely knew.

"You're gonna have to speak up, Lucinda," Donna said. She winked at Sarah, who had put the binoculars down, who never again wanted to find things closer than they were, not when things were really *farther away* than they should be, like Donna was farther away. *Lot #15. Symphony #26.* "I can't hear a single word you're saying," Donna said. She smiled a mischievous little smile at Sarah, but Sarah was listening to the chimes again, ghostly and faint, imagining how helpless they were, caught up in the strength of all that wind. She was listening for that sad and distant music that only angels can hear.

Lily King

Five Tuesdays in Winter

Mitchell's daughter, who was twelve, accused him of loving his books but hating his customers. He didn't *hate* them. He just didn't like having to chat with them, or lead them to very clearly marked sections (if they couldn't read signs, why were they buying books?) while they complained that nothing was arranged by title. He would have liked to have a bouncer at the door, a man with a rippled neck who would turn people away or quietly remove them when they revealed too much ignorance.

His daughter loved the customers. She sat behind the counter at the cash drawer every Saturday, writing up receipts in an illegible imitation of his own microscopic hand and chatting like an innkeeper. She was too tall and too sophisticated for a Maine preteen. She made him uneasy. She had recently learned the word "reticent" and used it on him constantly.

"Isn't he the most reticent person you've ever met?" she asked Kate, his only other employee.

"Maybe not the very most," Kate said, not looking up from her pricing.

"But he's—"

"That's enough, Paula," he said, then, feeling an unexpected pulse of blood to his cheeks, fled to the stockroom in back.

Mitchell had good ears, and just before he shut the door behind him, he heard Kate's gentle reprimand: "I think as a rule people don't like being spoken of in the third person."

He'd hired Kate three months ago. She'd recently moved to Portland from San Francisco for a man named Lincoln. They lived in a small apartment in the East End. On their machine, Lincoln sounded high-strung and full of anticipation, as if he only ever expected good news after the beep. Despite her strong résumé, Kate had unexpected gaps in her knowledge of books. She had never read *The Leopard* or *Independent People*. She had never even heard of Thomas Bernhard. Once he overheard a customer ask how many lines were in a sestina, and she didn't know. She was a reader (she borrowed and returned as many as ten books a week), but not a speller. On the dupe sheet, she wrote J. Austin and F. Dostoyevski. At the end of the day, when she stapled the credit-card receipts to the ticker-tape totals, she didn't always align the edges evenly. She let the pencils run out of lead. She had thin, sometimes dry lips, which she picked at when she was thinking deeply and which he would have liked to kiss.

Wanting to kiss Kate was like wanting a larger savings account for Paula's college education or one of those infallible computerized postal scales for mail orders. It was a persistent, irritating, useless desire. He had been on two dates since Paula's mother left. The first one, more than five years ago now, had been a setup, a friend of a friend. They'd gone to an Italian restaurant for pasta puttanesca. She'd picked out all of her capers and left them on the lip of her bowl, explaining that she was allergic to shellfish. Then she'd wanted to talk about his wife's departure. The story—his college buddy Brad coming to visit from Australia and leaving a week later with a box of live lobsters and Mitchell's wife—seemed to arouse her. He couldn't bear to take her out again and lost the mutual friend as a result. Thankfully, others had left him alone.

He hadn't been devastated when his wife walked out. People vanished. It had been happening all his life. His mother died when he was six, his father nine years later. His best friend from childhood, Aaron, had found a lump on his back—Mitchell himself had spotted it first on the beach—and he was dead by Labor Day. Even his favorite customer, Mrs. White, had died within a few years of the shop's opening.

Mitchell stood at the stockroom's one window and watched three gulls flap restlessly above the harbor. Thick broken slabs of ice, the size of mattresses, had been pushed to the shore by the tide. Out farther, beyond the frozen crust, the open water shimmered a luminous summer blue. In these kinds of cold spells everything seemed confused. Even the gulls overhead seemed lost.

Later that afternoon, Paula said, "Kate speaks Spanish." Kate demurred from where she was shelving, but Paula overrode her. "She does. Did you know that, Dad?"

"Mmm-hmmm." He was going through a mildewed carton a student had just brought in. They were good books, without writing or highlighting on any page, but the bottom edge of nearly every one had a pen and ink drawing of a hairy testicle.

"That's my icon, in my frat," the student said. "It's a—"

"I *know* what it is." Mitchell was sharp, even for Mitchell.

Paula glowered. She was trying to train him to be more forgiving of his patrons. That was her campaign, ever since she'd grown tall, learned words like reticent, and found him flawed.

After the frat boy had gone, Paula said, "I was thinking . . . Kate could help with my Spanish conversation."

Kate approached the counter as if she were a customer. "I'm not a teacher. I just lived in Peru for a couple of years."

"Are you fluent?"

He could see from her face that it was a rigid question. "By the time I left I could say pretty much anything I wanted. But it's been six years now."

She would have been living in Peru when his wife left. He hoped, with an uncomfortable swell of feeling, that she had been happy there, that if his and Paula's life had been redirected, like the course of a river, she had been the recipient of those higher waters. Full of this fervent thought, he headed, for a reason he'd forgotten, to anthropology.

Paula found him there, staring blankly at the spines on the shelf. "She said she could come on Tuesday evenings. Can she?"

"If you think it will help."

"I've *told* you Mr. Camargo never lets us speak."

He did not say that she'd never mentioned this before.

To the store, Kate wore faded, untucked shirts and jeans slashed at the knee. He was often tempted to tease her, tell her that just because she sold used books she didn't have to wear used clothes, but he thought she might snap back with a crack about the pittance he paid her, so he refrained. To the first Spanish lesson, however, Kate walked up the path to his door in wool pants the color of cranberries. Tuesday was her day off. Perhaps she'd had a late lunch date downtown with Lincoln. Worse, she might have had a job interview. It was an easy thing to find out. She was the type who could not take a compliment. If he told her she looked nice, she'd give the reason instead of saying thank you. But he was the type who could not give a compliment, so he just said hello and let her in.

Paula called from her room and he directed Kate down the hallway. The door clicked shut and he heard no Spanish, just peals of laughter, for the next half-hour.

He'd planned to do some paperwork before starting dinner, but when he sat down at his desk, he pulled out Kate's application instead. February 14th, 1968. Just as he'd remembered. She was well into her thirties, plenty old enough to be Paula's mother. So what was she doing in there, giggling like a seventh grader? Her birthday was coming up. On Valentine's Day, no less. Maybe she'd quit before then. She might expect a gift, or he might want to give her a little something and she'd take it the wrong way. Or Lincoln would.

They emerged from Paula's bedroom rosy-cheeked and watery-eyed, speaking gibberish. He quickly slipped the application back in its file.

"*Entonces, nos vemos el sábado, ¿no?*" Kate said.

"*¿Sábado? Sí.*"

They passed his desk without noticing him.

"*Bueno. Hasta luego, Paula.*" She added an extra half-syllable to his daughter's name.

"Adios, Caterina."

They kissed on both cheeks, as if in Paris.

He waved from his chair, not wanting to break the flow with the clunk of English.

When she came to their house the next Tuesday, she wrote down on a slip of paper (a bank receipt, he saw later, that stated she had $57.37 in her account) from her coat pocket her new address and phone number. She was moving closer to the store.

"With Lincoln?" Paula asked, and Mitchell for once was grateful for her prying.

"No," Kate said, as if she might say more, then didn't.

"Why not? He has such perfect teeth."

Paula read the question on Mitchell's face and said, "She showed me a picture of him."

Long after she'd gone, he got up from his reading to start supper and realized the slip of paper was still crushed in his hand.

The second and last date Mitchell had had since his wife left was with a woman who worked in the insurance office next to his store. Sometimes she'd come in when she got off work, and even though she talked too much and only looked at the oversized books with photos in any given section, he agreed to go to the movies with her when she got up the nerve to ask him. They chose a comedy, but she kept whispering in his ear right before every joke, so that everyone in the audience was always laughing except them. He'd come out of the theater excruciatingly unsatisfied, far more unsatisfied than a movie whose jokes he'd missed should have left him. He felt abstracted and disjointed, and it occurred to him that the sensation was only a slight magnification of what he felt all the time. He couldn't wait to get back to his car in the store parking lot and drive away. But she was in an entirely different mood. She nearly twirled down the street, swayed not too subtly against him, and asked if he'd like to get a coffee. He said no, without excuse.

The next day while he was unpacking a shipment of remainders in the stockroom, he heard her through the wall. She was on the phone with a friend. "No," she said, "it wasn't that bad. It was fun actually . . . Yeah, he is, but I kind of like that . . . (huge hoot of laughter) . . . I *do* . . . All right, details. Let's see . . . The high point? Oh God. Let's see . . . " Mitchell left the box half full and went back to the front of the store. That day he didn't stay till closing, but left at quarter of five. He did this for a week straight until one evening when his former employee, the employee before Kate, had a dentist appointment and he'd had to stay. She didn't come in. She never came in again. He saw her crossing the street once, and another time she was behind him at Westy's, the take-out place up the block, but they didn't speak. He couldn't say when he stopped seeing her altogether, when she must have left the insurance company, over a year ago, maybe two.

He listened to Kate's new message: *Hi. I'm not here. Say something funny and I'll get back to you.* But her voice was not hopeful. It was the voice of someone stuck in Maine for no good reason.

The only time he ever got any information about her was on Tuesdays and Saturdays. The rest of the week, without Paula, they worked together in the uninterrupted professionalism he'd established the first week of her employment. It was as if she'd never stood in his living room or giggled in Spanish with his daughter. He often hoped that Paula would bring up Kate's name in the evenings, let something slip about her he didn't know, but she never did. She spoke instead of teachers, friends, projects, a concert she wanted to go to. In history she was studying Watergate, and she wanted to know what he knew about it. His friend Aaron had been an intern in D.C. that summer of the hearings, the summer before Mitchell saw the hard knot on his spine. He and Aaron had talked on the phone a lot, sometimes until two or three in the morning, passionate talk about the implications of impeachment and then, that hot August, the resignations. Paula waited for Mitchell's version of the events, but what he remembered most now about Watergate was the feeling of being nineteen in a one-room apartment, and the sound, though it had been silent for so many years now, of Aaron's hyena laugh. Finally, when he began to describe the break-in, Paula said she already knew all that, and when he said that it was the end of an era, the government's undeniable breach of faith with its people, she said her teacher explained that, too. So he told her about his one-room apartment and how Aaron's laugh nearly broke his eardrums, and she was inexplicably satisfied.

On the third Tuesday, as Kate was leaving, the phone rang. Paula ran to answer it. It was for her, of course, so Mitchell walked their guest to the door alone. She was dressed up again; she had put her coat on carefully so as not to wrinkle her soft ivory shirt. She had thin, straight hair that she'd probably complained about (as Paula had about hers) all her life, but which was clean and shiny and soft-looking. Again he wanted to say how nice she looked, but instead said that he hoped she was keeping careful record of her tutoring hours. She nodded that she was and told him he didn't have to keep reminding her. He was embarrassed she remembered he'd said this before. It was his default line; it came out of his mouth when he wanted to say other things to her.

He watched her walk to her car which, during the lesson, had received a light coating of snow. He wondered if she'd brush off all the windows, or just the front and back. She didn't do any of them. She just got into the car, put on the wipers, and, without looking sideways to see him standing unconcealed at the window of his brightly lit living room, drove away.

"Kate has a date," Paula said, catching him in the act of watching her car disappear around the corner.

"Lincoln?" he asked hopefully, more comfortable with an old rival than a new one.

"They're over. With some guy she met at the store."

"My store?"

"She just said *tienda*, but I think so."

"She told you this in Spanish?"

"That's why she's here, isn't it?"

"Sí," Mitchell ventured uneasily.

The next day he told Kate she'd have to start addressing flyers for the sale he had every April.

"I don't mind at all, but you do know it's only the first of February."

He remembered her approaching birthday and the dilemma about Valentine's, and said, "There are over a thousand to send out, so we should get started on it."

He set her up in his office in the back, and waited on the thin stream of customers himself.

"Call if you need help," she'd said before he shut her in.

"I will." But he knew even if there was a line ten deep he wouldn't call.

Around two, a young man in a dark green parka came up to the counter. Mitchell knew he was going to ask for Kate, and when he did, he explained that she was busy at the moment. He was careful not to indicate in which direction she was so busy. Unperturbed, the man asked where the art section was, then slowly made his way toward it, lingering at the new arrival bin, the poetry shelves, mythology, psychology, before arriving at art. If he pulled out a book, he replaced it exactly as it had been, flush with the other spines and the edge of its shelf, just as Mitchell liked them. But he had bad posture, which made the bottom of the coat hang away from his body.

He could see Kate looking at her watch as she came out of his office. He couldn't think of any way to keep her from coming forward.

She looked down all the aisles until she found him.

"Hey," Mitchell heard her say.

"How're you doing?"

"A little disoriented." She flexed her hand, the one that had been addressing flyers for the past five hours. Her friend didn't ask why, and Mitchell was pleased that he shared this information with Kate alone. "Let's go," she said. Mitchell's spirits plummeted.

She hadn't mentioned leaving early. She had to stay until six. She came around the counter to get her coat and scarf. "I'm going to grab something at Westy's. Want anything?"

He'd forgotten all about lunch. "No," he said, even though he was suddenly starving. "Only mushroom soup."

It was a very small joke they had. Once, about four years ago, Westy's had served, for one day, the most delicious mushroom soup he'd ever tasted. They'd never offered it again, but he'd never stopped looking on the specials board for it, every time he went in. Occasionally he put in a request, but the teenager at the register clearly had no say over soups.

Commercial Street was covered in a thick, lumpy layer of ice, and they crossed it slowly, without touching. But they were talking a lot. Blue puffs came out of their mouths at the same time. They opened the door to Westy's and disappeared inside. They'd probably eat at one of the booths. He couldn't very well complain if once in the three months she'd been working there she ate her lunch there instead of bringing it back.

There was a couple in the far room whispering in fiction. He'd been pricing a stack of books he'd just bought from a composer, but now that Kate was gone he'd lost his concentration. He went down the aisle her friend had chosen, and pulled out, one by one, the books he'd looked at. Each one was a decent book in a sea, he acknowledged with familiar shame, of mediocre books. He would have liked to have an intensely intellectual selection—no confessional poetry, no massmarket psychology, no coffee-table crap. But as it was, business was precarious. Most intellectuals were like the composer: selling, not buying. A few days ago, a woman had come in with swatches of fabric and asked him to find books only in those colors. Last week a man had been looking for *War and Peace*, and when Mitchell explained that he was temporarily out of anything by Tolstoy, the man asked if he had it by anyone else. It was a terrible time for books.

"Hey, where are you?" She pulled on his sleeve. "I got it! Mushroom soup!" She held up two containers. She was smiling as wide as he'd ever seen. Her nose was red and dripping and beautiful. "It better be as good as you promised."

Hadn't she already eaten? Where was the guy in the green coat?

How much did he owe her? Questions swarmed, but stayed behind the tight knot in his mouth.

There was always one stool behind the counter and another that he used to prop open the door in summer, which now stood by the coat rack nobody ever used. He'd once wanted the store to be a homey place, the sort of place where you come in and hang up your coat and stay awhile, but it never had been. He'd never given any customer the impression that he wanted them to stay awhile. Kate found this other stool and dragged it around back, so that the two stools were now side by side, with a bowl of mushroom soup on the counter in front of each one.

He felt as if he would burst. He'd read about this feeling in novels, but he was sure he'd never experienced it. Meeting his wife had brought him pleasure, or a sort of relief, the mystery of whom to spend his life with solved—or so he'd thought. But he'd actually been fairly content before he met her, talking on the phone with Aaron, eating tuna in his little room, reading from the stacks of books borrowed from the store he now owned.

They took a long lunch. Customers, as always, were irritating and disruptive. They were worse in this kind of weather. There was a focus that went out of people's eyes. They often forgot what they were looking for and lingered absentmindedly in the aisles. When an elderly woman finally made it out the door, Kate grunted, imitating the way he had responded to her gratitude for finding her a book.

"It was *Middlemarch*," he explained.

"Which is a great book."

"I *know* it's a great book." He was aware of how much like Paula he sounded when he whined. "But shouldn't she have read it by now? She's only a hundred and thirty-seven years old."

"She could be reading it for the hundred and thirty-seventh time. Or she could be giving it to her granddaughter. Or great-granddaughter." She seemed amused, entirely uninterested in changing him. He knew it was like that at first, with anyone. He also knew it might mean that she didn't care about him at all.

He tried to think of what it really was that had bothered him about the old woman. For once in his life, the thought turned instantly to speech, before he could stop it. "I miss Mrs. White."

"What?"

"An old woman who used to come in here."

"What was she like?"

Mitchell hadn't thought about the actual Mrs. White in a long time. When he thought about her now it was just a feeling, not a person, just a deep longing. He hadn't known her very well. She used to sit on the hard pink chair in science, reading Stephen Jay Gould. They'd shared a laugh once, when a girl a few years older than Paula moved swiftly through the store to the picture of Thomas Pynchon that hung on the back wall, and burst into tears. It was the only picture of Pynchon available then, and not many people had ever seen even that, a reproduction of his high school yearbook photo, teeth like a donkey's. "The only person who should cry over that picture is his mother," Mrs. White had said.

Kate allowed him his silence. She didn't try to reframe the question or ask another. Mrs. White would have done the same thing. *What was she like?* She was like you, he realized, watching Kate bend to take a sip of her soup.

"She was like you," he said, incredulous.

The following day he couldn't bear her to be so far from him, and told her, at the risk of her finding more dates, that she didn't have to spend more than an hour a day addressing flyers. He stayed at the counter with her, but they spoke very little. He pored through the boxes of books people lugged in from their cars, she took money from the customers, and in between they priced in silence. He wanted to ask her if she was planning to move back to San Francisco, or somewhere else, but every time he rehearsed it in his head, it sounded like a boss's question and not a friend's. Just before closing, a customer came up to the counter and asked if they were related. "You two have the exact same kind of eyes," he told them. He was drunk and the comment was preposterous. Kate had warm, thick-lidded brown eyes, and his were a narrow, suspicious green. The man didn't have a coat and they watched him lurch away into the frozen air. They were careful not to look at each other's eyes. It was only yesterday, the day of the mushroom soup, but it was already far away.

Mitchell comforted himself with the thought of Saturday, the day after next, when Paula would be there with them. But that night she told him she had play practice in the morning—she'd been cast as Uncle Max in *The Sound of Music*—and that her friend Holly had invited her over afterwards.

Once he recovered from that blow, he saw on his calendar that the fourteenth of February fell on a Tuesday, the fifth Tuesday of Spanish lessons.

Saturday then Tuesday came and went, eventless. On Wednesday and on Friday it snowed. He woke up in the middle of the night thinking about snow clinging to the ends of Kate's hair and the slope of her back when she sat on the stool, then scolded himself until dawn. He tried to think of how to mention, offhand, to Paula that Kate's birthday was approaching. But, as usual, she was three steps ahead of him. "I completely forgot to tell you," she said at dinner. "I asked Kate to stay for dinner next Tuesday. It's her *cumpleaños*."

"Her birthday?" He feigned uncertainty.

"Have you been listening at the door, Dad?"

He wished he had the nerve.

"What should we get her?" Paula asked.

"How about a brooch?" he suggested.

"A brooch? What's that?"

"You know, a sparkly," he put his fingers on his chest, "pin thing."

"Oh my God. You are not serious."

"Then make her something."

"Like what?"

"I don't know. A drawing. A necklace. Or, what about doing what you used to do to the gravel?"

"Dad!"

Mitchell, remembering the hours Paula spent with her rock

polisher, lamented the loss of the driveway as a primary source of entertainment and gifts. He knew he'd have to drive Paula to the mall.

They saw Kate there that Sunday in the food court. She was eating a burrito, alone. Both he and Paula had the same irrational impulse to conceal themselves for fear that she would guess their purpose, and shadow her through the shops in order to discover her preferences. After lunch, she went to the perfume counters in Filene's. A saleslady offered her some powder on a brush, but Kate shook her head and said something that made the woman laugh. Mitchell's chest contracted slightly at being denied the words. Then they watched her weave through the smaller stores and their red streamers and glittering hearts and loud reminders with the words *Sweetheart* and *Someone Special.*

"She seems sad," Paula said.

Mitchell was relieved she'd noticed. He thought it was just his own wishful thinking.

Kate didn't buy anything. They watched her leave the mall, scan the parking lot for her car, then head toward it. There was nothing outside—not above or below or in the woods beyond the mall—that wasn't some shade of gray. The cold had eased and everything that had been solid was now a thick, filthy sludge.

"It's an awful time of year to have a birthday."

Paula agreed. They stood at the door Kate had walked through. She unlocked her car, lifted her long coat in behind her, shut the door, and sat for at least a minute before starting the engine. She'd been born in Swanton, Ohio. She'd had her appendix removed. She didn't like green peppers or people in costumes or Henry James. She had a mole on her head, just where her part began. With only this handful of facts, he admitted to himself as Paula drew hearts in the clouds she breathed on the plate glass, he'd begun to truly care for her.

They bought her a brooch and went home.

His wife had left because she claimed he was locked shut. She said the most emotion he'd ever shown her had been during a heated debate about her use of a comma in a note she'd left him about grocery shopping.

There was no reason why anything would be different, why he would be able to make anyone happier now. He was the same person. He'd always been the same person. He marveled how in books people looked back fondly to remembered selves as if they were lost acquaintances. But he'd never been anything but this one self. Perhaps it was because physically there'd been little change; he'd lost no hair, gained no weight, grown no beard. He'd read a great deal in the past twenty years, but nothing that threatened his view of the world or his own minuscule place within it.

Still, on the fifth Tuesday, as Mitchell made dinner during the lesson, the lasagna noodles quivered in his hands as he placed them in the pan. He was as nervous as a schoolgirl. He wondered where that expression came from, for he had never seen Paula ever behave this way. Nervous as a forty-seven-year-old bookseller was how the saying should go.

Kate had arrived with a small heart-shaped box of chocolates, which he'd set on a table in the living room. He'd been so startled by the gift that he hadn't taken in the rest of her, and now he couldn't picture her in Paula's room, sitting at the foot of the bed where they always sat (he'd often seen the indentation after she'd gone). Every now and then, as he went about preparing dinner, Mitchell glanced through the open doorway at the box of chocolates.

He was just putting the lasagna in the oven when Kate flew past.

"Where're you going?" he said, unable to conceal his horror as she flung her coat over her shoulders without bothering to fit her arms in the sleeves, and reached for the door.

"I'll be right back." The door slammed shut and he heard her holler from the walkway, "She'll be fine."

He went to his daughter's room. The door was open, but she wasn't in it. On her quilt on the bed was a dark red stain and a few pale streaks. Her bathroom door was shut. He stood in silence before it.

"I'm okay, Dad." She sounded like she was hanging upside down.

"You sure?" He couldn't control the wobble in his voice.

"Kate's gone to get some stuff."

He actually already had "stuff" in his bathroom; he'd bought it for her years ago, just in case. "That's good," he said.

He felt pleased that he was not overreacting, that he knew right away what had happened and hadn't called an ambulance. And then he looked down and saw the blood up close. He was holding the quilt in his arms. He didn't remember taking it off the bed. It was a quilt his mother had made and he had slept beneath as a child. The mottled stains seemed like warnings. Soon Paula would begin complaining that he didn't understand her, didn't appreciate her, didn't love her enough, when in fact he loved her so much his heart often felt shredded by it. But people always wanted words for all that roiled inside you.

"How do you feel?" he ventured.

"All right. Kinda weird."

"Your mother used to get terrible cramps." He waited for the clutch that came with talking about her, like someone had grabbed him by the chest hair. "She got headaches sometimes, too. She took extra iron. We probably still have some. They're green, in a white bottle." He waited, but the clutching feeling never came. "And she had a bullet birth when you were born, you know. Thirty-five minutes, I think. We barely made it to the hospital. Not that you want to be thinking of that right now." Sweat prickled his scalp. Shut up, he told himself. "One time she was wearing these white pants and—"

"Do you miss her, Dad?"

"No." He was astonished by the truth of it.

"I don't either, anymore. I feel like I *should* miss her. All I really remember is her walking me to school and holding my hand and giving me big hugs at the door. But I always knew the minute she turned her back I was out of her mind completely. She wasn't like you. I knew you were thinking about me always."

She was revising now, creating new memories out of what she was left with, but his eyes stung anyway.

When Kate came back from the pharmacy, he retreated to the kitchen. He could hear her coaching Paula, first in the bathroom and then through the door. At times her voice was serious and precise; other times they were both laughing. After a long while, she came in the kitchen. She caught him standing there in the middle of the room, doing nothing. She touched the quilt in his arms. "If I run cold water on it now, it won't stain."

"I'll do it." He went down the narrow back hallway to the laundry room with the big basin, and she followed. He never expected her to follow.

He turned on the faucet. "You may have to undo some stuff I told her while you were gone. I babbled on about iron and pregnancy and probably scared the lights out of her."

"You babbled? I thought you were the most reticent man in the world."

"Every forty-seven years or so I babble."

She still had her coat on. It must have started snowing again. Melted flakes glinted like stars all over her.

They had to do the quilt bit by bit, wringing out one part before starting on another. He wished, as in a fairy tale, the cloth would never end, and they could spend the rest of their lives washing and wringing.

He heard the timer buzz, then the oven door squeak open.

They hung the quilt on the fishing line he'd strung up years ago. When they were done he could do nothing but look at her. She looked carefully back. Paula called them to dinner, but they made no move toward the kitchen.

"Why do you think," he asked her, "that man said we have the same eyes?"

"Maybe he saw something similar in them."

"Like what?"

"Fear." She looked away. He'd forgotten how disappointing these conversations could be.

"Desire," she added quietly.

Love, he thought. It would come out soon enough. Words and feelings were all churned up together inside him, finding each other like lost parts of an atom. He didn't try to push them apart or away.

He let them float in the new fullness in his chest.

She brought her hand to his face. It wasn't the face other women had touched. The skin wasn't the same. His nerve endings had multiplied. He could feel each one of her fingers, their different sizes and temperatures. His stomach made a long slow twist in anticipation of all that his lips would feel.

He pulled Kate close, but Paula came around the corner then, and they jumped back. His daughter, however, was pleased by what she found. She took them each by the arm and led them to dinner. She'd lit a candle and poured apple juice into wineglasses. She'd put the heart of chocolates by his place. Lasagna sizzled in the center of the small table, and Kate was smiling. Mitchell felt that a long conversation was just beginning and, if only for this moment in his kitchen, if only for this one winter evening, he had a lot to say.

Richard Ford

Charity

On the first day of their Maine vacation, they drove up to Harrisburg after work, then flew to Philadelphia, then flew to Portland, where they rented a Ford Explorer at the airport, ate dinner at a Friendly's, then drove up 95 as far as Freeport—it was long after dark—where they found a B&B directly across from L. L. Bean, which surprisingly was open all night.

Before getting into the rickety canopy bed and passing out from exhaustion, Nancy Marshall stood at the dark window naked and looked across the shadowy street at the big, lighted Bean's building, shining like a new opera house. At one A.M., customers were streaming in and out toting packages, pulling garden implements, pushing trail bikes, and disappearing into the dark in high spirits. Two large Conant tourist buses from Canada sat idling at the curb, their uniformed drivers sharing a quiet smoke on the sidewalk while their Japanese passengers were inside buying up things. The street was busy here, though farther down the block the other expensive franchise outlets were shut.

Tom Marshall turned off the light in the tiny bathroom and came and stood just behind her, wearing blue pajama bottoms. He touched her shoulders, stood closer to her until she could feel him aroused.

"I know why the store's open 'til one o'clock," Nancy said, "but I don't know why all the people come." Something about his conspicuous warm presence made her feel a chill. She covered her breasts, which were near the window glass. She imagined he was smiling.

"I guess they love it," Tom said. She could feel him properly—very stiff now. "This is what Maine means. A visit to Bean's after midnight. It's the global culture. They're probably on their way to Atlantic City."

"Okay," Nancy said. Because she was cold, she let herself be pulled to him. This was all right. She was exhausted. His cock fit between her legs—just there. She liked it. It felt familiar. "I asked the wrong question." There was no reflection in the glass of her or him behind her, inching into her. She stood perfectly still.

"What would the right question be?" Tom pushed flush against her, bending his knees just a fraction to find her. He *was* smiling.

"I don't know," she said. "Maybe the question is, what do they know that we don't? What are we doing over here on this side of the street? Clearly the action's over there."

She heard him exhale, then he moved away. She had been about to open her legs, lean forward a little. "Not that." She looked around for him. "I don't mean that." She put her hand between her legs just to touch, her fingers covering herself. She looked back at the street. The two bus drivers she believed could not see through the shadowy trees were both looking right at her. She didn't move. "I didn't mean that," she said to Tom faintly.

"Tomorrow we'll see some things we'll like," he said cheerfully. He was already in bed. That fast.

"Good." She didn't care if two creeps saw her naked; it was exactly the same as her seeing them clothed. She was forty-five. Not so slender, but tall, willowy. Let them look. "That's good," she said again. "I'm glad we came."

"I'm sorry?" Tom said sleepily. He was almost gone, the cop's blessed gift to be asleep the moment his head touched the pillow.

"Nothing," she said, at the window, being watched. "I didn't say anything."

He was silent, breathing. The two drivers began shaking their heads, looking down now. One flipped a cigarette into the street. They both looked up again, then stepped out of sight behind their idling buses.

Tom Marshall had been a policeman for twenty-two years. They had lived in Harlingen, Maryland, the entire time. He had worked robberies and made detective before anyone. Nancy was an attorney in the Potomac County public defender's office and did women's cases, family defense, disabled rights, children at risk. They had met in college at Macalester, in Minnesota. Tom had hoped to be a lawyer, expected to do environmental or civil rights, but had interviewed for the police job because they'd suddenly produced a child. He found, however, that he liked police work. Liked robberies. They were biblical (though he wasn't religious), but not as bad as murders. Nancy had started law school before their son, Anthony, graduated. She hadn't wanted to get trapped with too little to do when the house suddenly became empty. The reversal in their careers seemed ironic but insignificant.

In his twenty-first year, though, two and a half years ago, Tom Marshall had been involved in a shooting inside a Herman's sporting goods, where he'd gone to question a man. The officer he partnered with had been killed, and Tom had been shot in the leg. The thief was never caught. When his medical leave was over, Tom went back to work with a medal for valor and a new assignment as an inspector of detectives, but that had proved unsatisfying. And over the course of six months he became first bored by his office routine, then alienated, then had experienced "emotional issues"—mostly moodiness—which engendered bad morale consequences for the men he was expected to lead. So that by Christmas he retired, took his pension at forty-three, and began a period of at-home retooling, which after a lot of reading led him to the idea of inventing children's toys and actually making them himself in a small workspace he rented in an old wire factory converted to an artists' co-op in the nearby town of Brunswick, on the Potomac.

Tom Marshall, as Nancy observed, had never been truly "cop-ish." He was not silent or cynical or unbending or self-justifying or given to explosive, terrifying violence. He was, instead, a tall, bean-poley, smilingly handsome man with long arms, big bony hands and feet, a shock of coarse black hair, and a generally happy disposition. He was more like a high-school science teacher, which Nancy thought he should've been, though he was happy to have been a cop once he was gone from the job. He liked to read Victorian novels, hike in the woods, watch birds, study the stars. And he could fix and build any- thing—food processors, lamps, locks—could fashion bird and boat replicas, invent ingenious furniture items. He had the disposition of a true artisan, and Nancy had never figured out why he'd stayed a cop so long except that he'd never thought his life was his own when he was young, but rather that he was a married man with responsibilities. Her most pleasing vision of her married self was standing someplace, *anyplace*, alongside some typical Saturday-morning project of Tom's— building a teak inlaid dictionary stand, fine-tuning a home-built go- cart for Anthony, rigging a timed sprinkling system for the yard—and simply *watching* him admiringly, raptly, almost mystically, as if to say "how marvelous and strange and lucky to be married to such a man." Marrying Tom Marshall, she believed, had allowed her to learn the or- dinary acts of devotion, love, attentiveness, and the acceptance of an- other—acts she'd never practiced when she was younger because, she felt, she'd been too selfish. A daddy's girl.

Tom had gotten immediately and enthusiastically behind the prospect of Nancy earning a law degree. He came home on flextime to be with Anthony during his last year of high school. He postponed vacations so she could study, and never talked about his own law- school aspirations. He'd rented a hall, staged a graduation party, and driven her to her bar exam in the back of a police car, then staged an- other party when she passed. He applauded her decision to become a public defender, and didn't gripe about the low pay and long hours, which he said were the costs of important satisfactions and of making a contribution.

For a brief period then, after Tom took his retirement and began work at the co-op, and Anthony had been accepted at Goucher and was interning for the summer in D.C., and Nancy had gotten on her feet with the county, their life on earth seemed as perfect as ever could be imagined. Nancy began to win more cases than she lost. Anthony was offered a job for whenever he graduated. And Tom dreamed up and actually fabricated two toy sculptures for four-year-olds that he surprisingly sold to France, Finland, and to Neiman Marcus.

One of these toys was a ludicrously simple dog shape that Tom cut out on a jigsaw, dyed yellow, red, and green, and drew on dog features. But he cut the shape in a way to effectively make *six* dogs that fitted together, one on the other, so that the sculpture could be taken apart and reassembled endlessly by its child owner. Tom called it Wagner-the-Dog, and made twenty thousand dollars off of it and had French interest for any new ideas. The other sculpture was a lighthouse made of balsam, which also fitted together in a way you could dismantle but was, he felt, too intricate. It sold only in Finland and didn't make any money. Maine Lighthouse he called it, and didn't think it was very original. He was planning a Web site.

The other thing Tom Marshall did once everything was wonderful was have an affair with a silkscreen artist who also rented space in the artists' co-op—a woman much younger than Nancy, named Crystal Blue, whose silkscreen operation was called "Crystal Blue's Creations," and who Nancy had been nice to on the occasions she visited Tom's space to view his new projects.

Crystal was a pretty little airhead with no personality of any sort who printed Maxfield Parrish–like female profiles in diaphanous dresses, using garish, metallic colors. These she peddled out of an electric blue van with her likeness on the side, usually to bikers and amphetamine addicts at fourth-rate craft fairs in West Virginia and southern Pennsylvania. Nancy realized Crystal would naturally be drawn to Tom, who was a stand-up, handsome, wide-eyed guy—the opposite of Crystal. And Tom might be naturally attracted to Crystal's cheapness, which posed as a lack of inhibition. Though only up to a point, she assumed—the point being when Tom stopped to notice there was nothing there to be interested in. Another encounter, of course. But along with that would quickly come boredom, the annoyance of managing small-change deceptions, and the silly look Crystal kept on her large, too-Italian mouth, which would inevitably become irritating. Plus the more weighty issues of betrayal and the risk of doing irreparable damage to something valuable in his—and Nancy's—life.

Tom, however, managed to look beyond these impediments, and to fuck Crystal in her silkscreen studio on an almost daily basis for months, until her boyfriend figured it out and called Nancy at her office and blew Tom's cover by saying in a nasal, West Virginia accent, "Well, what're we gonna do with our two artistic lovebirds?"

When Nancy confronted Tom—at dinner in an Asian restaurant down the street from the public defender's office—with a recounting of the boyfriend's phone conversation, he became very grave and fixed his gaze on the tablecloth and laced his large bony fingers around a salad fork.

It was true, he admitted, and he was sorry. He said he thought fucking Crystal was a "reaction" to suddenly being off the force after half his life, and being depressed about his line-of-duty injury, which still caused him discomfort when it rained. But it was also a result of pure exhilaration about his new life, something he needed to celebrate on his own and in his own way—a "universe feeling" he called it, wherein acts took place outside the boundaries of convention, obligation, the past, and even good sense (just as events occurred in the universe). This new life, he said, he wanted to spend entirely with Nancy, who'd sat composed and said little, though she wasn't thinking about Crystal, or Tom, or Crystal's boyfriend or even about herself. While Tom was talking (he seemed to go on and on and on), she was actually experiencing a peculiar sense of weightlessness and near disembodiment, as though she could see herself listening to Tom from a comfortable but slightly dizzying position high up around the red, scrolly, Chinese-looking crown molding. The more Tom talked, the less present, the less substantial, the less *anything* she felt. If Tom could've gone on talking—recounting his problems, his anxieties, his age-related feelings of underachievement, his dwindling sense of self-esteem since he quit chasing robbers with a gun—Nancy realized she might just have disappeared entirely. So that the problem (if that's what all this was—a problem) might simply be solved: no more

Crystal Blue; no more morbid, regretful Tom; no more humiliating, dismal disclosures implying your life was even more like every other life than you were prepared to concede—all of it gone in the breath of her own dematerialization.

She heard Tom say—his long, hairy-topped fingers turning the ugly, institutional salad fork over and over like a prayer totem, his solemn gaze fastened on it—that it was absolutely over with Crystal now. Her hillbilly boyfriend had apparently set the phone down from talking to Nancy, driven to Crystal's studio and kicked it to pieces, then knocked her around a little, after which the two of them got in his Corvette and drove to Myrtle Beach to patch things up. Tom said he would find another space for his work; that Crystal would be out of his life as of today (not that she'd ever really been *in* his life), and that he was sorry and ashamed. But if Nancy would forgive him and not leave him, he could promise her that such as this would never happen again.

Tom brought his large blue cop's eyes up off the table and sought hers. His face—always to Nancy a craggy, handsome face, a face with large cheekbones, deep eye sockets, a thick chin, and overlarge white teeth—looked at that moment more like a skull, a death's head. Not really, of course; she didn't see an actual death's head like on a pirate flag. But it was the thought she experienced, and the words: "Tom's face is a death's head." And though she was sure she wasn't obsessive or compulsive or a believer in omens or symbols as sources of illumination, she *had* thought the words—Tom's face is a death's head—and pictured them as a motto on the lintel of a door to a mythical courtroom that was something out of Dante. One way or another, this, the idea of a death's head, had to be somewhere in what she believed.

When Tom was finished apologizing, Nancy told him without anger that changing studios shouldn't be necessary if he could stay away from Crystal when she came back from Myrtle Beach. She said she had perhaps misjudged some things, and that trouble in a marriage, especially a long marriage, always came about at the instigation of both partners, and that trouble like this was just a symptom and not terribly important per se. And that while she didn't care for what he'd done, and had thought that very afternoon about divorcing him sim- ply so she wouldn't have to think about it anymore, she actually did- n't believe his acts were directed at her, for the obvious reason that she hadn't done anything to deserve them. She believed, she said, that what he'd done was related to the issues he'd just been talking about, and that her intention was to forgive him and try to see if the two of them couldn't weather adversity with a greater-than-ever intimacy.

"Why don't you just fuck *me* tonight?" she said to him right at the table. The word *fuck* was provocative, but also, she realized, slightly pathetic as an address to your husband. "We haven't done that in a while." *Though of course you've been doing it every day with your retarded girl- friend* were the words she'd thought but didn't like thinking.

"Yes," Tom said, too gravely. Then, "No."

His large hands were clasped, forkless, on the white tablecloth not far from hers. Neither moved as though to effect a touch.

"I'm so sorry," Tom said for the third or fourth time, and she knew he was. Tom wasn't a man distanced from what he felt. He didn't say something and then start thinking what it could mean now that he'd said it, finally concluding it didn't mean anything. He was a good, sin- cere man, qualities that had made him an exemplary robbery detec- tive, a superb interrogator of felons. Tom meant things. "I hope I haven't ruined our life," he added sadly.

"I hope not, too," Nancy said. She didn't want to think about ru- ining her life, which seemed ridiculous. She wanted to concentrate on what an honest, decent man he was. Not a death's head. "You proba- bly haven't," she said.

"Then let's go home now," he said, folding his napkin after dab- bing his mouth. "I'm ready."

Home meant he would fuck her, and no doubt do it with ardor and tenderness and take it all the way. He was very good at that. Crystal hadn't been crazy to want to fuck Tom instead of her nasal, crybaby boyfriend. Nancy wondered, though, why she herself ex- pected that now; why *fuck me?* Probably it was *fuck me* instead of *fuck you*. Since she didn't much want that now, she thought it would surely happen. It made her regretful; because she was, she realized, the very sort of person she'd determined Tom was not, even though she was not an adulterer and he was: she *was* a person who said things, then looked around and wondered why she'd said them and what their consequences could be, and (often) how she could get out of doing the very things she said she desired. She'd never exactly recognized this about herself, and now considered the possibility that it had just become true, or been made true by Tom's betrayal. But what was it, she wondered, as they left the restaurant headed for home and bed? What was that thing she was? Surely it was a thing anyone should be able to say. There would be a word for it. She simply couldn't bring that word to mind.

The next morning, Friday—after the night in Freeport—they ate breakfast in Wiscasset, in a shiny little diner that sat beside a large greenish river, over which a low concrete bridge moved traffic briskly north and south. The gilt-edged sign outside Wiscasset said it was THE PRETTIEST VILLAGE IN MAINE, which seemed to mean there were few houses, and those few were big and white and expensive-looking, with manicured yards and plaques by the front doors telling everyone when the house was built. Across the river, which was called the Sheepscot, white summer cottages speckled out through forested riverbank. This was Maine—small in scale, profusely scenic, annoyingly remote, exclusive, and crowded. She knew they were close to the ocean, but she hadn't seen it yet, even from the plane last night. The Sheepscot was clearly an estuary; gulls were flying upriver in the clear morning air, crisp little lobster craft, a few sailboats sat at anchor.

When they'd parked and hiked down toward the diner, Tom had stopped to bend over, peering into several windows full of house-for-sale pictures, all in color, all small white structures with crisp green roofs situated "minutes" from some body of water imprecisely seen in the background. All the locales had Maine-ish names. Pemaquid Point. Passamaquoddy something. Stickney Corner. The houses looked like the renter cabins across the river—places you'd get sick of after one season and then have to put back on the market. She couldn't gauge if prices were high or low, though Tom thought they were too high. It didn't matter. She didn't live here.

When he'd looked in at two or three realty windows, Tom stood up and stared down at the river beyond the diner. Water glistened in the light September air. He seemed wistful, but he also seemed to be contemplating. The salt-smelling breeze blew his hair against the part, revealing where it was thinning.

"Are you considering something 'only steps from the ocean'?" she said, to be congenial. She put her arm in under his. Tom was an enthusiast, and when a subject he wanted to be enthusiastic about proved beyond him, it often turned him gloomy, as though the world were a hopeless place.

"I was just thinking that everything's been discovered in this town," he said. "You needed to be here twenty years ago."

"Would you like to live in Wiscasset, or Pissamaquoddy, or whatever?" She looked down the sloping main street—a block of glass-fronted antique shops, a chic deli, a fancy furniture store above which were lawyers' and CPA offices. These buildings, too, had plaques telling their construction dates. 1880s. Not really so old. Harlingen had plenty of buildings that were older.

"I wish I'd considered it *that* long ago," Tom said. He was wearing tan shorts, wool socks, a red Bean's canvas shirt, and running shoes. They were dressed almost alike, though she had a blue anorak and khaki trousers. Tom looked like a tourist, not an ex-cop, which, she guessed, was the idea. Tom liked the idea of transforming yourself.

"A vacation is *not* to regret things, or even to think about things permanently." She tugged his arm. She felt herself being herself on his behalf. The street through town—Route 1—was already getting crowded, the bridge traffic slowing to a creep. "The idea of a vacation is to let your spirits rise on the breeze and feel unmoored and free."

Tom looked at her as though she'd become the object of his longing. "Right," he said. "You'd make somebody a great wife." He looked startled for saying that and began walking away as if embarrassed.

"I *am* somebody's wife," she said, coming along, trying to make it a joke, since he'd meant something sweet, and nothing was harmed. It was just that whatever was wrong between them caused unexpected events to point it out but not identify it. They loved each other. They knew each other very well. They were married people of good will. Everything was finally forgivable—a slip of the tongue, a botched attempt at lovemaking, a conversation that led nowhere or to the wrong place. The question was: what did all these reserves of tender feeling and kind regard actually *come to*? And not come to? Walking down the hill behind her husband, she felt the peculiar force of having been through life only once. These three days were to determine, she understood, if anything more than just this minimum made sense. It was an important mystery.

Inside the Miss Wiscasset Diner, Nancy perused *The Down-East Pennysaver*, which had a dating exchange on the back page. *Men seeking women. Women seeking men.* Nothing else was apparently permissible. No *Men seeking men.* Tom studied the map they'd picked up in the B&B, and which contained a listing of useful "Maine Facts" in which everything occasioned an unfunny variation on the state name: Maine Events. Mainely Antiques. Mainiac Markdowns. Maine-line Drugs. Roof Maine-tenance. No one seemed able to get over what a neat name the place had.

Out on the river, a black metal barge was shoving a floating dredger straight up the current. The dredger carried an immense bucket suspended on a cable at the end of an articulated boom. The whole enterprise was so large as to seem ridiculous.

"What do you suppose that's for?" Nancy said. The diner was noisy with morning customers and contained a teeming greasy-bacon and buttery-toast smell.

Tom looked up from his map out at the dredger. It would not get past the bridge where Route 1 crossed the river. It was too tall. He looked at her and smiled as though she hadn't said anything, then went back to his "Maine Facts."

"If you're interested, all the women seeking men are either 'full-figure gals over fifty,'" she said, forgetting her question, "or else they're sixteen-year-olds seeking mature 'father figures.' The same men get all the women in Maine."

Tom took a sip of his coffee and knitted his brows. They had until Sunday, when they were flying out of Bangor. They knew nothing about Maine, but had discussed a drive to Bar Harbor and Mount Katahdin, which they'd heard were pretty. Nancy had proposed to visit the national park, a bracing hike, then maybe a swim in the late-lasting-summer ocean if it wasn't too frigid. They'd imagined leaves would be turning, but they weren't yet because of all the summer rain.

They were also not able to tell exactly how far anything was from anything else. The map was complicated by quirky peninsulas extending back south and the road having to go up and around and down again. The morning's drive from Freeport had seemed long, but not much distance was covered. It made you feel foreign in your own country. Though they'd always found happiness inside an automobile—as far back as when Tom played drums in a college rock band and she'd gone along on the road trips, sleeping in the car and in ten-dollar motels. In the car, who they really were became available to the other. Guards went down. They felt free.

"There's a town called Belfast," Tom said, back to his map. "It's not far up. At least I don't think it is." He looked back at where the floating dredger was making its slow turn in the river, beginning to ease back toward the ocean. "Did you see that thing?"

"I don't get what 'down-east' means," Nancy said. Everything in the *Pennysaver* that wasn't a play on "Maine" had "down-east" somehow attached to it. The dating exchange was called "Down-East In Search Of." "Does it mean that if you follow one of the peninsulas as far as you can go south, you get east?"

This was a thing Tom should know. It was his idea to come here instead of the Eastern Shore place they liked. Maine had all of a sudden "made sense" to him—something hazy about the country having started here and the ocean being "primary" among experiences, and his having grown up near Lake Michigan and that never seeming remotely primary.

"That's what I thought it meant," Tom said.

"So what does Maine mean? Maine what?" she asked. Nothing was in the *Pennysaver* to explain anything.

"That I do know," Tom said, watching the barge turning and starting back downstream. "It means main *land*. As opposed to an island."

She looked around the crowded diner for their waitress. She was ready for greasy bacon and buttered toast and had wedged the *Pennysaver* behind the napkin dispenser. "They have a high opinion of themselves here," she said. "They seem to admire virtues you only understand by suffering difficulty and confusion. It's the New England spirit, I guess." Tom's virtues, of course, were that kind. He was perfect if you were dying or being robbed or swindled—a policeman's character traits, and useful in many more ways than policing. "Isn't Maine the state where the woman was shot by a hunter while she was pinning up clothes on the line? Wearing white gloves or something, and the guy thought she was a deer? You don't have to defend that, of course."

He gave her his policeman's regulation blank stare across the tabletop. It was an expression his face could change into, leaving his real face—normally open and enthusiastic—back somewhere forgotten. He took injustice personally.

She blinked, expecting him to say something else.

"Places that aren't strange aren't usually interesting," he said solemnly.

"It's just my first morning here." She smiled at him.

"I want us to see this town Belfast." He reconsulted the map. "The write-up makes it seem interesting."

"Belfast. Like the one where they fight?"

"This one's in Maine, though."

"I'm sure it's wonderful."

"You know me," he said, and unexpectedly smiled back. "Ever hopeful." He was an enthusiast again. He wanted to make their trip be worthwhile. And he was absolutely right: it was too soon to fall into disagreement. That could come later.

Early in the past winter Tom had moved out of their house and into his own apartment, a grim little scramble of white, drywalled rectangles that were part of a new complex situated across a wide boulevard from a factory-outlet mall and adjacent to the parking lot of a large veterinary clinic where dogs could be heard barking and crying day and night.

Tom's departure was calculatedly not dramatic. He himself had seemed reluctant, and once he was out, she was very sorry not to see him, not to sleep next to him, have him there to talk to. Some days she would come home from her office and Tom would be in the kitchen, drinking a beer or watching CNN while he heated something in the microwave—as though it was fine to live elsewhere and then turn up like a memory. Sometimes she would discover the bathroom door closed, or find him coming up from the basement or just standing in the back yard staring at the hydrangea beds as if he was considering weeding them.

"Oh, *you're* here," she'd say. "Yeah," he'd answer, sounding not entirely sure how he'd come to be present. "It's me." He would sometimes sit down in the kitchen and talk about what he was doing in his studio. Sometimes he'd bring her a new toy he'd made—a colorful shooting star on a pedestal, or a new Wagner in brighter colors. They talked about Anthony, at Goucher. Usually, when he came, Nancy asked if he'd like to stay for dinner. And Tom would suggest they go out, and that he "pop" for it. But that was never what she wanted to do. She wanted him to stay. She missed him in bed. They had never talked about being apart, really. He was doing things for his own reasons. His departure had seemed almost natural.

Each time he was there, though, she would look at Tom Marshall in what she tried to make be a new way, see him as a stranger; tried to decide anew if he was in fact so handsome, or if he looked different from how she'd gotten used to him looking in twenty years; tried to search to see if he was as good-willed or even as large and rangy as she'd grown accustomed to thinking. If he truly had an artisan's temperament and a gentle manner, or if he was just a creep or a jerk she had unwisely married, then gradually gotten used to. She considered the possibility of having an affair—a colleague or a delivery boy. But that seemed too mechanical, too much trouble, the outcome so predictable. Tom's punishment would have to be that she *considered* an affair and expressed her freedom of choice without telling him. In a magazine she picked up at the dentist's, she read that most women radically change their opinions of their husbands once they spend time away from them. Except women were natural conciliators and forgivers and therefore preferred not to be apart. In fact, they found it easy, even desirable, to delude themselves about many things, but especially about men. According to the writer—a psychologist— women were hopeless.

Yet following each reassessment, she decided again that Tom Marshall *was* all the things she'd always thought him to be, and that the reasons she'd have given to explain why she loved him were each valid. Tom was good; and being apart from him was not good, even if he seemed able to adjust to being alone and even to thrive on it. She would simply have to make whatever she could of it. Because what Nancy knew was, and she supposed Tom understood this, too: they were in an odd place together; were standing upon uncertain emotional territory that might put to the test exactly who they were as humans, might require that new facets of the diamond be examined.

This was a *very* different situation from the ones she confronted at the public defender's every day, and that Tom had encountered with the police—cut-and-dried, overdramatic and beyond-repair problems, where things went out of control fast, and people found themselves in court or in the rough hands of the law as a last-ditch way of resolving life's difficulties. If people wouldn't overdramatize so much, Nancy believed, if they remained pliable, did their own thinking, restrained themselves, then things could work out for the better. Though for some people that must be hard.

She had been quite impressed by how she'd dealt with things after Tom had admitted fucking Crystal d'Amato (her real name). Once Tom made it clear he didn't intend to persist with Crystal, she'd begun to feel all right about it almost immediately. For instance, she noticed she hadn't experienced awful stress about envisioning Tom bare-ass on top of Crystal wherever it was they'd done it (she envisioned a big paint-stained sheet of white canvas). Neither did the idea of Tom's betrayal seem important. It wasn't really a betrayal; Tom was a good man; she was an adult; betrayal had to mean something worse that hadn't really happened. In a sense, when she looked at Tom now with her benign, inquiring gaze, fucking Crystal was one of the most explicable new things she knew about him.

And yet, she realized, as spring came on and Tom remained in the Larchmere Apartments—cooking his miserly meals, watching his tiny TV, doing his laundry in the basement, going to his studio in the co-op—the entire edifice of their life was beginning to take on clearer shape and to grow smaller. Like a valuable box lost overboard into the smooth wake of an ocean liner. Possibly it was a crisis. Possibly they loved each other well enough, perhaps completely. Yet the strongest force keeping them together wasn't that love, she thought, but a matching curiosity about what the character of their situation was, and the novelty that neither of them knew for sure.

But as Tom had stayed away longer, seemingly affable and well-adjusted, she indeed had begun to feel an *ebbing*, something going out of her, like water seeping from a cracked beaker, restoring it to its original, vacant state. This admittedly did not seem altogether good. And yet, it might be the natural course of life. She felt isolated, it was true, but isolated in a grand sort of way, as if by being alone and getting on with things, she was achieving something. Unassailable and strong was how she felt—not that anyone wanted to assail her; though the question remained: what was the character of this strength, and what in the world would you do with it alone?

"Where's Nova Scotia?" Nancy said, staring at the sea. Since leaving Rockland, an hour back on Route 1, they'd begun glimpsing ocean, its surface calm, dense, almost unpersuasively blue, encircling large, distinct, forested islands Tom declared were reachable only by ferries and were the strongholds of wealthy people who were only there in the summer and didn't have heat.

"It's a parallel universe out there," he said as his way of expressing that he didn't approve of life like that. Tom had an affinity for styles of living he considered authentic. It was his one conventional-cop attitude. He thought highly of the Mainers for renting their seaside houses for two months in the summer and collecting fantastic sums that paid their bills for the year. This was authentic to Tom.

Nova Scotia was in her head now, because it would be truly exotic to go there, far beyond the green, clean-boundaried islands. Though she couldn't tell exactly what direction she faced out the car window. If you were on the East Coast, looking at the ocean, you should be facing east. But her feeling was this rule didn't apply in Maine, which had something to do with distances being farther than they looked on the map, with how remote it felt here, and with whatever "down-east" meant. Perhaps she was looking south.

"You can't see it. It's way out there," Tom said, referring to Nova Scotia, driving and taking quick glances at the water. They had driven through Camden, choked with tourists sauntering along sunny streets, wearing bright, expensive clothing, trooping in and out of the same expensive outlet stores they'd seen in Freeport. They had thought tourists would be gone after Labor Day, but then their own presence disproved that.

"I just have a feeling we'd be happier visiting there," she said. "Canada's less crowded."

A large block of forested land lay solidly beyond a wide channel of blue water Tom had pronounced to be Penobscot Bay. The block of land was Islesboro, and it, too, he said, was an island, and rich people also lived there in the summer and had no heat. John Travolta had his own airport there. She mused out at the long undifferentiated island coast. Odd to think John Travolta was there right now. Doing what? It was nice to think of *it* as Nova Scotia, like standing in a meadow watching cloud shapes imitate mountains until you feel you're *in* the mountains. Maine, a lawyer in her office said, possessed a beautiful coast, but the rest was like Michigan.

"Nova Scotia's a hundred and fifty miles across the Bay of Fundy," Tom said, upbeat for some new reason.

"I once did a report about it in high school," Nancy said. "They still speak French, and a lot of it's backward, and they don't much care for Americans."

"Like the rest of Canada," Tom said.

Route 1 followed the coast along the curvature of high tree-covered hills that occasionally sponsored long, breathtaking views toward the bay below. A few white sails were visible on the pure blue surface, though the late morning seemed to have furnished little breeze.

"It wouldn't be bad to live up here," Tom said. He hadn't shaved, and rubbed his palm across his dark stubble. He seemed happier by the minute.

She looked at him curiously. "Where?"

"Here."

"Live in Maine? But it's mortifyingly cold except for today." She and Tom had grown up in the suburbs of Chicago—she in Glen Ellyn, Tom in a less expensive part of Evanston. Their very first agreement had been that they hated the cold. They'd chosen Maryland for Tom to be a policeman because it was unrelentingly mild. Her feelings hadn't changed. "Where would you go for the two months when you were renting the house to the Kennedy cousins just so you could afford to freeze here all winter?"

"I'd buy a boat. Sail it around." Tom extended his estimable arms and flexed his grip on the steering wheel. Tom was in dauntingly good health. He played playground basketball with black kids, mountain-biked to his studio, did push-ups in his apartment every night before climbing into bed alone. And since he'd been away, he seemed healthier, calmer, more hopeful, though the story was somehow that he'd moved a mile away to a shitty apartment to make *her* happier. Nancy looked down disapprovingly at the pure white pinpoint sails backed by blue water in front of the faultlessly green-bonneted island where summer people sat on long white porches and watched the impoverished world through expensive telescopes. It wasn't that attractive. In the public defender's office she had, in the last month, defended a murderer, two pretty adolescent sisters accused of sodomizing their brother, a nice secretary who, because she was obese, had become the object of taunts in her office full of gay men, and an elderly Japanese woman whose house contained ninety-six cats she was feeding, and who her neighbors considered, reasonably enough, deranged and a health hazard. Eventually the obese secretary, who was from the Philippines, had stabbed one of the gay men to death. How could you give all that up and move to Maine with a man who appeared not to want to live with you, then be trapped on a boat for the two months it wasn't snowing? These were odd times of interesting choices.

"Maybe you could talk Anthony into doing it with you," she said, thinking peacefully again that Islesboro was Nova Scotia and every-one there was talking in French and speaking ill of Americans. She had almost said, "Maybe you can persuade Crystal to drive up and fuck you on your yacht." But that wasn't what she felt. Poisoning perfectly harmless conversation with something nasty you didn't even mean was what the people she defended did and made their lives impossi-ble. She wasn't even sure he'd heard her mention Anthony. It was pos-sible she was whispering.

"Keep an open mind," Tom said, and smiled an inspiriting smile.

"Can't," Nancy said. "I'm a lawyer. I'm forty-five. I believe the rich already stole the best things before I was born, not just twenty years ago in Wiscasset."

"You're tough," Tom said, "but you have to let me win you."

"I told you, you already did that," she said. "I'm your wife. That's what that means. Or used to. You win."

This was Tom's standard view, of course, the lifelong robbery-detective *slash* enthusiast's view: someone was always needing to be won over to a better view of things; someone's spirit being critically lower or higher than someone else's; someone forever acting the part of the hold-out. But she wasn't a hold-out. *He'd* fucked Crystal. *He'd* picked up and moved out. *That* didn't make her not an enthusiast. Though none of it converted Tom Marshall into a bad person in need of punishment. They merely didn't share a point of view—his being to sentimentalize loss by feeling sorry for himself; hers being not to seek extremes even when it meant ignoring the obvious. She wondered if he'd even heard her say he'd won her. He was thinking about something else now, something that pleased him. You couldn't blame him.

When she looked at Tom he was just past looking at her, as if *he'd* spoken something and *she* hadn't responded. "What?" she said, and pulled a strand of hair past her eyes and to the side. She looked at him straight on. "Do you see something you don't like?"

"I was just thinking about that old line we used to say when I was first being a policeman. 'Interesting drama is when the villain says something that's true.' It was in some class you took. I don't remember."

"Did I just say something true?"

He smiled. "I was thinking that in all those years my villains never said much that was true or even interesting."

"Do you miss having new villains every day?" It was the marquee question, of course; the one she'd never actually thought to ask a year ago, during the Crystal difficulties. The question of the epic loss of vocation. A wife could only hope to fill in for the lost villains.

"No way," he said. "It's great now."

"It's better living by yourself?"

"That's not really how I think about it."

"How do you really think about it?"

"That we're waiting," Tom said earnestly. "For a long moment to pass. Then we'll go on."

"What would we call that moment?" she asked.

"I don't know. A moment of readjustment, maybe."

"Readjustment to exactly what?"

"Each other?" Tom said, his voice going absurdly up at the end of his sentence.

They were nearing a town. BELFAST, MAINE. A black and white corporate-limits sign slid past. ESTABLISHED 1772. A MAINE ENTERPRISE CENTER. Settlement was commencing. The highway had gradually come nearer sea level. Traffic slowed as the roadside began to repopulate with motels, shoe outlets, pottery barns, small boatyards selling posh wooden dinghies—the signs of enterprise.

"I wasn't conscious I needed readjustment," Nancy said. "I thought I was happy just to go along. I wasn't mad at you. I'm still not. Though your view makes me feel a little ridiculous."

"I thought you wanted one," Tom said.

"One what? A chance to feel ridiculous? Or a period of *readjustment?*" She made the word sound idiotic. "Are you a complete stupe?"

"I thought you needed time to reconnoiter." Tom looked deviled at being called a stupe. It was old Chicago code to them. An ancient language of disgust.

"Jesus, why are you talking like this?" Nancy said. "Though I suppose I should know why, shouldn't I?"

"Why?" Tom said.

"Because it's bullshit, which is why it sounds so much like bullshit. What's true is that *you* wanted out of the house for your own reasons, and now you're trying to decide if you're tired of it. And me. But you want *me* to somehow take the blame." She smiled at him in feigned amazement. "Do you realize you're a grown man?"

He looked briefly down, then raised his eyes to hers with contempt. They were still moving, though Route 1 took the newly paved bypass to the left, and Tom angled off into Belfast proper, which in a split second turned into a nice, snug neighborhood of large Victorian, Colonial, Federal, and Greek Revival residences established on large lots along an old bumpy street beneath tall surviving elms, with a couple of church steeples anchored starkly to the still-summery sky.

"I do realize that. I certainly do," Tom said, as if these words had more impact than she could feel.

Nancy shook her head and faced the tree-lined street, on the right side of which a new Colonial-looking two-story brick hospital addition was under construction. New parking lot. New oncology wing. A helipad. Jobs all around. Beyond the hospital was a modern, many-windowed school named for Margaret Chase Smith, where the teams, the sign indicated, were called the SOLONS. Someone, to be amusing, had substituted "colons" in dripping blood-red paint. "There's a nice new school named for Margaret Chase Smith," Nancy said, to change the subject away from periods of readjustment and a general failure of candor. "She was one of my early heroes. She made a brave speech against McCarthyism and championed civic engagement and conscience. Unfortunately she was a Republican."

Tom spoke no more. He disliked arguing more than he hated being caught bullshitting. It was a rare quality. She admired him for it. Only, possibly now he was *becoming* a bullshitter. How had that happened?

They arrived at the inconspicuous middle of Belfast, where the brick streets sloped past handsome elderly redbrick commercial edifices. Most of the business fronts had not been modernized; some were shut, though the diagonal parking places were all taken. A small harbor with a town dock and a few dainty sailboats on their low-tide moorings lay at the bottom of the hill. A town in transition. From what to what, she wasn't sure.

"I'd like to eat something," Tom said stiffly, steering toward the water.

A chowder house, she already knew, would appear at the bottom of the street, offering pleasant but not spectacular water views through shuttered screens, terrible food served with white plastic ware, and paper placemats depicting a lighthouse or a puffin. To know this was the literacy of one's very own culture. "Please don't stay mad," she said wearily. "I just had a moment. I'm sorry."

"I was trying to say the right things," he said irritably.

"I know you were," she said. She considered reaching for the steering wheel and taking his hand. But they were almost to the front of the restaurant she'd predicted—green beaverboard with screens and a big red-and-white MAINELY CHOWDAH sign facing the Penobscot, which was so picturesque and clear and pristine as to be painful.

They ate lunch at a long, smudged, oilcloth picnic table overlooking little Belfast Harbor. They each chose lobster stew. Nancy had a beer to make herself feel better. Warm, fishy ocean breezes shifted through the screens and blew their paper mats and napkins off the table. Few people were eating. Most of the place—which was like a large screened porch—had its tables and green plastic chairs stacked, and a hand-lettered sign by the register said that in a week the whole place would close for the winter.

Tom maintained a moodiness after their car-argument, and only reluctantly came around to mentioning that Belfast was one of the last "undiscovered" towns up the coast. In Camden, and farther east toward Bar Harbor, the rich already had everything bought up. Any property that sold did so within families, using law firms in Philadelphia and Boston. Realtors were never part of it. He mentioned the Rockefellers, the Harrimans, and the Fisks. Here in Belfast, though, he said, development had been held back by certain environmental problems—a poultry factory that had corrupted the bay for decades so that the expensive sailing set hadn't come around. Once, he said, the now-attractive harbor had been polluted with chicken feathers. It all seemed improbable. Tom looked out through the dusty screen at a bare waterside park across the sloping street from the chowder house. An asphalt basketball court had been built, and a couple of chubby white kids were shooting two-hand jumpers and dribbling a ball clumsily. There was a new jungle gym at the far end where no one was playing.

"Over there," Tom said, his plastic spoon between his thumb and index finger, pointing at the empty grassy park that looked like something large had been present there once. "That's where the chicken plant was—smack against the harbor. The state shut it down finally." Tom furrowed his thick brow as if the events were grave.

An asphalt walking path circled the grassy sward. A man in a silver wheelchair was just entering the track from a van parked up the hill. He began patiently pushing himself around the track while a little girl began frolicking on the infield grass, and a young woman—no doubt her mother—stood watching beside the van.

"How do you know about all that?" Nancy said, watching the man foisting his wheelchair forward.

"A guy, Mick, at the co-op's from Bangor. He told me. He said now was the moment to snap up property here. In six months it'll be too pricey. It's sort of a last outpost."

For some reason the wheelchair rider she was watching seemed like a young man, though even at a distance he was clearly large and bulky. He was arming himself along in no particular hurry, just making the circle under his own power. She assumed the little girl and the woman were his family, making up something to do in the empty, unpretty park while he took his exercise. They were no doubt tourists, too.

"Does that seem awful to you? Things getting expensive?" She breathed in the strong fish aroma off the little harbor's muddy recesses. The sun had moved so she put her hand up to shield her face. "You're not against progress, are you?"

"I like the idea of transition," Tom said confidently. "It creates a sense of possibility."

"I'm sure that's how the Rockefellers and the Fisks felt," she said, realizing this was argumentative, and wishing not to be. "Buy low, sell high, leave a beautiful corpse. That's not the way that goes, is it?" She smiled, she hoped, infectiously.

"Why don't we take a walk?" Tom pushed his plastic chowder bowl away from in front of him the way a policeman would who was used to eating in greasy spoons. When they were college kids, he hadn't eaten that way. Years ago, he'd possessed lovely table manners, eaten unhurriedly and enjoyed everything. It had been his Irish mother's influence. Now he was itchy, interested elsewhere, and his mother was dead. Though this habit was as much his nature as the other. It wasn't that he didn't seem like himself. He did.

"A walk would be good," she said, happy to leave, taking a long last look at the harbor and the park with the man in the wheelchair slowly making his journey around. "Trips are made in search of things, right?" She looked for Tom, who was already off to the cashier's, his back going away from her. "Right," she said, answering her own question and coming along.

They walked the early-September afternoon streets of Belfast—up the brick-paved hill from the chowder house, through the tidy business section past a hardware, a closed movie theater, a credit union, a bank, a biker bar, a pair of older realtors, several lawyers' offices, and a one-chair barbershop, its window cluttered with high-school pictures of young-boy clients from years gone by. A slender young man with a ponytail and his hippie girlfriend were moving large cardboard boxes from a beater panel truck into one of the glass storefronts. Something new was happening there. Next door a shoe-store space had been turned into an organic bakery whose sign was a big loaf of bread that looked real. An art gallery was beside it. It wasn't an unpleasant-feeling town, waiting quietly for what would soon surely arrive. She could see why Tom would like it.

From up the town hill, more of the harbor was visible below, as was the mouth of another estuary that trickled along an embankment of deep green woods into the Penobscot. A high, thirties-vintage steel bridge crossed the river the way the bridge had in Wiscasset, though everything was smaller here, less up-and-going, less scenic—the great bay blue and wide and inert, just another park, sterile, fishless, ready for profitable alternative uses. It was, Nancy felt, the way all things became. The presence of an awful-smelling factory or a poisonous tannery or a cement factory could almost seem like something to wish for, remember fondly. Tom was not thinking that way.

"It's nice here, isn't it?" she said to make good company of herself. She'd taken off her anorak and tied it around her waist vacationer-style. The beer made her feel loose-limbed, satisfied. "Are we down east yet?"

They were stopped in front of another realtor's window. Tom was again bent over studying the rows of snapshots. The walk had also made her warm, but with her sweater off, the bay breeze produced a nice sunny chill.

Another Conant tour bus arrived at the stoplight in the tiny central intersection, red and white like the ones that had let off Japanese consumers last night at Bean's. All the bus windows were tinted, and as it turned and began heaving up the hill back toward Route 1, she couldn't tell if the passengers were Asians, though she assumed so. She remembered thinking that these people knew something she didn't.

What had it been? "Do you ever think about what the people in buses think when they look out their window and see you?" she said, watching the bus shudder through its gears up the hill toward a blue Ford agency sign.

"No," Tom said, still peering in at the pictures of houses for sale.

"I just always want to say, 'Hey, whatever you're thinking about me, you're wrong. I'm just as out of place as you are.' " She set her hands on her hips, enjoying the sensation of talking with no one listening. She felt isolated again, unapprehended—as if for this tiny second she had achieved yet another moment of getting on with things. It was a grand feeling insofar as it arose from no apparent stimulus, and no doubt would not last long. Though here it was. This beleaguered little town had provided one pleasant occasion. The great mistake would be to try to seize such a feeling and keep it forever. It was good just to know it was available at all. "Isn't it odd," she said, facing back toward the Penobscot, "to be seen, but to understand you're being seen wrong. Does that mean . . ." She looked around at her husband.

"Does it mean what?" Tom had stood up and was watching her, as if she'd come under a spell. He put his hand on her shoulder and gently sought her.

"Does it mean you're not inhabiting your real life?" She was just embroidering a mute sensation, doing what married people do.

"Not you," Tom said. "Nobody would say that about you."

Too bad, she thought, the tourist bus couldn't come by when his arm was around her, a true married couple out for a summery walk on a sunny street. Most of that would be accurate.

"I'd like to inhabit mine more," Tom said as though the thought made him sad.

"Well, you're trying." She patted his hand on her shoulder and smelled him warm and slightly sweaty. Familiar. Welcome.

"Let's view the housing stock," he said, looking over her head up the hill, where the residential streets led away under an old canopy of elms and maples, and the house fronts were white and substantial in the afternoon sun.

On the walk along the narrow, slant, leaf-shaded streets, Tom suddenly seemed to have things on his mind. He took long surveyor's strides over the broken sidewalk slabs, as though organizing principles he'd formulated before today. His calves, which she admired, were hard and tanned, but the limp from being shot was more noticeable with his hands clasped behind him.

She liked the houses, most of them prettier and better appointed than she'd expected—prettier than her and Tom's nice blue Cape, the one she still lived in. Most were pleasant variations on standard Greek Revival concepts, but with green shutters and dressy, curved, two-step porches, an occasional widow's walk, and sloping lawns featuring shagbark hickories, older maples, thick rhododendrons, and manicured pachysandra beds. Not very different from the nice neighborhoods of eastern Maryland. She felt happy being on foot where normally you'd be in the car, she preferred it to arriving and leaving, which now seemed to promote misunderstandings and fractiousness of the sort they'd already experienced. She could appreciate these parts of a trip when you were *there*, and everything stopped moving and changing. She'd continued to feel flickers of the pleasing isolation she'd felt downtown. Though it wasn't pure lonely isolation, since Tom was here; instead it was being alone *with* someone you knew and loved. That was ideal. That's what marriage was.

Tom had now begun talking about "life-by-forecast"; the manner of leading life, he was saying, that made you pay attention to mistakes you'd made that hadn't seemed like they were going to be mistakes before you made them, but that clearly *were* mistakes when viewed later. Sometimes very bad mistakes. "Life-by-forecast" meant that you tried very hard to feel, in advance, how you'd feel afterward. "You avoid the big calamities," Tom said soberly. "It's what you're supposed to learn. It's adulthood, I guess."

He was talking, she understood, indirectly but not very subtly about Crystal-whatever-her-name-had-been. Too bad, she thought, that he worried about all that so much.

"But wouldn't you miss some things you might like, doing it that way?" She was, of course, arguing *in behalf* of Tom fucking Crystal, in behalf of big calamities. Except it didn't matter so much. She was at that moment more interested in imagining what this street, Noyes Street, would look like full in the teeth of winter. Everything white, a gale howling in off the bay, a deep freeze paralyzing all activity. Unthinkable in the late summer's idyll. Now, though, was the time when people bought houses. Then was the time they regretted it.

"But when you think about other people's lives," Tom said as they walked, "don't you always assume they're making fewer mistakes than you are? Other people always seem to have a firmer grasp of things."

"That's an odd thing for a policeman to think. Aren't you supposed to have a good grasp on rectitude?" This was quite a silly conversation, she thought, peering down Noyes Street in the direction of where she calculated *she* herself lived, hundreds of miles to the south, where she represented the law, defended the poor and friendless.

"I was never a very good policeman," Tom said, stopping to stare up at a small, pristine Federalist mansion with green ornamental urns on both sides of its high white front door. The lawn, mowed that morning, smelled sweet. Lawn mower tracks still dented its carpet. A lone, male homeowner was standing inside watching them through a mullioned front window. Somewhere, on another street, a chain saw started then stopped, and then there was the sound of more than one metal hammer striking nails, and men's voices in laughing conversation at rooftop level. Preparations were in full swing for a long winter.

"You just weren't like all the other policemen," Nancy said. "You were kinder. But I do *not* assume other people make fewer mistakes. The back of everybody's sampler is always messier than the front. I accept both sides."

The air smelled warm and rich, as if wood and grass and slate walls exuded a sweet, lazy-hours ether mist. She wondered if Tom was getting around in his laborious way to some new divulgence, a new Crystal, or some unique unpleasantness that required the ruin of an almost perfect afternoon to perform its dire duty. She hoped for better. Though once you'd experienced such a divulgence, you didn't fail to expect it again. But thinking about something was not the same as caring about it. That was one useful lesson she'd learned from practicing the law, one that allowed you to go home at night and sleep.

Tom suddenly started up walking again, having apparently decided not to continue the subject of other people's better grip on the alternate sides of the sampler, which was fine.

"I was just thinking about Pat La Blonde while we were down at the chowder house," he said, staying his course ahead of her in long studious strides as though she was beside him.

Pat La Blonde was Tom's partner who'd been killed when Tom had been wounded. Tom had never seemed very interested in talking about Pat before. She lengthened her steps to be beside him, give evidence of a visible listener. "I'm here," she said and pinched a fold of his sweaty shirt.

"I just realized," Tom went on, "all the life that Pat missed out on. I think about it all the time. And when I do, everything seems so damned congested. When Pat got killed, everything started getting in everything else's way for me. Like I couldn't have a life because there was so much confusion. I know you don't think that's crazy."

"No, I don't," Nancy said. She thought she remembered Tom saying these very things once. Though it was also possible she had thought these things *about* him. Marriage was that way. Possibly they had both felt the same thing as a form of mourning. "It's why you quit the force, isn't it?"

"Probably." Tom stopped, put his hands on his hips, and took in an estimable yellow Dutch Colonial sitting far back among ginkgos and sugar maples, and reachable by a curving flagstone path from a stone front wall to its bright-red, perfectly centered, boxwood-banked front door. "That's a nice house," he said. A large black Labrador had been lying in the front yard, but when Tom spoke it struggled up and trotted out of sight around the house's corner.

"It's lovely." Nancy touched the back of his shirt again, down low where it was damp and warm. The muscles were ropy here. She was sorry not to have touched his back recently. In Freeport, last night.

"I think," Tom said, and seemed reluctant, "since that time when Pat was killed, I've been disappointed about life. You know it?" He was still looking at the yellow house, as if that was all he could stand. "Or

I've been afraid of being disappointed. Life was just fine, then all at once I couldn't figure out a way to keep anything simple. So I just made it more complicated." He shook his head and looked at her.

Nancy carefully removed her hand from the warm small of his back and put both her hands behind her in a protective way. Something about Tom's declaration had just then begun to feel like a prologue to something that might, in fact, spoil a lovely day, and refashion everything. Possibly he had planned it this way.

"Can you see a way now to make it *less* complicated?" she said, looking down at her leather shoe toes on the grainy concrete side-walk. A square had been stamped into the soft mortar, and into the middle of it was incised PENOBSCOT CONCRETE—1938. She was pur-posefully not making eye contact.

"I do," Tom said. He breathed in and then out importantly.

"So can *I* hear about it?" It annoyed her to be here now, to have something sprung on her.

"Well," Tom said, "I think I *could* find some space in a town like this to put my workshop. If I concentrated, I could probably dream up some new toy shapes, maybe hire somebody. Expand my output. Go ahead with the Web-site idea. I think I could make a go of it with things changing here. And if I didn't, I'd still be in Maine, and I could find something else. I could be a cop if it came to that." He had his blue, black-flecked eyes trained on her, though Nancy had chosen to listen with her head lowered, hands behind her. She looked up at him now and created a smile for her lips. The sun was in her face. Her temples felt wonderfully warm. A man in khaki shorts was just exiting the yellow house, carrying a golf bag, headed around to where the black Labrador had disappeared. He noticed the two of them and waved as if they were neighbors. Nancy waved back and redirected her smile out at him.

"Where do *I* go?" she said, still smiling. A brown-and-white Belfast police cruiser idled past, its uniformed driver paying them no mind.

"My thought is, you come with me," Tom said. "It can be our big adventure." His solemn expression, the one he'd had when he was talking about Pat La Blonde, stayed on his handsome face. Not a death's face at all, but one that wanted to signify something different. An invitation.

"You want me to move to Maine?"

"I do." Tom achieved a small, hopeful smile and nodded.

What a very peculiar thing, she thought. Here they were on a street in a town they'd been in fewer than two hours, and her estranged husband was suggesting they leave their life, where they were both reasonably if not impossibly happy, and *move* here.

"And why again?" she said, realizing she'd begun shaking her head, though she was also still smiling. The roof workers were once more laughing at something in the clear, serene afternoon. The chain saw was still silent. Hammering commenced again. The man with the golf bag came backing down his driveway in a Volvo station wagon the same bright-red color as his front door. He was talking on a cell phone. The Labrador was trotting along behind, but stopped as the car swung into the street.

"Because it's still not ruined up here," Tom said. "And because I know too much about myself where I am, and I'd like to find out something new before I get too old. And because I think if I—or if we—do it now, we won't live long enough to see everything get all fucked up around here. And because I think we'll be happy." Tom suddenly glanced upward as if something had flashed past his eyes. He looked puzzled for an instant, then looked at her again as if he wasn't sure she would be there.

"It isn't exactly life-by-forecast, is it?"

"No," Tom said, still looking befuddled. "I guess not." He could be like an extremely earnest, extremely attractive boy. It made her feel old to notice it.

"So, am I supposed to agree or not agree while we're standing here on the sidewalk?" She thought of the woman pinning clothes to a line, wearing white gloves. No need to reintroduce that, or the withering cold that would arrive in a month.

"No, no," Tom said haltingly. He seemed almost ready to take it all back, upset now that he'd said what he wanted to say. "No. You don't. It's important, I realize."

"Did you plan all this," she asked. "This week? This whole town? This moment? Is this a scheme?" She was ready to laugh about it and ignore it.

"No." Tom ran his hand through his hair, where there were scatterings of assorted grays. "It just happened."

"And if I said I didn't believe you, what then?" She realized her lips were ever-so-slightly, disapprovingly everted. It had become a habit in the year since Crystal.

"You'd be wrong." Tom nodded.

"Well." Nancy smiled and looked around her at the pretty, serious houses, the demure, scenically shaded street, the sloped lawns that set it all off just right for everybody. If you seek a well-tended ambience, look around you. It was not the Michigan-of-the-East. Why wouldn't one move here? she thought. It was a certain kind of boy's fabulous dream. In a way, the whole world dreamed it, waited for it to materialize. Odd that she never had.

"I'm getting tired now." She gave Tom a light finger pat on his chest. She felt in fact heavy-bodied, older even than she'd felt before. Done in. "Let's find someplace to stay here." She smiled more winningly and turned back the way they'd come, back down the hill toward the middle of Belfast.

In the motel—a crisp, new Maineliner Inn beyond the bridge they'd seen at lunch, where the room offered a long, unimpeded back-window view of the wide and sparkling bay—Tom seemed the more bushed of the two of them. In the car he'd exhibited an unearned but beleaguered stoicism that had no words to accompany its vulnerable-seeming moodiness. And once they were checked in, had their suitcases opened, and the curtains drawn on the small, cool, spiritless room, he'd turned on the TV with no sound, stretched out on the bed in his shoes and clothes, and gone to sleep without saying more than that he'd like to have a lobster for dinner. Sleep, for Tom, was always profound, congestion or no congestion.

For a while Nancy sat in the stiff Naugahyde chair beside a table lamp, and leafed through the magazines previous guests had left in the nightstand drawer: a *Sailing* with an article on the London-to-Cape-Town race; a *Marie Claire* with several bar graphs about ovarian cancer's relation to alcohol use; a *Hustler* in which an amateur artist-guest had drawn inky moustaches on the girls and little arrows toward their crotches with bubble messages that said *Evil lurks here*, and *Members Only*, and *Stay with your unit*. Naughty nautical types with fibroids, she thought, pushing the magazines back in the drawer.

There was another copy of the same *Pennysaver* they'd read at breakfast. She looked at more of the "Down-East In Search Of"s. *Come North to meet mature Presque Isle, cuddly n/s, sjf, cutie pie. Likes contradancing and midnight boat rides, skinny-dipping in the cold, clean ocean. Possibilities unlimited for the right sjm, n/s between 45 and 55 with clean med record. Only serious responses desired. No flip-flops or Canucks plz. English only.* Touching, she thought, this generalized sense of the possible, of what lay out there waiting. What, though, was a lonely *sjf* doing in Maine? And what could a flip-flop be that made them so unlikeable? Cuddly, she assumed, meant fat.

She wished to think about very few things for a while now. On the drive across from Belfast she'd become angry and acted angry. Said little. Then, when Tom was in the office paying for the room while she waited in the car, she'd suddenly become completely *un*-angry, though Tom hadn't noticed when he came back with the key. Which was why he'd gone to sleep—as if his sleep were her sleep, and when he woke up everything would be fixed. Peaceful moments, of course, were never unwelcome. And it was good not to complicate life before you absolutely had to. All Tom's questing may simply have to do with a post facto fear of retirement—another "reaction"—and in a while, if she didn't exacerbate matters, he'd forget it. Life was full of serious but meaningless conversations.

On the silent TV a golf match was under way; elsewhere a movie featuring a young, smooth-cheeked Clark Gable; elsewhere an African documentary with tawny, emaciated lions sprawled in long brown grass, dozing after an offstage kill. The TV cast pleasant watery light on Tom. Soon oceans of wildebeests began vigorously drowning in a muddy, swollen river. It was peaceful in the silence—even with all the drownings—as if what one heard rather than what one saw caused all the problems.

Just outside the window she could hear a child's laughing voice and man's patient, deeper one attempting to speak some form of encouragement. She inched back the heavy plastic curtain and against the sharp rays of daylight looked out at the motel lawn, where a large, thick-bodied young man in a silver wheelchair, wearing a red athletic singlet and white cotton shorts—his legs thick, strong, tanned and hairy as his back—was attempting to hoist into flight a festive orange-paper kite, using a small fishing rod and line, while a laughing little blond girl held the kite above her head. Breeze gently rattled the kite's paper, on which had been painted a smiling oriental face. The man in the wheelchair kept saying, "Okay, run now, run," so that the little girl, who seemed perfectly seven, jumped suddenly, playfully one way and then another, the kite held high, until she had leaped and boosted it up and off her fingers, while the man jerked the rod and tried to winch the smiling face into the wind. Each time, though, the kite drooped and lightly settled back onto the grass that grew all the way down to the shore. And each time the man said, his voice rising at the end of his phrases, "Okay now. Up she goes again. We can do this. Pick it up and try it again." The little girl kept laughing. She wore tiny pink shorts and a bright-green top, and was barefoot and brown-legged. She seemed ecstatic.

He was the man from the park in town, Nancy thought, letting the curtain close. A coincidence of no importance. She looked at Tom asleep in his clothes, breathing noiselessly, hands clasped on his chest like a dead man's, his bare, brown legs crossed at the ankles in an absurdly casual attitude, his blue running shoes resting one against the other. In peaceful sleep his handsome, unshaved features seemed ordinary.

She changed the channel and watched a ball game. The Cubs versus a team whose aqua uniforms she didn't recognize. Her father had been a Cubs fan. They'd considered themselves northsiders. They'd traveled to Wrigley on warm autumn afternoons like this one. He would remove her from school on a trumped-up excuse, buy seats on the first-base line, and let her keep score with a stubby blue pencil. The sixties, those were. She made an effort to remember the players' names, using their blue-and-white uniforms and the vinyl outfield wall as fillips to memory thirty years on. She could think of smiling Ernie Banks, and a white man named Ron something, and a tall, sad-faced, high-waisted black man from Canada who pitched well but later got into some kind of police trouble and cried about it on TV. It was too little to remember.

Though the attempt at memory made her feel better—more settled in the same singular, getting-on-with-it way that standing on the sunny street corner being misidentified by a busload of Japanese tourists had made her feel: as if she was especially credible when seen without the benefit of circumstance and the encumbrances of love, residues of decisions made long, long ago. More credible, certainly, than she was here now, trapped in East Whatever, Maine, with a wayward husband on his way down the road, and suffering spiritual congestion no amount of life-by-forecast or authentic marriage could cure.

This whole trip—in which Tom championed some preposterous idea for the sole purpose of having her reject it so he could then do what he wanted to anyway—made her feel unkind toward her husband. Made him seem stupid and childish. Made *him* seem inauthentic. Not a grownup. It was a bad sign, she thought, to find *yourself* the adult, whereas your lifelong love-interest was suddenly an overexuberant child passing himself off as an enthusiast whose great enthusiasm you just can't share. Since what it meant was that in all probability life with Tom Marshall was over. And not in the way her clients at the public defender's saw things to their conclusions—using as their messenger-agents whiskey bottles, broom handles, car bumpers, firearms, sharp instruments, flammables, the meaty portion of a fist. There, news broke vividly, suddenly, the lights always harsh and grainy, the volume turned up, doors flung open for all to see. (Her job was to bring their affairs back into quieter, more sensible orbits so all could be understood, felt, suffered more exquisitely.)

For her and for Tom, basically decent people, the course would be different. Her impulse was to help. His was to try and then try harder.

His perfidy was enthusiasm. Her indifference was patience. But eventually all the enthusiasm would be used up, all the patience. Possibilities would diminish. Life would cease to be an open, flat plain upon which you walked with a chosen other, and become instead cluttered, impassable. Tom had said it: life became a confinement in which everything got in everything else's way. And what you finally sought became not a new, clearer path, but a way out. Their own son no doubt foresaw life that way, as something that should be easy. Though it seemed peculiar—now that he was away—to think they even *had* a son. She and Tom seemed more like each other's parents.

But, best just to advance now toward what she wanted, even if it didn't include Tom, even if she didn't know how to want what didn't include Tom. And even if it meant she *was* the kind of person who did things, said things, then rethought, even regretted their consequences later. Tom wasn't, after all, trying to improve life for her, no matter what he thought. Only his. And there was no use talking people out of things that improved their lives. He had wishes. He had fears. He was a good-enough man. Life shouldn't be always trying, trying, trying. You should live most of it without trying so hard. He would agree *that* was authentic.

Inside the enclosed room a strange, otherworldly golden glow seemed to fall on everything now. On Tom. On her own hands and arms. On the bed. All through the static air, like a fog. It was beautiful, and for a moment she wanted to speak to Tom, to wake him, to tell him that something or other would be all right, just as he'd hoped; to be enthusiastic in some hopeful and time-proven way. But she didn't, and then the golden fog disappeared, and for an instant she seemed to understand *slightly* better the person she was—though she lacked a proper word for it, and knew only that the time for saying so many things was over.

Outside, the child's voice was shouting. "Oh, I love it. I love it so much." When Nancy pulled back the curtain, the softer light fell across the chair back, and she could see that the wheelchair man had his kite up and flying, the fiberglass fishing rod upward in one hand while he urged his chair down the sloping lawn. The bare-legged child was hopping from one bare foot to the other, a smashing smile on her long, adult's face, which was turned up toward the sky.

Nancy stood and snapped on the desk lamp beside Tom's open suitcase. One bright, intact, shrink-wrapped Wagner dog and one white Maine Lighthouse were tucked among his shirts and shaving kit and socks. Here was also his medal for valor in a blue cloth case, and the small automatic pistol he habitually carried in case of attack. She plucked up only the Wagner dog, returned the room to its shadows, and stepped out the back door onto the lawn.

Here, on the outside, the air was fresh and cool and only slightly breezy, the sky now full of quilty clouds as though rain were expected. A miniature concrete patio with blue plastic-strand chairs was attached to each room. The kite, its slant-eyed face smiling down, was dancing and tricking and had gained altitude as the wheelchair man rolled farther away down the lawn toward the bay.

"Look at our kite," the little girl shouted, shading her eyes toward Nancy and pointing delightedly at the diminishing kite face.

"It's sensational," Nancy said, shading her own eyes to gaze upward. The kite made her smile.

The wheelchair man turned his head to view her. He *was* large, with thick shoulders and smooth rounded arms she could see under his red singlet. His head was round, his thick hair buzzed short, his eyes small and dark and fierce and unfriendly. She smiled at him and for no reason shook her head as though the kite amazed her. An ex-jock, she thought. A shallow-end diving accident, or some football collision that left him flying his kite from a metal chair. A pity.

The man said nothing, just looked at her without gesture, his expression so intent he seemed unwilling to be bothered. She, though, felt the pleasure to be had from only watching, of having to make no comment. The cool breeze, the nice expansive water view to Islesboro, a kite standing aloft were quite enough.

Then her mind flooded with predictable things. The crippled man's shoes. You always thought of them. His were black and sockless, like bowling shoes, shoes that would never wear out. He would merely grow weary of seeing them, give them away to someone more unfortunate than himself. Was this infuriating to him? Did he speak about it? Was the wife, wherever she might be, terribly tired all the time? Did she get up at night and stand at the window, staring out, wishing some quite specific things, then return to bed un-missed? Was pain involved? Did phantom pains even exist? Did he have dreams of painlessness? Of rising out of his chair and walking around laughing, of never knowing a chair? She thought about a dog with its hind parts attached to a little wheeled coaster, trotting along as if all was well. Did *anything* work down below, she wondered? Were there understandings, allowances? Did he think his predicament "interesting"? Had being crippled opened up new and important realms of awareness? What did *he* know that she didn't?

Maybe being married to him, she thought, would be better than many other lives. Though you'd fast get to the bottom of things, begin to notice too much, start to regret it all. Perhaps while he was here flying a kite, the wife was in the hotel bar having a drink and a long talk with the bartender, speaking about her past, her father, her hometown, how she'd thought about things earlier in life, what had once made her laugh, who she'd voted for, what music she'd preferred, how she liked Maine, how authentic it seemed, when they thought they might head home again. How they wished they could stay and stay and stay. The thing she—Nancy—would not do.

"Do you want to fly our kite?" the man was saying to her, his voice trailing up at the end, almost like Tom's. He was, for some reason, smiling now, his eyes bright, looking back over his hairy round shoulder with a new attitude. She noticed he was wearing glasses— surprising to miss that. The kite, its silky monofilament bellying upward in a long sweep, danced on the wind almost out of sight, a fleck upon the eye.

"Oh do, do," the little girl called out. "It'll be so good." She had her arms spread wide and up over her head, as if measuring some huge and inconceivable wish. She was permanently smiling.

"Yes," Nancy said, walking toward them. "Of course."

"You can feel it pulling you," the girl said. "It's like you're going to fly up to the stars." She began to spin around and around in the grass then, like a little dervish. The wheelchair man looked to his daughter, smiling.

Nancy felt embarrassed. Seen. It was shocking. The spacious blue bay spread away from her down the hill, and off of it arose a freshened breeze. It was far from clear that she could hold the kite. It *could* take her up, pull her away, far and out of sight. It was unnerving. She held the toy Wagner to give to the child. That would have its fine effect. And then, she thought, coming to the two of them, smiling out of flattery, that she would take the kite—the rod, the string—yes, of course, and fly it, take the chance, be strong, unassailable, do everything she could to hold on.

Richard Russo

Monhegan Light

Well, he'd been wrong, Martin had to admit as Monhegan began to take shape on the horizon. Wrong about the island, about the ferry. Maybe even wrong to make this journey in the first place. Joyce, Laura's sister, had implied as much, not that he'd paid much attention to her, cunt that she was. Imagine, still trying to make him feel guilty so long after the fact of Laura's death, as if *he* was the one who'd been living a lie for twenty-five years. He could still see her smirking at him. "Poor Martin," she'd said after telling him, with surprisingly little reluctance, where Robert Trevor was to be found. Almost as if she *wanted* Martin to meet the man. "You just don't get it, do you?"

Of all the things that Joyce's sort of woman said about men, Martin disliked the he-just-doesn't-get-it riff most of all. For one thing it presupposed there was something to get, usually something obvious, something you'd have to be blind not to see. And of course the reason you couldn't see it—as women were happy to explain—was that you had a dick, as if that poor, maligned appendage were constantly in a man's line of sight, blocking his view of what women, who were not similarly encumbered, wanted him to take notice of, something subtle or delicate or beautiful, at least to their way of thinking. If you didn't agree that it was subtle or delicate or beautiful, it was because you had a dick. You just didn't get it.

But he *had* been wrong about the island. He'd imagined Monhegan as harboring some sort of retreat or commune inhabited by starving, self-deluded, talentless fringe painters like Joyce. Wannabes.

(Not that Robert Trevor, alas, was one of those.) But a quick scan of the brochure had shown him that he was wrong. This was no commune. The artists who summered here were not hoping to "arrive" one day; they already had. The island's other claim to fame was its hiking trails, for which he was grateful. Otherwise, how could he have explained to Beth his sudden urge to visit this particular island.

The woman in question had closed her eyes and reclined her head over the back of the seat so that her smooth throat was exposed to the weakening September sun. Her long hair hung straight down, spilling onto the top of a backpack that a young man sitting behind them had wedged between the seats. Martin gave the boy an apologetic smile, and received in return a shrug of camaraderie that suggested the boy understood about pretty women who were careless with their hair.

No, Beth was not the sort of girl, Martin reassured himself, who became suspicious. In fact, her ability to take in new data without apparent surprise was one of her great life skills. An arched eyebrow seemed to represent the extreme end of her emotional range when it came to revelation, and to Martin's way of thinking, there was much to be said for such emotional economy, especially in a woman. Beth never said I-told-you-so, even in an I-told-you-so situation, of which the ferry was the latest.

The whole trip, hastily arranged after the shoot had wrapped, was not going smoothly. Both legs of the flight east had been full, which meant they'd not been able to sit together. Martin had been of the opinion that flyers were generally happy to switch seats so that people who were traveling together could sit together, but such requests, they discovered, were far more likely to be honored in order to seat a child next to his mother than to place a middle-aged man next to his fetching, far younger traveling companion. Martin had also been of the opinion that they'd have no trouble picking up a car in Portland, having no reason to know that there was a convention in town. So, instead of heading directly up the coast, they'd spent a day in Portland in a very shabby motel waiting for a rental to become available. And now the ferry.

"I think I've discovered why they don't take cars," Martin told her, gesturing with the tourist brochure. He'd assured her yesterday that all the ferries along coastal Maine took automobiles, and that now, after Labor Day, they probably wouldn't even need a reservation. "There are no roads on the island."

Of course there was a downside to Beth's emotional reticence. That arched eyebrow of hers did manage to convey, perhaps by intention, perhaps not, that she wasn't greatly surprised if you got something wrong, because she understood you, knew you better than you knew yourself, and therefore *expected* you to be wrong about a lot of things. Glancing over at her now, Martin was rewarded with the precise arched eyebrow he'd anticipated, its meaning unmistakable. Fortunately there was also a trace of a smile, and in that smile a hint of generosity that distinguished her from professional bitches like Joyce. Both might come to the same conclusion—that you didn't get it—but only one of them held it against you.

"No paved roads, anyway," he continued, after Beth allowed her eyes to close again sleepily. "Except for the summer, there are only seventy-five full-time residents on the island. Five children attend the local school."

Beth didn't open her eyes when she spoke. "I wonder if they have a special program for gifted kids."

Martin chuckled. "Or a remedial one, come to that."

She didn't smile, causing Martin to wonder if he'd misread her remark. He'd assumed she meant it to be funny, since it was, but one never knew. "She looks perfect for you, Martin," Joyce had remarked yesterday, though Beth had remained in the car while Martin climbed the front porch steps and rang the bell. "How clever of you two to find each other."

"They suggested that visitors bring a flashlight, since power outages are pretty common," he said, looking up from the brochure. "I don't suppose you've got a flashlight on you?"

At this, Beth pulled the material of her tube top away from her chest to check. From where Martin sat, her entire right breast was exposed for a full beat before she allowed the elastic to snap back into place. The young man seated behind them had chosen that precise moment to stand up, which meant that he must have gotten an even better view.

"Hey," he whispered, once the boy had wandered over to the railing. "This ain't L.A."

"It's not?" she said, feigning astonishment. "Really?"

"Okay, fine," he said. "But people have different attitudes about things in New England." California born and bred, Martin had been to the Northeast only a couple of times, both on shoots, once to southern Connecticut, which didn't feel much like New England, and once to Boston, which felt like most other big cities. But Puritanism had flowered in this same rocky soil, hadn't it? And after driving up the coast of Maine from Portland, Martin thought he understood why people who lived in such a harsh, unforgiving landscape might come to sterner conclusions about sex and life in general than they did in, say, Malibu.

"Well, old man, I've spent a lot of money on these boobs."

Which was true. And not just her boobs either, Martin was certain. Beth was a firm believer in fixing whatever ailed you and also, come to think of it, a believer in firmness. At thirty-five her body was taut and lean, her long legs tanned and ropelike, her stomach flat from thousands of murderous crunches. Her breasts, truth be told, were a little too firm, at least for Martin, better to look at than to caress. Whatever she'd done to them caused her nipples to be in a constant state of erection. If the boy over at the rail had gotten a good look, he'd already had the best of them.

"In California," Martin's friend Peter Axelrod was fond of saying wistfully, "ugliness is gradually being bred out of the species." And beauty along with it, Martin sometimes thought. Living in L.A. and working in "the industry," Martin saw many beautiful women, and even the most beautiful were anxious about some supposed flaw, from Audrey Hepburn's eyebrows to Meryl Streep's nose. On the set he'd witnessed many a tearful, whispered conversation in which an actress would explain how that next shot would reveal or emphasize some terrible imperfection she was determined to conceal. Axelrod, whose face had been badly burned in childhood, handled them as well as anybody. "Look at me," he'd say quietly. "Look at this face and then tell me *you're* ugly." They loved him for that, sometimes, Martin suspected, even sleeping with him out of gratitude. Back in his director's chair, he'd give the actress a few minutes to compose herself, explaining to the waiting crew, in his most confidential tones, "Everybody wants to be perfect. I certainly hope this isn't a perfect movie we're making." Whereupon he would be assured it wasn't.

Strangely, when Axelrod himself wed, late in life, the woman he married might have been Beth's sister, a flawless beauty some twenty years his junior with a face and body whose perfect symmetry seemed computer-generated. Which probably meant that men, ultimately, *were* to blame. That's certainly what Joyce would say. It was men, after all, who were responsible for setting the standards of feminine beauty. Someday, Martin felt certain, it would be discovered what women were responsible for, though probably not in his lifetime.

When he looked up from his brochure, Martin saw that the island's lighthouse had come into view above the dark line of trees, so he got up and went over to the rail for a better look. A few minutes later, the ferry rounded the southernmost tip of the island and chugged into the tiny harbor with its scattering of small buildings built into the hillside. High above and blindingly white, the lighthouse was straight out of a Hopper painting, presiding over a village starkly brilliant in its detail. Martin could feel his eyes welling up in the stiff breeze, and when he felt Beth at his elbow, he tried to wipe the tear out of the corner of his left eye with the heel of his hand, a gesture he hoped looked natural. She must have noticed, though, because she said, "Don't be jealous, babe. God lit this one."

It wasn't until they'd disembarked from the ferry, until they located their bags on the dock and started up the hill toward the second-best accommodations on the island, that Martin turned back and saw the name painted on the ferry's transom: *The Laura B.*

He'd told Beth nothing of his wife, except that she'd died several years ago and that they'd stayed married, he supposed, out of inertia. Beth seemed content with this slender account, but she rarely wanted more information than Martin had already offered about most anything. He would have concluded that she was genuinely incurious except that sometimes, if he'd been particularly evasive, she'd pose a follow-up question, days or even weeks after the fact, as if it had taken her all that time to realize he'd not been terribly forthcoming. Worse, she always remembered his precise words, which meant he couldn't plead misunderstanding when a subject got unpleasantly revisited. Often her questions took the form of statements, as was the case now.

"That woman didn't appear to like you very much," she observed over her chicken Caesar salad.

They were the only two people in the dining room. They'd checked in just after two and were told that the dining room was closed, though the young woman working in the kitchen said she supposed, inasmuch as they were guests of the hotel, they might be fed something if what they wanted wasn't too complicated. Martin had ordered a bowl of chowder, figuring something of that sort was probably what the woman had in mind. Beth had ordered the chicken Caesar, which was what she would have ordered if the woman had been mute on the subject of what they might and might not have. When she brought their food a few minutes later, the woman said that the last seating for dinner would be at seven-thirty, which either registered or not with Beth, who didn't look up from the trail map she was studying. She'd changed into hiking clothes in their room.

Martin was about to remark that it was Beth herself whom the cook wasn't fond of when it occurred to him that she'd been referring to Joyce.

"She was Laura's sister," he said, as if it was common knowledge that all sisters despised their brothers-in-law by natural decree.

"Did you fuck her?" Beth asked around a bite of blackened chicken breast.

"Joyce?" Martin snorted.

"Well, I assume you were fucking your wife," Beth pointed out, not unreasonably. Martin might have corrected her, but did not. "Besides, men have been known—"

"I'll try to forgive that unkind and entirely unwarranted suspicion," he said, blowing on his chowder, the first spoonful of which had burned his tongue.

"This is an excellent Caesar salad," Beth said.

"Good," he told her. "I'm glad."

"Now you're mad at me."

"No."

"Tell me," she said, leaving him to wonder for a full beat whether she intended to change the subject or forge ahead. Change it, was Martin's guess, and he was right. "What will you be doing while I'm climbing the island's dangerous cliffs, which this publication warns me not to do alone?"

He decided not to take this particular bait. "I thought I'd take some pictures, maybe visit a gallery or two. See if I can locate a bottle of wine for dinner." The hotel, they'd been informed upon checking in, had no liquor license.

"One dinner without wine wouldn't kill us, actually," Beth said.

"How do you know?"

"Well, it's true I'm only guessing."

Martin studied her until she pushed her plate away. As usual, about half her food was untouched. In all of the time they'd been to-gether, nearly a year now, Martin had never known her to finish a serving of anything. In restaurants known for small portions, Beth would order twice as much food and still leave half. Laura, he recalled, had eaten like a man, with appetite and appreciation.

Then a thought struck him. "When have I ever been unable to an-swer the bell?" he asked. "Any bell."

Beth gave him a small smile, which meant that their argument, if that's what this was, was over. "I'm not overly fond of boxing metaphors applied to sex," she said, taking one of his thumbs and pulling on it. "It's not war."

Like hell, Martin thought.

"But yes," she conceded, "you *do* answer every bell, old man."

"Thank you," Martin said, meaning it. The question he'd asked had been risky, he realized, and he was glad the danger had passed.

"I'm going back to the room for some sunscreen," she said,

pushing her chair back. "I'll be taking the 'A' Trail—"

Martin whistled a few bars of "Take the 'A' Train."

"—in case I need rescuing."

Watching her cross the room, he had a pretty good idea what the sunscreen was for. She'd sunbathe on a rock, topless, in some secluded spot, while the young fellow from the ferry scrutinized her through binoculars from an adjacent bluff. *You could go with her*, he said to himself. *There's nothing preventing you.*

But there was.

From what he'd read in the brochure, roughly a third of the houses on the island had to be artists' studios, though to the casual eye they looked no different from the other houses inhabited, presumably, by lobstermen and the owners of the island's few seasonal businesses. All of the buildings were sided with the same weathered gray shingles, as if subjected, decades ago, to a dress code. He'd half expected to discover that Joyce had lied to him, but Robert Trevor's studio was right where she said it would be, at the edge of the village where the dirt road ended and one of the island's dozen or so hiking trails began. Martin had watched Beth disappear up another of these half an hour ago, purposely waiting until he was sure she hadn't forgotten something and wouldn't return until early evening.

Trevor's studio was unmarked except for a tiny sign with his last name to the left of the door, which was open. Martin was about to knock on the screen door when he heard a loud crash from around back of the house. There, on the elevated deck, Martin found a large man with a flowing mane of silver hair, dressed in paint-splattered jeans and an unbuttoned denim work shirt. He was teetering awkwardly on one knee, his other leg stretched out stiffly in front of him like a prosthesis, trying to prop up a rickety three-legged table with its splintered fourth leg. Jelly jars and paintbrushes were strewn everywhere. One small jar, which according to its label had originally contained artichoke hearts, had described a long, wet arc over the sloping deck and come to a teetering pause at the top of the steps before thumping down all five, coming to rest at Martin's feet.

He picked it up and waited for Robert Trevor—clearly this man was the artist himself—to take notice of him. The wooden leg fell off again as soon as the man, with considerable difficulty, got back to his feet and tested the table. "All right, be that way," he said, tossing the leg aside and collapsing into a chair that didn't look much sturdier than the table. It groaned under his considerable weight, but ultimately held. Martin saw that Robert Trevor was sweating and his forehead was smudged with several different colors of paint from his palette. There was an easel set up next to the table, and Trevor studied the half-finished canvas resting there, a landscape, as if rickety furniture were the least of his problems.

It took him a minute to sense Martin's presence at the foot of his deck, and even then he didn't react with as much surprise as Martin himself would have displayed had their situations been reversed. The painter nodded at Martin as if he'd been expecting him, and he did not get up. "You," he said, running his fingers through his hair, "would be Laura's husband."

"Martin."

"Right, Martin."

"Joyce called you?"

Trevor snorted. "I don't have a phone. That's one of the many beauties of this place." He paused to let this vaguely political observation sink in. "No, the sun went behind a cloud and I looked over and there you were. I made the connection."

Okay, Martin thought. So that's the way it's going to be.

The sun *had* disappeared behind a cloud in that instant, and Martin thought of Beth walking along the cliffs on the back side of the island. She'd be disappointed now, lacking an excuse to sunbathe topless.

"I'm going to need that, Martin," the painter told him, indicating the artichoke jar.

"Can I come up?" Martin asked.

"Have you come to murder me?" Trevor asked. "Did you bring a gun?"

Martin shook his head. "No, no gun. I just came to have a look at you," he said, pleased that this statement so nicely counterbalanced in its unpleasantness the painter's own remark about the sun.

Trevor apparently appreciated the measured response as well. "Well, I guess I'll have to trust you," he replied, finally struggling to his feet.

Martin climbed the steps to the deck, where there was an awkward moment since neither man seemed to relish the notion of shaking hands.

"There's another of those jars under the table, if you feel nimble," the man said. "I could do it myself but it would take me an hour."

Martin fetched that jar and two others while Trevor picked up his brushes, arranging them in groupings that made no sense to Martin, then added solvent to each of the jars from a tin can. Martin, crouching low, managed to wedge the leg back in place fairly securely, then stood up.

"I didn't mean for you to stop work," he said, realizing that this was what was happening.

The painter regarded him as if he'd said something particularly foolish. He was a very big man, Martin couldn't help noticing; he had a huge belly, but was tall enough to carry the weight without appearing obese. He'd probably been slimmer before, when he and Laura were lovers. Martin hadn't doubted that this was what they were from the moment he unpacked the painting.

"The light's about finished for today, Martin," the other man shrugged. "The best light's usually early. The rest is memory. Not like that bastard business you're in."

So, Martin thought. Laura had talked about them. First she'd fucked this painter and then she'd told him about their marriage and their lives.

"What's that term movie people use for the last good light of the day?"

"Magic hour?"

"Right. Magic hour," Trevor nodded. "Tell me, is that real, or just something you people made up?"

"It's real enough."

"Real enough," Trevor repeated noncommittally, as if to weigh the implications of "enough." "Well, if you aren't here to murder me, why don't you have a seat while I get us a beer. And when I come back, you can tell me if *my* Laura's 'real enough' to suit you."

She had arrived professionally wrapped and crated, and when Martin saw the return address on the label, he set the parcel aside in the corner of his study. Joyce had always been an unpleasant woman, so it stood to reason that whatever she was sending him would be unpleasant. She'd called a week earlier, telling him to expect something but refusing to say what. "I wouldn't be sending it," she explained, "except I hear you have a new girlfriend. Is it serious, Martin?"

"I don't see where it's any of your business, Joyce," he'd told her, glad to have this to say since he didn't have any idea whether he and Beth were serious or not. Still, it was something of a mystery how Joyce, who lived clear across the country, could have heard about Beth to begin with. Why she should care was another. What she'd sent him, crated so expertly against the possibility of damage, was a third, but all three mysteries together aroused little curiosity in Martin. That the parcel contained a painting was obvious from its shape and packaging, but he'd idly assumed that talentless, bitter Joyce herself was the painter.

So he'd left the package unopened for more than a week. Beth had been curious about it, or maybe just intrigued by his own lack of interest. She loved presents and received a great many, it seemed to Martin, although the majority were from her doting father, a man not much older than Martin himself. Daddy, as she referred to him, lived in Minnesota with a wife his own age, and Martin, thankfully, had never met either of them. Beth displayed little urgent affection for her parents, though her eyes always lit up when one of her father's packages arrived. "You never buy me presents, Martin," she sometimes said, feigning complaint, when she opened one of these. "Why is that?"

Whatever instinct prevented Martin from opening the painting in front of Beth, he was grateful for it as soon as he tore the outer covering off the skeleton of protective latticework. Seeing Laura there, just behind the cross-hatched slats, he had to suppress a powerful urge to lock the front door and pull the curtains shut against the brilliant California sunlight. After she was uncrated and leaning against the wall, he'd remained transfixed for a long time—he couldn't afterward be sure how long—and for almost as long by Robert Trevor's signature in the lower right of the canvas. He didn't need the signature, of course, to know that Joyce was not the painter. She hadn't anything like this measure of talent, for one thing. For another, she never would've seen Laura like this. It wasn't just his wife's nakedness, or even her pose, just inside an open doorway, light streaming in on her, all other objects disappearing into shadow. It was something else. The painting's detail was minutely photographic where the light allowed, yet it was very much "painted," interpreted, Martin supposed, an effect no camera eye could achieve. Joyce would've gotten a charge out of it, he had to admit, when the spell finally broke. The sight of him kneeling before Laura would have covered both her trouble and the expense.

"So what was it?" Beth asked when she returned from work that evening. He'd opened a bottle of white wine and drunk half of it before he heard the garage door grind open and Beth's Audi pull inside.

"What was *what*?" he said, affecting nonchalance.

She poured herself a glass of the wine, regarded him strangely, then held up a splintered slat from the latticework he'd broken into small pieces over his knee and stuffed into one of the large rubber trash cans they kept in the garage. Had he forgotten to put the lid on? Or was it Beth's habit to examine the trash on her way in each evening, to see if he'd thrown away anything interesting?

"Something hateful," he finally said, believing this to be true, then adding, "Nothing important," as pure a lie as he'd ever told.

She nodded, as if this explanation were sufficient and holding her wineglass up to the light. "Not our usual white," she remarked, after taking a sip.

"No."

"A hint of sweet. You usually hate that."

"Let's go to Palm Springs for the weekend," he suggested.

She continued to study him, now clearly puzzled. "You just finished shooting in Palm Springs. You said you hated it."

"It'll be different now," he explained, "with us gone."

"So, Martin," Trevor said when he returned with two bottles of sweating domestic beer, a brand Martin didn't realize was even brewed anymore. He'd partially buttoned his blue denim work shirt, Martin noticed, though a tuft of gray, paint-splattered chest hair was still visible at the open neck. The man sat in stages, as if negotiating with the lower half of his body. "Have I seen any of your films?"

"*My* films?" Martin smiled, then took a swallow of cold, bitter beer. "I'm not a director, Robert."

The man was still trying to get settled, lifting his bad leg straight out in front of him by hand, clearly annoyed by the need to do so. "When I was inside, I was trying to remember the word for what you are. Laura told me, but I forgot."

"Cuckold?" Martin suggested.

Robert Trevor didn't respond right away. This was a man whose equilibrium did not tilt easily, and Martin found himself admiring that. His eyes were a piercing, pale blue. Laura, naked, had allowed him to turn them on her. "Now *there's* a Renaissance word for you," Trevor said finally. "A Renaissance notion, actually."

"You think so?" Martin said, pressing what he felt should have been his advantage. "Have you ever been married, Robert?"

"Never," the painter admitted. "Flawed concept, I always thought."

"Some might say it's people who are flawed, not the concept."

Robert Trevor looked off in the distance as if he were considering the merit of Martin's observation, but then he said, "Gaffer! That's what you are. You're a gaffer."

Martin had to restrain a smile. Clearly, if he'd come all this way in hopes of an apology, he was going to be disappointed. The good news was that this was not—he was pretty sure—what he had come for.

"Laura explained it all to me one afternoon," Trevor explained.

"Actually, I'm a D.P. now," Martin said, and was immediately ashamed of his need to explain that he'd come up in the world.

Trevor frowned. "Dip?" he said. "You're a dip, Martin?"

"Director of photography."

"Ah," the other man said. "I guess that makes you an artist."

"No," Martin said quietly. "Merely a technician."

He'd been called an artist, though. Peter Axelrod considered him one. He'd gotten an urgent call from Peter one night a few years ago, asking Martin to come to the set where he was shooting a picture that starred a famously difficult actor. It was a small film, serious in content and intent, and for the first three weeks the director and star had been embroiled in a quiet struggle. The actor was determined to give a performance that would be hailed as masterfully understated. To Peter's way of thinking, his performance, to this point, was barely implied. Worse, the next day they'd be shooting one of the pivotal scenes.

Martin found his old friend sitting alone in a makeshift theater near the set, morosely studying the dailies. Martin took a seat in the folding chair next to him and together they watched take after take. After half an hour, Peter called for the lights. "There's nothing to choose from," he complained, rubbing his forehead. "He does the same thing every fucking take, no matter what I suggest."

To Martin, perhaps because he could focus on one thing while his friend had to juggle fifty, the problem was obvious. "Don't argue with him. He's just going to dig his heels in deeper, the way they all do. You want a star performance, light him like a star, not like a character actor."

Peter considered this advice for all of about five seconds. "Son of a *bitch*," he said. "David's in cahoots with him, isn't he." David, a man Martin knew well, was Peter's D.P. on the film. "I should shit-can the prick and hire you right this second."

Martin, of course, had demurred. The following week he was starting work on another picture, and Peter's offer wasn't so much literal as symbolic, a token to his gratitude. "You just saved this picture," he told Martin out on the lot. "In fact, you just saved me."

The two men were shaking hands then, when Peter remembered. "I was sorry to hear about Laura," he said, looking stricken. "It must have been awful."

"Pretty bad," Martin admitted. "She weighed about eighty pounds at the end."

The two men looked around the lot. "Movies," the director said, shaking his head. "I wonder what we'd have done if we'd decided to live real lives and have real careers."

"You love movies," Martin pointed out.

"I know," Peter had admitted. "God help me, I do."

"Merely a technician," Trevor repeated now, improbably seated across from Martin on the opposite coast. He'd already drained half his beer, while Martin, never a beer drinker, had barely touched his. "Well, I wouldn't worry about it. In the end, maybe that's all art is. Solid technique with a dash of style."

"I don't much feel like talking about aesthetics, Robert."

"No, I don't suppose you do," the painter said, running his fingers through his hair. "Joyce told me she sent you that painting. I'd have tried to talk her out of that, had I known."

"Why?"

"Because Laura wouldn't have wanted her to. Funny to think of them as sisters, actually. Joyce always seeking vengeance. Laura anxious to forgive."

Which was true. Martin had seen photos of them as little girls, when it was hard to tell them apart. But by adolescence Laura was already flowering into the healthy, full-figured, ruddily complected woman she would become, whereas Joyce, pale and thin, had begun to look out at the world through dark, aggrieved eyes. When Martin had seen her yesterday, it was clear that not one of her myriad grievances had ever been addressed to her satisfaction.

"So, Robert. How long were you and my wife lovers?"

Trevor paused, deciding how best, or perhaps whether, to answer. "Why would you want to know that, Martin? How will knowing make anything better?"

"How long?"

After a beat, the painter said, "We had roughly twenty years' worth of summers."

Right, Martin thought. The worst, then. Odd that he couldn't remember whether Laura had ever directly deceived him, or whether she'd simply allowed him to deceive himself. He'd assumed that she needed this time with her sister each summer. That she never asked him to come along, given his opinion of Joyce, he'd considered a kindness.

"A month one year. Six weeks the next. I painted her every minute I could, then kept at it when she was gone."

Yes. The worst. This was one of the things he'd needed to know, of course. "How many are there?"

"Paintings?" Trevor asked. "A dozen finished oils. More watercolors. Hundreds of studies. The one Joyce sent you might be the best of the lot. You should hang on to it."

"Where are they?" he asked, then nodded at the studio. "Here?"

"At my farm in Indiana."

"You never sold any of them?"

"I've never *shown* any of them."

"Why not?"

"She wouldn't allow it when she was alive. Joyce kept the one you have in the guest room Laura used when she visited. Laura made her promise never to show anyone."

"She's been dead for several years now."

"Also, there were your feelings to consider."

Martin snorted. "Please. You want me to believe you gave that a lot of thought?"

"Not even remotely," Trevor admitted. "Laura did, though. And . . . after her death . . . I started thinking of the pictures as private. When I die will be time enough."

"So nobody knows about them?"

"You do. Joyce. My New York agent *suspects*, and I've given instructions concerning them to my attorney." He finished his beer, then peered into the bottle as if, there at the bottom, the names of others who knew about the paintings might be printed. "That's what you should prepare yourself for, Martin. I've never pursued fame, but it appears I've become famous anyway, at least in certain circles. When I die, Laura's going to become a very famous lady. Everybody loves a secret. In fact"—at this he smiled and put the bottle down, turning to look at Martin—"you might want to option the movie rights."

"Did you know she was dying?"

"She told me when she was first diagnosed, yes. I painted her that summer, like always."

Martin massaged his temples, the tips of his fingers cool from holding the beer bottle.

"She insisted. And of course I wanted to. I couldn't not paint her. I would have, right to the end, had that been possible."

"Why?"

"Why paint her disease, you mean?"

No, that wasn't what he'd meant, not exactly, though he was ashamed to articulate further. "Why paint her at all, Robert? That's what I've been wondering. She wasn't what you'd call a beautiful woman."

Trevor didn't hesitate at all. "No, Martin, she wasn't what *you'd* call a beautiful woman. She was one of the most beautiful women *I've* ever laid eyes on."

Yes, Martin thought. That was obvious from the moment he'd opened the crate. And his next question was the reason he'd come so far. "Why?" he heard himself ask. "What was it about her?"

"I thought you didn't want to talk about aesthetics, Martin," the painter replied.

That night, Martin and Beth ate by candlelight in the inn's small dining room. The candles were a matter of necessity. The storm had blown up out of nowhere, or so it seemed to Martin. The sun had disappeared behind that first cloud when he'd arrived at Trevor's studio; by the time he'd left, an hour later, the sky was rumbling with dark, low thunderheads from horizon to horizon. The painter, predicting that the island would lose power, had insisted that Martin take a flashlight with him. "Just leave it in the room," he'd instructed. "I run into Dennis and Pat all the time. They can return it whenever." When Martin smiled at this and shook his head, Trevor read his thought and nodded in agreement. "Island life, Martin. Island life."

He had walked with Martin as far as the gate, an effort that clearly cost him. "What's wrong with your leg, Robert?" Martin asked as he lifted the latch to let himself out.

"It's my hip, actually. It needs replacing, they tell me. I'm thinking about it."

Martin remembered the battered table Trevor used for his paints, the broken leg he continued to prop under it. Unless he was very much mistaken, Trevor wasn't the sort of man who put much faith in "replacement."

"You didn't come to visit her," Martin remarked—one last-ditch attempt at censure—after the gate swung shut between them.

"No."

"You could have," he said. "You could have shown up with Joyce, claiming to be an old friend. I wouldn't have known."

"I thought about it," Trevor admitted. "But I had it on excellent authority that I wasn't needed. You rose to the occasion, is what I heard."

In the distance, a low rumble of thunder.

"That's what our friend Joyce can't quite forgive you for, by the way," he continued. "Your devotion during those last months enraged her. Up to that point, she'd always felt perfectly justified in despising you."

"You mean I rose to the occasion of her death, but not her life?"

"Something like that," Trevor nodded. "But look at it this way. You got a damn good painting out of that woman's need to punish you."

"I don't know what to do with it, though," Martin said. "I had to rent one of those self-storage units out in the valley."

"Air-conditioned, I hope."

Martin smiled. "It's the only thing in there."

"I'd love to have it back, if you don't want it."

"It'll be even harder to look at now," he admitted, though he knew he'd never return the painting to Trevor. "That look of longing on her face. The way she was standing there. I'm always going to know it was you she wanted to come through that door."

"Wrong again, Martin." Trevor was leaning heavily with both hands on the gate now, letting Martin know that a handshake wasn't any more necessary now than it had been earlier. It suddenly dawned on Martin that the man had to be in his seventies. "I was the one who *did* come through that door. You were the one she was waiting for."

"So," Beth said, digging into her steak with genuine appetite. At least, Martin thought, she wasn't one of those L.A. girls who always order fish and drink nothing but mineral water. "Were you worried about me?"

"Yes," he said. He'd been waiting for her in a rocking chair on the inn's front porch, the sky growing blacker and blacker, when she came striding down the dirt path. She'd no more than sat down next to him than the air sizzled with electricity and the first bolt of lightning cleaved the sky.

"You forget I'm from Minnesota," she said, pointing her fork at him. "I spent the first twenty years of my life watching storms. And how was your lazy afternoon, old man?"

"Fine."

"Just fine?"

"I visited a studio. Took some photos. Like I said."

"You should've come with me. The path through the forest is strewn with fairy houses."

"With what?"

"Little houses built of bark and leaves and pebbles. By children, I suppose, if you don't believe in fairies. People leave pennies near the ones they like best. Isn't that sweet? I can see why Laura loved it here."

Martin just stared at her.

"Well . . . that's why we came all this way, right? This island was your wife's favorite place in the whole world, and this is your way of saying good-bye."

"I didn't know you—"

"I'm not *stupid*, Martin. I know how much you loved her."

But I didn't. The words were right there to be spoken, and for a heartbeat Martin thought he'd already said them. But if he did, how would he ever stop? How would he keep from adding, *Any more than I love you.*

Richard Russo

They used Robert Trevor's flashlight to wind their way up the narrow, pitch-black staircase to locate their room on the third floor. Undressing in the dark, they lay in the canopied bed and watched the sky through the open window. Though the storm had moved out to sea, it still flickered on the distant horizon, and every twenty seconds or so the beam from the lighthouse swept past.

"What do you think?" Beth said. "Should we stay an extra day?"

"If you like," he said. "Whatever you want."

"It's up to you."

After a moment he said, "I called Peter while you were out. He needs me to start work earlier, by the second week of rehearsal instead of the third, if possible. He didn't come right out and say so, but that's what he wants."

"What do *you* want?"

"I wouldn't mind heading back."

"Fine with me."

"Let's, then."

A few minutes later she was snoring gently in the crook of his arm. For a long time Martin lay in the dark thinking about Robert Trevor's farm in Indiana, if there was such a place, and the countless versions of Laura he claimed to have stored there. And he thought too about Beth, the poor girl. She had it exactly backwards, of course. This trip wasn't so much about saying good-bye to his wife as saying hello. He'd fallen in love with her, truly in love, the moment he'd uncrated the painting back in L.A. and seen his wife through another man's eyes. Just as Joyce had known, somehow, that he would.

What folly, Martin couldn't help concluding, bitterly, as he contemplated the lovely young woman sleeping at his side; it was his destiny, no doubt, to sell her short as well. What absolute folly love was. Talk about a flawed concept. He remembered how he and his junior high friends—all of them shy, self-conscious, without girlfriends—used to congregate in the shadow of the bleachers to evaluate the girls at Friday night dances. The best ones were taken, naturally, which left the rest. "She's kind of pretty, don't you think?" one of his friends, or maybe Martin himself, would venture, and then

122

it would be decided, by popular consensus, if she was or she wasn't.

That they were leaving in the morning was a relief to Martin. He preferred the West Coast, and he was looking forward to working on Peter's new picture, which was to star an actress they'd both worked with shortly after Laura's death. That script had called for partial nudity, and the actress, who'd recently had a baby, fretted constantly about how she would look. "Trust me," Peter had told her. "Nobody's going to see anything. They're just going to think they do. Because this man"—he pointed to Martin—"is an artist."

The next evening, the three of them sat on folding chairs watching the dailies of the scene that had so frightened her. They'd shot only three takes, and midway through viewing the first, the actress— she *was* one of the most beautiful women Martin had ever laid eyes on, and never more beautiful than right then—began to relax, intuiting that it was going to be all right. Still, he couldn't have been more surprised when she took his hand there in the darkness, leaned toward him and whispered, without ever taking her eyes off the screen, "Oh, I love you, I love you, I love you."

Ellen Cooney

See the Girl

Her face was close to the window. She was a traveler, on her way to something brand new. She felt lucky that the Tri-Valley Medical Center was far outside town, in a suburb near the city. She had never been in a city, but that was all right.

She saw the suburb first in a blur from the highway, through long, deep rows of fir trees, and through slants of daylight and shadows, which never repeated a pattern, but were always shifting and changing.

It looked as quiet as a village in a model toy railroad, with a feel in the air of a hush. There weren't factories. It was not the kind of neighborhood where people blew car horns. You could never hear people's television sets through their windows. You would have to be quieter out here than at home.

But still, it might be a good place to live. People at the clinic were going to say, "Ronda, we'll buy a new house for you and your mom, and we'll put it wherever you want," and Ronda would probably pick the suburb. The reason they would be saying this would be the healing. They would want to give Ronda a present, out of happiness and amazement. They would take up a collection for this. The new house would look like the house in the book where the rabbit says good night to everything. But there would not be a bowl of hot mush, like in the story, which Ronda would find disgusting. The healing was still a secret.

The houses of the suburb were like racks in a department store of good wool coats, racks and racks of them, with aisles between them for browsing. They were different sizes, with different collars, buttons, pockets, and belts, but basically, they were all the same coat; and so what if, when you bought one, you had to go through the winter looking just like everyone else, like you were going through life all together, wearing uniforms. Ronda's mom wouldn't like this at first, but she could learn to enjoy it.

The Tri-Valley Medical Center was all cement. The houses of the suburb were white, gray, shades of brown, light blue, brick-red, and the pinkish tone of brick painted over with white, as if the walls were standing there blushing. There were woodlots of high old spruces and pines. It smelled like Christmas. There were wide flat lawns, big yards, paved-over driveways, smooth roads. No one stuck out. No one had fights, or had a husband who was married to a bar stool, or went to court to get divorces, or had children who looked like lizards and trolls, like you saw all the time at the clinic.

The drive up north on the highway, straight up from the bottom of the valley, where the town was, was like driving up the side of a bowl. This was the best part. Just when it seemed to Ronda that she would never reach the rim, she'd be on it: all the trees looked higher, and the buildings and houses spread out, and the open spaces had opened up even more; and then the sky would come suddenly nearer.

The weather on the rim was so clear today, Ronda sat back and relaxed. "Flip it back, Mom!" she cried, and her mother reached up and pushed back the visor of the windshield. Then the clouds were so close, they were floating one inch above the steering wheel. This, Ronda knew, was a perfectly excellent sign.

Now she rode on her mother's broad back the way she liked it—piggyback, or turtle-back, because that's what she was, with the casts on; she was partly a turtle. Ronda smelled her mother's sweat, and her hair. She was careful not to let her arms get wrapped the wrong way around her mother's neck, and not to jerk back suddenly. She could travel long distances in this manner without a single wrong move. She knew everything about holding on, and everything about flinging back her head to feel the air rushing by, and everything about pressing herself in, with her eyes shut tight, when the important thing to do was just hide, so that no one could see her at all, unless she let them.

She was on her way to being healed. There was a very short time to keep waiting, but she was starting to feel impatient.

"Faster, please, faster," said Ronda.

Why it was happening that this was the day she'd be healed, she didn't know. There was no particular reason. She'd been lying in her bed one night, looking out the window like always, but not at anything special, just the night. She had said to herself, as normally as anything, "Oh, when Leon takes my casts off this time, I'll be healed." She just knew. That was all.

Leon Johnson was the cast-and-brace man. He was strict, especially when he was using his saw. He had a list of parents who he allowed in the brace room, to stand by their children and hold their hands, but the names of Ronda's parents weren't on it.

Ronda didn't hold this against Leon. If she were him, she wouldn't let them in there, either. She was not afraid of Leon, although many other people were. He was old, and had enormous hands, and long, thin fingers, all crusted in the nails with bits of plaster, which sprinkled out sometimes as if his fingers were snowing. He wore a long cotton coat, buttoned up to his chin, and every time he saw Ronda, he said the same thing. He called her "my little mermaid." He said, "How come you don't have an H, like everyone else who has your name?"

It was a joke with them. "Because I got my name from a Ronald," she answered, and his eyes would open wide, in alarm and anxiety.

"Oh, my poor little mermaid, was it for Reagan?"

And Ronda would say, "Don't insult me." This was what she'd heard her dad say once, at a gas station, when a guy her dad didn't know had struck up a conversation with him at the pump, and had asked the same question. The name of Ronda's father was Ronny Bailey.

"You're hurting me," said Ronda's mother. "You're digging your spurs into me. Cut it out."

"Ask me right, and I will," said Ronda. She could whisper directly in her mother's ear because that's where her face was.

"Ronda Rondalla Rondaronia, please," said Ronda's mother. "If you don't stop digging your spurs into me, I will throw you out the window."

"OK, Mom," said Ronda.

They were not really spurs. They were bolts on the heels of the leg casts for the metal bar that she had worn every night since the surgery. The bar was exactly the width of Ronda's bed. The space between Ronda's legs with the bar on was a triangle, like a wishbone from a chicken, if a wishbone had a bottom line. The cast of each leg was stained a little: some pee had dripped down, accidentally, but there wasn't any type of bad smell. Ronda had swabbed her skin at the tops of the casts every day with cottonballs soaked with alcohol. The alcohol smelled like the hospital.

It was strange to call the part of your leg that runs down the back a hamstring. The name of Ronda's surgeon was Dr. Pellegrino. He wasn't the chief. He did not have white hair, like chiefs were supposed to. Dr. Pellegrino was the one who went inside her, plucked her strings, and released them. They were still in her legs, though. "Ronda, your strings are too tight, so when we put you to sleep this time, I am going to release them." He was Italian. He never said "ham." He knew it was a stupid way to talk about bodies, but he may have found this out from the chief.

It used to be difficult to have to sleep every night on her back. Her bed was next to a window. Ronda knew exactly what the sky looked like, all gray and white combined, when it was almost morning. That was when the sky was most quiet; it looked like silver and snow mixed together. Then the stars blinked out. They still were up there, though. So was the moon. One night, and she will never forget this, the moon was at the top of her window like a silver banana.

The best of the stars, she felt, were the ones that made a W, which looked like a crown, a real crown. Was that why people invented crowns, in the old days, for kings and queens? Maybe. It would have been better, on the nights when the moon was like a face, if the crown of those stars was on its head. That would have really been something.

But the moon wasn't ever near the W, in any shape at all, so Ronda put her own face there instead. Ronda had never seen herself so happy as she looked when she was up in the sky.

Except for the tiny bit of pee, the plaster of Ronda's casts, even after seven weeks, was as white as a clean piece of paper. Ronda did not allow decorations on her casts, not even a little drawing in Magic Marker by her dad, who was good at drawing helicopters, airplanes, X-wing fighters like on *Star Wars*, rockets, hot-air balloons, and blimps like in the Super Bowl.

Ronda's mother was not a horse. She was a mother, and her name was Patsy Bailey. But Ronda liked it better when her mother was the one who brought her to the clinic. Her father would have pushed her in a wheelchair. This was because a man could get hernias from carrying children, and a woman could not. But her father would change his clothes from whatever he'd been wearing around his house; he would have fixed himself up. You would think that this should have been the other way around, but it wasn't.

Ronda's mother said "cerebral palsy" like this: "ser-*ree*-brul *paul*-zee." Her father said, "*seb*-rah-ball-*paul*-zee." It was another way that they were different, besides the fact that they lived in different houses.

Ronda's mother stopped cold. Someone was coming. One of the social workers who wasn't Beryl might have spotted them, or a doctor, or a physical therapist, or a nurse. Ronda waited to be shouted at. They were always saying to Ronda's mother, "Don't be carrying her like that! Don't be carrying her like that!"

It was Beryl, though, coming toward them from down the hall. It was good to see her. Beryl was the kind of person who, when you talked to her, she said, "Oh, I know what you mean," and you knew she was telling the truth, unlike many other people.

Beryl was the only person at the clinic Ronda's mother could stand. After she talked to Beryl, Ronda's mother did not walk away all knotted-up, all edgy, muttering to herself, as if her jaw hurt, "Goddamn professionals, I hate them all." Ronda's father felt the same. Even though Ronda's father lived alone now, Ronda always knew his point of view.

As for Ronda, she loved Beryl absolutely. When Ronda got down on the living room rug at home with her Barbies, Kens, G.I. Joes, Legos, blocks, and Lincoln Logs, and played the game of "Tornado at the Hospital," which could take a whole day, because, before she wrecked it, she had to carefully, realistically build it, she made Beryl a doll she would rescue. Ronda herself played the part of the tornado. She would also save Leon, and the Ken who was chief, but not her own doctor, which her mother found unacceptable.

"You should show that Italian who operates on you some respect," her mother said, when he died. The dolls who represented Ronda's parents didn't always survive. She was sorry about this, but sometimes they were blown to the back of the sofa, they were thrown behind a chair, they were suffocated, they lost limbs, they were hurtled through the hall into the bathroom. Ronda tried to play fair. She had to be careful about never disfavoring one parent over the other, which could really upset them. Except for the secret that she was keeping today, she was not the kind of person who kept secrets.

"Patsy and Ronda, hey, I heard you'd be here today," Beryl said.

Beryl was a large-bosomed, big-voiced, short, heavy woman, and older than Ronda's mom: her hair was all gray, but soft. Ronda was used to seeing it long. It used to hang down to Beryl's shoulders, all loose, streaming this way and that, like porcupine hair.

But Beryl had had a haircut—no, not just a haircut. She'd had it all cut off to almost nothing. Ronda had the feeling that, maybe everyone who saw Beryl should jump to their feet and salute her, but the haircut looked good on her. Ronda kept looking at Beryl's hair. She had to, to be sure not to spill out the news of what was just about ready to happen to her. Ronda wanted everyone to be surprised. She wanted to see what their eyes would be like—Beryl's, her mother's, everyone's—when she came out from the brace room, and then they saw her.

"It looks fantastic, Beryl. Do you have gel on, or what," said Ronda's mother.

"I don't need it," said Beryl.

Ronda wanted to compliment Beryl, too, but just then a woman's voice came over the intercom, saying, "Gertrude Stein to Admissions, please. Miss Stein to Admissions, please."

Beryl looked up at the ceiling; a flush came over her face. Ronda's mom said, "What's the matter?"

"That's me," said Beryl. "I'm going to kill her. I'm going down there, and I'm going to kill her. She's been doing this to me all day." Then Beryl turned around and walked away.

"See you later on!" cried Ronda. Then it was quiet again. "Drink," said Ronda in her mother's ear. They were standing close to a water bubbler.

"If I had to bend down to let you get one, I would never get up again," said Ronda's mother. "And you know what would happen? Everyone would think we were twins, and I'd go out of my mind."

"You," said Ronda.

"Sweetheart, the kind of drink I want, it's not in there."

Ronda patted her mother's head. It was hot outside but the air-conditioning in the clinic was on. Still, her mother kept sweating. She was big. She was the biggest mother Ronda had ever seen. Her hair was so wet. Maybe she was *partly* a horse. Ronda tried to make her mother feel better. "If you're very good, you can have a cold beer when we go home, Mom," Ronda whispered, and her mother said, "Don't be talking like that around here."

"But you're going to be happy," Ronda whispered.

"Well, after today, you'll be lighter," said Ronda's mom.

They started moving again. Ronda's mother had her same old brown canvas jacket on, and dungarees, and brown, scuffed-up leather boots, like a man's. Wearing those boots had been a big mistake. They were slowing her down. Ronda tried harder to keep her feet out, away from her mother's ribs. But she urged her mother on.

"*Hurry*," said Ronda. She thought about how, when Leon took her casts off the last time, and the time before that, and the time before that, and the time before that, her legs were all limp and grayish-white, not like real legs, but like fishes. They were scaly and hairy and strange. They were as skinny as goat legs, with a new set of scars, like marks branded into her skin, joining up with the old ones.

Was that the right number of times? Ronda counted up all her surgeries. She ticked them off with her fingers, at her mother's neck, but not so that her mother felt it. It was right. The surgery on her strings had been her fifth.

Her fifth! That was the number of stars in the W! That was why today was the day!

"Oh," Ronda said to herself. She could not believe she hadn't seen this before. If she could have let go of her mom, she would have thumped herself on the head.

What would she look like? She could not imagine how her legs would look today when Leon was through with her. As part of the healing, the scars could have all disappeared. If they hadn't, though, it wouldn't matter. She had decided to not be fussy about details, and not to be expecting the impossible.

Soon it will be over. She'll come out from the brace room. Someone will cry, "Look at Ronda, she doesn't have C.P. anymore!" That was how most people said it, "see-*pee*," which Ronda found repulsive, but, from now on, she wouldn't care.

A stir would rise up in the hall, with everyone craning their necks to catch sight of her. The big double doors outside the waiting room would open up a little wider, by themselves, with a whooshing. She would pass through the doors so quickly, it would seem that her feet were only air. She would know how to do this. She had practiced in her mind. She would quietly sit by her mother again. Her mother would be crying and gasping, both at once; she would throw back her head and make really loud noises. But Ronda would not be embarrassed. The people who hadn't been healed yet would turn to her and say, "Way to go, Ronda Bailey." They would say, "We're not jealous of you."

And the white-haired chief of Orthopedics, who never once came into the waiting room, would come. He would come out to see her himself. No one would resent the special treatment. Everything would become very quiet. He would look all around until he saw where she was sitting, and he would stroll to her, and the expression on his face would turn softer, not at all how he normally looked. He would bend to kiss her hand. He would hold out his arm to her. A light would come into his eyes.

"Congratulations," he would say. "Where would you like your new house?"

Oh, and Beryl would be in there as well. Beryl and the chief would walk with Ronda together, like the mother and father of Sleeping Beauty. They would walk all around the waiting room.

After the healing, when Ronda gets up from her chair, her body will be curving and straight, both at once, as if a line and a circle had joined together, somehow. Then everyone will be looking at her. If they clapped and cheered for her, she would know what to do. She would bow, way down low, and stand up again even straighter, because her legs will have learned how to hold her, and there she will be.

They had reached the last hall before the brace room. It felt as if a great rush of air had entered Ronda's ears. She held on, though. There was one minute left to keep waiting. "Giddy *up*," Ronda said to her mom.

Susan Kenney

The Death of the Dog and Other Rescues

It's a typical Saturday morning in October. Linnie's due at a birthday party at noon, but I've rushed into town with both kids to get sneakers, and we're late so I'm feeling pressed and a little cross at David, who had a fit in the shoe store because he couldn't find new sneakers that looked and felt exactly like his old ones; and I'm worried about the three other little girls I'm supposed to pick up, waiting all dressed up wondering what happened to us, and the little girl whose party it is thinking no one is going to come, so as I turn into the driveway I say over my shoulder to Linnie, "Now as soon as I stop the car you jump right out, run in, and get dressed as fast as you can, because we're late."

"I don't want to be late," she wails, tears jumping out of her eyes.

"Well, it's too late not to be late now, so just do it," I answer sharply. David is scrunched down in the backseat glaring at me in the rearview mirror, elbows jammed down on the new sneakers box with the old sneakers inside, not talking.

Phil looks up, smiling. He's out in his shorts mowing the lawn for what he fervently hopes is the last time of this long Indian summer we got in trade for the real summer that never came. It's so warm he's not wearing a shirt; he's finally gotten over his self-consciousness about the big scar from his operation, and his whole upper body is tan and greased with sweat, the scar looping up from his shorts and across his ribs with a little jog at the end like an upside-down hockey stick. The truth is, it's barely noticeable now, especially when he's tan. The dog is lying beside the driveway, panting slightly in the heat; he bumps his tail on the ground as our wheels crunch down the driveway. He can't hear us because he's deaf now, but he feels our vibrations and turns his head in our direction as we pass, tail gyrating wildly. He's very old, fifteen, in fact, but the same foxy bright-eyed collie face he had as a young dog looks up expectantly to see who's here. Even now in his old age he is in truth a handsome dog, a rake, a pirate, an Errol Flynn of a dog. We've had him all our married life and even before, ever since he was a puppy almost too young to stand on all fours, his back legs not quite strong enough to hold up his rear end.

Phil waves briefly, cantilevers the mower around, and starts back down the grass. He's left the gas can and funnel at the edge of the driveway not far from the dog, who is also at the edge just off the grass, out of the way of the mower

As I yank on the brake and hop out of the car to open the kids' door I think how peaceful it all is, what a nice day we have here, and isn't everything going well?

But there's the party, and we're late. "Come on, Linnie, let's step on it. Crying doesn't get you anywhere."

"I don't know where the present is." She sniffles. I hold the back door open with one hand over her head to let her pass.

"I hate my new sneakers," David mutters, ducking under my arm. He has an additional grievance. "I want to go too. I never get to go anywhere."

"You weren't invited," I say from the middle of the cupboard where I've stashed the present for the birthday girl.

"Mom! Mom!" Linnie screams hysterically from upstairs. "I need you!"

"Just for the ride," David says glumly as I run upstairs to Linnie.

Inside of three minutes we are all running back out to the car. The doors slam, one, two, three, the motor roars, the radio blares, the kids are squabbling and I can't hear a thing, can't even think, and I jam the car into reverse and back up fast, bump, crunch, right over some hard but hollow object that crumples under my wheels. "What's that! What's that?" the kids holler, peering all around, and I look up through the windshield to see Phil, a horrified look on his face, waving franti-cally at me, gesticulating wildly as though we were in some terrible imminent danger. He's shouting at me, but the windows are rolled up and the radio is blaring and the kids are yammering so loud I can't hear him, so I try to read his lips as he pantomimes disaster, something about the door, but all the doors are shut, I heard them, and then I realize I must have run over the loaded gas can and we are going to catch fire and explode so, always quick to respond to danger, I shove the gear into forward and pull ahead crunch, crunch, buckle, away from the ruined gas can and the leaking gas so we won't explode, pull forward out of danger and turn off the ignition so we're safe. No one can say I don't react well in a crisis.

But Phil has really gone crazy now, dancing and whirling and hopping up and down, bending forward with his hands over his stom-ach as though he were going to throw up, then standing up with his eyes closed and flinging one arm out as if he were throwing a Frisbee in a gesture of what I take to be despair, and I watch him, puzzled, be-cause haven't I done the right thing?

But of course not, because it's not the gas can that has gotten up, moved and flopped its old arthritic bones down in a heap behind the car where I never thought to look. It's not the gas can I have run over, crunching and crumpling it not once but twice, coming and going this bright fall day—it's the dog.

II

He was always a handsome dog. This line, a joke between Phil and me because it was so literally true, has for some reason always reminded me of my father. There is a photograph of the dog in his younger days lying on the lawn in what we always called his noble-dog pose, nose lifted, eyes staring off in the distance, a faintly ironic, tolerant, ever-so-slightly self-conscious expression on his face. There is a similar photograph of my father when he was very young and very handsome, dressed to the nines in white sharkskin coat and knickerbockers, sitting in a lawn chair with his legs crossed, cigarette dangling casually from his fingers. He looks wonderful, one eyebrow cocked wittily, like a blond Robert Taylor without the mustache. Someone has just said to him, "Jim, you are a handsome dog," and he is regarding that person with a tolerant, amused, ironic smile as if to say, Yes, I know, but it doesn't really matter, that's just the way I am.

When Phil and I were first married and had no children, the dog went everywhere with us. People would stop us on the street and say, "Oh, what a pretty dog!" then mystify us by asking "Is he ugly?" and when we shook our heads, bewildered, not understanding at first that they meant his temper, not his beauty, they'd reach down to stroke his white ruff, his blond fur, scratch behind his foxy ears, admire his dainty paws. Cars would slow down, children across the street would tug at their mothers' sleeves and call out, "Look, a little Lassie! A little Lassie, see?" Actually he was not a little Lassie at all, except for his color and markings, not even close. In fact, he was a collie-shepherd mix with big limpid brown eyes and a wedge-shaped shepherd nose, pointy upright ears, and long but not really shaggy fur. But some genetic accident had made him look, as so seldom happens with mixed-breed dogs, as though he had got that way on purpose. We always thought he was a throwback to those first small, wiry, blunt-nose mountain collies before they were bred up to size with coats like llamas, torpedo noses, and beady little snake eyes on the sides of their heads. Because he was a crossbreed, we knew that there would never be another one quite like him. Even if he fathered puppies, which in his green and salad days running loose he certainly must have, he would not breed true.

We got him unexpectedly when he was very small, his whole litter abandoned in Phil's sister's dorm at college, brought home while we were visiting and given the bum's rush from Phil's mother's kitchen right into our car for the trip back up to Cornell. And there he stayed for all our travels, at first so little he curled up under the seat with only his wedge-shaped nose sticking out in front; then, as he grew bigger, under my feet in the front footwell where as a grown dog he just fit and felt secure. In a paroxysm of graduate school cuteness we named him Collie Cibber after the eighteenth-century poet laureate and enemy of Pope, and in some ways he lived up to his name. He was a fop, a dandy, the only dog I've ever seen licking his fine white paws clean and then polishing his face just like a cat. He went everywhere with us, was well known, even legendary, on campus for herding students into our classes, nipping officiously at their ankles, rounding them up and ushering them through the door, then thumping down with a resigned and drawn-out groan across the doorway, stretching out on his back with his legs sticking up, underbelly exposed, and ostentatiously going off to sleep, punctuating my lectures with an occasional snore. When the bell rang at the end of class he invariably leaped bolt upright, startled and sleepy-faced, abashed, then recovered himself, shook down his fur, and stood sentry by the door as the students filed out. For years after the children came, first David, then Linnie, he refused to acknowledge their existence, would never come when they called or lift a paw to shake their hands as he did ours, suffered by no means gladly their maulings and pettings. He was our first and in his eyes remained our only child, was one of us, never seeming to take in the fact that he was much the furriest, and generally although not always ate and slept on the floor. And he was perfect, charming, bright, intelligent, yes, a handsome dog.

III

Ever since my father died suddenly away from home when I was twelve, I have felt that it was my responsibility to keep everyone around me safe. This has meant saving them when necessary, at the very least hovering somewhat officiously, a walking first-aid manual, rapid extricator and rehabilitator of lost causes. Phil has called this my rescuer complex, but, complex or not, I can't help believing deep down that whatever is lost can be recovered, what is broken can be mended, and what is gone replaced; at least it's worth a try. So over the years I have tracked down within minutes children missing from the school bus at the appointed stop, yanked out drowning ones before they could inhale a single drop of water, righted capsized sailboats, glued back together broken objects, recovered a single dropped earring of little real but great sentimental value from the middle of a well-used tennis court. Quick off the blocks, I have rescued no later than the third thump around the dryer a cat suicidally fond of sleeping in odd places. I have toughed it out with barely a murmur in countless waiting areas, emergency rooms, ICUs, stood close and watchful while my husband struggled through the numerous nearly fatal complications of a botched and messy operation for a tumor the size of a dumbbell in his belly, clutching his hand and muttering "Don't leave me" while I nagged the doctors with questions gleaned from medical textbooks—What does this mean? Have you checked that? What happens next, and are you positively absolutely sure?— determined not to lose him the way we did my father. Now I, who have weathered any number of these crises and near-misses without losing control, I, the cool, the calm, the take-charge person, leap screeching out of the car with my two hands simultaneously trying to cover my eyes, my ears, my mouth, run screaming hysterically into the house and up the stairs as fast and as far away as I can get, howling at the top of my lungs, "Oh, no, dear God, not the dog, please, not the goddamned dog!" In my carelessness and haste, I, the rescuer, the caretaker, have run over and killed my own dog.

I finally skid to a halt upstairs in the bedroom that overlooks the driveway. I creep over to the window, cautiously uncovering one eye, ready to leap back if it's too awful, and take a look.

Phil is bending over the dog, who is lying in some sort of heap in the middle of the driveway. Then Phil takes a step back and I stare in disbelief. The dog is not dead after all.

In fact, he is sprawled more or less upright in a version of his stately noble-dog pose, swinging his head around and looking a little dazed, obviously trying to figure out what hit him. He looks pretty much the same, and I can't quite believe it; can it be we've both been spared? Then I notice his hindquarters aren't quite right; they are askew and slightly flattened, one leg sticking out behind at an awkward angle. No, he has definitely been run over. I watch, holding my breath, expecting him to expire before my eyes, while Phil reaches forward. The dog sniffs at his hand, his tail starts to twitch, then gyrate slightly, whisking up a little cloud of gravel. He is wagging his tail. Wow, I think, that's a good sign, his tail still works, his spine must not be crushed. In the back of the car the children gaze in fascinated horror, their noses pressed against the rear window. I go into the bathroom and throw up.

But the dog is still alive. I have not killed him, at least not so far. He's hurt, of course, but what is broken can be mended. I splash water on my face and go downstairs, sidle over to the car; I still can't go near the dog. I yell to Phil that I'm going to take the kids on up to the Lanes' and to the party, that he should call the vet. As I back around past him he shakes his head as though to say, Don't get your hopes up. On the way up the road I consider the probability that even though he is not dead, the dog is so badly hurt he will have to be put to sleep when we take him to the vet's. How many dogs can get run over and survive? So this reprieve is only temporary; the reckoning comes soon.

When I arrive at the Lanes' house I am in a terrible state. The three little girls are lined up beside the driveway with their presents clutched to their smocked bosoms, looking anxious. I can hardly talk, but Joyce just nods; Phil has called ahead with the news. She is sympathetic; once she ran over a kitten, which proceeded to get up, shake itself, and dance loosely toward her with its crushed bones, then leaped straight into the air and died at her feet. She felt terrible for weeks, still dreams of it sometimes. "Come on, shove over," she says. "I'll drive."

Everyone piles into the car, and we drive back down the road and stop at the top of our driveway. I get out and she pulls away in the direction of the birthday party, but not before I hear Katie's shrill voice: "Did Sara really squash Cibber flatter than a pancake?" I walk down the drive, forgetting that with the car gone we have no way to transport the dog to the vet's eleven miles away.

The dog is still alive, breathing fast and whimpering, one leg stuck out behind at that funny angle, otherwise apparently intact, if a little flat. There is no blood, no splintered bone. "Sorry, old man, I didn't mean to," I say as I walk over to him. He does not bump his tail this time, only blinks up at me desperately, his breath rasping. Oh, oh, I think, progressive trauma; we're losing him. We've got to do something. I bend down and put a hand out toward him.

"Don't touch him," Phil says quickly. I look up to see that he is holding a towel to his neck, and there is blood congealing on his bare shoulder. He shrugs. "I wanted to get him away before you came back so you wouldn't have to see him, but when I tried to pick him up he whipped right around and bit me on the neck." He takes the towel away and I see the two deep toothmarks oozing blood, no more than an inch from Phil's carotid artery. "Do you fucking believe it?" Phil says by way of conversation. I shake my head; I fucking don't. I look back down at the dog, who is making impatient weeping noises like faint radar bleeps as if to say, Well, don't just stand there, do something. He peers around at his rear end and his front paws contract as he digs into the gravel, trying to stand up. Old as he is, this is not easy in the best of circumstances, and now it is clearly impossible. He shifts his front paws, gazes up faintly puzzled at the two of us, and groans.

"I'll get a blanket," I tell Phil, and run into the house, thinking about first aid for shock and keeping the victim warm.

"Do you think we can move him?" I ask Phil after I've covered the dog up.

"We'll have to," Phil says. "The vet can't make house calls; the trauma truck is in the shop. Besides, they don't come out this far."

So we have to drive the dog into town, but that's all right, because Phil will have to go to the emergency room anyway to get his neck sewed up. We need a car, and ours is gone to the birthday party. Just then our neighbor down the street arrives with his son. They have heard my screams and want to know if they can help. He and Phil and the son confer over the dog's head about what to do, and because they seem able to take care of everything, I wander back inside, out of earshot. But I watch out the window while the three of them tie the dog's mouth shut with an old nylon stocking, arrange him on a blanket sling, and hoist him into the back of our neighbor's brand-new Volvo station wagon. I peer out the window until they're out of sight, and when Joyce arrives with the car I drop her and David at her house and follow the others into town.

IV

And after all that, the dog is not only not dead, according to the vet he is not even dying, or in immediate danger of it. The vet on call, a short stocky woman with small hands, tells me there are no other contiguous eight inches of dog I could have run over without killing him outright. I have run over the pelvic arch, breaking it in three places, and there may be some kidney and bladder damage, some nerve and muscle bruising, but it's not too bad, considering. A close call, she says, and of course his age will be a factor in recovery, but they'll keep him under sedation and quiet for a few days until the bones can set—you can't put a cast on a dog's ass, or anyone else's, for that matter—and then we can take him home and go from there. So things are clearly not as bad as we first thought. "You're a lucky dog," she says as she gathers up the dog, his nose still tied shut, and starts out back with him. "You'd better get that seen to," she says casually over her shoulder to Phil, "before you bleed to death." Phil blinks and goes pale; he is no stranger to the possibility of bleeding to death. But of course she's only kidding. "Call us tomorrow," she shouts from the back room. "We'll probably know better then." And that's it; she and the dog are gone.

Phil and I stand there, flabbergasted. I can't believe it. A fifteen-year-old dog run over and squashed flat, and we can pick him up in a few days? It seems incredible, too good to be true, but naturally I'm relieved. Still, after our trip to the emergency room—five stitches, not a record, only average for us—as we drive home in the dark I prepare myself for the worst. The dog may not recover, he may not walk again, life may not be worth living to him as an invalid, a cripple. Phil has always been more adamant on this issue than I, especially since his illness; he is a confirmed quality-of-lifer. So I try to face up to the fact that we may finally have to make a decision we have been dreading these last few years as the dog has grown more stiff and feeble, the time when—if he did not die a sudden and natural death the way my first dog Barney did at fourteen, his age and mine, conveniently expiring in seconds on the living room rug—we would have to say the word and have him put to sleep. I have contemplated this and decided I would want to be there to see him out, the good old friend. The vet has not said anything about putting the dog to sleep, not even as a remote possibility, but just in case, I say to Phil as we drive along, "He's had a good life, at least there's that. He's been a happy dog. So if it does come to that it's not so bad." I hear a sniffle next to me, and look over to see the tears rolling down Phil's cheeks, along his jaw, and into the gauze bandage. Choked up but dry-eyed—lately I seem to have lost the knack of tears—I say, "Come on, you know, he's really just a dog." Phil nods, but I can tell it doesn't help one bit.

V

Still, rescued for the moment from the worst consequences of my own haste and negligence, I ponder this latest in a long series of other such near-misses and close calls, so many, in fact, that I have come to think of myself as some sort of lightning rod for disasters that don't quite happen, or turn out at the last moment not to be so bad. We are certainly no strangers to the odd laceration, the quick and bloody trip to the emergency room with thumbs held over pressure points, towels and ice packs pressed to rapidly rising lumps and contusions. Oddly enough, these stitches of Phil's are his first, not counting the ones from his operation. David at age ten has had his head split open twice, has put his hand through the glass storm door, cutting it badly in three places, and nearly taken the top of his thumb off within minutes of acquiring his new Swiss army knife. I am in second place with the scar—now barely visible—over my eyebrow from falling into the garbage can when I stepped on one of David's toy trucks, and Linnie is a distant fourth with two tiny stitches on the bridge of her nose where David whacked her accidentally last winter with the snow shovel. These are the near-misses—the eye not put out, the artery not sliced, the tendon unsevered—dreadful possibilities that you never think of until after it's all over, and you just wipe your brow and sigh deeply with relief that it wasn't worse. Even more unsettling are the close calls, those terrible calamities that somehow are revoked after you have accepted the reality of their happening, fully entered into the altered state of post-disaster consciousness, the ones that give you that strange sense of dissociation, as though you might be dreaming that they didn't happen because they are so awful, but in a little while you will wake up and find they have. So the children do *not* roll out and get smashed dead at sixty miles an hour through the back door of the station wagon I have carelessly left unlatched in my hurry to get somewhere. Thanks to a friend with quick reflexes who grabs her arm before she can pull it back through, Linnie does *not* lacerate and scar her hand for life after putting it through the other glass storm door panel we have not had the sense to replace after David's accident. And the tender skin at the back of David's knee is *not* after all impaled on the rusty barbed-wire fence six miles from help as in our panic we at first believed, but only pinched between two prongs, the skin hardly even broken, and even though after I have freed him he falls over in a dead faint from sheer fright, he recovers almost immediately.

So the dog run over but not killed is only the latest in a long list of these bizarre remissions, close calls, near-misses, lost causes not so lost after all. And I wonder sometimes what I have done to deserve this peculiar brand of good fortune, or if in fact it is a kind of test, a punishment, to be always coming up short of real disaster, always running to the rescue, always compelled to see what I can do. And do I keep at it because it somehow seems to work?

On the kitchen table among the other odds and ends I find this note printed in my daughter's hand. It's the beginning of a story she has to write for school. "A mother is telling her daughter to keep trying and not to give." That's as far as she's gotten, but it makes me wonder if I have done my children any favors by instilling—not only that, but apparently demonstrating—this attitude of "keep trying and not to give." Whatever is broken can be mended, whatever is lost can be replaced, whatever is missing can be found, whatever is sick can be healed. It's all done with mirrors after all, and there's no such word as can't. But, I often wonder, by jumping on my horse and riding in all directions, usually to some, if not complete, avail, have I given them an impression of life that is not really true? How will they know, if and when the time comes, how to give? How will I? Sometimes in my worst daydreams I imagine a plane crash or shipwreck in the middle of a dark cold ocean, the four of us floating survivors with no hope of rescue, or a nuclear bomb blast not too near but near enough, so that it's just a matter of time before the death cloud hits. I imagine them clinging to me, looking at me, asking, "What are we going to do?" And for once there will be nothing, absolutely nothing, I can do.

VI

Four days after the accident I go to pick up the dog. Our regular vet is there, the one who's taken care of the dog all these years. He's kind but not a sentimentalist, and when he sees me he just shakes his head. "I was sorry to hear what happened; I know how crazy you are about that dog."

"He's a good old friend," I say in a slightly choked-up voice. But I don't cry. After all, it's just a dog, and there are worse things than running over your own dog, particularly if the dog survives.

The vet brings the dog out, his mouth tied shut with a strap, puts him in the back of the car for me. The dog's eyes look wild and desperate; he growls at the vet, nudges him sharply with his tied-up nose; if it weren't for the strap he'd bite him for sure. "You'll have to tie his jaw shut whenever you move him," the vet says. "He's pretty strong for an old dog, and he sure knows how to use those teeth." He slams the door shut. "Give me a call in about a week, let me know how he's doing," he says through the window, then adds ominously, "if he's making any progress." That's it; I drive home with the dog.

The kids and Phil have set up a bed in the kitchen, a camp mattress, David's old sleeping bag, the smelly blanket the dog sometimes curls up on, and newspapers all over. The red plastic dog dish and a ceramic bowl for water—over the years he has become accustomed to drinking from the toilet bowl, but that's out of range for the time being—are neatly arranged at one end of the bed. I lug the dog in, protesting through his tied-up teeth, and lay him down, untie the strap from his nose. He just lies there panting, his head and chest erect, front paws parallel, looking from one of us to the other. He whimpers a little, then groans, staring up at me. But there is no way, I tell myself, that he could know I did it, just a sudden dark shadow, a heavy crushing weight, and pain. No, he couldn't know. But just the same I'll make it up to you, old man, I promise silently. I will make you better; I will make you well.

As it turns out, it's just as well I've made this solemn vow, because the dog will not let anyone else come near him, even to tie up his mouth. He growls and snaps at Phil and the kids if they so much as put a hand out. He will not let me pick him up with his mouth untied. Clearly unable to help himself, he snaps at me and then sinks his head down sheepishly, apologetic. He submits, blinking in humiliation, when I come toward him with the nylon stocking, but lets me tie it around his nose and behind his ears, so I can pick him up.

At first he cries all night. For a while I sit with him, but I keep falling asleep in the chair, so I go upstairs and collapse into a stupor, in which I still hear him yelping and moaning faintly throughout the night. In the morning I find him at one end of his bed, as far as he can get from the puddles and piles of dog shit, looking up at me with that bright foxy look, shifting his front paws in restless expectation as though to say, Let's get on with it.

And get on with it we do. I learn to recognize a certain tone of whimper and restless scrabbling as a signal he wants to go out, so I tie his mouth, hoist him up—for an old arthritic bony dog he's still no lightweight—take him outside, where he does his business lying down. There are accidents, but fewer and fewer as we get our signals straight, and picking him up seems to hurt him less and less. He does not complain much, eats and slurps up water, and watches us all go in and out, following us with the same old bright foxy look, still interested, so I can hardly believe what the vet has told us, that he's not only deaf but nearly blind. When I call the vet to tell him how things are going he listens carefully, then says the last thing I want to hear. "I'm worried about those legs. If he's not using them in a month, you may want to reconsider your options." I go all limp and wobbly at this, but the vet goes right on in his matter-of-fact voice. "Meanwhile, just let him take the lead, go at his own rate. If he wants to get better, he'll let you know."

Let him take the lead, I tell myself after I've hung up. Fine. What could be more reasonable? But I worry about the legs, about the dog's not walking, and what will happen then.

One morning in early November about three weeks after the accident, I come down early to find the dog all the way across the kitchen, squatting in front of the back door. He is straining upright, his back legs still sprawled awkwardly on the floor, scrabbling feebly. He looks at me, then points his nose up toward the doorknob and cries to be let out. Taken aback, I open the door and watch as he struggles through the opening, the two hind legs pushing like flippers behind. He gets all the way out the door and several feet beyond before he gives up. As I pick him up to lug him the rest of the way, he grunts and his nose grazes back against my cheek, but he does not bite me. Outside on the grass I stand him on his feet and hold his back end, and for the first time he pisses standing up, the way he did at first when he was a puppy, before he learned to lift one leg. I remember one time in particular when he jerked his leg so high he overbalanced, fell backward, and caught himself right in the eye. The next time I take him out and hold him up, he takes two faltering steps forward before his rear end keels over onto the ground. But I'm elated; he's walking, or will be soon, and when I call the vet to tell him, he says, "That's a good sign; that's good."

All through the next month as fall turns into winter I lug the dog out, following behind with one hand on either side of his skinny rear, holding it up as he staggers along. The legs both work now, though he still drags one, but I can't let him go, because the weight of his hips on the tottery old legs gradually tilts over the weak side and he goes down, subsiding slowly over to the ground the way he did when he was small. Then I have to set him back up again, but he will walk as long as I hold on, so I trot along behind him like a child playing train, eventually going all over the yard while he sniffs the snow for gossip, until finally my back can't take it anymore and I concoct a kind of sling for under his belly. Watching me trot after him, holding the contraption up, Phil shakes his head and says, "That's the first time I ever actually saw someone going around with his ass in a sling."

After a while the dog is strong enough to get around with me hanging onto the tip of his tail as though it were a leash. My in-laws come to visit, and my father-in-law sneaks out early one morning, takes a picture of me in my bathrobe, down vest, and rubber snow boots trailing around behind the dog in the snow, holding his tail up like a plume. My mother-in-law comments, "Such devotion, I never would have believed it. You're certainly making it up to him. But don't your feet get cold?"

I shake my head, although they do, but that is little enough to pay for this miraculous recovery, little enough as expiation for my sins.

VII

"Well, old man," I hear Phil murmur as he lets the dog out one morning the next fall, "you may outlive me yet." The dog looks back at him, then staggers out and down the porch steps, rickety on his old pins, but no more than any sixteen-year-old arthritic dog, to do his morning rounds. He has, according to the vet, recovered as fully as possible from the accident, but the effects of old age, weak kidneys and arthritis are creeping up on him, and he is getting frailer. A bad liver infection he contracted in the spring did not help much, and he has had several fits in the last few months, which the vet regards as warning signs of progressive terminal kidney failure. He has told Phil that it is just a matter of time; most dogs his size don't live past twelve, let alone sixteen. When Phil asks him what to do, the vet shrugs, says we'll know when it's time, that we will be able to tell when his life is not worth living to him anymore. So we watch and wait, but so far it does not seem the time has come and we think we'll let him have this one last summer, and when winter comes, then it will be time. He is as he was, if frailer, and in fact in the late summer after we change his diet the fits come less frequently. He still seems pleased to be alive, and it seems he'll go on forever, in his contracted world. He does not go out of the yard now, and he can't get up the stairs to sleep under our bed the way he used to, falling to his belly with a crash and thumping on his elbows as far in as he could get. He sleeps downstairs now, on a blanket in the study next to my chair. He seems perfectly happy in this world of downstairs and around the yard, places he knows intimately by smell and feel, if no longer by sight and sound.

Anyway, it is Phil we're concerned with now. The tumor has recurred and the local doctors, at a loss, have at our insistence agreed to send Phil to a big cancer center in Boston to have his case reevaluated, to see if something can be done. The doctors here are worried about his kidneys—or rather kidney, since we now know that one was mistakenly removed during the operation two years ago. So Phil is home now, and we are waiting for a bed. When one is free, Phil's parents will come up to stay with the children, and Phil and I will drive to Boston. Phil is not hopeful, and thus his comment to the dog, not meant for anyone to hear. He knows I don't want to hear things like that, believing as always where there's life there's hope; his fatalism is balanced by my refusal, with what I consider to be ample precedent, to declare the game is over, at least in public and out loud.

Contemplating Phil's illness and what we have come to so soon, Phil not even forty yet, I see this as the apotheosis of a childhood fantasy, conceived not too long after my father died, while we were still living in Toledo, before my mother gave up on living by ourselves and we all moved back with my grandmother and my aunt in Skaneateles, in what I have come to think of as the house of widows.

In the street in back of us on River Road there was a big boy, a bully, head of a gang of children in a subdivision neighborhood—the Island Avenue gang. Although I played with many of the kids in the gang, I was never invited to belong, by virtue of my address as well as my timidity. The bully and his cohorts used to tease me unmercifully on the way home from school, and I was a natural and satisfactory victim, quick to respond and especially to cry. My mother told me I had to learn to fight my own battles, and the worst thing I could do was to talk back or cry. I must let them know they didn't bother me one bit. I was to turn the other cheek, as my father used to say, so one day I did just that, leaning back against the fence nonchalantly as they passed, chanting, "Sticks and stones will break my bones, but words will never hurt me," while rather prominently looking the other way. In an instant the bully had whipped off his leather belt and whacked me across the face with the buckle end. It laid the skin above my eye right open, narrowly missing my eyeball and, as my outraged mother later told the parents of the bully, nearly blinding me for life. Naturally I was forbidden ever to play with the Island Avenue hooligans again, those ruffians, and for a long time my mother drove me to school the long way around.

My fantasy was this: In one of my lonely walks through the woods of the abandoned filtration plant up the road, I would come upon the bully, laid out cold, having fallen from a high branch of one of the trees that had been allowed to grow up on the reserve. He lay there either unconscious or with a broken leg, or both. And of course it was up to me to save him, which I did in any number of ways, the most implausible of which involved my carrying him piggyback all the way to Island Avenue. The upshot always was that I would rescue him somehow, and become the heroine of the gang.

This, I now recognize, was the original formulation of my rescuer complex, a conversion into fantasy of my feeling that I should somehow have prevented my father's death, either by not letting him go away from home or by being there when the heart attack hit, so he'd know someone was there and wouldn't die. But I failed at this, and the conviction of my original powerlessness developed into an irresistible impulse to rescue everything and everyone in sight.

Certainly life has given me ample opportunity to exercise this impulse, but over the years I have gotten better at moderating it somewhat—take, for instance, my mother's last psychotic episode six years ago when she wound up in yet another paranoid frenzy in an Auburn motel. It was the seventh go-round in as many years—the second in a little over a year—and my sister had washed her hands of the whole thing and was on her way to Colorado. But instead of jumping in the car and driving ten hours to get there and take care of things, even though it was once again my turn, after pondering the problem for a while, I finally sent the motel owner a card with several phone numbers and the message: "In case of any trouble with Martha Gilead, please contact the following." Sure enough, three days later a social worker from the psychiatric ward at Auburn General called me with the news that my mother was there, they were putting her back on lithium, and everything was going to be just fine. We'd heard that many times before, but oddly enough this time they were right, or close enough. There have been one or two lapses since, but she has generally been getting better and better. She came through her mastectomy five years ago with no trouble, and even showed up unexpectedly when Phil was in the hospital for so long after his operation to help me with the kids, just like anybody else's mother. She's helping to put my sister Fran through medical school; last spring she took a bus down to see my brother and his family, and even went by herself into Philadelphia to see the Garden Show. She writes letters now which, if a little scrawly at times, are funny ha-ha, not funny peculiar, so that I sometimes feel I am getting glimpses of the way she must have been when she was young and first married to my father. I think I have a better understanding of what she must have gone through in her sad life, and it seems possible now that, after all these years, we may even have resumed that old uncomplicated childhood mother-daughter relationship so abruptly short-circuited nearly thirty years ago. So it seems that after all our combined efforts over the long haul, she is finally rescued for good.

But the situation with Phil makes all these other rescues seem like dress rehearsals, mere warm-ups. The doctors have told us he is dying, has perhaps six months, a year at most to live. If his words to the dog are any indication, he feels some parallel in their predicaments, though Phil is only thirty-nine, and the dog in people years is upwards of a hundred and two, and of course, the dog is just a dog. But both of them are waiting for a sign that says, "It's time to give."

While we are waiting, we go about our business, to work, to school, or in Phil's case, sailing, since he has taken a medical leave from the college. The days stretch on, the pathology reports criss-cross the medical establishment, and one day I notice a growth in the dog's mouth that is interfering with his chewing. Since nothing else is going on at the moment, I load him in the car and take him to the vet's. It's the first time we've been there since his liver infection in the spring, and he quivers and trembles and looks pathetic, but acquiesces finally in his elderly dignified way.

The vet is horrified when he looks in the dog's mouth. "Oh, Jesus," he says, baring his teeth in a grimace of pained discovery. The growth is large and black, a piece of the dog's inner lip, looking like a giant slug of chewed-up licorice bubble gum. "Melanoma," the vet mutters. "Not good."

It doesn't sound good to me either. Melanoma is a cancer in humans, and a friend of ours has just died of it at the age of forty-one.

"Pretty advanced," the vet goes on. "He's probably got it other places, too. Why didn't you bring him in before?"

"Could it be something else?" I ask, ignoring his implication. The question's worked before. In fact, sometimes I think it works for every-thing except death itself.

"Nope," the vet says nonnegotiably as he gets out his tools, a huge hypodermic and a vial. Suddenly I'm overtaken by a terrible suspicion.

"You're not going to put him to sleep, are you?"

"Of course," the vet says, holding up the vial and sucking the pale green fluid back into the huge needle.

"But, but . . ." I throw an arm protectively over the dog, who looks up at me curiously, the iridescent cataracts in his eyes catching the light, momentarily clouding the bright puppy look. "Just like that? But . . . but we haven't even discussed it," I say desperately. The fact is, I'm not ready for this.

"What's there to discuss?" the vet says imperturbably. "If I don't put him to sleep for this, he'll squirm all over. I don't think you can hold him. And I've felt those teeth too many times before."

I stare at the vet. Dumb. Put him to sleep. Right. For the

operation. He's going to remove the growth and send us on our way, reprieved again. I nod, and he grabs a front leg, jabs the needle in while I hold the dog's nose.

But there is not even time for a struggle, the odd snap; as soon as the needle hits his skin the dog goes limp, without even time to shut his eyes, which roll back and shine dully up at me, sightless under peaky eyebrows. He looks dead, and I think in horror that the vet has killed him, either by accident or—knowing me—by design.

"Is he dead?" I gasp.

"Of course not," the vet says as he turns toward an instrument that resembles a blowtorch. "Just out cold."

The blowtorch thing is in fact an electric cauterization needle, and the vet burns away the tumor while I hold the dog, his body limp as a fur rug, his head lolling, the tongue hanging to one side like a slab of veal. I count his teeth; some are missing, some broken. Dogs should not outlive their teeth, I think, such an indignity. But he's got plenty left. "When will he wake up?" I want to know.

"In an hour or so. He'll be pretty shaky for a while. You got any errands downtown?" The vet hangs up the electric scalpel, finished. The growth is gone, or near enough. "I can't promise you much in the long run, though. These things are generally lethal," he says, looking at me seriously. "It won't be long. You might want to talk it over with your husband. It may be time."

But when I pick the dog up later that afternoon he's wide awake and frisky, still the same old dog with his foxy, handsome face. He skitters across the floor in his eagerness to get out of there, staggers out to the car and hops into his place in the front footwell, next to my feet, and home we go. I don't mention to Phil what the vet told me; there will be time to do that later when we get Phil squared away himself. The dog's all right for the time being, and it's not winter yet.

VIII

And the end of the story is this:

It's been almost two weeks since Phil and I drove down to Boston to the hospital, but all the tests are in now, and the operation is scheduled for tomorrow. It's old home week in Phil's room, doctors coming over from the Institute: surgeons, endocrinologists, oncologists, nephrologists, radiologists, anesthesiologists, not to mention nurses, nurse's aides, student nurses, all wanting to wish him well. He's very popular around here—someone they can cure, or hope they can. And the phone calls come in from all over, too: Maine, Vermont, New Jersey, California. His hometown doctor has called, some friends have called, his sisters have called.

Phil lies there, his cheeks pudgy from all the fluids they've pumped into him to offset the anticipated effects of tomorrow's surgery. He's also chock-full of Valium, grinning cheerfully. Besides the doctors, two friends are visiting; it's a three-ring circus. I haven't been here very long myself; in fact, I just got back after spending two days at home with Phil's parents and the kids.

Finally everyone leaves, and then the phone rings again. "You get it," Phil says. "I'm tired of talking." It's almost time for his body shave and the enema they've promised him to get his bowels whistle-clean, "just in case."

I pick up the phone. "Sara, is that you?" It's Phil's mother, and she sounds so upset I decide on the spot I'm not going to let her talk to Phil. But it's me she wants. "Listen, I'm sorry to bother you at a time like this, but it's about the dog. I don't know what's wrong, but he had a fit in the study and he's messed himself and all over the floor, poor soul, and he's lying in it and can't get up." In the background I can hear yelping and howling, shouting of several voices: Pop and the kids. "When we went to help him he tried to bite Pop," she finishes, her voice trailing off into a quaver. "We don't know what to do."

I stand there gripping the phone, thinking, I just don't believe it. The phone hums, the dog yelps, and I hear Pop's voice raised faintly: "No, no, don't go near him!"

The phone sniffles, clears its throat, waiting. "Sara?" I shut my eyes, my head buzzing angrily. They're asking me what to do, for chrissake? What do they expect, me to drive back up tonight and rescue the goddamned dog? Can't they deal with this themselves? It's the night before Phil's operation, and they can't cope with a stupid dog?

"I hate to bother you at a time like this," my mother-in-law repeats, "but we thought you should know."

For once I'm speechless.

"Sara?" my mother-in-law says timidly after a moment. Phil is looking at me, his head lifted off the pillow, alarmed.

"The dog is sick," I say with my hand over the phone. "They're all hysterical." Phil's head flops back, his eyes closed. He looks relieved. "I thought it was one of the kids," he says.

Meanwhile, not used to being stuck for an answer, I'm thinking furiously. It's eight o'clock at night. The clamor at the other end of the phone squawks in my ear; all hell has broken loose. "Okay, look," I say as calmly as I can to Phil's mother. "If you're afraid to go near the dog, call Punch next door or Joyce up the street—the dog knows both of them—and ask them to come and help you. See if you can get him in the car and take him straight to the vet's. Then call me back. Call me back no matter what."

They call me back ten minutes later. Nobody's home, not Punch, not Joyce, not even the vet. "Well, just shut the doors and leave him until tomorrow morning," I say at last. "There's nothing else anybody can do."

"Poor soul," my mother-in-law says. "I feel so bad for him."

"There's nothing I can do," I tell her, unable to keep the exasperation out of my voice any longer.

"I know, Sara, I know," she says wearily. "We just thought you ought to know. Can I speak to my son now?"

I hand the phone over to Phil, and that's the end of that.

Over the next couple of days I'm at the hospital constantly, during the eight hours of Phil's operation and his subsequent stay in the intensive care unit. I hardly think about the dog. When I call with the good news that the operation was an apparent success, they tell me almost as an afterthought that the man from the general store down the street came over the next morning to help Pop get the dog into the car, but at the last minute he got up and walked into the car under his own power, God bless him, so maybe things aren't so bad. But he cried all night, and they're all exhausted. They'll let me know what happens, and everything's under control.

Meanwhile, Phil is recovering but in a lot of pain, and both of us have to struggle with the horrors, remembering the other operation and its aftermath. But he amazes everyone with his rapid progress, his eagerness to get up and get going, back on his feet. I spend most of my time there. The nurses let me stay beyond the ten minutes at a time, because by now they know I won't scream and cry and faint into the forest of IVs and monitors around his bed, and besides, my presence seems to help. I don't cry at all; I haven't yet and I don't now, because things are looking up. One day runs into the next in ICU, but he makes rapid progress. One minute I am watching Phil, vacant-eyed and dopey, trying to stand up between two stocky nurses; the next time I see him he's walked around the whole unit and is talking about sending out for a pizza. The nurses joke about not knowing what to do for him since no one ever eats real food in ICU. But they are short of beds in the step-down unit where Phil goes next, and they want to keep him in here one more day. So I leave for Cambridge, thinking how relaxed and jolly it all is, and how everything is going so well.

But when I get back to our friends' house where I'm staying there's a message: "Call home." And it's the dog. The vet has called that morning, Sunday, to find out what we want to do. The dog is suffering, sick and retching, can't stand up. I'm supposed to call him. "His life is a misery to him," my mother-in-law says sadly, and I can guess what it is the vet wants me to say. And so I call the vet.

"The dog is really in bad shape, full of tumors, advanced kidney failure," he says in his matter-of-fact, professional, but not unsympathetic voice. "There's no point in prolonging this. I hate to see him suffer this way."

He wants my permission; all I have to do is say the word—two words, actually: Do it. And I remember the times Phil and I talked about this, how we would want to be there, and my throat dries up and my tongue cleaves to the roof of my mouth, and I can't say anything at all.

"I've got to think about it," I say finally. "I don't know what to do."
I explain to the vet what's going on down here, Phil still in intensive
care, that I can't leave right now.

"He wouldn't know you," the vet says. "He's really out of it,
doesn't know much of anything anymore." He pauses, waiting. "But it's
entirely up to you."

Still I can't do it. I try to remember the last time I saw the dog,
whether I even noticed him, patted him and said good-bye. It's a familiar feeling, this guilt, and I have to remind myself he's just a dog.

"I've got to think it over," I say finally in my crabbed voice, aware
of the vet's silent disapproval on the other end. He thinks that this is
sentimental bullshit, and in a way it is. "I can't decide now, I just
can't," I tell him apologetically. "Let me sleep on it, and I'll call you in
the morning.

And then I go to bed, but I don't sleep, and in fact this is the worst
night I've spent since we came down to Boston. Somehow the dog's
trouble has gotten lost in all this other business, but he's been such a
good old friend and can it be there's no time to spare after all these
years to see him out? I toss and turn, arguing with myself he's just a
dog, he wouldn't know I was there, it's silly, stupid, a waste of time and
energy. In the midst of all this, I remember the time not long ago
when I took him in to have the growth removed and thought the vet
had killed him, that he was dead just like that, right before my eyes.
And I think that is how it would be, the first shot that puts him out in-
stantaneously, with no pain, and then the second one that stops the
heart. He'll never know what hit him. Not a bad death, so quick, so
humane, and how can it be worth it for me to drive all the way back
up there just for those few seconds? And have I made it up to him, I
wonder in the dark? Did I really make him better, and was it worth it
to him, even though it's come to this? And all the time I'm thinking
this, I know it's not the dog I need to rescue; it's me.

In the morning I've made up my mind. I'm driving up. I call the
hospital to get a report on Phil; he's been moved out of intensive care,

his condition satisfactory, stable. I dial the vet's number to let him know I'm coming.

And the vet says, "I'm afraid it's out of your hands. The dog passed away in his sleep last night. I found him this morning. So it's all been decided for you."

"Thanks," I croak, barely able to hang up the phone. I cross over to the couch, bury my face in my hands, and start to cry—sudden loud, wet, uncontrollable sobs.

"Oh, my God!" my friend Jane shrieks as she stops dead in the doorway of the room, her hands flying to her face in a pantomime of anticipated horror. "Oh, my God, Sara! Oh, no! What's happened, what's wrong?"

Of course, seeing me crying, she thinks it's Phil. I look up at her, damp and trembling with these my first, my only, and my ancient tears, and say, "No, it's all right. It's just the dog. It's just the god-damned dog."

And this is what I've learned about the dead: It is not always their absence that haunts us. So I still hear the clink of a chain collar against a porcelain bowl, the skittering of toenails across a wooden floor, the thump and sigh of a weary dog flopping his old bones down next to my chair. I feel the presence of those old bones under my chair, under my feet. Under my wheels.

Elaine Ford

Elwood's Last Job

They didn't hear him over the roar of the washers and the flopping of clothes in the dryers, so he said it again, louder this time. "Nobody move. This is a stickup."

The Widow Balch looked up from the afghan square she was knitting and saw Elwood Tibbetts standing in the doorway with a plaid cloth suitcase in his hand. In the other he held what appeared to be a gun. Mrs. Balch peered over her half-moons. "Stop that foolishness, Elwood," she said.

"It ain't foolishness." He stepped into the laundrymat and set the suitcase down. Then he turned the lock in the glass door behind him.

By now Elwood had the attention of Rena Guptill and Mandy Clukey, who were seated in molded orange chairs near Mrs. Balch's. In her third-grade-teacher voice, which she hadn't lost in twenty years of retirement, Mrs. Balch said, "Put that away, now, Elwood. It's not polite to go waving guns around, even if it is a toy."

"This ain't a toy," Elwood said.

True, the gun had the heavy, black, sober look of an honest-to-goodness weapon. "Where'd you get it?" Mandy asked.

"Never you mind."

Must have sent away for it, Mandy thought, from one of those mail-order places that advertise in gun magazines. She pictured Elwood laboriously penciling the address on a rumpled envelope, enclosing a money order he would have bought at the post office. Elwood worked there, sweeping the place out and emptying the trash bins. You could also see him shoveling snow at the Congregational Church or in summer mowing its lawn and trimming the hedges. He was a hulking, paunchy man with little in the way of a chin and shoulders sloped from decades of menial jobs.

"Why would you want to rob a laundrymat?" Mandy said. "Nothing worth taking in this crummy place."

"She's got that right. Left my diamond tiara at home, ha ha." Rena found a cigarette and lit up, in spite of the flyspecked sign that forbade bare feet, shirtlessness, smoking, overloading the washers, dyeing, and loitering.

Suddenly Elwood took aim at the change machine, pulled the trigger, and fired. BLAM. Mrs. Balch dropped a stitch and Mandy the damp copy of *House and Garden* she'd been thumbing through. In the center of the machine was a hole like a belly button where once a lock had been.

When their eardrums had recovered from the blast, Mrs. Balch said, "My stars," and Rena said, "Well, there. I guess you showed that ole change machine. Just let it try to cough back our raggedy bills now."

From his pocket Elwood drew a black plastic garbage bag. "You," he said to Mandy, "over here." Mandy was eight months pregnant, her first kid, and these days you practically needed a winch to budge her. In addition, she was not used to taking direction from Elwood Tibbetts. She had trouble wrapping her mind around this departure from the normal order of things. However, she heaved herself out of her chair and waddled toward the change machine.

Elwood handed the bag to Mandy and pried up the machine's hinged door. He ordered her to scoop quarters out of the three metal troughs inside the machine, which were the size of smallish shoe boxes, upended. "Holy shit," she exclaimed. There were way more quarters inside this machine than Mandy would ever have imagined, enough to do the whole town's wash, maybe the whole county's wash—and dry it, too. Encouraged by the sight of the gun, she got to work, and fistfuls of coins began to go tumbling into the bag, ringing merrily. The bag got heavier and heavier.

In fact, Elwood had underestimated the combined weight of a serious quantity of coinage. As Mandy was finishing emptying the last trough, the bag's bottom seam burst open, and a torrent of quarters poured onto dirty linoleum. Some rolled under the chairs Mrs. Balch and Rena were sitting on.

"Dang," Elwood said. "'S'posed to be a heavy-duty bag." Pointing the gun in turn at all three ladies, Elwood looked around the laundrymat. He seized a pillowcase from one of the baskets and tossed it to Mandy. "Okay," he said, "pick up them quarters."

"Why don't you get Rena to do it? I'm in no condition to go crawling around on the floor."

"I've got a bad back," Rena said. "Elwood knows about my back, don't you, Elwood? Remember how I always mention it when I see you in the P.O.?"

"You won't get away with this," Mandy said to Elwood. With a groan she knelt and began to gather heaps of quarters into the pillowcase. She wondered how come nobody in Clip'n'Curl next door had heard the shot. She wondered how come nobody arrived with their laundry and pulled on the door handle and peered through the glass and sized up the situation and ran to call the sheriff. It seemed like everyone in town had magically vanished, leaving the three ladies to the mad whims of Elwood Tibbetts.

"What are you going to use the money for?" Mrs. Balch asked conversationally, fishing for the dropped stitch.

"I ain't sayin'."

Mrs. Balch noticed Elwood was sweating in the moist heat of the laundrymat. His sparse straight hair was all mussed. She remembered when he was in her third-grade class and he always hid slumped in the back row so as not to be called on. The other boys picked on him because he was slow and because he couldn't throw or catch a ball to save his soul, and she'd felt sorry for him, but when teachers butted into children's affairs it only made life worse for the victim. You just had to pray the tormentors outgrew the nonsense before too much damage was done. Mrs. Balch recalled that one of Elwood's classmates was killed in Vietnam. Another drowned, dragged from his lobster boat by his own gear. But most of them moved away, because they couldn't find work here that paid enough. Elwood was one of the few left in town.

"I bet you're running off with somebody," Rena said. With her pinkie nail she picked a shred of tobacco out from between two front teeth. You could see the gold inlay in her dog tooth. "The new checkout girl in Conklin's Variety, maybe."

"No girls," Elwood said with conviction, as if he'd already considered such a plan and decided a female companion would be more trouble than she'd be worth. Based on his experience with his mother, Rena thought, he'd be right. Nasty old biddy, Gladys Tibbetts. One of the washers screeched to a halt, and Rena said, "That's my load. Mind if I put it in the dryer?" She squashed her butt under her shoe. "I'm kinda in a hurry," she added, explaining that she'd promised to bake two lemon meringue pies for tonight's Vets Club supper. She figured Elwood would be bound to respect the Vets, if not her.

"I guess that would be okay," Elwood said reluctantly. "Just don't try anything."

The gun trained on her, Rena wheeled one of the laundrymat's carts over to the washer and removed a tangle of sheets and underwear from its innards. Behind her, Mandy crawled under a chair to retrieve a quarter. The knees of her maternity pants were now filthy from the floor, which hadn't been mopped in years, possibly decades. Her bleached hair was coming undone from its rollers.

This is like a movie, Mandy thought, dragging the heavy pillowcase behind her. She tried to picture what would happen next. The sheriff would burst in, guns blazing. Or the most unlikely one of the hostages—yes, she decided, they were actually hostages—would disarm the gunman and save the day. That would have to be Mrs. Balch, but Mrs. Balch was proceeding with her afghan as calmly as if this was just an ordinary occurrence on an ordinary day. Mandy's baby kicked her bladder, and she realized she had to pee.

Rena stuffed her wash into one of the dryers, then remembered she was out of change. She waved a dollar bill, which looked as if it had been through some previous wash itself, in Elwood's direction. "Could I turn this in for some of the quarters in the pillowcase?" she asked. "As you know, the change machine has a little problem at the moment." Without waiting for a reply, Rena handed the bill to Mandy and received four quarters, which she deposited in the coin slots. Her sheets and underwear began to rotate behind the dryer's foggy window.

Back in her chair, Rena said, "So, are you planning on taking the loot over to the Union Trust? You know what Monica's going to say when you show up with that pillowcase there? Monica's going to say, 'Where'd you get all them quarters, Elwood? Whaja do, rob the laundrymat? Ha, ha.'"

"Ain't taking 'em to the bank."

"What *are* you going to do?"

Not that it was any of their business, but he'd be on the 11:45 bus to Bangor. And from there on the next bus out of town. Never coming back, neither.

All three ladies absorbed this for a while. None of them could imagine the town without Elwood Tibbetts cutting the church lawn in crooked swaths. Or standing in front of the nursing home in red and black wool jacket and matching hat with earflaps, selling homemade crafts like reindeer lawn ornaments he'd constructed out of birch logs. Or raising a cloud of dust in your face in the post office, smiling bashfully if you bothered to pass the time of day with him.

Mandy hauled herself to her feet and thrust the pillowcase at Elwood. Must be hundreds of bucks' worth of coins in there, she thought, but he was so numb he didn't know he wouldn't get very far on that. She plunked herself back in a chair, hoping she'd get to pee soon, now that he had what he came for.

Not quite yet, though. The next thing Elwood did was to extract a wad of paper money maybe three inches thick from the machine. The ladies' eyes bugged. Here they'd thought all he was getting was quarters, a lot of quarters to be sure, but still, pocket change. Actual bills—including fives and tens—were a whole different kettle of fish. Calmly, Elwood dropped the wad into the pillowcase. While they were still digesting the size of the take, Elwood held the sack open in front of the three ladies, who sat in a row in their molded orange chairs. He was like a kid trick-or-treating, a large middle-aged kid toting a gun. "Put your stuff in," he said. "Money, any jewelry you got on you, any other val'ables."

"Why Elwood," Mrs. Balch said. "Robbing the laundrymat is one thing, but robbing us is quite another. We're your friends."

"Naw," he said. "You ain't."

Mrs. Balch remembered the D-minus she'd given the boy in penmanship, although he'd struggled so hard even to hold the pen properly, never mind form the letters. She wrestled her wedding ring off her finger and dropped it in the pillowcase. In her pocketbook, she knew, was a ten-dollar bill and some singles. She added the pocketbook, then the garnet earrings she'd inherited from her mother. Mrs. Balch wondered sadly if she'd ever see them again.

Rena remembered all the times she'd walked past Elwood's pitiful little stall in front of the nursing home and never bought a thing—well, why should she have? Bunch of junk. Into the pillowcase went her purse with the forty dollars she'd been about to spend for the week's groceries, then her diamond engagement ring, which she'd been wearing on her right hand for three years, ever since she and Phil went their separate ways. Dammit, she might not be married anymore, but she'd *earned* that ring. She didn't like the way this was going at all.

Mandy remembered how she and her friends used to shout *Hey, Smellwood, where'd you lose your chin?* at him as they rode past on their bikes. She didn't have a wedding ring, not yet, but she had two hundred dollars she'd just taken out of the ATM to give to Donnie Dorr, who was adding a porch onto her trailer and would work for less if you paid him under the table. She put the wallet containing those crisp new twenties into the pillowcase, plus her beloved gold chain anklet engraved with her initials. Geez, she needed to pee so bad. And now she felt sort of sick to her stomach, nervous sick. She always thought Elwood was harmless, poor old doofus, but maybe she'd been wrong.

"Elwood, dear," Mrs. Balch said, "if you go your mother will miss you terribly. Why don't you reconsider? Maybe the laundrymat people will overlook the damage you did to their change machine if you give the money back directly."

Rena glared at Mrs. Balch. Reminding him of his witch of a mother was the last thing to convince him not to bolt.

"You'll be leaving behind witnesses, you know," Mrs. Balch went on in a kindly voice. "The police will put up a roadblock and arrest you long before the bus gets to Bangor."

Christ on a crutch, Rena thought. Why did she have to bring up the subject of witnesses? Who knew what Elwood was capable of, bashful grin or no? He could shoot them as easy as any change machine. "Shut the hell up, you old windbag," she hissed at Mrs. Balch.

"There's no need to be rude," Mandy said, beginning to sniffle.

"You can shut *your* mouth too," Rena said, "like you should've shut your legs when that worm digger came around, and would've if you had any sense."

Mandy wailed.

"That was not at all a kind thing to say," Mrs. Balch said to Rena. "No wonder Phil Guptill took off the way he did."

"Get up," Elwood said.

"What?" Mrs. Balch asked.

"Get up. Now." Keeping the gun on them, Elwood went to the glass door and unlocked it. Then, the pillowcase slung over his shoulder as if he was some kind of deranged Santa Claus, the plaid suitcase in his left hand, he marched the ladies past the rows of washers to the back of the laundrymat and out the rear door. Behind the laundrymat was an alley surrounded by a plank fence, where none of the ladies had ever been. It was empty except for two dented trash cans and some dead leaves from last fall. Chilly out here, for May, on account of a breeze off the bay. Blackflies had already hatched, and a few of them began to menace the ladies' ears.

"My driver's license," Rena said suddenly. "You've got my driver's license in that pillowcase. And my MasterCard."

"Don't worry. You won't be needing them anytime soon. You and you," he said to Rena and Mandy, "sit." Elwood took a roll of duct tape and a pair of scissors out of the suitcase and gave them to Mrs.

Balch. Pointing the gun at her, he explained how she was to tape up the other ladies' mouths and wrists and ankles as they huddled on the cold concrete.

"My back," Rena whimpered, "you remember about my back, don't you?" but Elwood paid no attention. Mrs. Balch had prided herself on the values she taught her third graders (*a job well done is worth two half done; a job worth doing is worth doing well*), and she executed a thorough and efficient job of disabling the other witnesses. Next Elwood taped up his old teacher, every bit as competently as she could have done it herself. Humming a cheerful but unrecognizable tune, he unzipped the suitcase. He took out a floppy denim hat and clapped it on his head. Then he returned the duct tape and the scissors to the suitcase, along with the gun. With effort he crammed in the pillowcase. Once he'd zipped up the suitcase the bulge wasn't that conspicuous. It could have been his winter jacket and some of his mother's fruitcakes, wrapped well, packed to give him sustenance on his journey. "You have a good day now," he said to the three mummified ladies. Suitcase in hand, he unlatched the rear gate and closed it securely behind him.

The ladies heard cars and trucks go up and down Main Street. They heard the Bangor bus roar to a stop in front of Clip'n'Curl and shortly thereafter take off again. Gulls screamed overhead. Blackflies swarmed and bit the flesh below their ears. Rena was dying for a cigarette. Mrs. Balch thought about her laundry mildewing in the washer and the chicken parts defrosting in her kitchen sink, probably going to end up spoiled. Mandy made a sorry little puddle on the cement beneath her.

Finally they heard a squad car's siren approaching from Route 1A, turning the corner onto Main Street, and abruptly terminating in front of the laundrymat. The sheriff must have been at the other end of the county when he heard about the heist over his shortwave radio, up to Lubec or Calais, and that's what took him so long to get here. They'd be rescued now. But nobody came to the rear door of the laundrymat. After a while they heard the squad car drive away.

They thought Elwood might get pretty far, after all.

Bill Roorbach

A Job at Little Henry's

Richard Milk thought about the stolen money all weekend, planned different speeches, different ways of dealing with Dewey Burke on Tuesday when Dewey Burke was due to show up. Richard wanted to explode in Dewey's pocked face, but yelling wasn't going to work. Better to quietly ask that jailbird to admit the theft, then offer to let him work it off, solemnly hear his promises, and maybe no longer allow him in the house.

Such were Richard's thoughts all weekend—a long weekend, as it happened, Richard following Gail to no fewer than six Memorial Day picnics and dinners and dances—the problem of Dewey Burke crowding into every crevice left by more immediate concerns. And, in truth, Richard found these thoughts of Dewey refreshing, this new trouble much easier to think about than Lester Molina or the rocky going of late with Gail.

Late Monday night, Richard moved the money jar out of the kitchen, put it in Gail's desk, put a few bucks in it to get it started again. That ridiculous money jar—the habit of a twenty-two-year marriage. Right now, they were trying to put together enough spare dimes and quarters and dollar bills and occasional fives to buy a good chunk of next year's spring trip to Florida.

On Tuesday, Memorial Day weekend was over and Gail went to work. She was the area coordinator in School Administrative District 98, LaDoux County, Maine, which meant she was busy nearly every minute of every day, and which meant that she and Richard were comfortable enough, despite his recent troubles: Richard was out of work. Up until six weeks ago he'd been chief designer at Molina Log Homes, an enormous prefabricating operation that beardy Molina had started in his back-to-the-land days, hippie days. Now it was a small empire, stretching across the top of America clear to Montana. Richard had designed every home they marketed, designed them for beauty, designed them for comfort, designed them for the earth-friendly aspects Molina Log Homes advertised, designed them for profit too, and so that logs could be shipped pre-cut aboard ever smaller trucks. Lester had talked lugubriously for an hour about housing starts and the shaky economy, but his theatrically sad eyes couldn't hide what had really happened: Richard Milk had drawn all the designs Lester Molina needed to do his huge business forever, and so Lester had let him go.

Oh, yes, on Tuesday the long weekend was over. Richard stood in the yard an hour after breakfast (Gail long gone in her safe red Saab), just stood and looked at the hills across the way. The thief Dewey turned up exactly on time. Richard saw him coming up the road, slouching up the road with his bouncing reform-school swagger. Richard felt calm, told himself a few encouraging words, tried a sentence out: *I'll understand if you don't want to admit it right away, but . . .*

Then the bum was at the door, saying it was a decent day—in fact, saying just those words, with no inflection at all, no way to sense the man: "Decent day."

"Nice'un," Richard said, "yup." He found himself talking the way Dewey did, just as he found himself talking like Koreans he'd met in the city, just as he found himself talking like Texans when he and Gail had lived down there. Gail saw this cultural echolalia (that was the phrase she used, sometimes gently, usually not) as a lack of boundaries, as the symptom of a man with no self. Richard saw it as his quite firm self's private brand of mockery, something he did unconsciously to nearly everyone, especially people he regarded as less sophisticated. In any case, it was something he meant to cut out.

Dewey had no more conversation in him, turned and walked back around the house to the shed, pulled out a shovel and rake, and headed over to the corner of the woodlot to continue exactly where he'd left off last Thursday, digging out the old compost, putting it cartload by cartload on the garden. Richard followed him more slowly, choosing words: *But don't worry, we understand, we know a call for help when we hear it. You've worked for us faithfully for over a year. You won't be fired. We only want . . .* what? What did they want? Gail hadn't seemed the least bit concerned. "We'll have to get rid of him," was all she said, meaning that Richard had to get rid of him, of course.

"Dewey?"

"Mister?"

"Dewey, there's something I want to talk to you about."

"Right."

"Dewey, we're concerned. You've offended our trust. Let me put it bluntly: Gail and I know you stole our money." That didn't sound right—too confrontational. "Dewey, this really . . . pisses me off. You stole from us."

"Didn't either."

"Dewey, you stole forty-five dollars on Tuesday and fourteen on Thursday."

"The fuck I did." Dewey stabbed the shovel into the compost and straightened, looked square at Richard. His eyes were as cold and deep and dark as the deep-woods quarry ponds in Avon to which Richard and Gail had made the strenuous hike last summer with the intention of swimming. They had not swum. The place was beautiful and what one once thought of as secluded, the water green and clear and very deep, but there were too many beer cans and lots of trash and diapers and those grotesque, mud-splattered, off-road trucks parked halfway up the sides of boulders for show and twenty people who looked like Dewey Burke, people like Dewey everywhere, a circus of tattoos and hidden weaponry.

Something firmer: "Dewey, listen, you're caught. Now if you'd just take a minute to think about it . . . I mean, you're caught. We caught you. You stole our money. Dewey, listen to me. You stole from us."

The look on Dewey's face went cloudy, then black. He stepped toward Richard and swung his arm—that's what Richard saw, the arm. The tattooed fist seemed to arrive separately, and too early, arrived right at Richard's nose and sent him into a vague and fuzzy time warp in which everything Dewey did seemed extremely slow and purposeful, almost inevitable, certainly unstoppable. Richard didn't fall, didn't take a fighter's stance, just put a hand to his face in amazement. "Jesus, Dewey." And that fist came back, hitting Richard's hand, knocking his own soft palm into his own hard cheekbone. "That's enough."

"Don't tell *me*," Dewey spouted, and swung again, this time hitting Richard's eye so precisely that the fist (tattooed B-A-D-D across the knuckles) blocked the light for a moment. A strong punch to his stomach (L-U-C-K) finally knocked Richard down.

Dewey stopped. "You say sorry," Dewey said. "Say it." He loomed over Richard, threatening with his marked fists as Richard sat up.

"Jesus, Dewey."

Dewey whirled—some kind of homespun martial-arts move— whirled and kicked Richard in the side. Richard's ribs made a deep internal crunch, and hurt sharply, so he lay down. Dewey kicked him again, this time on the butt, then once more, sharply on the thigh. "Sacka shit," Dewey said. He stood over Richard a moment, waiting for the slightest twitch, a single word, the tiniest reason to resume the beating, then seemed to decide that Richard was through and walked off with the same slow swaggering slouch as always.

The sheriff's deputy who turned up late in the afternoon sat in his car for five minutes talking on the radio, only opened his door when Richard came out of the house. By now both of Richard's eyes were black, and of course his nose hurt. He didn't think his ribs were broken, but he'd begun to consider a call to Dr. LeMonteau (pronounced locally as Lemon Toe) to ask about his leg, which ached deeply, ached to the bone. Gail wasn't going to believe this.

"Looking good," the deputy said, swinging his legs out of the car but remaining seated. He pulled a thick notepad from his shirt pocket, produced a pen.

"Thank you," Richard said.

"Dewey Burke's one tough rabbit, sir. I'd think twice about fighting him again."

"I wasn't *fighting* him. He attacked me. Right back there. Punched me over and over, kicked me in the leg, knocked me down, all because I confronted him about some money he'd stolen." Into Richard's voice crept the clipped quality of the deputy's. He tried to cut it out: "He stole money from us in two days of work: forty-five dollars the first time—we hoped maybe it had just been misplaced—fourteen the second time, which is when I decided to talk to him about it."

The deputy put on a practiced skeptical frown. He hadn't written a word on his pad. "You have proof he stole it?"

"Well, of course. He was the only one here. Both Tuesday and Thursday."

"Your kids didn't take it?"

"The kids are in college, sir, both of them."

"You keep your doors locked?" The deputy had a cast to his eye, seemed to be looking over Richard's shoulder.

"Well, not generally, not when we're around, of course. Probably seldom. Mostly just when we're away."

"So anyone could have come right in and took the money, correct?"

"But who on earth would do that?"

"Drug addicts."

Richard wearily smiled, gave a good-natured shake of his head: "You're getting a little outlandish, sir."

"Friends of your kids, maybe."

Richard struggled to stay calm. Here in rural Maine, his children had found themselves viewed negatively as artsy types, and the deputy would certainly know that fact, know exactly how long Ricky's hair was, and see in his mind the many colors of Cindy's tie-dyed shirts, see the kids' sweet bunch of friends gathered playing Frisbee in the little park near the county court building. "My children's friends are among the most honest in town, Mr. Springer."

"Just borrowing a few bucks, maybe. Don't get weepy—I'm just looking for the facts here, and the facts is you don't have any evidence that Dewey Burke stole anything whatsoever at all."

Richard had learned to stay quiet a minute when insulted or angry, and so he did, stood quietly, looking away from the deputy, who looked away from him, still holding his unpoised pen and his empty pad, still making no sign that he'd get out of the car to investigate.

Finally Richard said, "Let's get to the point. I was attacked. A dangerous felon is loose."

"Would you like to press charges?"

"Do I need to press charges?"

"Well, in the case of fights, generally, we won't make an arrest unless there's been property damage."

"This wasn't a fight, Mr. Springer, as I've repeatedly told you."

"You mean you didn't get a single punch in?"

"I told you, sir, it was not a fight."

"Well. If you want to make a federal case out of it . . ." The deputy swung his legs back into the car, shut his door, sat staring out the windshield, seeming to try to decide whether to say what he was about to say. Then quietly, confidentially: "You'll want to know that if old Dew gets arrested for anything, anything at all, he's going back to jail for a wicked long time."

Gail Milk got home late because of the monthly school board meeting, home to a darkened house. She found Richard on the kitchen floor holding his leg. Soon, in the emergency room at LaDoux County Hospital, they learned that he had suffered a hematoma, an intermuscular blood clot, which, as Doctor LeMonteau said, could certainly be unbearably painful, but which wasn't particularly dangerous, unless the clot were to loosen and travel through the chambers of Richard's heart and to his brain, where it would certainly kill him. Dr. LeMonteau said this was unlikely. Richard had two cracked ribs as well, not much to do for that, just rest and heal.

Thursday morning, about the time Dewey would normally have appeared, a youngish woman came instead. Her hair looked partly washed. She appeared weary but intelligent, too, very bright in the eyes, something Richard was ashamed not to expect from the depths of a mobile home surrounded by old snow machines and car parts and doghouses. Her breasts were hard not to notice—large and upstanding under her T-shirt, her nipples walleyed under the worn cloth. Her legs and hips were as unnaturally narrow as an undernourished child's. Dewey's girlfriend. Holding a rhubarb pie.

Richard accepted the pie as solemnly as it was offered, stood in the doorway holding it, facing the unpretty woman.

She spoke earnestly: "Mr. Milk, Dew says sorry for fucking you up. He's really sorry. But he just didn't steal from you and that's what got him off. He just didn't steal nothing. Never has. That's not his thing. And he's been in trouble plenty so when he's finally straightened out it just flipped him out. Know what I mean? God, you look awful."

"It's not so bad."

"So can he come back to work?"

Tuesday Dewey was back. He went immediately to the compost pile and resumed what he'd been doing a week past when Richard had confronted him: shoveling humus into the Milks' red yard cart. Richard watched from the kitchen window, remembering the woman, and feeling himself to be a soft touch, sentimental even: he wanted to help Dewey, this thug in the garden. What was that all about? The man worked no faster or slower than he had before. He never looked up at the house, just shoveled the compost, wheeled the cart to the garden, spread the rich new earth. By midmorning he was done, had turned to the rototilling.

Normally, Dewey stopped for lunch—came up to the house, politely washed up at the kitchen sink, took the sandwich Richard offered, and ate it alone outside. Today, Dewey skipped lunch altogether. He got the lawn mower out and paced the big lawn with it, stopping frequently to empty the bag of clippings into a new pile in the compost bin.

Richard tried to get to his studying. He meant to pass the architecture boards this fall. He'd failed twice out of grad school, then got the job with Molina and quit trying. The studying would comprise a full-time occupation till October. Richard sat at his drawing board and opened two books. He stared at the wall, stared at the pages of the books, put his face in his hands, pushed back in his chair, thought of making an elaborate lunch, inviting Dewey in for a little of what Gail liked to call *rapprochement*, gazed back at the books, at the wall, at the floor. He had to get a look at Dewey—make sure Dewey seemed all right. The man mowed the lawn in record time, stood sweating by the toolshed, making a cigarette with shreds of tobacco from his tattered pouch. Six dollars an hour wasn't much for all Dewey did. Six dollars an hour was slave wages. No wonder the poor guy was so full of fury.

Gail thought Richard was a fool, had said so during a heated exchange in the breakfast nook—"A fool and more of a masochist than I thought!"—but Richard wasn't going to back down this time. Richard felt something grand growing in him, felt he'd risen past revenge, transcended fear, had turned his other cheek, had experienced true compassion for the first time in all his days, something that arose in some way to do with being fired, for sure, but something to do with Dewey's fists, as well, something to do with the sharp points of Dewey's shoes.

"You are a dolt," Gail had said in anger (later she would apologize, with kisses). "A *dunderhead*. And you are deluding yourself. Get your architect's license—please!—pass that loser's exam, and then, *get a job*, and you won't need to pay people to punish you for your *failures!*"

"You and your cheap psychology," Richard had replied. "Who's punishing whom around here?" But he would forgive Gail, too. He was capable of that.

Alone at home on Saturday (Gail at a high school track meet—her endless cheery obligations, the children far away at their respective wild college towns), Richard puttered awhile, feeling cheerful, nearly healed. He whistled and felt positively euphoric, his turn at compassion having knocked depression from his shoulder.

He studied distractedly, drew buildings in the allotted ninety minutes while his oven timer ticked, drew based on what he knew the regents of the architecture board would want to see. Richard worked despite himself till lunch, then stood in the yard looking at all the good Dewey had wrought. And suddenly, he had to see the man, take compassion past forgiveness to the next step: friendship. Richard felt the warm light of understanding surround him—he was not above Dewey; they had only had different luck in life. At length, he collected Dewey's lank girlfriend's untouched pie from the refrigerator, slid it from its pan (just a foil thing, not even the right size for a pie— Probably saved from some frozen meal, Richard thought, then scolded himself), slid it into the compost bucket. He washed the tin: one needed an excuse for visiting along the Avon Road.

Pie tin in hand, Richard walked quickly down the road, suddenly aware of his new boating shoes, his bright socks, his purple shorts. Soon he was back in his house, searching his closet for clothes to wear to Dewey's. And in a black T-shirt from his son's drawer, blue jeans, work boots (both jeans and boots mortifyingly unscathed by work), Richard knocked on Dewey's trailer door. The knock was superfluous: four dark dogs straining at their chains bellowed Richard's presence, all bright teeth and rage.

Dewey had friends over. One of them, a large fellow in a clean shirt, came and blocked the door. "Yeah?" he said.

"I'm a neighbor," Richard said. "Just out walking around, thought I'd stop by, bring back this pie tin."

The man in the door looked him over.

Richard said, "Dewey here?"

"Dewey ain't."

The dogs barked hoarsely, now, strangling themselves on their collars on chains. Something was going on in the small living room behind the big fellow.

Dewey came up silently behind Richard, having somehow sneaked out of the trailer and come around the back side, startled him with a rough tap on the shoulder. Richard spun.

Dewey looked disgusted, said, "Oh, it's you."

"Yup. Me."

"You all better?"

"I'm okay, I guess." He gave a smile in anticipation of an apology, but an apology didn't come, and the men simply stood, a dooryard tableau, still as stumps. "I brought back your pie plate."

"Go in. Jim, s'okay."

The big man—Jim—stepped back. At the kitchen table a younger fellow hulked, staring. He had something hidden in his lap. Seeing Richard, seeing Dewey behind him, the kid breathed, relaxed, put two stout handguns on the table. Jim gave a flat laugh: huh huh huh. Richard noticed that the place was very clean, very tidy (cheaply furnished, to be sure), decent, nice.

"Have a sit," Dewey said.

Richard wanted to say no thanks, wanted to run out the door, but didn't want to appear to be shaken by the presence of the firearms, which were, after all, perfectly legal, so far as he knew. He said, "Going hunting?" This lame gambit turned out to be a hilarious joke, the laughter from Dewey and his pals long and hard and followed by a kind of formally granted but clearly temporary acceptance.

Dewey broke out a six-pack of Piels beer, and soon Richard was drinking his second can. By noon he was sharing yarns about college drinking exploits (these didn't seem as funny or racy as they did in other company), listening to yarns in turn, stories wherein car windows were smashed, and this guy's head was cracked against a wall, and in which women were objectified and African-American people disparaged, and Asians named gooks, the wife of the President of the United States called a cunt, the President himself a fag. It seemed all three men were on parole, and all three for violent crimes just short of murder. Despite which (if even true), they were funny men, good at stories. How bad could they actually be? They were men operating without the benefit of education, without breaks, without hope. Barely aware how drunk he was becoming, Richard saw himself saving them. Compassion! They had a certain nobility, he began to think; they were almost saints.

Even drunk he could hear what Gail would say about that idea: These men are insane. These men, she would say, are dangerous. Gail had always been blind that way, always blind, a snob. Richard rose, holding his beer can foaming in front of him. "I lost my job," he announced, a kind of toast.

Dewey nodded in real fellow feeling, sympathy Richard hadn't gotten yet from anyone.

So Richard went on, told the whole story: Molina's perfidy! The heartless phone call! The lousy severance package! The kids' college bills!

When Richard was done, the boys were with him one hundred percent, pounded his back in sympathy, riffed a long time hilariously on the theme of destroying Lester Molina, rocked the table with their laughter, pictures of Molina filling the air of the trailer kitchen: Molina with his head in a toilet, his balls in a vise, his house on fire, his car in a pond.

At one o'clock the woman who'd delivered the pie came out of the back room, appeared as if from exile, carrying a little boy, four or maybe five or even six years old, too old, in any case, to need to be carried. But she never put him down. Impassive, she made plain white-bread sandwiches and held her boy and exerted a huge presence in the room in silence. The men only drank their beer while she worked, the conversation embarrassed to a halt in front of her.

So Richard said, "What's the boy's name?" He had drunk four beers.

No reply.

Richard tried again: "The kid, what's his name?"

"That's Don't He," big Jim said.

"What?"

"That's Don't He."

"Dewey and Don't He," the kid with the guns said, and he and Jim laughed.

"Don't he look like Dewey?" Jim said.

"Do he or don't he?" the young man—Baker—said.

Dewey said, "Leem alone," but his voice was mild; this wordplay was some kind of old joke.

"Don't He," Jim said one more time.

The woman put the sandwiches on the table. The child stayed in the crook of her arm. His mother didn't glower, exactly, but the look on her face was no longer impassive. Something murderous was alive in her. She said, "He's Jeremy Charles, like his grandfather."

Richard said, "Hi, Jeremy," and the kid buried his face in his mother's neck.

She went back into the bedroom, closed the door.

The men ate. When his sandwich was gone, Richard began to think of graceful exit lines. Jim got up and went outside. Richard heard him piss, heard him open the door of his truck, cheered with the others when he saw the bottle of Old Granddad, though it didn't actually make him glad.

Later, Richard would puke on the side of the Avon Road, then again at the end of his driveway, holding his sore ribs, then twice in his bathtub, where Gail would find him; but for now the afternoon stretched ahead, and the stories were good, and he enjoyed the company of what through his newfound compassion he'd revisualized suddenly as good men—rough men, surely, maybe not the smartest guys on the face of the earth, but men he chastised himself for misjudging.

Dewey stopped coming to work. And because Dewey had no phone, it seemed to Richard after a couple of weeks that another visit to the trailer down the road was in order. He needed Dewey's help around the yard, he told himself. And he told Gail the same, when she said they were better off rid of Dewey forever: "You'd think he was your only friend," she said. "You'd think you didn't notice that he stole from us and beat your face and then made you sick with alcohol when you tried to reach out to him."

"Well, with your schedule I do need the company."

Gail sighed at this pale jest, this introduction of an old issue between them.

"Kidding," Richard said. "I'm only kidding. But really. I'm just going over to see if he wants work. I'll just go see him, that's all. I think the guy needs help. I think the guy *needs* me."

Gail hugged Richard with big teacherly warmth, said, "Well, fine.

Go get Dewey. But don't come home barfing your guts out!" This last was the kind of joke she made to announce the end of an argument.

Richard laughed, remembering that day. Somehow the puking had given him a feeling of youth, had brought him back to a time when what was sensible didn't usually turn out to be what was right or needed.

So on a Saturday in July he dressed as a biker, left Gail to her preparations for that afternoon's 4-H luncheon, and headed on foot down the Avon road. He hoped Dewey would be home. He hoped big Jim and Baker would be there. He hoped Jeremy Charles—Don't He—would be there with his protective mom. And maybe today he'd have a beer. Maybe today he'd have a beer and then another, and then as much whiskey as Dewey. Who was to say he shouldn't? And maybe today he'd make more of the jokes he'd made, and the guys would laugh as they had before, and maybe tomorrow he'd be sick. Maybe he would, and what was wrong with that?

No one answered his knock at the trailer door. He waited, knocked, and waited some more, then gave up. As he walked away, Dewey tapped him on the shoulder, having appeared from nowhere and silently behind him. When Richard turned, Dewey pretended to hit him with a left, L-U-C-K, then stabbed him with a pretend knife in a tightly squeezed right. Dewey didn't smile. A normal person would smile after a joke like that, Gail might say. But Richard knew what Gail did not: Dewey was a roughshod gem.

Richard said, "Just wondered if you wanted to come back and work."

"I got another job."

"Ah. Well, good. Good for you. Where?"

"It's decent."

Richard looked out over the trailer, Dewey looked out toward the road, a perfect silence in the dryness of the day. Finally, too eagerly, Richard said, "Got any beer?"

Dewey shook his head. "No way. You?"

Richard just shook his head. He made a decision, said, "Naw. But let's go get us some." Screw it: "And we can do us up some whiskey, too."

Dewey said nothing, but went back into his trailer for a long minute. When he returned, the two men walked in silence back to Richard's. Gail had left. Good. They climbed into the new minivan. Dewey didn't want to go to the store in town, insisted they go all the way out to the general store in Leslie, a twenty-mile drive.

"Why not?" Richard said. He'd never stopped in Leslie, a one-store town up past the lakes.

To the Leslie store in silence. And in silence Richard and Dewey stood in front of the shelves of liquor, Richard feeling the money in his pocket, knowing he'd be the one to have to pay. Dewey picked out a *half-gallon* of expensive whiskey, the most expensive they had, then motioned for Richard to pick his own. So Richard did, adding the prices in his head, shrugging it off: sixty bucks, so what? They walked to the counter, waited behind another customer, a woman who had a hundred questions about birdseed. Dewey nudged Richard, nodded subtly, meaningfully. Richard nodded back, as if he knew the meaning in that nod. When the counter person bent to find the price list for sunflower seed, Dewey leapt at the door, burst outside, ran to the van carrying his whiskey. The woman at the counter stood up and looked after him, looked quizzically at Richard. He paused, felt the money in his pocket, said, "Uhm . . ."

Then he jumped, too—burst out the door, into the hot sun, ran across the pavement. Behind him he heard the woman say "Hey!" and that was all. She didn't even run after them. Probably she was calling the cops.

Dewey had taken the driver's seat so Richard had to adjust his flight at the last second and hop in the passenger side of his own little van. He flung Dewey the keys, and before anyone could get a good look they were out of there in a blasting cloud of front-wheel-drive dust and gravel, out of there and flying down Route 2 faster than Richard had ever dared drive. Somewhere before New Sharon, Dewey fishtailed off the highway and into the mouth of a dirt road and they bounced in the ruts to the woods.

"Jesus," Richard said.

Dewey said, "Never pay for a drink." He slowed down on the

awful road. At a bend in the Sandy River, far from the main road, far from any house, far from responsibility and fear, high up on a bluff over mild rapids, Dewey parked. He opened his bottle and drank.

Richard's breathing slowed gradually. He opened his own bottle, hefted it to his lips. The whiskey turned him hot. Careful not to smile, he said, "That was a blast."

They watched the river.

"'A blast,'" Dewey said, mocking him. Then he was quiet. After several good slugs from his huge bottle he said, "Think you got the nuts for a real job?"

Richard knew what Dewey meant. He straightened and used his own voice, an architect's voice: "The nuts? I would say, yes. The desire, no."

"Same thing," Dewey said.

"Shit, Dew. Forget it."

"I have this idea."

"Dew, forget it."

They drank from the ungainly bottles and watched the river and hardly said anything at all. Before long Richard found himself unable to prevent a smile, kept grinning and laughing and patting his bottle of booze. "I'm as happy as I've been in years," he said.

Dewey seemed barely to hear him.

Because Richard had wondered aloud whether Dewey was married, big Jim called him Wedding Bells. Soon this was shortened to Bells, which seemed to stick. Happily, huge Jim was in the back of the minivan during the hour's ride to Little Henry's in Port Lawrence. Back there all his jabs and jibes and nervous patter seemed contained.

Little Henry's was a rural convenience store, and Dewey had learned somehow that on Sundays the owner was stupid enough to keep all the money from the whole busy tourist weekend in a little safe in back—as much as $10,000 (which to Richard didn't sound like as grand a sum as it clearly did to Dewey and Jim)—such a little safe that Dewey knew Jim could lift it and carry it. Jim had been carrying rocks around for weeks—rocks twice the weight of the safe—and was ready.

Richard was to be the driver. Late nights he found it shocking that he'd agreed to this. But the plan and his place within it had fallen together incrementally, ineluctably. Richard had drunk with the boys and enjoyed the conversations—been part of the conspiracy. He honestly thought it was just talk, Sherwood Forest kind of stuff, thought nothing was ever going to come of it, thought Jim was putting enormous rocks in the van as a kind of conceptual exercise, nothing more. Yet, there was a precise night Richard had said yes. A precise night he'd taken Dewey's hand and shaken it a long damn time and said yes right in Dewey's dark eyes. Dewey's logic had been unassailable: young Baker was back in jail (he'd punched his piggish parole officer in the neck), and the gang needed a driver; Richard's minivan was perfect (wood paneling even, cute, like something you'd drive nuns in); Richard (here Dewey's voice dropped solemnly) was by now part of the gang, and it was like the marines, or the muskefuckingteers: all for one, one for all.

So Richard had clasped Dewey's hand, said yes. The very next morning, pleading at Dewey's door, Richard tried to make it no. But Dewey Burke put an arm around Richard's neck and dragged him roughly into the trailer's kitchen, pulled a big carving knife out of a broken drawer, poked the point into Richard's forehead, drawing blood, touching skull. He said: "You gonna quit?" After a very long pause Dewey let go, put the knife away, said he was kidding, said, "Go ahead, Third Eye. Quit if you want."

Richard hadn't quit, so really he'd said yes twice. By day, the decision left him exhilarated. Nights, he slept poorly, wanted to wake Gail, desperately wanted to shake Gail from her overworked exhaustion and slumber and confess all. By day, he watched her drive off to meetings and laughed at himself: if he ever woke her she would only say he was a dope and too idle, turn back to sleep and in the morning drive off to her meetings just the same. At night he thought of Dewey's woman, thought of Dewey's kid, thought of his own kids, planned how he'd back out of this thing, how he'd tell Gail, then Dewey, how easy that would really be.

But by day he did the research required of him: the exact mileage from Little Henry's to the state police barracks, the exact mileage to the Port Lawrence Police Department, the exact mileage to the Ledyard County Sheriff's office, the exact distance on Route 2 from Little Henry's to home, the exact distance on the circuitous Route 124, the distance to all of twelve different logging roads they might disappear on, the distance to two gravel pits and a quarry in which they might hide if (Dewey's grave concern) ". . . the pigs went bullshit."

Oh, Richard liked the excitement, liked having such a fine secret from Gail. He liked his acceptance by folks who had never noticed him at all. He liked how his wardrobe had changed (black T-shirts, a big black belt, heavy boots). He liked the way he'd stopped fitting in at Gail's many luncheons and dinners, liked how easy it was to skip them. And he loved his afternoons at Dewey's: the camaraderie, the hilarity, the feeling these guys would take care of him.

They'd all been to Little Henry's twice now, knew where the safe was (behind a white door that said EMPLOYEES ONLY and hard against a grimy toilet that the clerk had let Richard use); knew that Sunday night the kid at the counter (named Pete) would be alone; knew that the nearest police station (actually the Port Lawrence Town Office) was nearly eleven miles from the store; knew that the Sunday night police shift was the lightest of the week (one cop, who hung out in the station with the lady dispatcher, drinking coffee); knew that the much more professional state police tended to stay toward the coast and the interstate. The gang made a bunch of contingency plans, even practiced a couple of routes home, worked their way to the night they'd picked: July 23.

A hot night. Richard drove, wishing fervently that he'd said no when no was still possible. Dewey and Jim insisted on displaying their big handguns in the car. Saints wouldn't need guns. They buffed them up, stared at them, called them maggies and bones. Baker, languishing in prison, had donated his firepower to the cause in exchange for a ten percent cut. Richard had opted not to go lumpy, as the boys put it, not to carry a gun, because he couldn't use one if he had one, and had no intention of shooting or threatening anyone, no intention of getting out of the car, for that matter. He would sit there in jacket and tie, as planned, and earn his thirty percent quietly.

So in the parking lot at Little Henry's, the night dark, Richard waited. He watched the mirrors, but no one else drove in. Dead night. Almost quitting time. He saw Dewey through the big store window, Dewey rummaging through the potato chips. He couldn't see Jim. He couldn't see the clerk, either, which was the idea: if he couldn't see the clerk, the clerk couldn't see him, couldn't see the vehicle for an ID. It had been Richard's idea, in fact, to smear mud on the license plates. No one in the mirrors.

Richard needed something for his stomach, needed to crap, needed something to eat, needed the next fifteen minutes to be over, fast. He saw Dewey step to the counter with a bag of popcorn. He saw big Jim step up too, saw Dewey yank the gun from his pants, saw Jim do the same from his, big guns in their hands, now Dewey yelling something Richard could almost hear. They waved the guns and shook them, fingers on the triggers, looking profoundly evil. Richard moaned with fear. No one in the mirror. Gail in the den at home, furious with him for going drinking again. Dewey leaning over the counter, handfuls of bills and checks and food stamps, looking mean, saying something. The kid clerk must be lying down now, as per their plan. Jim out of the picture, gone to get the safe. In the mirror, nothing. Richard remembered his job, leaned across the armrest into the back of the van, slid the side door open so the van would be ready to accept the safe. Dewey stuffing his pockets with cash. No sign of Jim. *Shit*: cop car, entering the lot slowly, no flashing lights, no siren.

Richard thought about honking the horn, realized that might seem suspicious. He got out of the van, oddly calm, walked into the store, announced it: "Cops."

Jim was just coming out of the bathroom backwards, carrying the safe an inch off the floor. Clearly it was heavier than the rocks he'd been practicing with.

"Cops," Richard said again, more loudly. He stood like a customer at the counter, looked casually out. Two policemen, staties, as Dewey called them, big men, one of them smiling, finishing some joke as he climbed out the car.

Dewey said, "Go behind. Like you work here." He ducked down in one of the small aisles.

Richard stepped behind the counter. The clerk lay in old receipts with his face to the linoleum, panting. Jim left the safe in the middle of the floor, hopped back into the bathroom.

The cop came in.

"Hello," Richard said.

"New guy," the cop said, perfectly jocular. "What'd they? Fire Pete?"

The kid on the floor said "Here!" Said, "Robbing! Guns!"

The cop didn't even have time to look confused or respond before Dewey stood and blasted at him. The shot was bad, smashed the big store window. The second shot was better, seemed to catch the statie's shoulder. The gun was loud in that little place, louder than the practice shots.

"Jesus," Richard cried. He was going to jail forever. He was going to die. Gail in the warm den right now, feet up, with a book.

The cop wheeled and fell to the floor and scurried forward, pushing the door open. His partner was quick, was on the radio, was out of the car, and both of them were behind it with guns drawn before Jim got out of the bathroom. He'd missed what happened, maybe thought Dewey had got it, ran to the door with his gun waving, opened the door even as he saw the situation, took several bullets in his chest, and fell. The kid on the floor at Richard's feet—Pete— flinched but didn't try to move.

Dewey peeked over the tampons, said, "Get over here, Bells."

But Richard couldn't.

Dewey waved the gun: "Get your shit-dick over here!"

Richard put his hands in the air so the cops would see he was unarmed, stepped from behind the counter. Dewey leapt behind him, put the gun to his neck, said "Go to the door."

The cops were out there holding their huge guns, scared, trying to peer into the store.

Richard had to step in Jim's blood to make the door, could hear something gurgling in Jim's big body.

"Out," Dewey said.

Richard pushed the glass door open with his belly, gun at his neck, hands in the air. "I'm an architect," he called. "I'm an architect."

"I'll shoot him," Dewey said.

"Put it down," one cop said.

"Put yours down," Dewey said. "Yours, or I shoot the architect."

Richard could see the cops weren't going to shoot, saw how young they were. Dewey led him around the van. They climbed in through the open side door, Dewey firmly pressing the gun to Richard's temple.

"Go," Dewey said, once Richard was in the driver's seat. The cops looked helpless. The one who'd been shot slumped against the cruiser, a hand pressed to his bleeding shoulder.

Richard backed up slowly into the dark street, backed up so that Dewey was never exposed. The cops didn't move till he put the van in drive and pulled out, then he saw them tumble into their car. Dewey said, "Fuck." Money stuck out of his jacket pockets.

Richard said, "Jim . . ."

"'I'm an architect,'" Dewey said. He climbed in back, opened the sliding door, and before the cops were far enough out of the parking lot to see, he leapt from the van and rolled onto someone's lawn. Richard had a glimpse of him rising and running, kept driving. The cruiser's lights began to flash; in seconds the cops were close behind. Richard put his hand out the window to show that it was he, the architect, and slowly pulled to a stop in front of a farmhouse.

He climbed from the car, hands in the air, stepped toward the cops. They climbed out both sides of their car, aimed their guns at the beautiful new minivan.

"He jumped out," Richard said. "He's gone."

"Get over here," the uninjured cop said.

Richard kept his hands up, made a couple more steps.

"He's gone?" the cop said.

"Jumped out," Richard said. "He ran into the woods back there."

"You're a lucky man," the shot cop said.

"Hostage is free," the other cop said, into the radio.

Dewey was caught two months later trying to cash one of the checks from Little Henry's, caught on the very day that Richard passed his architecture exams. In court, just before Christmas, Dewey never looked at Richard once, never said a word to implicate him, confirmed Richard's story, the story Dewey must have read in the newspaper or seen Richard give on TV: two thugs, one of them an acquaintance, had commandeered Richard's van right in his driveway and made him take them to Port Lawrence at gunpoint. It was a pretty good story, and no one but Gail ever questioned it: she knew Richard had planned some kind of outing with those drunken fools that night, but even she would never begin to suspect the whole truth, just thought some drinking game had got out of hand.

Richard didn't sleep a full night till spring, waited for the lady at the Leslie general store to come forward, waited for that kid Pete to remember that it was Richard who'd announced the cops, but the store lady never peeped, and Pete in court had called Richard brave, a hero.

Dewey is serving forty years. Jim is dead. Richard the hero mows Dewey's yard when he can, and he talks to Dewey's woman (who's not saying what she knows about that night); she's got an okay job now at the turning mill in Wilton. And Richard helps her with her many chores, takes the little boy out fishing, pays a bill or two quietly, and thinks she's begun to regard him without suspicion. She's even agreed to let him add a porch for her (it's a design he'd like to try out, he says; it's just a prototype; of course it's free), agreed to let him clear the lot of car parts and dogshit and glass. He tells her he owes her—he owes Dewey—and it's on those terms she allows him in.

Carolyn Chute

"Ollie, Oh . . ."

Erroll, the deputy who was known to litter, did not toss any Fresca cans or Old King Cole bags out this night. Erroll brought his Jeep to a stop in the yard right behind Lenny Cobb's brand-new Dodge pickup. The brakes of Erroll, the deputy's, Jeep made a spiritless dusty squeak. Erroll was kind of humble this night. The greenish light of his police radio shone on his face and yes, the froggishly round eyes, mostly pupil because it was dark, were humble. His lips were shut down over his teeth, which were usually laughing and clicking. Humbleness had gone so far as to make that mouth look almost *healed over* like the holes in women's ears when they stop putting earrings through. He took off his knit cap and lay it on the seat beside the empty Fresca can, potato chip bag, and cigar cellophanes. He put his gloved hand on the door opener to get out. But he paused. He was scared of Ollie Cobb. He wasn't sure how she would take the news. But she wasn't going to take it like other women did. Erroll tried to swallow, but there was no saliva there to work around in his throat.

He looked at Lenny Cobb's brand-new Dodge in the lights of his Jeep. It was so cold out there that night that the root-beer-color paint was sealed over every inch in a delicate film like an apple still attached, still ripening, never been handled. Wasn't Lenny Cobb's truck the prince of trucks? Even the windshield and little vent windows looked heavy-duty . . . as though congealed inside their rubber strips, thick and deep as the frozen Sebago. And the chrome was heavy as pots. And the plow! It was constricted into travel gear, not yet homely from running into stone walls and frost heaves. And on the cab roof an amber light, the swivel kind, big as a man's head. Of course it had four-wheel drive. It had shoulders! Thighs. Spine. It might still be growing.

The Jeep door opened. The minute he stood up out in the crunchy driveway he wished he had left his cap on. The air was like paper, could have been thirty below. His breath leaving his nose turned to paper. It was all so still and silent. With no lights on in Lenny Cobb's place, a feeling came over Erroll of being alone at the North Pole. Come to his ears a lettucelike crispness, a keenness . . . so that to the top arch of each ear his spinal cord plugged in. A cow murred in the barn. One murr. A single note. And yet the yard was so thirsty for sound . . . all planes gave off the echo: a stake to mark a rosebush under snow . . . an apple basket full of snow on the top step. He gave the door ten or twelve thonks with his gloved knuckles. It *hurt*.

Ollie Cobb did not turn on a light inside or out. She just spread open the door and stood looking down at him through the small round frames of her glasses. She wore a long rust-colored robe with pockets. The doorway was outside the apron of light the Jeep head-lights made. Erroll had to squint to make her out, the thin hair. It was black, parted in the middle of her scalp, yanked back with such efficiency that the small fruit-shape of her head was clear: a lemon or a lime. And just as taut and businesslike, pencil-hard, pencil-sized, a braid was drawn nearly to her heels . . . the toes, long as thumbs, clasped the sill. "Deputy Anderson," she said. She had many teeth. Like shingles. They seemed to start out of her mouth when she opened it.

He said: "Ah . . ."

Erroll couldn't know when the Cobb house had rotted past saving, yet more certain than the applewood banked in the stove, the smell of dying timbers came to him warmly . . . almost rooty, like carrots . . .

"What *is* it?" she said.

He thought of the great sills of that old house being soft as carrots. "Lenny has passed away," he said.

She stepped back. He was hugged up close to the openness of the door, trying to get warm, so when the door whapped shut, his foot was in it. *"Arrrrr!"* So he got his foot out. She slammed the door again. When he got back in his Jeep, his coffee fell off the dash and burned his leg.

II

The kitchen lights came on. All Ollie's white-haired children came into the living room when she started to growl and rub her shoulder on the refrigerator. This was how Ollie grieved. She rolled her shoulders over the refrigerator door so some of the magnetic fruits fell on the floor. A math paper with a 98 on top seesawed downward and landed on the linoleum. The kids were happy for a chance to be up. "Oh, boy!" they said. All but Aspen, who was twelve and could understand. She remained at the bottom of the stairs, afraid to ask Ollie what the trouble was. Aspen was in a lilac-color flannel gown and gray wool socks. She sucked the thumb of her right hand and hugged the post of the banister with her left. It was three-fifteen in the morning. Applewood coals never die. All 'round the woodstove was an aura of summer. The socks and undershirts and mittens pinned in scores to a rope across the room had a summer stillness. They heard Ollie growl and pant. They giggled. Sometimes they stopped and looked up when she got loud. They figured she was not getting her way about something. They had seen the deputy, Erroll, leave from the upstairs windows. They associated Erroll with crime. Crime was that vague business of speeding tickets and expired inspection stickers. This was not a new thing. Erroll had come up in his Jeep behind Ollie a time or two in the village. He said "Red light" and she bared her teeth at him like a dog. She was baring her teeth now.

There was an almost Christmas spirit among the children to be wakened in the night like that. There was wrestling. There was wriggling. Tim rode the dog, Dick Lab. He, Dick Lab, would try to get away, but hands on his hocks would keep him back. Judy turned on the TV. Nothing was on the screen but bright fuzz. The hair of them all flying through the night was the torches of after-dark skiers: crackling white from chair to couch to chair to stairway, rolling Dick Lab on his side, carouseling twelve-year-old Aspen, who sucked her thumb, Eddie and Arnie, Tim and Judy.

The herdsman's name was Jarrell Bean. He was like all Beans, silent and touchy, and had across his broad coffee-color face a look that made you suspect he was related somehow, perhaps on his mother's side, to some cows. The eyes were slate color and were of themselves lukewarm-looking, almost steamy, very huge, browless, while like hands they reached out and patted things that interested him. He inherited from his father, Bingo Bean, a short haircut . . . a voluntary baldness: the father's real name was also Jarrell, killed chickens for work and had the kind of red finely lined fingers you'd expect from so much murder. But Bingo's eyes everybody knows were yellow and utility. It was from his mother's side that Jarrell the herdsman managed to know what tact was. He came to the Cobbs' door from his apartment over the barn. He had seen the deputy Erroll's Jeep and figured Lenny's time had come. He was wearing a black-and-red-checked coat and the spikes of a three-day beard, auburn. It was the kind of beard men adrift in lifeboats have. Unkind weather had spread each of the hairs its own way.

He had traveled several yards through that frigid night with *no hat*. This was nudity for a man so bald.

In his mouth was quite a charge of gum. He didn't knock. The kitchen started to smell of spearmint as soon as he closed the door behind him. Ollie was rolled into a ball on the floor, grunting, one bare foot, bare calf, and knee extended. He stepped over the leg. He made Ollie's children go up the stairs. He dragged one by the arm. It howled. Its flare of pale hair spurted here and there at the herdsman's elbow. The entire length of the child was twisting. It was Randy, who was eight and strong. Dick Lab sat down on the twelve-year-old Aspen's ankles and feet, against the good wool. Jarrell came down the stairs hard. His boots made a booming through the whole big house. He took Dane and Linda and Hannah all at once. Aspen kept sucking her thumb. She looked up at him as he came down toward her, seeing him over her fingers. She was big as a woman. Her thumb in her mouth was longer and lighter than the other fingers from twelve years of sucking. He fetched her by the blousey part of her lilac gown. She came away from the banister with a snap: like a Band-Aid from a hairy arm . . . "Cut it out!" she cried. His hands were used only to cattle. He thought of himself as *good* with cattle, not at all cruel. And yet with cattle what is to be done is always the will of the herdsman.

III

When Jarrell came downstairs, Ollie was gone. She had been thinking of Lenny's face, how it had been evaporating for months into the air, how the lip had gotten short, how the cheeks fell into the bone. While Jarrell stood in the kitchen, he picked up the magnetic fruits and stuck them in a row on the top door of the refrigerator. He figured Ollie had slipped into her room to be alone.

He walked out into the yard, past Lenny's new root-beer-color truck. He remembered how it roared when Leo at the Mobil had fiddled with the accelerator and everyone—Merritt and Poochie and Poochie's brother and Kenny, even Quinlan—stood around looking in at the big 440 and Lenny was resting on the running board. Lenny's neck was getting much too small for his collar even then.

Jarrell went up to his apartment over the barn, his head stinging from the deep-freeze night, then his lamp went out and the yard was noiseless.

Under the root-beer truck Ollie was curled with her braid in the snow. She had big bare feet. Under the rust-color robe the goose bumps crowned up. Her eyes were squeezed shut like children do when they pretend to be sleeping. Her lip was drawn back from the elegantly twisted teeth, twisted like the stiff feathers of a goose are overlaid. And filling one eyeglass lens a dainty ice fern.

IV

It was Ollie whose scheduled days and evenings were on a tablet taped to the bathroom door. Every day Ollie got up at 4:30 A.M. Every evening supper was at 5:45. If visitors showed up late by fifteen minutes, she would whine at them and punish them with remarks about their character. If she was on her way to the feed store in the pickup and there was a two-car accident blocking the road up ahead, Ollie would roll down the window and yell: *"Move!"*

Once Aspen's poor body nearly smoked, 102 temperature, and blew a yellow mass from her little nose holes . . . a morning when Ollie had plans for the lake . . . Lenny was standing in the yard with his railroad cap on and his ringless hands in the pockets of his cardigan, leaning on the new root-beer truck . . . Ollie came out on the porch where many wasps were circling between her face and his eyes looking up: "She's going to spoil our time," Ollie said. "We've got to go down to the store and call for an appointment now. She couldn't have screwed up the day any better." Then she went back inside and made her hand like a clamp on the girl's bicep, bore down on it with the might of a punch or a kick, only more slow, more deep. Tears came to Aspen's eyes. Outside Lenny heard nothing. Only the sirens of wasps. And stared into the very middle of their churning.

Oh, that Ollie. Indeed, Lenny months before must have planned his cancer to ruin her birthday. That was the day of the doctor's report. All the day Lenny cried. Right in the lobby of the hospital . . . a scene . . . Lenny holding his eyes with the palms of his hands: "Help me! Help me!" he wailed . . . she steered him to a plastic chair. She hurried down the hall to be alone with the snack machine . . . HEALTHY SNACKS: apples and pears, peanuts. She despised *him* this way. *This* was her birthday.

V

In the thirty-below-*zero* morning jays' voices cracked from the roof. Figures in orange nylon jackets hustled over the snow. They covered Ollie with a white wool blanket. The children were steady with their eyes and statuesque as they arranged themselves around the herdsman. Aspen held the elbow of his black-and-red coat. Everyone's breath flattened out like paper, like those clouds cartoon personalities' words are printed on. It may have warmed up some. Twenty below or fifteen below. The cows had not been milked, shuffling and ramming and murring, cramped near the open door of the barn . . . in pain . . . their udders as vulgar and hard as the herdsman's velvet head.

VI

At the hospital surgeons removed the ends of Ollie's fingers, most of her toes, and her ears. She drank Carnation Instant Breakfast, grew sturdy again, and learned to keep her balance. She came home with her thin hair combed over her earholes. In the back her hair veiled her ruby coat.

She got up every morning at 4:30 and hurtled herself out to the barn to set up for milking. Jarrell feared every minute that her hair might fall away from her missing ears. He would squint at her. Together they sold some of the milk to the neighborhood, those who came in cars and pulling sleds, unloading plastic jugs and glass jars to be filled at the sink, and the children of these neighbors would stare at Ollie's short fingers. Jarrell: "Whatcha got today, only two . . . is ya company gone?" or "How's Ralph's team doin' now? . . . that's good ta hear," or "Fishin' any good now? I ain't heard." He talked a lot these days. When they came around he brightened up. He opened doors for them and listened to gossip and passed it on. They teased him a lot about his lengthening beard. Sometimes Tim would stand between Jarrell and Ollie and somehow managed to have his hands on the backs of Jarrell's knees most of the time. As Ollie hosed out the stainless-steel sink there in the wood and glass white room, Tim's eyes came over the sink edge and watched the water whirl.

At night Jarrell would open Mason jars and slice carrots or cut the tops off beets. Ollie would lift things slowly with her purply stubs. She set the table. She would look at Jarrell to see if he saw how slick she did this. But he was not looking. The children, all those towheads, would be throwing things and running in the hall. There had come puppies of Dick Lab. Tim and a buff puppy pulled on a sock. Tim dragged the puppy by the sock across the rug. Ollie would stand by the sink and look straight ahead. She had a spidery control over her short fingers. She once hooked small Marsha up by the hair and pressed her to the woodbox with her knee. But Ollie was wordless. Things would usually go well. By 5:45 forks of beets and squash were lifted to mouths and glasses of milk were draining.

After supper Jarrell would go back to his apartment and watch *Real People* and *That's Incredible* or *60 Minutes* and fall asleep with his clothes on. He had a pile of root beer cans by the bed. Sometimes mice would knock them over and the cans would roll out of the room, but it never woke him.

Jarrell could not go to the barn in the morning without thinking of Lenny. He would go along and pull the rows of chains to all the glaring gray lights. He and Lenny used to stand by the open door together. The black and white polka-dot *sea* of cows would clatter between them. And over and between the blowing mouths and oily eyes, Lenny's dollar-ninety-eight-cent gloves waved them on, and he'd say: "Oh, girl . . . oh, girl . . ." Their thundering never ever flicked Lenny's watered-down auburn hair that was thin on top. And there were the hairless temples where the chemotherapy had seared from the inside out.

Jarrell could recall Lenny's posture, a peculiar tired slouch in his pea coat. Lenny wore a watch cap in midwinter and a railroad cap in sweaty weather and the oils of his forehead were on the brims of both.

Jarrell remembered summer when there was a big corn-on-the-cob feast and afterward Lenny lay on the couch with just his dungarees on and his veiny bare feet kicking. His hairless chest was stamped with three black tattoos: two sailing ships and a lizard. Tim was jumping on his stomach. A naked baby lay on its back, covering the two ships. Lenny put his arm around the baby and it seemed to melt into him. Lenny's long face had that sleepy look of someone whose world is interior, immediate to the skin, never reaching outside his hundred and twenty acres. That very night that Lenny played on the couch with his children, Jarrell left early and stayed awake late in his apartment watching Tim Conway dictating in a German accent to his nitwit secretary.

Jarrell heard Ollie yelling. He leaned out his window and heard more clearly Ollie rasping out her husband's name. Once she leaped across the gold square of light of their bedroom window. Jarrell knew that Lenny was sitting on the edge of the bed, perhaps with his pipe in his mouth, untying his gray peeling work boots. Lenny would not argue, nor cry, nor turn red, but say ". . . oh, girl . . . oh, Ollie, oh . . ." And he would look up at her with his narrow face, his eyes turning here and there on his favorite places of her face. She would be enraged the more. She picked up the work boot he had just pulled off his foot and turned it in her hand . . . then spun it through the air . . . the lamp went out and crashed.

Lenny began to lose weight in the fall. In his veins white blood cells soared. The cancer was starting to make Lenny irritable. He stopped eating supper. Ollie called it fussy. Soon Ollie and Jarrell were doing the milking alone. Sometimes Aspen would help. Lenny lay on the couch and slept. He slept all day.

VII

One yellowy morning Ollie made some marks on the list on the bathroom door and put a barrette on the end of her braid. She took the truck to Leo's and had the tank filled. She drove all day with Lenny's face against her belly. Then with her hard spine and convexed shoulders she balanced Lenny against herself and steered him up the stairs of the Veterans' hospital. She came out alone and her eyes were wide behind the round glasses.

VIII

Jarrell had driven Lenny's root-beer Utiline Dodge for the first time when he drove to the funeral alone. Lenny had a closed casket. The casket was in an alcove with pink lights and stoop-shouldered mumbly Cobbs. They all smelled like old Christmas cologne. There must have been a hundred Cobbs. Most of the flowers around the coffin were white. Jarrell stood. The rest were sitting. The herdsman's head was pink in the funny light and he tilted his head as he considered how Lenny looked inside the coffin under the lid. Cotton was in Lenny's eyes. He probably had skin like those plaster-of-Paris ducks that hike over people's lawns single file. He was most likely in there in some kind of suit, no pea coat, no watch cap, no pipe, no babies, no grit of Flash in his nails. Someone had undoubtedly scrubbed all the cow smell off him and he probably smelled like a new doll now. Jarrell drove to the interment at about eighty to eighty-five miles per hour and was waiting when the headlighted caravan dribbled into the cemetery and the stooped Cobbs ambled out of about fifty cars.

IX

Much later, after Lenny was dead awhile and Ollie's fingers were healed, Ollie came into the barn about 6:10. They were running late. The dairy truck from Portland was due to arrive in the yard. Ollie was wearing Lenny's old pea coat and khaki shirt with her new knit pants. Tim was with her. Tim had a brief little mouth and freakish coarse hair, like white weeds. His coat was fastened with safety pins. Ollie started hooking up the machines with her quick half-fingers. They rolled like sausages over the stainless-steel surfaces. Jarrell, hurrying to catch up, was impatient with the cows when they wanted to shift around. Ollie was soundless but Jarrell could locate her even if he didn't see her, even as she progressed down the length of the barn. He had radar in his chest (the heart, the lungs, even the bladder) for her position when things were running late. God! It was like trying to walk through a wall of sand. Tim came over and stood behind him. Tim was digging in his nose. He was dragging out long strings of discolored matter and wiping it on his coat. One cow pulled far to the right in the stanchion, almost buckling to her knees as a hind foot slipped off the edge of the concrete platform. The milking machine thunked to the floor out of Jarrell's hands. Ollie heard. Her face came as if from out of the loft, sort of downward. *Her hair was pulled back* caught up by her glasses when she had hurriedly shoved them on. *She did not have ears. He saw for the first time they had taken her ears.* His whole shape under his winter clothes went hot as though common pins were inserted over every square inch. He squinted, turned away . . . ran out of the milking room into the snow. The dairy truck from the city was purring up the hill. The fellow inside flopped his arm out for his   routine wave. Jarrell didn't wave back, but used both hands to pull himself up into the root-beer truck, slid across the cold seat, made the engine roar. He remembered Lenny saying once while they broke up bales of hay: "I just ordered a Dodge last week, me and my wife . . . be a few weeks, they said. Prob'ly for the President they'd have it to him the next day. Don't it *hurt* to wait for somethin' like that. Last night I dreamed I was in it, and was revvin' it up out here in the yard when all of a sudden it took off . . . right up in the sky . . . and all the cows down in the yard looked like dominoes."

X

That afternoon Jarrell Bean returned. He came up the old Nathan Lord Road slow. Had his arm out the window. When he got near the Cobb place he ascended the hill in a second-gear roar. As he turned in the drive he saw Ollie in Lenny's pea coat standing by the doorless Buick sedan in which the hens slept at night. She lined the sights of Lenny's rifle with the right lens of her glasses. One of her sausage fingers was on the trigger. She put out two shots. They turned the right front tire to rags. The Dodge screamed and plowed sideways into the culvert. Jarrell felt it about to tip over. But it only listed. He lay on the seat for a quarter of an hour after he was certain Ollie had gone into the house.

Aspen and Judy came out for him. He was crying, lying on his stomach. When they saw him crying, their faces went white. Aspen put her hard gray fingers on his back, between his shoulders. She turned to Judy . . . Judy, fat and clear-skinned with the whitest hair of all . . . and said: "I think he's sorry."

XI

Ollie lay under the mint-green bedspread. The window was open. All the yard, the field, the irrigation ditches, the dead birds were thawing, and under the window she heard a cat digging in the jonquils and dried leaves. She raised her hand of partial fingers to her mouth to wipe the corners. She had slept late again and now her blood pressure pushed at the walls of her head. She flipped out of the bed and thunked across the floor to the window. She was in a yellow print gown. The sunrise striking off the vanity mirror gave Ollie's face and arms a yellowness, too. She seized her glasses under the lamp. She peered through them, downward . . . *startled*. Jarrell was a few yards from his apartment doorway, taking a pair of dungarees from the clothesline. There were sheets hanging there, too, so it was hard to be sure at first . . . then as he strode back toward his doorway, she realized he had nothing on. He was corded and pale and straight-backed and down front of his chest dripped wet his now-full auburn beard. The rounded walls of his genitals gave little flaccid jogglings at each stride and on all of him his flesh like unbroken yellow water paused satisfyingly and seldomly at a few auburn hairs. On top, the balded head, a seamless hood, trussed up with temples all the way in that same seamless fashion to his eyes that were merry in the most irritating way. Ollie mashed her mouth and shingled teeth to the screen and moaned full and cowlike. And when he stopped and looked up, she screeched: *"I hate you! Get out of here! Get out of here!"*

She scuttled to the bed and plunked to the edge. Underneath, the shoes that Lenny wore to bean suppers and town council meetings were still crisscrossed against the wall.

XII

That summer Jarrell and the kids played catch in the middle of the Nathan Lord Road. Jarrell waded among them at the green bridge in knee-deep water, slapped Tim a time or two for persisting near the drop-off. They laughed at the herdsman in his secondhand tangerine trunks and rubber sandals. He took them to the drive-in movies in that root-beer truck. They saw *Benji* and *Last Tango in Paris*. They got popcorn and Good and Plentys all over the seat and floor and empty paper cups were mashed in the truck bed, blew out one by one onto different people's lawns. He splurged on them at Old Orchard Beach, rides and games, and coordinated Aspen won stuff with darts: a psychedelic poster, a stretched-out Pepsi bottle, and four paper leis. Then under the pier they were running with huge ribbons of seaweed and he cut his foot on a busted Miller High Life bottle . . . slumped in the sand to fuss over himself. It didn't bleed. You could see into his arch, the meat, but no blood. Aspen's white hair waved 'round her head as she stooped in her sunsuit of cotton dots, blue like babies' clothes are blue. She cradled his poor foot in her fingers and looked him in the eye.

Ollie *never* went with them. No one knew what she did alone at home.

One afternoon, Ollie stared through the heat to find Jarrell on the front porch, there in a rocking chair with the sleeping baby's open mouth spread on his bare arm. Nearly grown puppies were at his feet. He was almost asleep himself and mosquitoes were industriously draining his throat and shirtless chest. On the couch after supper the little girls nestled in his auburn beard and rolled in their fingers wads of the coarse stuff. The coon cat with the abscesses all over his head swallowed whole the red tuna Jarrell bought for him and set out at night on an aluminum pie plate. Jarrell whenever he was close smelled like cows.

XIII

Ollie drove to the drugstore for pills that were for blood pressure. Aspen went along. The root-beer truck rattled because Jarrell had left a yarding sled and chains in the back. Ollie turned her slow rust-color eyes onto Aspen's face and Aspen felt suddenly panicked. It seemed as though there was something changing about her mother's eyes: one studied your skin, one bored dead-center in your soul. Aspen was wearing her EXTINCT IS FOREVER T-shirt. It was apricot colored and there was a leopard's face in the middle of her chest.

"Do you want one of those?" Ollie asked Aspen, who was poking at the flavored ChapSticks by the cash register.

"Could I?"

"Sure." Ollie pointed somewhere. "And I was thinking you might like some colored pencils or a . . . you know . . . movie magazine."

Aspen squinted. "I would, yes, I would."

A trio of high-school-aged Crocker boys in stretched-out T-shirts trudged through the open door in a bowlegged way that made them seem to be carrying much more weight than just their smooth long bones and little gummy muscles. One wore a baseball cap and had sweat in his hair and carried his sneakers. He turned his flawless neck, and his pink hair cropped there in a straight line was fuzzy and friendly like ruffles on a puppy's shoulders where you pat. He looked right at Aspen's leopard . . . right in the middle and read: "Extinct is forever."

His teeth lifted in a perfect cream-color line over the words and his voice was low and rolled, one octave above adulthood. Both the other boys laughed. One made noises like he was dying. Then all of them pointed their fingers at her and said: "Bang! Bang! Bang!" There are the insightful ones who realize a teenager's way of flirting, and then there was Aspen who could not. To see all the boys' faces from her plastic desk at school was to Aspen like having a small, easily destructible boat with sharks in all directions. Suddenly self-conscious, suddenly stoop-shouldered as it was for all Cobbs in moments of pure hell, Aspen stood one shoe on top of the other and stuck her thumb in her mouth. There is something about drugstore light with its smells of sample colognes passing up like moths through a brightness bigger and pinker than sun that made Aspen Cobb look large and old, and the long thumb there was nasty looking. The pink-haired Crockers had never seen a big girl do this. They looked at each other gravely.

She walked over to where her mother was holding a jar of vitamin C. Her mother was arched over it, the veils of her thin black hair covering her earholes, falling forward, and her stance was gathering, coordinated like a spider, the bathtub spider, the horriblest kind. She lifted her eyes. Aspen pulled her thumb out of her mouth and wiped it on her shirt. Ollie put her arm around Aspen. She never did this as a rule. Aspen looked at her mother's face disbelievingly. Ollie pointed with one stub to the vitamin C bottle. It said: "200% of the adult minimum daily requirement." Aspen pulled away. The Crocker boys at the counter looked from Ollie's fingers to Aspen's thumb. But not till they were outside did they shriek and hoot.

On the way home in the truck Aspen wished her mother would hug her again now that they were alone. But Ollie's fingers were sealed to the wheel and her eyes blurred by the glasses were looking out from a place where no hugging ever happened. There was a real slow Volkswagen up ahead driven by a white-haired man. Ollie gave him the horn.

XIV

The list of activities on the bathroom door became more rigidly ordered . . . with even trips to the flush, snacks and rests, and conversations with the kids prescheduled . . . peanut butter and saltines: 3:15 . . . clear table: 6:30 . . . brush hair: 9:00 . . . and Ollie moved faster and faster and her cement-color hands and face were always across the yard somewhere or in the other room . . . singular of other people. And Jarrell looked in at her open bedroom door as he scooted Dane toward the bathroom for a wash . . . Ollie was *cleaning out the bureau again; the third time that week* . . . and she was doing it very fast.

In September there was a purple night and the children all loaded into the back of the truck. Randy strapped the baby into her seat in the cab. The air had a dry grasshopper smell and the truck bed was still hot from the day. Jarrell turned the key to the root-beer-color truck. "I'm getting a Needham!" he heard Timmy blat from the truck bed. He pulled on the headlights knob. He shifted into reverse. The truck creaked into motion. The rear wheel went up, then down. Then the front went up and down. Sliding into the truck lights was the yellow gown, the mashed gray arm, the black hair unbraided, the face unshowing but with a purple liquid going everywhere from out of that hair, the half-fingers wriggling just a little. She had been under the truck again.

From the deepest part of Jarrell Bean the scream would not stop even as he hobbled out of the truck. Oh, he feared to touch her, just rocked and rocked and hugged himself and howled. The children's high whines began. They covered Ollie like flies. As with blueberry jam their fingers were dipped a sticky purple. The herdsman reached for the twelve-year-old Aspen. He pulled at her. Her lids slid over icy eyes. Her breath was like carrots into his breath. He reached. And her frame folded into his hip.

Lewis
Robinson

Finches

I met Dayna during my short stint working for the veterinarian Stanley Perez. Stanley provided a delivery service for his clients, and I drove Stanley's truck, returning healed animals to their owners. We did a lot of large-animal work, lots of cows. I wore a uniform, white coveralls with a zipper from the crotch to the neck and the words STAN THE ANIMAL MAN over the breast pocket. I had a radio, too, clipped to my side. I had held other jobs requiring uniforms—I'd worked at a Speedy Lube, and as the mate on an island ferry, and as a prep cook at Robey's Family Restaurant in Springdale. But I felt that wearing a uniform while driving a truck put me in a different league. I was the master of valuable cargo, I had a flexible schedule, I was iden-tifiable as a man with places to go, a man with a distinct and enviable purpose. I was impatient with the animals, and wary of them, but otherwise, I thought the job was aces.

I didn't know Dayna, but I was bringing her bird back. It was a parakeet that had been treated for parasites, and I had it in a cage on the seat beside me in Stanley's rig. Typically, I'd have hung the cage from a hook in the back of the truck, but at lunchtime I'd filled the back with finches. They were flitting around, uncaged.

Dayna lived out the Sligo Road, in the sardine factory, a three-story chalk-colored building with a service elevator. Stanley told me she was from New York City, which meant a sardine factory apart-ment was the perfect place for her. You move up to Maine from a city like New York and you want to be reminded every second of where you are. There are many ways to do this: move next to a hockey rink, or across the road from a chicken farm, or within earshot of a sawmill. All of these options are available in Point Allison. But Dayna wanted to see the ocean, so she lived on the third floor of the sardine factory, where the bosses' offices had once been—the landlord had taken out the walls, and through six-foot-high south-facing windows you could see the Royal River widen into the bay.

It had been raining for three days, but now the sky was clearing, the mist had risen, clouds were gathering and rolling away to the east. I parked by the old loading dock at the factory, which hadn't been used in years—lupines sprouted through cracks in the concrete platform. I sat in the quiet of the truck, letting the sun heat the side of my face. When I closed my eyes, I heard the parakeet scratching and fumbling in its cage, which I'd covered with a black felt blanket so as not to upset him in transit. The noises made me want to get the delivery over with, so I walked around to the passenger side and hefted the spherical cage in both arms. The service elevator was just inside the factory's back entrance. When I stepped in and closed its metal gate, the bird spoke.

"Up and down," it said.

"I suppose you think you know where you are," I said.

"Up and down," said the bird.

"I mean, that's really great, you can sense where we are even though you can't see."

The bird's wings clicked against the cage. I waited for it to say something else, imagining its expression under the black cloth, resolute and aloof.

"Okay, fine," I said.

People loved getting their pets back. Like a magician, I removed the cloth when Dayna answered the door. "Oh, Winston, look at you. You're a healthy little beast," she said.

"Winston, Winston, Winston, Winston," said Winston.

These are the differences I see between city women and women from Maine: city women eat vegetables, they can't drive in snow, and they're used to witnessing human indecencies of the public kind rather than the more horrifying private kind. Dayna was definitely from a different part of the world, despite her baseball cap, her bare feet, her tan arms. She moved in a practiced way; she was used to being watched. There was no hesitation in her gestures, nothing wild or desperate.

The apartment looked like a yard sale—it seemed she had no interest in putting things away.

"Oh, if you have a minute, you probably know a lot about this," she said. I was still holding Winston's cage as Dayna walked from the door to the window in her kitchen. There was a hole the size of a hockey puck in the screen. She raked at it with her fingers. "I'm having problems with my squirrels."

And that was another thing: there was an immediate familiarity; she spoke to me as though she knew me. That's from the city. She spoke to me as though she knew my name, knew my brothers, knew about the trouble I'd had with amphetamines in high school, and that nevertheless I'd made it to college, and that there I'd desired women but hadn't had much luck with them.

"I'm Jim," I said.

"Dayna," she said, and she put out her hand, so I propped the cage on my thigh and grabbed her fingers awkwardly. "Here's the problem. I started feeding them, and now they've chewed through my window screen. They even come inside to pee. I came back one afternoon and found a puddle on the counter, like motor oil. They must be sick, don't you think? And they eat everything. They eat my soap and my ant traps and my paper towels."

"You shouldn't have fed them," I said.

"But they expect it now."

"Who cares? That's not your problem."

"But it's my fault they expect it," she said.

"No," I said. "Just stop feeding them." I felt very confident in this.

"What about that?" she asked, pointing at the hole in the screen.

"Rat traps," I said. "That'll do it."

"You're a veterinarian?" she asked.

"I drive the truck," I said.

Winston was glancing at me, craning his neck, then looking away, moving in that twitchy, nervous way birds do. I set the cage down, resting it against Dayna's refrigerator. The job made me hate animals; they were always disapproving and disappointed with me. When they judged, they judged harshly. Those who spend only fleeting time with animals don't notice the judgment—when you have a pet, a pet you feed and speak to in baby talk, it appears to love you. In my daily contact with anonymous animals, though, I learned otherwise. I found that animals have the same deep-seated resentments, the same nagging sense of failure that people do. They have less fear, less shame, but they are equally petty, equally irrational and loathsome.

"Rat traps?" said Dayna. "But they've been like my pets. I just want to get them to behave."

"They're taking advantage of you, Dayna," I said.

She stared at the hole in the screen and bent the frayed strands back to smooth its edges.

Before Dayna there was Andrea, when I worked at Robey's in Springdale—we'd fool around in the walk-in cooler. I'd be sitting on a milk crate and she'd sit in my lap; we'd kiss, she'd bite my ears, then she'd pull down her black uniform pants and I'd pull down mine and she'd say *Will you park the pink Cadillac?* and I would say yes. But I always felt as though she was very far away. I had no idea what we were doing together. We didn't seem to have any real interest in each other at all. We'd gone to see *The Karate Kid* and she'd fallen asleep. She spent all her extra money on cocaine, which only made her nostalgic. Then she left town; she moved to Tucson without saying good-bye. Not long afterwards, I got fired. Robey caught me taking a nap behind the restaurant, out by the dumpsters.

"Could you help me hang Winston's cage?" asked Dayna.

"My pleasure," I said.

Stanley rarely checked up on me, and when he did—by radio—I would sometimes claim engine trouble if I was behind in the delivery schedule, if I'd been wasting time. There were days when I took two-hour picnics on the rocks under the Point Skyler Bridge. Stanley was getting somewhat suspicious. He questioned me more, which made me more interested in fucking off during the workday. That's a problem I have, generally speaking: if people expect me to disappoint them, I'll do my best to meet their expectations.

"I had it in the bedroom, but I guess I could change that," said Dayna.

"Oh, yes," I said. "Definitely."

"You don't think I should have it in the bedroom?"

"Doesn't the bird talk a lot?"

"But I like how Winston talks," she said.

"Winston, Winston, Winston, Winston," said the bird.

But then I noticed the progress I'd made. Dayna wasn't looking at me, just quickly meeting my eye, then turning away, toward Winston, or toward the floor. This was a foothold. She was acting less urban, less fluid; I saw a glimmer of loneliness; I saw her on a Sunday morning listening to the radio and content to be in this new town (which was all I'd ever known), looking at the mouth of the harbor, watching the lobstermen steam eastward, toward the outer islands, thinking, *This is good, this is just what I needed*—when in fact what she needed was me.

Winston's movement had caused the cage to roll quietly against a pile of jackets in the kitchen doorway. He had left his trapeze perch, which was upside down, and he was clutching the bottom of the cage. He looked miffed.

"Do you have an extra hook? We could hang the cage right in the corner of the living room," I suggested.

"What about the kitchen? That might be nice. Then I could talk to him when I cook," she said.

"Well—"

"What?"

"I don't think that's quite what you want to do."

"I have a hanging basket for onions. I could take that down and use the same hook."

"But it's the kitchen. Doesn't the bird, um . . . have smells?"

She looked at me like I'd plucked Winston and was spit-roasting him. "Winston is extremely clean."

My radio crackled. A transmission came through.

"You on there, Jim?" It was Stanley.

I held up a finger of apology to Dayna, then clicked the talk button, like a pro. "Gotcha, Stanley," I said.

"Where are you?" Stanley asked.

"Out the Sligo Road. Helping that client with her parakeet."

"You buy some finches today?" he asked.

I looked at Dayna while resting my finger gently on the talk button.

Stanley came through again. "Jim?"

Then I pushed down the button. "I'm not reading you, Stanley. Come again?"

"Finches. You buy some finches at Winkman's earlier today?"

"Finches. Yes, I did. I picked up a few finches earlier today. At Winkman's."

"What's going on, Jim?" asked Stanley.

"Well, Stanley, I'm with a client now. I'm in her kitchen, to tell you the truth. Doing an installation. Putting a cage up. I'll call you back shortly. Over and out."

"In the kitchen?" Stanley asked, but I didn't click back again. "You call me, Jim," he said. "When you're done. Over and out."

"Now I'm curious," said Dayna. She walked to the living room, so I picked up Winston's cage and followed her. She sat on the arm of the couch, and I was towering over her in my coveralls with the cage in my arms.

"Where are they?" she asked.

"They?"

"The finches."

"They're out in the truck," I said. I had always wished to be a better liar, especially with people I was attracted to. It made things easier, it seemed, if you could bend the truth in a smooth and natural way. The problem was, I actually didn't know what I was doing with the finches. I wasn't sure why I'd bought them. I was at Winkman's, picking up a case of cat toys for Stanley, when I'd seen the birds—the kind that sit on telephone wires—Winkman had a new walk-in cage full of them. Winkman's is this dark place, lit mostly by neon fish tanks, but I could see the birds clearly, they were the size of those large marshmallow peanuts, and they were fluttering their wings against each other, angry about their predicament, somewhat confused. Edgy. Jerking their swivel heads at notched increments, as though in constant disbelief. They made me nervous.

"Hey, hey! It's Stan the Animal Man," Winkman had said. The guy was an asshole. He was a hippie, but for no better reason than that it allowed him to be careless and lazy. He had a mangy beard and kept a boa constrictor draped over his shoulders. He called the snake Bootsie.

"Jim," I said. "It's Jim, not Stan."

"You're gonna be a vet, though, right, Jimmy? Jimmy the Animal Man? You'll take over when Stan's done?"

"No," I said. We'd been through this before. "I need some cat toys."

Winkman stroked the snake. *Yes,* Winkman seemed to say, *I have a twelve-foot killer wrapped around my neck, and the killer is my friend, and I can kiss it and call it Bootsie.* I didn't care. He always spoke to me in the chipper voice of a game-show host. I was sure the snake hated Winkman, too, wanted to eat him, and I wished for that.

"Well, we've got squeakers, fuzz balls, rubber mice, furry mice, fuzzy dice, and the Kitty Kong," said Winkman.

"Get me what Stanley usually gets," I said.

"The usual," said Winkman.

The snake raised its head and snapped out its flashy red tongue three times.

"Bootsie," said Winkman. "You gorgeous, gorgeous, beautiful devil. You smell me? Is that what you smell?"

I tried to look as bored as possible.

"Oh, Bootsie," Winkman continued. "My beauty. You're hungry

for birds, aren't you? You love them so much, don't you, Boots?" The snake's head rested on the counter. Its skin didn't look shiny enough. I could tell Bootsie thought the both of us were fools.

Winkman passed me a cardboard box. "Will that be all?"

"And twenty finches," I said. "Put them on Stanley's account." For some reason I just needed to get them out of that store.

And now, at Dayna's, I pictured the finches in the truck: they'd calmed down, they'd found places to perch and rest, they were waiting in the dark, preening, rustling their wings.

Winston was clinging to the side of the cage, agitated. He pecked at the zipper of my coveralls.

"Winston! Be nice," said Dayna.

"Winston, Winston," said Winston. Then he went back at it.

Dayna walked to the kitchen and returned with a large screw-in hook and a pair of pliers.

"Let's put it in here," she said. "You're probably right about the kitchen." She kicked us a path to the corner of the room, clearing aside stray sneakers, bags of cat litter, and coffee-stained Styrofoam cups.

She carried two chairs to the corner, and I stood on one with the cage in my arms and she stood on the other, installing the hook.

With her arms reaching above her head, I looked at her breasts, and she glanced down and caught me looking, and I looked up at the hook. We both looked at the hook. When it was ready, sunk deep in the ceiling, I steadied my feet on the chair and lifted the cage from my chest to eye level. As Dayna used the pliers to try to catch the cage's handle on the hook, Winston was staring me down.

"Hurry," I said.

"I'm trying," she said.

I looked at Dayna through the bars of the cage. She held a stubborn, determined look while working to get the handle in place; her eyes narrowed.

Winston was making his unsteady way toward me, clutching a horizontal bar in one claw and a vertical one in the other, shuddering his wings for balance. His beak approached my nose.

"Oh . . . crap . . ." I said.

"Almost there," she said.

Winston cocked his head to the side, then came at me. I turned my cheek to the bird, and his beak bumped against it. I was holding my breath.

"Got it," she said, and I let go, pushing away from Winston and losing my footing. When I hit the floor, one of my ankles turned and I landed on my ass. Dayna looked down, confused, and there was a beat of silence, then the cage—and Winston—was moving quickly toward me. I took it hard on the chest.

"Oh!" cried Dayna.

Winston and I didn't speak. The hook had ripped through the plaster. He was flying as best he could inside the sphere. He flapped and flapped, furious. The cage had knocked the wind out of me.

"Jeez, I'm sorry," she said.

There was a pain in my ribs when I took a breath and I felt a burn on my chin, but I tried to motion that I was okay.

"No, really, you must be hurt," she said. "Oh, man, you're bleeding." She looked genuinely upset as she climbed down and ran to the bathroom.

It's funny: I take the fondness I remember, the good feelings I have about her, and I think about walking into her kitchen then, the wind knocked out of me, looking for a glass of water. I remember the empty box of instant spuds on her electric range, the sink full of crusty plates, every cabinet and drawer open. I have a general, queasy feeling of regret when I think of it now, not for the particulars—I couldn't find a clean cup, didn't want to rummage further, so I moved quietly back out to the living room—but for the whole thing, falling in love with her, the beginning, the end. The end.

She taped an oversized gauze pad to my chin, and she propped Winston's cage on the ground in the corner, with a bag of cat litter wedged against it so it wouldn't roll.

"Little beast," I said.

"Winston, Winston, Winston, Winston," said Winston. I imagined the bird on the shoulder of a pirate, chatting away while I walked the plank.

Dayna took an armload of laundry off her couch for me, and she sat against the wall, on a pile of magazines.

"How did you get this job?" she asked

"You know how things are around here," I said, stupidly.

"No, I don't," she said.

"Everyone knows everyone," I said. "Stanley thought I was the right one for the job." In the corner of my eye, I saw a squirrel, which I thought at first was a cat—its gray tail rose from behind a stack of World Books. "Look," I said.

Dayna turned around. "Here they are again," she said. She shifted her weight, and the magazines loosened beneath her, spilling over on both sides.

It froze and looked at us. I felt my stomach chill. I reached inside my breast pocket for my tape measure, which I cocked back in my throwing hand, and looked at Dayna. "Okay?" I asked her. She said nothing, but she nodded, grimly. I fired the tape measure at the squirrel. It thudded against the far wall, leaving a cracked pockmark in the plaster, and the squirrel flinched but held its ground.

Dayna and I looked at the squirrel, and the squirrel returned our gaze, fiercely, with its black marble eyes. Dayna had her back against the foot of the couch now. We stared in silence. I was sitting on the couch, with my hands on my knees, and her shoulder was just inches from me. I lifted my hand and pressed the back of it against her arm, trying to get her attention, but she didn't turn around, she was watching the squirrel. I thought this was very weird, that she wasn't turning around, and that I wasn't taking my hand away.

"Hey," I said, and the squirrel left its post, returning to the kitchen. "Do you want to go for a ride in the truck?"

She turned and scrunched her eyebrows at me. "Not so much. Why?"

"I was thinking I could show you around," I said.

"Why did you buy those birds, anyway?" she asked. "Really."

"You go to Winkman's, then you'll know. The guy's a criminal."

"Are you going to keep them at your house?" she asked.

"Probably," I said. But I needed a cage, and I didn't really want them around. I just hadn't liked the idea of Winkman's snake eating them. It's not as though I was saving them—who knows if I could treat them any better—I was just acting on a strong urge to get them out of Winkman's reach.

"Well, I can't go now, if that's what you're asking," she said.

"Have you been over to Soper Island?" I asked.

"Nope," she said.

"Well, you've got to go," I said.

"Do I? Why's that?" she asked. She was like that.

"Well," I said, "it's worth it. I promise."

"I'd need to be back by seven," she said.

"No problem. We'll do a quick loop," I said.

It seemed to be a really tough decision for her. "All right," she said, finally.

I radioed Stanley.

"Hey, boss," I said.

"Where are you?" asked Stanley.

"I've got to run a quick errand, then I'll be back. Go ahead home, if you want. I'm off the clock."

"I want to talk to you, Jim," he said.

"See you tomorrow, Stanley," I said, and I clicked off the radio.

My problem has always been anticipation. I expect the best, and I expect the worst. The bad part is the expecting. Even then, as I radioed Stanley, I looked at Dayna—a real beauty, the kind that makes you hurt, makes you want to apologize—and I saw my future. Attachment. Pain. Things being thrown at me in a motel room at four in the morning.

Later, on the Point Skyler Bridge, driving north toward the cliffs near Soper Island, I glanced at Dayna in the passenger seat, and I watched her as she stared at the view. What she was looking at was the best vista in all of Point Allison. I was proud she liked it. The light at that time of day was perfect, so I put on my hazards, slowed to a stop, and snapped the air brakes. From that spot exactly you could see the water white against the rocks on Soper, then the green shallows, then the deep black water in the middle of the channel. And of course everywhere else, spruce and pine trees. The air was cool but the sun was still warm. The cars behind me honked, and a pickup truck clipped by us and its driver told me to fuck myself. I asked Dayna to come with me to the rear of the truck, and there I clicked open the padlock, hopped on the bumper, and grabbed the nylon strap to pull open the door. I hesitated. Then I looked at Dayna. She stood tentatively with her arms folded, no smile. But this fact remained: she was there, with me, waiting. After pulling open the door, I jumped from the bumper, landing beside her, and put my hand on her arm, and when I kissed her, the gauze pad brushed her chin. Her lips didn't move and she frowned. "Hey," she said. "The finches."

The sun was just below the trees on Point Skyler. Wind blew from the south, whistling by the bridge towers. Cars sped around us on the left. The interior of the truck was in shadows; we couldn't see a thing. Nothing burst from the truck. We looked in silence.

Then they came, all of them, in uneven rows—much tinier, it seemed, than when I'd bought them—they hopped from the darkness to the bumper. One after the next they dropped in a brief free fall from the truck, caught the updraft, and vanished through the suspension cables. They dipped under the bridge, or shot north up the river, too quick to see.

I wanted another chance to watch them, but it was over, they had all flown away.

A year after we broke up, I attended a wedding in Bangor and Dayna was there. I'd never seen her in heels. She was nearly as tall as I was, and not having talked to her for all that time—well, she looked perfect. She was wearing glasses, and her eyes were cold.

I approached her after three glasses of beer. She was sitting on a white plastic chair at the edge of the tent, alone, having a cigarette away from the crowd.

"Hiya," I said.

"Hi," she said.

"Great band, huh?"

"Sure," she said.

You see, I'd been the one to cut things off, which is to say I'm fairly brain dead when it comes to staying happy. With a good enough ramp, just about anyone can jump twelve buses on a motorcycle. Sticking the landing, though—that's something else entirely.

I said, "Listen, Dayna, we both know I'm the one who messed it all up—"

She rolled her eyes.

"I could apologize. I have apologized, and it's crap. I know," I said.

"Jim, are you drunk?" she asked.

"The thing is, we were so close."

"Yes, we were."

"And I haven't even talked to you in a year."

"Nope."

"Isn't it crazy? We have two years together, we're together almost every day, and then zilch. Nothing. Total strangers. What I mean is—"

"What?"

"I miss knowing you."

She scrunched up her nose. "Why should that matter?"

I thought about that one. The best part had been the beginning, when everything was unknown. I wasn't proud of that. "How's Winston?" I asked.

"Winston? He's gone. I released him off the bridge," she said.

"Really?"

"No, you dope. Not really."

"Winston's still around?"

"Yes." She was smirking; she seemed pleased with herself.

"Can we dance?" I asked.

"Jesus," she said, and shook her head.

"Well, come on. Just a dance."

"As long as you shut up. No more talking."

"Agreed," I said.

People were filtering out of the tent to smoke cigarettes and look at the stars. It was a warm night with a breeze. Dayna really looked fantastic. We didn't hold hands. We faced each other, not dancing, just swaying there, sometimes bumping into other dancers. She looked over my shoulder, and I couldn't read her eyes at all. When the song ended, I touched her arm and had a flash of hope, thinking we'd get back together, but it must have just been the feeling of not knowing her at all.

Debra Spark

A Short Wedding Story

—with debts to Martin Buber's *The Legend of the Baal Shem Tov*

Her trip to London was purely for pleasure, but Rachel Rubenstein did have a goal. She wanted to buy presents for her nephews, something fun that wouldn't cost too much. She found what she was looking for at the grocers: chocolate eggs with prizes inside. They were from Germany. Or maybe it was Switzerland. Anyway, they were hollow chocolate eggs, lined with white, as if the shell were on the inside. Rachel cracked open a few, while she was still in London, to make sure they'd please. She found tiny puzzles, small one-toothed monsters, itty-bitty tops. Perfect. Only her eggs melted by the time she got home, so she gave the kids little misshapen brown lumps of . . .

"You know what I'm thinking those look like," her sister Greta began.

"I'd like that to be one of those thoughts you leave unexpressed."

"Gotcha," Greta said.

So Rachel wasn't surprised—not entirely—by the foil-wrapped chocolate egg in Mamie Bess's effects. She associated such items with Europe. Ditto Mamie, who had come from Poland to Queens in the 1930s and stayed there till earlier this morning, when death had forced her removal to a Long Island cemetery. Not that Mamie was actually in Long Island. She'd joined the Everlasting, if Rabbi Cohen—he of the spittley lips and saggy cheeks—could be trusted. Rachel wasn't sure she believed in such things, but it was enough that

Mamie did. The last time they'd spoken, it was about a date Rachel had gone on.

"So?" Mamie had said. "You mind me asking what he's like?"

"I don't know," Rachel said. She was in her late twenties and vague when it came to her personal life. It seemed altogether possible that she might never have one. "A doctor and Jewish, so it should be good, but I just couldn't get much of a conversation going with him." The man had been the grandson of one of Bess's friends. Rachel was in a period of welcoming blind dates, no matter what quarter they came from.

"He doesn't need to be perfect. Perfect isn't for here. That's for the *yenne velt.* You know what that means? It's Jewish. It means the other side."

Rachel smiled. She hadn't known that Bess had notions about the afterlife. She'd never mentioned it before. There was definitely a life-is-for-the-living philosophy that ran through the family. Rachel didn't really like talking about her nonexistent romantic life with her grandmother, but she did add, "He doesn't need to be perfect. But I should be able to talk to him, don't you think?"

"Mmm," Bess mused. Then said, "Talking's overrated."

The chocolate egg made Rachel think of a jar that Bess had kept in the pantry of her old house in Queens. Bess had lived there before moving to the Long Island condo in which Rachel was now boxing up her belongings. The jar had been full up of candies that didn't exist anywhere save in Mamie's closets. Say "M&M" in the old Queens house, and you might be speaking a foreign tongue. But on Bess's shelves, there were always containers stuffed full of hard candies that dissolved into soft cakey centers and strange mints that turned into chocolates the longer you sucked. Rachel didn't have any memory of chocolate eggs, but here was one now. She peeled it immediately. She was immoderately greedy for sweets, though dutifully embarrassed by this fact. The chocolate was old, dusty white, the way chocolate gets after many years. Rachel sniffed. It smelled only vaguely of cocoa; it might have been a chocolate egg from the old country. But it clearly wasn't solid. It felt, in her fingers, like those KinderEggs she'd found in London. There might even be a Cracker Jack–type prize inside. Age—when it came to candy—didn't worry her. She nibbled the top of the egg and imagined she heard someone cry, "*Gevult.*"

The egg didn't surprise Rachel, but the little rabbi inside the egg certainly did.

"Shalom," he called, half in warning, so she wouldn't bite further.

"Oh, my," Rachel cried, and put the egg down, a little repulsed, as if it was a tiny mouse rather than a holy man crawling over a fence of chocolate to greet her. "Simon," he called. "Master of the Name."

"What?" she said. "What?" She felt momentarily dizzy and put her hand to her head. Had she had enough water today? Once, when she was in college, she'd gotten so dehydrated she'd started hallucinating.

"My name," he said. "I was just translating for you. Simon Baal Shem."

"A-ha," Rachel said, as if in assent. Could a figment of your imagination make up something—like a name—that would never occur to you? Probably not.

Rachel wasn't all that religious herself, but she'd had a bat mitzvah, way back when, and a few things had trickled down to her from visits with Bess and her occasional foray into the synagogue in Maine, where she lived. "The Baal Shem?" she said now. "Wasn't he . . . ?" The founder of Chasidism, she was about to say, but the rabbi interrupted her.

"He was the Baal Shem *Tov.* The Holy One. I'm not him. In the Middle Ages, Baal Shem was a name given to any Jewish rabbi who might be a miracle worker."

"And you're one of them."

"I'm one of them," he said.

"But it's not the Middle Ages."

"Well," Simon said, brushing a shard of chocolate from his shoulders, "if you want to get stuck on details." He had a dark mustache and dark hair—both almost as black as the fleck of fabric he wore as a skullcap—but his beard was flecked with white. His woolly head of hair discomfited her, resembling, as it did, the hair of one of the divorced parents at the daycare center where she worked. Rachel was always half-hoping he'd ask her out.

"How long have you been in there?"

"What's time to someone inside an egg?"

"Oh," Rachel said earnestly. "I guess I don't know." He looked at her expectantly. The flat mournful planes of his cheeks made her think of a Modigliani painting. Below them, his long beard looked like two separate beards, two pennant flags hanging from his chin.

Rachel didn't know what to say. "What sort of miracles do you do?"

"I don't like to brag."

"No," she said. "I suppose you wouldn't." Rachel's mind was blank. She tried to call up an appropriate question, but everything she might ask—everything about which she was genuinely curious—struck her, for some reason, as off-limits. Or too silly. Who, for instance, had sewn the little dark suit he was wearing? Out of what ancient workshop came his mildly scuffed miniature shoes? She didn't ask. And yet she wasn't at ease with the quiet, though the rabbi sat peaceably looking at her, as if talk or no talk, it was all the same to him. At length, Rachel decided to treat him like any guest.

"Can I get you, maybe, something to eat?"

"That would be welcome."

"I don't know what's here." She opened Bess's refrigerator, felt a stab of pain at the prune juice and cottage cheese there. The freezer had an iced-up bag of frozen ravioli. She turned for the cabinets, and in the end, the rabbi contented himself with the better part of a garbanzo bean as a snack.

"So," Rachel said, as he chewed contentedly, "is there a … is there a reason why you're here?"

"Perhaps," the rabbi said but didn't elaborate.

Rachel knew which way was up. A miracle worker was no genie in the bottle, and even if he were, a rabbi required righteous behavior. Selflessness at the least, though she did have the urge to rub his head and ask him if he could help her meet a nice guy. Or lose a few pounds. Or reverse the state of the mutual fund into which she'd poured her meager retirement savings. A rush of shame came over her as the rabbi sat down, leaning his back against the pot of a jade plant, and cooling himself in the shade of its leaves.

"Lovely," the rabbi said, tugging the dark gabardine of his suit over his hips and crossing his feet at his ankles. It looked like he intended to stay awhile.

"In the morning, the men from the auction house will be coming to sell all this," Rachel gestured to what remained unpacked—a table full of brandy snifters on which dust had settled permanently, a coffee table cluttered with porcelain figurines, a closet of old housecoats, a giant painting of three mermaids. There were nametags—Shira, Jenny, Greta, Samuel, Tova—attached to various pieces of furniture and the large oval mirror in the hallway. Most of the bigger items were going to a grandchild or great-grandchild. Rachel was supposed to take the grandfather clock, though there really wasn't enough room for it in her apartment. For the time being, it was going to Greta's. "If you don't mind, I have to . . . "

"Please . . . ," the rabbi said, gesturing as if to say she should continue doing what she'd been doing. "For the moment, I'd just like to watch."

The evening continued almost as if Rachel were alone. The rabbi stood only once to resettle himself into an old bag of white beans on the kitchen table, as if it was some giant throw pillow from the '70s. As he moved, he muttered in Yiddish, and when Rachel turned to the sound of his words, he looked up—his gaze was disarmingly direct—to say, "You speak Jewish?"

"No," Rachel admitted.

"Oh," the rabbi said, and didn't translate his words.

Rachel spent the night in Bess's old bed, felt the discomfort of this acutely, though Bess had lived a good, long life, and death at age ninety-two was no tragedy. (Who, if Rachel, didn't know this? A young woman who flinched at the evening news and fretted over tragedies near and far: an abduction in Florida, the cancer in her boss's breast, the bomb in Jerusalem. Oh, good Lord.) Still, she'd miss the old woman. Bess had been a true friend, someone with whom Rachel had always talked warmly and frankly.

For the rabbi, Rachel found a 250-count box of wooden matches, the contents of which she tossed into a trash bag already full with overstretched sweaters, worn slippers, and a disarming box of Depends undergarments. Probably no one knew what Bess had suffered in the end. Rachel dug a purse-size container of tissues from her handbag, and the rabbi accepted this for a mattress, and an old embroidered handkerchief of Bess's late husband for a blanket.

"You want maybe to hear a story?" the rabbi asked on their second night in Bess's apartment. The place had been cleared of all belongings, save Rachel's suitcase and a sleeping bag and pillow that she'd brought from her apartment in South Portland, Maine. A phone snaked from the wall to the pillow. In the morning, Rachel would wind up the phone and drop the key off with the president of the condo association.

"I'd like that."

"But first a candle you must light."

Rachel looked around the empty condo. "But . . . "

The rabbi was insistent.

"I don't have a candle."

"Then we wait."

"Well, no," Rachel said, "let me go see if I can find a neighbor."

Once out in the dim hallway, though, Rachel realized she didn't really have the courage to bother a neighbor for something like this. A cup of milk for baking, yes, but a candle? It seemed too rude, and she'd have to ask for a holder as well.

When she came back empty-handed, the rabbi said, "A carved potato you could use for a candleholder."

Rachel nodded. She did have a jackknife.

"You should try maybe apartment 4F," the rabbi said sagely, and Rachel, thinking that perhaps miracle workers could see through walls, went up to the fourth floor and knocked.

An old man with a bristly gray-black mustache answered the door. His right side was partially paralyzed, and he leaned so dramatically into the strength of his left, he looked as if he might tip over.

"I'm terrible sorry to bother you," Rachel began. "I'm the grand-daughter of Bess Seidman. She lived in 2B?"

"Oh, *yeees,*" the man said. "Come in. I'm so *sooor-ry* to *lose* her." What-ever had ruined the right portion of his body had given him a peculiar drawl, a habit of holding onto syllables a beat longer than he should. At the same time, his voice had the cartoony sound of an audiotape played at the wrong speed. "*Yooouur* grandmother was a *good soul.*"

Rachel's eyes teared up. "I know," she said. Fear had forestalled her own grief. If she gave into it, then what? "It" being not just her sorrow but her sense that all the grown-ups were gone now. And, Lord, they'd left her own idiot generation in charge.

"Everyone in the building loved her. If someone got *saaad,* we always sent them *to her.* She could cheer anybody up. She knew how to look on the bright *side* of things. You know?"

Rachel did, though she hadn't always loved her grandmother for this quality. When Rachel's own parents had died (seven and eight years earlier, of two separate cancers, courtesy of the toxins that were the state of New Jersey), her grandmother had said, "They had their life. That was their life, and you have to feel blessed for it."

"Easy enough to say," Rachel had groused to her sister Greta, "when you've already been treated to eighty-five years." But then she'd tried to grow into the wisdom of her grandmother's words. She had to find a way to accept the loss of her parents, after all. She didn't—as Greta sometimes pointed out—have any other choice.

"Come in and sit," the old man said. "I'm Howie Rosengren."

"I can't stay. I just needed to ask a favor."

"Anything," the man said. "And ac-shually I have something for you." He walked, dragging one foot, back into his apartment, and Rachel followed. He pulled a card from a wallet resting on top of a bookcase. "This here," he said, as he handed it to her, "is my *son's* busi-ness. Rosengren and Sons, though I don't do the work anymore. You go down to the shed . . . you don't even *both-er* with a *phone* call, but go straight there and ask for Jeremy. That's my little one's littlest one. You tell him you need a *marker* for your *grandma,* and he'll make it for you. Tell him I said to give you a *good discount.*"

"Oh, that's OK," Rachel said. "I actually have a name from Bess's rabbi for the gravestone."

Mr. Rosengren made a contradictory farting sound with his lips. "Pfft, no," he said. "That rabbi is a fool. I don't *want* you *going* to him." Rachel was taken aback by the command in his words. Why exactly did he imagine he had the right to order her around on such private business? "You *go* to my *grandson*."

"Well, thank you," she said reluctantly, and asked for what she'd come.

"Candle? Sure, we got candles." He limped farther into the apartment and returned with a stub of a maroon candle and a box of matches. "I hope this will *do*."

"I'm sure it will." She paused. "You wouldn't happen to have an old potato, too?"

"In my time," began Rabbi Simon, once Rachel was back in the apartment, and they were seated cross-legged on the floor around the impromptu light of the guttering candle, "my days were the Lord's, but my hours were with horses. I took horses from the field and trained them for town and to make the runs from our city to the coast. One day, a man came to me with an untrainable horse. Me? What did I care? I had heard this before. *Nu?* I could tame a horse. But this horse. *Oy gut*. I worked for days, then weeks. Still, the first time the horse draws a carriage, over it goes. The people inside were hurt. A young boy's legs . . . crushed." The rabbi shook his head gravely. His face gleamed red in the light of the flame above him. " 'This horse is for the slaughterhouse,' I said. But the horse's owner said no, and so I worked on. What choice did I have? But you know how it goes. At the sight of me, the horse would stamp and kick. I lost hope. I went about my house with gloom. How could I rest knowing that through my failures, I had hurt another living thing? Finally, a stranger, he comes to my farm. 'I'll change your horse's ways,' he tells me. 'Who's stopping you?' I say. He goes out to my barn, and within minutes he is back. 'You will have no problem with him any longer,' he says. Well, this I didn't believe. But out I go and hitch the horse to a carriage to give the stranger a ride back to town. The horse trots happily. 'What did you do?' I asked the stranger.

" 'I went to him with an open heart.'

" 'And me too,' I said. 'Didn't I go to him with an open heart? For this is the way of the people of the Lord.'

" 'I went to him with an open heart and no desire for his learning,' the stranger said. 'And so he learned.' "

Rachel wasn't one to keep secrets, but the following week back at the Busy Bees childcare center, where she had served as art instructor to the pre-K set for almost six years, she didn't feel quite ready to announce that she had a pocket-sized rabbi living with her. The people at the center weren't Jewish—few people in the state were—and if they found her dreidl craft projects exotic, what would they make of this? Rachel didn't know herself what she thought of the circumstances, and after her first inquiry about the rabbi's purpose, she asked no further questions, supposing it best simply to attend to his needs. He had a fondness for "communing with nature," and she took him to the small strip of greenery that surrounded Country Creek Estates— the name for the complex that housed her one-bedroom apartment, all she could afford on her sparse salary. It wasn't a great place—the walls too thin, the cockroaches likely to travel from a neighbor's apartment no matter how clean she kept her own cabinets, the inhabitants (all of them) in someway damaged. There was a cab driver who'd been waiting ten years to save enough money to return to college; an angry blind woman who sometimes asked Rachel to read her the newspaper; and a born-again Christian who lived upstairs and who had the bland cheerfulness and dutiful work habits of a man who—in another country and at another time—might be inclined to kill her.

And there was another reason she didn't say anything: a reticence had fallen over her since her stay in New York. It might have been a delayed grief at Mamie's passing, or the curiousness of her situation, but she was aware that she was having trouble talking to people. Real trouble, though ordinarily she thought of her easy manner with others as her greatest (well, actually, her only) gift. With children, the gift had always been most pronounced—she could draw out the non-talkers, soothe the fussy, engage the frenetic—and around Christmas she knew that hers would be the box at school most full of personal thanks for her talents. There were children who came back, even now that they were ten, just to say hi. And children and parents alike flushed with pleasure when they saw her in the grocery store. "Oh, Miss Rubenstein," they cried, as if both elder and younger parties were shocked to find she lived outside the walls of the daycare center. Of course, her charms worked on the young and the married and seemed to elude the unmarried male, but now even those charms were gone, and she found herself with the same blank head she'd had when first asking the rabbi questions about himself. It was as if she'd suddenly forgotten—but forgotten for all circumstances—what it was she meant to say.

Rachel called her old college roommate to chat. In Maine, she'd never developed the sort of fond friends she'd had in college or just after, when she lived with a bevy of roommates in Boston. She blamed the state itself. In Maine, people liked their privacy. You couldn't tell when they'd interpret friendliness as crossing a boundary.

"How's work?" Rachel asked Jessica.

"So-so."

"And George?"

"He's fine."

And then Rachel felt stumped. Did Jessica not like her phone calls? Maybe it wasn't Maine. Maybe she was the only one left, the only unattached person left who still needed friends.

"And you?" Jessica said.

But what could she say? That she had a kosher action figure living with her?

"Feigele," the rabbi said. Dear. He had quickly lapsed into terms of endearment for Rachel. "Yes," Rachel finished washing her face and leaned down to where he was, his black shoes dampening in a small puddle at the edge of the sink.

"I have for you another story. In fact, I have for you four stories."

"Four?"

"Yes, one I already told you. So three more. But all in good time."

"OK," Rachel said. She sat down on the edge of the bathtub. "Well?"

"Not now. Before you hear, you have to stop waiting to hear."

Back when she was in junior high school, in Elizabeth, New Jersey, a group of girls had been given the assignment of taking care of an egg for a week. They had to have the egg with them at all times—or get a babysitter, if they wanted to go somewhere where it wouldn't be convenient to have a raw egg in tow. The idea, of course, was to frighten the girls out of pregnancy. Only it wasn't an assignment that girls like Rachel were given. You had to be fast—or fast in the minds of the teacher—to get an egg, and Rachel had always felt slighted at not being chosen for the exercise. Now, though, she thought she had a sense of what those teenage girls had gone through, for Rabbi Simon could not be left at home. She'd tried it, on that first day of work after she returned from New York, and she'd come home to a terrified rabbi. The cockroaches had formed an ugly band and approached him where he sat, gnawing on a crouton at the kitchen table. He bowled one bug over with the stale bit of bread, then raced for the leg of the table. He'd made it into Rachel's bedroom and had hid there, behind the wheel of the bed, till Rachel returned. What portion in heaven for someone responsible for terrifying a man right out of worship and into the fearful muttering Rabbi Simon was doing when Rachel dropped her purse on her mattress? Who knew, but a week into his stay, Rachel was carrying him everywhere. Still, she kept him her secret, taking more breaks than normal from work, if only so she could go to the bathroom and pull the rabbi out of her pocket. After a day or two, the routine made him moody—"One must search for a bright light in these dark times," he mumbled—and Rachel anxious. How could she keep the rabbi in the light and go to work?

"From the time he was born," the rabbi began one night, and Rachel knew this was the start of his second story, "Rabbi Judea Lev was a serious child. His days he spent working the fields, and his nights with books. But light or dark, he was always thinking about how to get closer to his God. One day, his family goes to the lake. It's hot, *nu*? And old times, new times, a hot man wants to cool down. But *oy gut!* A whirlpool pulls Lev under. At first for air he gasps but then he drinks the water, and darkness comes. After there is a light like no other, and Lev begins to ascend to it. His soul pines for the light like a schoolboy for his mother, and as he rises, he hears the fish and even the plants about him, all speaking in their secret tongue. But for the boy the language is not a secret. Everything he understands. Then he hears a voice say, 'Not yet.' A hand grabs his ankle and pulls him up, up through the water, and he is suddenly in the arms of a strange man, and his mother is beside the man, crying and thanking him. Lev sees his mother's relief, but even so, he knows what he has lost, and as hard as he studied before, he promises himself he will study harder yet."

"You know what bugs me about that story?" Rachel began. The rabbi looked shocked, as if an objection to the story weren't possible. "It suggests getting closer to God is good, which I wouldn't argue with, but it also suggests death is the path. Doesn't it?"

The rabbi looked at her curiously and said, "No."

Rachel opened her mouth to protest, but the phone rang. It was her sister Greta, calling to remind Rachel about the marker for Bess's grave.

"Speaking of death," Rachel said.

"What?" Greta cried.

"Nothing. A dumb joke. Yeah, I'll do it. I didn't think there was any rush." The Jewish tradition was to unveil the stone on the first anniversary of the death. Rachel put her sister on speakerphone, so the rabbi could listen in on the conversation.

"No, but, let's just . . . Well, you don't know how long it will take for the stonecutter to do the work, and what if you forget when the time gets near and . . . "

"OK," Rachel said. Greta's manner was to take care of a task before it had even been assigned to her, and Rachel's had always been to wait to the last minute. "I'll do it before the month is up."

"And the clock? When are you going to get that?"

"Soon."

"When soon?"

"Ohhh," Rachel said. The truth was she had an uneasy relationship with things, even in the best of times. She didn't like to be encumbered. If she had to, Rachel could still fit almost everything she owned, minus a few pieces of furniture, into her Ford Escort. It was a point of pride with her.

"Your basement isn't going anywhere, is it? Can't you just keep it there?"

"Rachel," Greta said, aggrieved. "It's less room here than you think. Come on."

Greta was the older of the two sisters and seemed to feel that her three-year seniority and marriage gave her the rights of parenthood when it came to Rachel. What this meant, most recently, was that Greta had controlled all aspects of Bess's funeral, insisting on a catered reception, though Rachel's own way would have been homier. She'd have asked Bess's friends to bring casseroles to the apartment. "A potluck funeral?" Greta had said, incredulous. But that's what Bess would have preferred. Or so Rachel thought. After all, Bess never liked being served by waiters or advised while in a department store, but then Rachel remembered that Bess had taken her and Greta out for Chinese food after their father's funeral. It had seemed positively surreal, Bess saying, "Girls, what do you want. Eggrolls? Spare ribs?" What they wanted was their father, but Bess didn't let conversation turn to him. He was gone, they were here now, and they had to get on with things, so did they or didn't they want chicken with cashew nuts?

"OK," Rachel said now, hoping her lack of specificity about what she was assenting to would buy her more time. "Well, I've got to go." She clicked the phone off its speaker function and turned her back to the rabbi.

"You always say that when you want to hang up," Greta accused.

"No really," Rachel protested, and then because it wasn't truly a lie, she whispered, "I've got a guy here."

"Oooo," Greta said interested. "I'll call tomorrow!"

"More important than Torah," the rabbi said as Rachel hung up the phone, "is family happiness."

"Yes?" Rachel said, on the edge of being irritated.

"A trip to New York," he pressed his tiny palm to his chest, as if waylaid by a sudden fit of indigestion, "is what I'm suggesting."

The nature of the rabbi's awareness of history suggested he'd been interred in chocolate sometime after the Holocaust but before the '50s. So while computers needed to be explained to him—and cell phones and color TVs—he knew his way around New York and was disappointed only by what he didn't find. In the streets of the Lower East Side, where the rabbi had asked to go, no radios tuned themselves to WEDV. "I used to love that show, what's-it-called," the rabbi said when Rachel pulled him out of her purse, and sat him down on her lunch table. ("Cool doll," the waitress had said, fingering the stud in her nose, as if it were a pimple she hoped to pop.) "I know!" the rabbi remembered. "Yiddish Melodies in Swing. That was a good one." The rabbi actually hadn't wanted to have lunch at a deli. He'd wanted a hot dog from Nathan's. But that chain was long gone, and the rabbi was put off by vegetarian Rachel's description of hot dogs as "cow cheeks and assholes."

"Very un-lady-like," he had said.

On the ascending ladder toward God, Rachel had clearly descended a rung. And yet she was aware of purposely having used the word "asshole" to test the limits of the rabbi's patience with . . . well, not her exactly, but her milieu, the world in which she lived.

They'd settled on the warren-like Ratner's, where they shared a plate of potato pancakes and applesauce amid the lunchtime din. Rachel hid the rabbi behind a napkin dispenser and figured people could make their own guesses about why she seemed to be addressing the ketchup bottle. Outside, the stores were stuffed to bursting with imitation leather luggage, cheap jeans, and T-shirts with rude slogans. Here, waiters barely stopped to ask patrons what they wanted before tucking their pads into their waistbands and racing for the kitchen.

"Do you like this place?" Rachel asked the rabbi. The wisdom of your stories won't work here, she wanted to say. I wish it would, but the world's just too complicated.

He wiped the corners of his mouth on a piece of a napkin, folded his hands neatly before him. He kept his air of decided calm no matter what was happening around him. "It'll do," he said.

Greta lived in Maplewood, New Jersey, with her husband Philip and their two sons. After lunch and a brief tour of the lower part of the city—past the matzoh factory, by Gus's Pickles and the *shul*—Rachel joined Philip for the trek from his downtown office back to the suburbs. It had been on the edge of rain all afternoon—a chilly wind had accompanied Rachel and the rabbi on their rounds—and now the sky began to unburden itself. Rachel and Philip skittered along the sidewalk to the garage where he parked his car, the day's newspaper serving as a makeshift umbrella for Philip, Rachel resigned to getting soaked.

"How was your day?" she asked, as they settled into the car, the wet strands of her hair whapping her cheeks like some sort of practical joke the day had played on her.

"Fine."

Philip was a skinny tax lawyer, and even in the best of times, Rachel found him sour and overly obsessed with money.

"What's up with the kids?"

Philip glanced over at her. Was he annoyed?

"You know," Rachel said cajolingly, "I'm asking for the Cute Report. What new things are they doing or saying?" For each kid at the daycare, Rachel could find a thousand answers for this question. Max was talking about the way monsters made themselves skinny, so they could fit under his bedroom door at night. Jason had been looking at a book of trucks the other day, and when Rachel approached, he'd said matter-of-factly, "Hi, I'm just enjoying the fun." Little Sarah had looked up from the craft table just yesterday and said, "Miss Rubenstein, this Play-Doh is freaking me out."

"The boys?" said Philip. "The usual."

But there was no usual with little kids. That—Rachel thought, half-consciously bookmarking her notion to share with the rabbi later—was part of the fun. Normally, Rachel would have persisted in her effort to draw Philip out. She could usually get him to complain vociferously about some colleague at work, but she felt too irritated to open her mouth. He could ask her about *her* kids, couldn't he? The ones at the daycare? Or ask her something about art . . . or, well, anything, but that would mean he'd have to place just a teeny bit of value on one thing that she did. Which he couldn't. They'd crossed over the bridge, and Rachel turned her head to look back at Manhattan. Bess had always held that the rain cleaned the city off. From this distance, it did seem sparkly, though her few hours of wandering with the rabbi had left her feeling grubby. Occupying yourself in New York was exhausting; you had to bring so much vigilance to even a decision to rest on a bench. "Well," Rachel said, a sort of sigh, then settled into her own silence, a quiet that seemed to content Philip. At least, he didn't do anything to break it till they arrived in Maplewood.

Over dinner, in Greta's small but neat ranch house with its mammoth leather sofa and chairs—forest green cushions stuffed beyond reason, as if for a giant's derriere—Rachel found new things to dislike about her brother-in-law, though it was six years into Greta's marriage, and Rachel thought she'd long completed the tally. Philip snapped at Greta for failing to pick up the dry cleaning earlier in the day and then reprimanded her as she went to eat a third chocolate-chip cookie. "Didn't the kids make those for Rachel?"

"Well, I wasn't planning on eating the whole plate," Rachel put in.

"Still," Philip said, his mouth tightening.

Little bastard. No wonder she hadn't been able to make conversation with him.

But perhaps the problem wasn't all with Philip. For after dinner, even Greta seemed beyond Rachel's reach. The sisters sat and watched the boys play a game that involved making and destroying a town that they had nicknamed "Big City Adventure." Ordinarily, Rachel and Greta would chatter on about books they'd read or old friends or their cousins. Now, Rachel was telling a story about their cousin Katrina. After ten years of marriage, she had finally met her husband's father. The man had been an alcoholic and homeless—a couch surfer, sleeping on friends' couches, and moving (with all his belongings in a single cardboard box) from apartment to apartment. The whole history fascinated Rachel. At the very least, it explained some glitches in her cousin's husband's character, but Greta didn't seem to much care. She was sitting heavily on a stepstool in the playroom, when normally she'd be bustling about, throwing trucks back into the play chest, and stacking puzzle boxes on the bookshelf.

Rachel stopped her narrative, mid-sentence. "Are you all right?"

"Yeah. Just tired."

Of course, Rachel thought, but when her sister didn't return her to her story with a question, she wondered if she'd been talking too much, if at the very moment she thought she'd been entertaining, her sister thought she was going on and on.

"So," Rachel said, as if she was going to start up again, but she didn't continue. A dark mood overtook her. She might be heading for one of those stretches (it had happened to her twice in the past) when she stood outside of all her everyday actions, and everything that ordinarily seemed normal and easy seemed strained and false. Even basic sentences felt hard to put together, the drastic imprecision of her own speech—she never quite found the words to say what she meant—newly intolerable. It was best not to dwell in this way, but once she got going it was hard to stop.

Eventually Greta said, "Tonight I'll let David sleep in a sleeping bag in Matthew's room. That way you don't have to take the couch."

It wasn't yet nine, but Rachel turned in, relieved not to have to try anymore with her sister.

Once in David's bedroom, Rachel thought to confess her feelings. Who else but a holy man to help her with her struggles? But she couldn't articulate her thoughts, and they merged with a general feeling of hopelessness. There was such a brief time of enjoying the fun before the years of ambition and unrealized ambition and then the suffering (whatever portion you were allotted) before you died. Everybody she knew wanted their life to be a stepping-stone to something else, and no one was happy with where they landed. And what of it? That was life. It didn't matter really. Or it wouldn't matter if there was only someone to talk to about it.

Rachel put on her nightgown, then pulled the rabbi, sweaty and lint-covered, from her purse.

"Well, what do you think?" Rachel said dispiritedly.

"I couldn't hear!" he said, seeming to sense how her emotions had dimmed with the day.

Rachel had an urge to pick up a phone and call Bess. "Hello. 1-800-THE-GREAT BEYOND?" Without fully realizing it, Rachel had leaned into her grandmother Bess's authority—the authority of greater experience—as if it were a ledge on which she might prop herself. Greta was family, but she couldn't fill that role. She was too much in the midst of life herself to offer any help with it. Rachel put the rabbi's matchbox bed on the night table, then peeled back the Winnie the Pooh sheets of her nephew's bed.

"Maybe I'm just missing my grandma." She turned toward the wall, so the rabbi could dress for bed. He slept in some doll clothes Rachel had filched from the daycare: blue footsie pajamas patterned with red French horns. Complete with a matching cap.

"All set," the rabbi called. "You were saying?"

"My grandma Bess." Rachel lay back in bed, an arm pressed against her left eye—she was allergic to something in this room. Above her head, a mobile of planes twirled and slowly settled. "Once, one of the teachers at the daycare said to me, 'You know what you have is a compassion disorder.' The morning paper had reported the death of one hundred and twelve people in a plane crash, and I couldn't get my head off the tragedy. 'You can't think about that stuff,' Bess used to tell me when she found me fretting over such things. 'If you think about that stuff, you go crazy.' She wasn't trying to comfort me. She was telling me to stop it." And Rachel had liked it—Bess's instructions, a reminder, however cruel, from above: life isn't for the dead.

The rabbi didn't respond, and Rachel felt something—a clot of grief or loneliness—stick in her throat. Her thoughts were so natural to her; could it be that others really didn't share them; that when she confessed what was closest to her heart, she was really being a pain in the neck? Rachel reached over and clicked off the lamp.

The light from the moon cut through the window, and the rabbi formed a shadow puppet of himself on the wall. "Well," he said at last, sitting up in his bed as he spoke. His pajama cap sat lopsided on his head, like a half-collapsed soufflé. "We're travelers, so I'll tell you the story of a traveler."

Herschel Schtok wanted to learn the Law. He'd grown up in the country among peasants. Prayers he knew to recite, but Hebrew? He could not read a word. When he was old enough, he went to town and set himself up as a shopkeeper. Now begin his studies. One day he hopes to visit the synagogue in Karyek. No one knows Karyek anymore, but in its day, it was known for the holiness of its citizens. And the rabbi of Karyek was the holiest of them. There were rumors . . . things you wouldn't believe. That in his holiest of fervors, he left the earth entirely and flew through the air, though some said it wasn't flying really, but hopping, and that he did it when he was full of the joy of the Lord. A kind of a skip. What does it matter? Herschel wanted to meet this rabbi. Surely such a man could tell him how best to continue his studies. So Herschel wrote ahead and made for himself an appointment with the rabbi. Soon it was all set. The Sabbath hence Herschel would celebrate in Karyek. On Saturday after sundown, he'd go to the shul, when it was permitted to ask the rabbi questions.

A peasant, he knows how to wake up early, and so Herschel gets up before the sun on the day of his trip. He knows, too, about weather, so he gives himself three extra days for travel. Might not a rainstorm wash out his road? And how reliable is a horse anyway? Hershel rides as far as he can on his first night, and just when he fears he has traveled too far into the wilderness, that there will be no place for him to stay the night, he comes across a small inn at the foot of a mountain.

239

The innkeeper comes to the door. He is a large man in a peasant blouse and tight boots and pants. He wipes his hands on his shirt, leaving two brown stains by his ribs, then holds out his palm to greet Herschel.

"I'll just be staying the single night," Herschel explains. "I need to get to Karyek by Sabbath."

"And why not spend the Sabbath with me?"

"I am going to see a very holy man," Herschel explains. "It is my life's journey."

"So be it," the man says, and shows him to his room.

Herschel pays at once. He will be up before the innkeeper in the morning, as he intends to put as many miles between him and the mountain before nightfall. He travels all day, but he doesn't come across another inn, and at dusk, when he happens to turn his head around—strangeness of strangeness—he sees the inn in which he'd slept the previous night. Herschel, he doesn't know what to think, but he turns back and enters the inn for a second time. He explains again to the innkeeper that he needs a room, that he intends to meet a holy man by the next Sabbath. Again, the innkeeper says, "And you don't wish to spend your Sabbath with me?"

"Don't joke with me, sir," Herschel cries. "Something has happened, and my senses are bedeviled, and I must keep to my true path."

Herschel departs early the next morning. Perhaps he took a circular road on the previous day? Today, he will pay more attention and make sure he does not double back. The Sabbath is drawing closer, and he does not think he will get a second chance, in this life, to speak to the Karyek rabbi, so that as he travels even the leaves seem to give voice to his fears, rustling, as they appear to, about time and how little time each man has on earth. It is Friday, and Herschel's road goes through no towns. The day hurries past, and soon it is almost dusk. Finally, he sees a light in the distance. He pushes his horse forward. He has arrived at the little inn again.

"I see you have chosen to spend the Sabbath with me after all," the innkeeper says as he helps Herschel unsaddle his horse.

Herschel, he is in despair, but he knows to respect an invitation, so he says, "I'd be honored."

The innkeeper's wife—a girl whom Herschel had not seen during either of his previous visits—greets him before the hearth. She sprinkles salt on the table, brings out a challah, wine, and candles. The innkeeper says the blessings and Herschel joins in, his voice hoarse with grief over his failure. The Sabbath meal is a thick bean and bread soup, and despite himself, Herschel enjoys both it and the innkeeper's wife's quiet chatter.

When he turns in for the evening, though, he cannot rest. His mind turns over all that has happened to him, and he can find no reason for the confusion that has led him in circles. He rises to walk outside, for in the past, walking in the night air has calmed him. When he steps outside, he sees the innkeeper, holy book in hand, reading at the foot of the mountain, while from the sky comes a shaft of light. Looks, maybe, like a sunbeam and falls on the ground where he stands, a soft gray at his ankles, but as the light travels up his body, it grows brighter and whiter, till his head and the blond curls there are in the purest of white light, so pure that it hurts Herschel's eyes, and he has to look down to the man's feet, which are no longer quite on the ground.

All through this long story, Rachel had watched the rabbi's shadow and not the man himself. She turned to him now and let herself wish (out loud) that he'd stay with her forever. It was a kind of a love she felt for him, she supposed. Since he'd arrived, she'd been forming the idea—it only emerged into full consciousness now, with his story—of the rabbi as some version of Bess. Which meant, of course, Rachel wasn't as untethered from knowledge as she'd imagined herself earlier in the evening. What was a rabbi if not a source of wisdom?

"Me?" the rabbi said. "I'm just a visitor with you. I won't stay much longer. That's the point of the story."

"It is?" Rachel said. She'd been an English major in college and knew a little bit about literary interpretation. She didn't see one bit of evidence for the rabbi's reading of his own tale.

"It is," the rabbi said. "Absolutely."

She slept heavily, then woke in the middle of the night, wondering what the rabbi's story meant. She half-expected to turn and see him floating above his matchbox bed, his head consumed with ethereal light, but when she did peek over, he was fast asleep, his forefinger pressed to his chin, as if in contemplation of his next thought.

When she woke, the rabbi was gone.

"Oh, no," she cried. She hadn't thought he meant he was going to leave her so soon.

"Morning," Greta called and stuck her head into the bedroom. "Want some French toast? Is . . . What's the matter? You look upset."

"Nothing. Give me a few seconds, and I'll be out."

She showered and pulled on her clothes. As she went to get her lipstick from her bag, she heard a tiny *"Got mayner!"* Then a "Help!"

The rabbi was stuck in her wallet.

"What're you doing?"

"I was trying to get this," he said. He was pulling on a business card that she'd stuffed into her wallet. "The whole thing closed over on me."

Rachel freed the rabbi, then stuck him in her blouse pocket.

The card he'd been trying to get was for Rosengren & Sons. "Remember, you've got to go see this Jeremy fellow."

"What?" Rachel looked at the card. "Oh, that's right. The man in Bess's apartment building. I'm pretty sure Greta's already got someone to make the marker."

But she didn't, it turned out. So as they sat at breakfast, eating their French toast, Rachel passed the card over to Greta and said, "I know it's a schlep. But let's go over to Long Island and see what this guy's stuff looks like. I hear he does good work."

Greta shrugged an OK. "Oh," she cried, "I almost forgot. I have something for you." She went out of the room and came back with a big wrapped box.

"What is it?"

"It's a present. For you."

Rachel felt the lie of this instantly. Greta's presents were invariably because Greta liked to shop, not because Greta had divined something Rachel wanted.

Philip came in. "Morning," he said, taking a gulp of coffee. Everything about the man seemed parsimonious. Too selfish to even add a "good" to his "morning."

"So open it already," Greta said of the present.

It was a toaster. But not just a toaster. It was a toaster that was more like a village, with a built-in clock, a mini oven, and a microwave.

"Greta," Rachel said, regretting the whine in her own voice, "I don't have room for this. You've seen my place."

"But you've been doing your toast in the oven. You told me yourself."

"I just don't need it. You're always getting me things I don't need."

Greta huffed. "You know the reason you're not married is you don't want to grow up. Grown-ups have toasters. It doesn't mean you've become a part of the capitalist patriarchy. It just means you can have some toast for breakfast." It was true Rachel resisted owning things. And that she had never liked change. It was a family joke that she'd wept—at age six—when they'd traded in the old two-door sedan for the four-door Buick. "But I like the old one," she'd kept crying.

"Say thank you," Philip said. "Why can't you just say thank you?"

Rachel stared at him with open dislike. He'd always felt optional—not like real family—and when Greta said things that made Rachel wonder about their marriage, she didn't have any fearful sense of what would happen to her sister's world if they split up. When her parents and when Mamie had died, it was as if piece by piece, the foundation below Rachel crumbled, and now she was just a house floating in air. When Philip went away, everything felt more, rather than less, solid, like things were returning to their natural way of being.

Rachel didn't say thank you. She turned from Philip and said evenly, "How am I going to be able to carry this on the train?"

"You never heard of the mail?" Greta said. "I'll mail it to you."

*　　*　　*

"You wanna drive?" Greta offered, as they headed for the car. It wasn't an apology, but it was something. Neither sister liked to be the passenger when the other was driving. Greta thought Rachel rode the brake too much. Rachel thought Greta was always about to plow into the car in front of her.

"No, thanks. You'll never be able to read this." Rachel lifted the paper onto which she had scribbled directions to the Rosengren & Sons shed. After the contretemps about the toaster, she'd gone to call Jeremy Rosengren.

"My granddad said to come down here?" Jeremy had asked affably. "That doesn't sound right. We've got a showroom in town. The number's 824-8120." But when Rachel called, an answering machine said they were closed for the week. Rachel called Jeremy back. "Closed?" he said, dumbfounded. "Well, you can come down here if you want. I've got a book of monuments—photos of the things we've done in the last few years—but it'd be better to wait the week." Rachel explained her situation—only in town for a few days. "Well, OK," Jeremy said cautiously, "though it's not the way we normally do it."

Greta navigated from New Jersey to Long Island, then Rachel took over, consulting her directions, and getting progressively more carsick as they drove. There was something impossibly hard to take about the way shops and chain stores were heaped up on the side of the roads here. And then there were the endless signs screaming about sales and bargains.

"Why is it Long Island always makes me want to barf?"

"You really are turning into a Maine girl."

"Should it say anything?"

"What?"

"The marker. Should it say anything, or should it just have Bess's name and the dates?"

"What would it say?"

"I don't know. 'She was loved.' Something like that."

"But we didn't write anything on any of the other markers. If hers says something, then it'll be like the others weren't loved."

"I suppose. But she was."

"Was what?"

"Loved."

"Well, I know that. Why are we arguing about that?"

"I don't know." Rachel felt abruptly like crying.

They finally found the dilapidated building that was Rosengren & Sons located behind a large office supply store in Port Washington. At least they found a big wooden shed with a chipping, rusty sign announcing MONUMENTS–MARKERS–LETTERING–REPAIR. The slabs of granite by the entrance door offered their own clue that they'd come to the right place.

They pushed through the door. Inside, there was some sort of pit, surrounded by corrugated metal. Two giant cranes hovered above. An unidentifiable mechanical whirring came from somewhere deep within the room. There were three large stones in the pit before them. To their left stood a few battered old wooden chairs and a desk cluttered with Styrofoam cups and soda cans.

"They're supposed to do excellent work," Rachel added, half-apologetic, though, of course, she didn't know if this was true. She called into the room, "Jeremy?"

"Un-huh," a voice answered, and a head stuck out from behind the largest of the three stones in the pit. "That's me. Are you Rachel?"

"Yes—you gave me directions this morning?"

"That was me."

Jeremy wiped his hands on an old gray rag, then came toward them, his hand extended. He was tall and slim, with a big grin that seemed less about his happiness to meet her than his amusement at something—perhaps his own ears, which stuck out of his head and made him look all the more goofily pleased by the world. "Normally people go to the sales office to see the markers, but I can show you stuff. Have a seat." He gestured to the chairs near them.

You wouldn't expect a man who deals in death all day to be so happy, Rachel thought.

As if he'd divined her thoughts, Jeremy smiled and said, "It's good to be in the business of helping people remember their loved ones. Let me show you some of your choices." He pulled a three-ring notebook out of a drawer. Greta held her arms out to receive the book, but he passed it into Rachel's hands.

"We'll look together," Rachel said and started flipping through the pages.

Greta explained, "We already have a family monument with the last name, so we're just looking for a marker with her name and dates." She sounded defensive, as if she expected Jeremy to try to talk her into more than what she wanted. "And she just died, so the unveiling is still a year away."

"Your grandfather told us to come to you. He lives in the same building with Bess. Where she used to live, I mean." Rachel was quiet, then added, "Of course."

Jeremy scratched the back of his head contemplatively. "And did he say I should give you a big discount?" His voice took on his grandfather's inflections, and he gave two brief karate chops to the air, as if marking out a space in front of his chest where the words might hang.

Rachel had been wondering how she'd slip that piece of information into the conversation. She bobbed her head.

"Of course," Jeremy said. Rachel thought of the small business card that Philip always flashed at the crowded fish restaurant where he and Greta liked to eat. It said that he was a friend of the owner and should be seated right away. Philip always flipped the card out of his wallet rather grandly, and the waitress nodded at the card; probably the owner gave them to everyone he met.

"Well, " Jeremy went on, "normally I just do the carving. I'm not in sales. But, sure, you can have a big discount." He smiled. "There's a reason I'm not in sales."

Greta looked at him uncertainly.

"Your grandma. Was she the one who always made raisin kugel?" The sisters shook their head no.

"And she wasn't in the book group?"

"No, she was," Rachel said. "The Jewish book group?"

"Yeah, that always cracked me up. They would only read biographies. 'What about a novel?' I'd say to my grandfather. 'There are lots of good Jewish novels out there.'

"'You never heard that truth is stranger than fiction?' he'd say. 'I stick to the strange stuff.'"

Greta cleared her throat and pointed to the book before them. "Maybe we should get back to . . ."

"Un-huh. Well, we can set the stone whenever. That's allowed. You'll see there are more formal and less formal things in there. We can do it as plain as you want, though normally there's a candelabra for the women. Sometimes words."

"Like what words?" Rachel said, livening at this suggestion. Even if the others didn't have anything, she wanted something for Bess.

"Normally we write—in Hebrew—'May her soul be bound with the bundle of light.'"

Rachel looked at Jeremy and smiled.

"That's it. That's exactly what I want."

Greta looked at Rachel. She had never known her sister to make a quick decision. "Well, then," she said, "I can't disagree."

When people asked, and they inevitably did ask, "How did you meet your husband?", this was the story that Rachel told, the story of picking out the gravestone marker; the way she'd thrilled to Jeremy's suggestion about the words for Bess. "May her soul be bound with the bundle of light." Yes, exactly, as if Bess had resurrected herself, for one tiny moment, in the form of this stranger, to remind Rachel that she wanted to comport herself in death as in life. By looking on the sunny side, and all that. But there was more, of course. There was the tentative way Jeremy called Rachel, later that day, and apologizing profusely, asked if she wouldn't like to have dinner sometime. And the way she, also apologizing, since she had to go back to work that Monday, said, "How about right now?" She had liked the anecdote about the book club. They had met halfway, taking the respective trains in from Long Island and New Jersey, and ate at Grand Central's

Oyster Bar, so they wouldn't have to waste any time walking around finding a place. He'd ordered French onion soup and spooned it onto his fettuccini. Rachel grimaced. "This sticking to the strange stuff runs in the family, I see."

Jeremy shrugged and put his spoon down. She shouldn't have been rude. Still, before their dinner was up, he had taken Rachel's hand and said, "Will you see me again? If you just say yes, then I don't have to worry about asking you later." They'd exchanged phone numbers and e-mails, and Rachel had come back to the city the very next week. It wasn't so easy conducting a romance in front of a rabbi, and she'd left her friend tucked into a drawer at Greta's for that second date. Then Jeremy came to Maine. They'd gone for a walk around the bay in Portland, Rachel pointing out the lighthouses and fireboats, Jeremy thrilling at the most ordinary things: the pile of lobster traps behind a restaurant, the friendliness of people on their path. Already they were writing their own history. "I just felt I had to see you again," Jeremy said about what had impelled him to call her, at Greta's, the night of their first meeting. He was usually quite shy with girls.

They married at a nature center in Maine. After the wedding ceremony, Rachel and Jeremy were conducted to a small room—it was normally some sort of administrative office—where they were expected to spend their first married moments relating to one another, before the onslaught of the party that Greta and Jeremy's family had planned.

Jeremy kissed Rachel. "Don't hold it against me that these are my first words to you as a husband."

"Yeah?"

"I really got to use the bathroom."

Rachel laughed. "Go down the back hall—then you can use the one upstairs without anyone seeing you."

Jeremy rolled his eyes at himself, hummed a line of "Isn't It Romantic?" and hurried out the door. All Rachel's clothes from the morning—her handbag and her summer dress—were piled on a filing cabinet. Outside, two bright yellow goldfinches were perched on a bird feeder. She turned for her handbag and took out the little rabbi.

"It was beautiful. I'm sorry you couldn't have heard it. But it went so fast. I can't believe it's over." Jeremy's dad had tripped when he stood to read the blessing, and there was an uneasy tittering until everyone realized he wasn't hurt. Her two nephews had made very cute flower boys, not scattering the petals, but throwing them over their heads like confetti.

"Mazel tov," the rabbi said. "Remember you once asked me what sort of miracles I do?"

"Yes?"

"I can make a man who doesn't have to go to the bathroom go to the bathroom."

"Oh," she said. "I think I can do that, too. I learned this trick at summer camp where you put a kid's hand in warm water, not that I'd ever—"

"I have a story to tell you."

"Now?" She had yet to be in the position of not wanting to hear the rabbi's words, but at the moment her mind was on other things.

He paid no attention to the incredulity in her voice and began in the same measured tones he'd begun all his stories. "*Feigele*, you will think this a strange story to tell you on your wedding day, for it is a terrible tale. You know, of course, the world is full of horrors, and for the Jews that has meant, at times, a pogrom. You know pogrom?"

"I know what it is, if that's what you're asking. I haven't, you know, myself, personally—knock wood and all—ever been subjected to a—"

"I'll tell you about Mendel Agar, who had a wife who he loved beyond all reason. His hand was always in hers, if you came to call at the house. If she stood to do a chore, he would rise to help, and she would do the same for him."

"Oh, so this is going to be Mendel Agar's tips for the newly married?"

The rabbi held up a little finger, as if to indicate she shouldn't have interrupted. "But if you chanced to come on a Sabbath, you would see a very peculiar sight. They prayed together at home, but when they prayed, they looked like one who was dead. Their breathing became so slow it seemed to stop, and their skin turned cool. One day a visitor presumed them dead and sent for help, but when the help came, the couple was awake and blowing away the smoke of the Havdalah candle.

"Mendel, he lives in Russia, and comes to Russia a terrible time for the Jews. One evening, a band of men arrive, and they give him this choice: You give to us the Jewish boys of your classroom, we want to have ourselves a little massacre, or we kill you. In the morning, the men will come for the boys."

"Mendel's a schoolteacher?"

"Yes, didn't I say?"

"Like me."

"No, not like you. Did I say like you? Listen. The next day the men come for Mendel, but they find him . . . already dead. And his wife, too. Or so it seems, for the two are deep in prayer, sending up their soul's voices to God, so this terrible thing, it should not be. Into their prayers comes the knowledge that the boys will be killed anyway. Mendel's choice, they understand, is no choice at all. So they pray for the souls of the boys. And for their own souls. They pray no one else will be hurt. They pray so long and so hard that their breath gets slower and slower and slower; their cheeks grow paler and paler and paler. Then they stop.

"It has never been done before, this thing that Mendel and his wife have done, but they have done it. They have prayed themselves into oblivion. Now when a neighbor chances by and thinks they are dead, they really are dead."

"You sound impressed," Rachel says.

"God gives burdens—also shoulders."

"Dead shoulders," Rachel thinks to say, but she hasn't planned for theological debate on her wedding day.

"So *bubele*," the rabbi says, then scurries up her arm and onto her shoulder, so he can reach over to pat her turned cheek with his dime-sized hand, "you let me finish, no?"

Rachel smiles a yes—she has routinely had his whole body in her hand, moving him from here to there, but this is the first time he's actually touched her. She returns the rabbi to the desk before her, and he seats himself on a stack of brochures that read NATURE DISCOVERY PROGRAMS. "Mendel and his wife, their souls are not easy, and as good as they were in their days on earth, they do not enter into the Everlasting. First, Mendel is reborn into the home of a New York gravestone engraver, and his wife is reborn into the home of a pharmacist in New Jersey. All their days they feel as if they are looking for someone, and all their days they never find this person. Other people marry and have children, and still they are alone, or talking with those who can never truly understand their words. It happens this way for many years. They once almost meet by the side of a lake in Maine, where the boy has gone with a friend for a week away from the city. They once almost meet in a subway car that grinds to a halt on a hot summer day. They once see each other in a sporting goods store, where she is buying sneakers and he is purchasing a basketball. Then, but you know the end of the story yourself—"

Rachel turned to the sound of Jeremy coming back through the door. She was still half-smiling at what the rabbi had to say, and not yet thinking to hide him back in her purse. She had planned to tell Jeremy about the rabbi sooner or later. But when she swiveled back to thank the rabbi for his story, he was gone, his little yarmulke and prayer shawl were gone, and it was time for the couple to go out to join their guests for a piece of chocolate cake.

Stephen King

The Reach

"The Reach was wider in those days," Stella Flanders told her great-grandchildren in the last summer of her life, the summer before she began to see ghosts. The children looked at her with wide, silent eyes, and her son, Alden, turned from his seat on the porch where he was whittling. It was Sunday, and Alden wouldn't take his boat out on Sundays no matter how high the price of lobster was.

"What do you mean, Gram?" Hal asked, but the old woman did not answer. She only sat in her rocker by the cold stove, her slippers bumping placidly on the floor.

Hal asked his mother: "What does she mean?"

Lois only shook her head, smiled, and sent them out with pots to pick berries.

Stella thought: She's forgot. Or did she ever know?

The Reach had been wider in those days. If anyone knew it was so, that person was Stella Flanders. She had been born in 1884, she was the oldest resident of Goat Island, and she had never once in her life been to the mainland.

Do you love? This question had begun to plague her, and she did not even know what it meant.

Fall set in, a cold fall without the necessary rain to bring a really fine color to the trees, either on Goat or on Raccoon Head across the Reach. The wind blew long, cold notes that fall, and Stella felt each note resonate in her heart.

On November 19, when the first flurries came swirling down out of a sky the color of white chrome, Stella celebrated her birthday.

Most of the village turned out. Hattie Stoddard came, whose mother had died of pleurisy in 1954 and whose father had been lost with the *Dancer* in 1941. Richard and Mary Dodge came, Richard moving slowly up the path on his cane, his arthritis riding him like an invisible passenger. Sarah Havelock came, of course; Sarah's mother Annabelle had been Stella's best friend. They had gone to the island school together, grades one to eight, and Annabelle had married Tommy Frane, who had pulled her hair in the fifth grade and made her cry, just as Stella had married Bill Flanders, who had once knocked all of her schoolbooks out of her arms and into the mud (but she had managed not to cry). Now both Annabelle and Tommy were gone and Sarah was the only one of their seven children still on the island. *Her* husband, George Havelock, who had been known to everyone as Big George, had died a nasty death over on the mainland in 1967, the year there was no fishing. An ax had slipped in Big George's hand, there had been blood—too much of it!—and an island funeral three days later. And when Sarah came in to Stella's party and cried, "Happy birthday, Gram!" Stella hugged her tight and closed her eyes

(*do you do you love?*)

but she did not cry.

There was a tremendous birthday cake. Hattie had made it with her best friend, Vera Spruce. The assembled company bellowed out "Happy Birthday to You" in a combined voice that was loud enough to drown out the wind . . . for a little while, anyway. Even Alden sang, who in the normal course of events would sing only "Onward, Christian Soldiers" and the doxology in church and would mouth the words of all the rest with his head hunched and his big old jug ears just as red as tomatoes. There were ninety-five candles on Stella's cake, and even over the singing she heard the wind, although her hearing was not what it once had been.

She thought the wind was calling her name.

"I was not the only one," she would have told Lois's children if she could. "In my day there were many that lived and died on the island. There was no mail boat in those days; Bull Symes used to bring the mail when there was mail. There was no

*ferry, either. If you had business on the Head, your man took you in the lobster boat.
So far as I know, there wasn't a flushing toilet on the island until 1946. 'Twas Bull's
boy Harold that put in the first one the year after the heart attack carried Bull off
while he was out dragging traps. I remember seeing them bring Bull home. I remember
that they brought him up wrapped in a tarpaulin, and how one of his green boots
poked out. I remember . . ."*

And they would say: *"What, Gram? What do you remember?"*

How would she answer them? Was there more?

On the first day of winter, a month or so after the birthday party,
Stella opened the back door to get stovewood and discovered a dead
sparrow on the back stoop. She bent down carefully, picked it up by
one foot, and looked at it.

"Frozen," she announced, and something inside her spoke another
word. It had been forty years since she had seen a frozen bird—1938.
The year the Reach had frozen.

Shuddering, pulling her coat closer, she threw the dead sparrow
in the old rusty incinerator as she went by it. The day was cold. The
sky was a clear, deep blue. On the night of her birthday four inches of
snow had fallen, had melted, and no more had come since then. "Got
to come soon," Larry McKeen down at the Goat Island Store said
sagely, as if daring winter to stay away.

Stella got to the woodpile, picked herself an armload and carried
it back to the house. Her shadow, crisp and clean, followed her.

As she reached the back door, where the sparrow had fallen, Bill
spoke to her—but the cancer had taken Bill twelve years before.
"Stella," Bill said, and she saw his shadow fall beside her, longer but
just as clear-cut, the shadow-bill of his shadow-cap twisted jauntily off
to one side just as he had always worn it. Stella felt a scream lodged
in her throat. It was too large to touch her lips.

"Stella," he said again, "when you comin' 'cross to the mainland?
We'll get Norm Jolley's old Ford and go down to Bean's in Freeport just
for a lark. What do you say?"

She wheeled, almost dropping her wood, and there was no one
there. Just the dooryard sloping down to the hill, then the wild white

grass, and beyond all, at the edge of everything, clear-cut and somehow magnified, the Reach . . . and the mainland beyond it.

"Gram, what's the Reach?" Lona might have asked . . . although she never had. And she would have given them the answer any fisherman knew by rote: a Reach is a body of water between two bodies of land, a body of water that is open at either end. The old lobsterman's joke went like this: know how to read y'compass when the fog comes, boys; between Jonesport and London there's a mighty long Reach.

"Reach is the water between the island and the mainland," she might have amplified, giving them molasses cookies and hot tea laced with sugar. "I know that much. I know it as well as my husband's name . . . and how he used to wear his hat."

"Gram?" Lona would say. "How come you never been across the Reach?"

"Honey," she would say, "I never saw any reason to go."

In January, two months after the birthday party, the Reach froze for the first time since 1938. The radio warned islanders and mainlanders alike not to trust the ice, but Stewie McClelland and Russell Bowie took Stewie's Bombardier Skiddoo out anyway, after a long afternoon spent drinking Apple Zapple wine, and sure enough, the Skiddoo went into the Reach. Stewie managed to crawl out (although he lost one foot to frostbite). The Reach took Russell Bowie and carried him away.

That January 25 there was a memorial service for Russell. Stella went on her son Alden's arm, and he mouthed the words to the hymns and boomed out the doxology in his great tuneless voice before the benediction. Stella sat afterward with Sarah Havelock and Hattie Stoddard and Vera Spruce in the glow of the wood fire in the town-hall basement. A going-away party for Russell was being held, complete with Za-Rex punch and nice little cream-cheese sandwiches cut into triangles. The men, of course, kept wandering out back for a nip of something a bit stronger than Za-Rex. Russell Bowie's new widow sat red-eyed and stunned beside Ewell McCracken, the minister. She was seven months big with child—it would be her fifth—and Stella, half-dozing in the heat of the woodstove, thought: *She'll be crossing the Reach soon enough, I guess. She'll move to Freeport or Lewiston and go for a waitress, I guess.*

She looked around at Vera and Hattie, to see what the discussion was.

"No, I didn't hear," Hattie said. "What *did* Freddy say?"

They were talking about Freddy Dinsmore, the oldest man on the island (two years younger'n me, though, Stella thought with some satisfaction), who had sold out his store to Larry McKeen in 1960 and now lived on his retirement.

"Said he'd never seen such a winter," Vera said, taking out her knitting. "He says it is going to make people sick."

Sarah Havelock looked at Stella, and asked if Stella had ever seen such a winter. There had been no snow since that first little bit; the ground lay crisp and bare and brown. The day before, Stella had walked thirty paces into the back field, holding her right hand level at the height of her thigh, and the grass there had snapped in a neat row with a sound like breaking glass.

"No," Stella said. "The Reach froze in '38, but there was snow that year. Do you remember Bull Symes, Hattie?"

Hattie laughed. "I think I still have the black-and-blue he gave me on my sit-upon at the New Year's party in '53. He pinched me *that* hard. What about him?"

"Bull and my own man walked across to the mainland that year," Stella said. "That February of 1938. Strapped on snowshoes, walked across to Dorrit's Tavern on the Head, had them each a shot of whiskey, and walked back. They asked me to come along. They were like two little boys off to the sliding with a toboggan between them."

They were looking at her, touched by the wonder of it. Even Vera was looking at her wide-eyed, and Vera had surely heard the tale before. If you believed the stories, Bull and Vera had once played some house together, although it was hard, looking at Vera now, to believe she had ever been so young.

"And you didn't go?" Sarah asked, perhaps seeing the reach of the Reach in her mind's eye, so white it was almost blue in the heatless winter sunshine, the sparkle of the snow crystals, the mainland drawing closer, walking across, yes, walking across the ocean just like Jesus-out-of-the-boat, leaving the island for the one and only time in your life on *foot*—

"No," Stella said. Suddenly she wished she had brought her own knitting. "I didn't go with them."

"Why *not?*" Hattie asked, almost indignantly.

"It was washday," Stella almost snapped, and then Missy Bowie, Russell's widow, broke into loud, braying sobs. Stella looked over and there sat Bill Flanders in his red-and-black-checked jacket, hat cocked to one side, smoking a Herbert Tareyton with another tucked behind his ear for later. She felt her heart leap into her chest and choke between beats.

She made a noise, but just then a knot popped like a rifle shot in the stove, and neither of the other ladies heard.

"Poor *thing*," Sarah nearly cooed.

"Well shut of that good-for-nothing," Hattie grunted. She searched for the grim depth of the truth concerning the departed Russell Bowie and found it: "Little more than a tramp for pay, that man. She's well out of *that* two-hoss trace."

Stella barely heard these things. There sat Bill, close enough to the Reverend McCracken to have tweaked his nose if he so had a mind; he looked no more than forty, his eyes barely marked by the crow's-feet that had later sunk so deep, wearing his flannel pants and his gum-rubber boots with the gray wool socks folded neatly down over the tops.

"We're waitin' on you, Stel," he said. "You come on across and see the mainland. You won't need no snowshoes this year."

There he sat in the town-hall basement, big as Billy-be-damned, and then another knot exploded in the stove and he was gone. And the Reverend McCracken went on comforting Missy Bowie as if nothing had happened.

That night Vera called up Annie Phillips on the phone, and in the course of the conversation mentioned to Annie that Stella Flanders didn't look well, not at all well.

"Alden would have a scratch of a job getting her off-island if she took sick," Annie said. Annie liked Alden because her own son Toby had told her Alden would take nothing stronger than beer. Annie was strictly temperance, herself.

"Wouldn't get her off 'tall unless she was in a coma," Vera said, pronouncing the word in the downeast fashion: *comer.* "When Stella says 'Frog,' Alden jumps. Alden ain't but half-bright, you know. Stella pretty much runs him."

"Oh, ayuh?" Annie said.

Just then there was a metallic crackling sound on the line. Vera could hear Annie Phillips for a moment longer—not the words, just the sound of her voice going on behind the crackling—and then there was nothing. The wind had gusted up high and the phone lines had gone down, maybe into Godlin's Pond or maybe down by Borrow's Cove, where they went into the Reach sheathed in rubber. It was possible that they had gone down on the other side, on the Head . . . and some might even have said (only half-joking) that Russell Bowie had reached up a cold hand to snap the cable, just for the hell of it.

Not 700 feet away Stella Flanders lay under her puzzle-quilt and listened to the dubious music of Alden's snores in the other room. She listened to Alden so she wouldn't have to listen to the wind . . . but she heard the wind anyway, oh yes, coming across the frozen expanse of the Reach, a mile and a half of water that was now overplated with ice, ice with lobsters down below, and groupers, and perhaps the twisting, dancing body of Russell Bowie, who used to come each April with his old Rogers rototiller and turn her garden.

Who'll turn the earth this April? she wondered as she lay cold and curled under her puzzle-quilt. And as a dream in a dream, her voice answered her voice: *Do you love?* The wind gusted, rattling the storm window. It seemed that the storm window was talking to her, but she turned her face away from its words. And did not cry.

"But Gram," Lona would press (she never gave up, not that one, she was like her mom, and her grandmother before her), "you still haven't told why you never went across."

"Why, child, I have always had everything I wanted right here on Goat."

"But it's so small. We live in Portland. There's buses, Gram!"

"I see enough of what goes on in cities on the TV. I guess I'll stay where I am."

Hal was younger, but somehow more intuitive; he would not press her as his sister might, but his question would go closer to the heart of things: "You never wanted to go across, Gram? Never?"

And she would lean toward him, and take his small hands, and tell him how her mother and father had come to the island shortly after they were married, and how Bull Symes's grandfather had taken Stella's father as a 'prentice on his boat. She would tell him how her mother had conceived four times but one of her babies had miscarried and another had died a week after birth—she would have left the island if they could have saved it at the mainland hospital, but of course it was over before that was even thought of.

She would tell them that Bill had delivered Jane, their grandmother, but not that when it was over he had gone into the bathroom and first puked and then wept like a hysterical woman who had her monthlies p'ticularly bad. Jane, of course, had left the island at fourteen to go to high school; girls didn't get married at fourteen anymore, and when Stella saw her go off in the boat with Bradley Maxwell, whose job it had been to ferry the kids back and forth that month, she knew in her heart that Jane was gone for good, although she would come back for a while. She would tell them that Alden had come along ten years later, after they had given up, and as if to make up for his tardiness, here was Alden still, a lifelong bachelor, and in some ways Stella was grateful for that because Alden was not terribly bright and there are plenty of women willing to take advantage of a man with a slow brain and a good heart (although she would not tell the children that last, either).

She would say: "Louis and Margaret Godlin begat Stella Godlin, who became Stella Flanders; Bill and Stella Flanders begat Jane and Alden Flanders and Jane Flanders became Jane Wakefield; Richard and Jane Wakefield begat Lois Wakefield, who became Lois Perrault; David and Lois Perrault begat Lona and Hal. Those are your names, children: you are Godlin-Flanders-Wakefield-Perrault. Your blood is in the stones of this island, and I stay here because the mainland is too far to reach. Yes, I love; I have loved, anyway, or at least tried to love, but memory is so wide and so deep, and I cannot cross. Godlin-Flanders-Wakefield-Perrault . . ."

That was the coldest February since the National Weather Service began keeping records, and by the middle of the month the ice covering the Reach was safe. Snowmobiles buzzed and whined and sometimes turned over when they climbed the ice-heaves wrong. Children tried to skate, found the ice too bumpy to be any fun, and went back to Godlin's Pond on the far side of the hill, but not before little Justin McCracken, the minister's son, caught his skate in a fissure and broke his ankle. They took him over to the hospital on the mainland where a doctor who owned a Corvette told him, "Son, it's going to be as good as new."

Freddy Dinsmore died very suddenly just three days after Justin McCracken broke his ankle. He caught the flu late in January, would not have the doctor, told everyone it was "Just a cold from goin' out to get the mail without m'scarf," took to his bed, and died before anyone could take him across to the mainland and hook him up to all those machines they have waiting for guys like Freddy. His son George, a tosspot of the first water even at the advanced age (for tosspots, anyway) of sixty-eight, found Freddy with a copy of the *Bangor Daily News* in one hand and his Remington, unloaded, near the other. Apparently he had been thinking of cleaning it just before he died. George Dinsmore went on a three-week toot, said toot financed by someone who knew that George would have his old dad's insurance money coming. Hattie Stoddard went around telling anyone who would listen that old George Dinsmore was a sin and a disgrace, no better than a tramp for pay.

There was a lot of flu around. The school closed for two weeks that February instead of the usual one because so many pupils were out sick. "No snow breeds germs," Sarah Havelock said.

Near the end of the month, just as people were beginning to look forward to the false comfort of March, Alden Flanders caught the flu himself. He walked around with it for nearly a week and then took to his bed with a fever of a hundred and one. Like Freddy, he refused to have the doctor, and Stella stewed and fretted and worried. Alden was not as old as Freddy, but that May he would turn sixty.

The snow came at last. Six inches on Valentine's Day, another six on the twentieth, and a foot in a good old norther on the leap,

February 29. The snow lay white and strange between the cove and the mainland, like a sheep's meadow where there had been only gray and surging water at this time of year since time out of mind. Several people walked across to the mainland and back. No snowshoes were necessary this year because the snow had frozen to a firm, glittery crust. They might take a knock of whiskey, too, Stella thought, but they would not take it at Dorrit's. Dorrit's had burned down in 1958.

And she saw Bill all four times. Once he told her: "Y'ought to come soon, Stella. We'll go steppin'. What do you say?"

She could say nothing. Her fist was crammed deep into her mouth.

"Everything I ever wanted or needed was here," she would tell them. "We had the radio and now we have the television, and that's all I want of the world beyond the Reach. I had my garden year in and year out. And lobster? Why, we always used to have a pot of lobster stew on the back of the stove and we used to take it off and put it behind the door in the pantry when the minister came calling so he wouldn't see we were eating 'poor man's soup.'

"I have seen good weather and bad, and if there were times when I wondered what it might be like to actually be in the Sears store instead of ordering from the cat- alog, or to go into one of those Shaw's markets I see on TV instead of buying at the store here or sending Alden across for something special like a Christmas capon or an Easter ham . . . or if I ever wanted, just once, to stand on Congress Street in Portland and watch all the people in their cars and on the sidewalks, more people in a single look than there are on the whole island these days . . . if I ever wanted those things, then I wanted this more. I am not strange. I am not peculiar, or even very eccentric for a woman of my years. My mother sometimes used to say, 'All the difference in the world is between work and want,' and I believe that to my very soul. I believe it is better to plow deep than wide.

"This is my place, and I love it."

One day in middle March, with the sky as white and lowering as a loss of memory, Stella Flanders sat in her kitchen for the last time, laced up her boots over her skinny calves for the last time, and wrapped her bright red woolen scarf (a Christmas present from Hattie three Christmases past) around her neck for the last time. She wore a suit of Alden's long underwear under her dress. The waist of the drawers came up to just below the limp vestiges of her breasts, the shirt almost down to her knees.

Outside, the wind was picking up again, and the radio said there would be snow by afternoon. She put on her coat and her gloves. After a moment of debate, she put a pair of Alden's gloves on over her own. Alden had recovered from the flu, and this morning he and Harley Blood were over rehanging a storm door for Missy Bowie, who had had a girl. Stella had seen it, and the unfortunate little mite looked just like her father.

She stood at the window for a moment, looking out at the Reach, and Bill was there as she had suspected he might be, standing about halfway between the island and the Head, standing on the Reach just like Jesus-out-of-the-boat, beckoning to her, seeming to tell her by gesture that the time was late if she ever intended to step a foot on the mainland in this life.

"If it's what you want, Bill," she fretted in silence. "God knows I don't."

But the wind spoke other words. She did want to. She wanted to have this adventure. It had been a painful winter for her—the arthritis, which came and went irregularly, was back with a vengeance, flaring the joints of her fingers and knees with red fire and blue ice. One of her eyes had gotten dim and blurry (and just the other day Sarah had mentioned—with some unease—that the firespot that had been there since Stella was sixty or so now seemed to be growing by leaps and bounds). Worst of all, the deep, griping pain in her stomach had returned, and two mornings before she had gotten up at five o'clock, worked her way along the exquisitely cold floor into the bathroom, and had spat a great wad of bright red blood into the toilet bowl. This morning there had been some more of it, foul-tasting stuff, coppery and shuddersome.

The stomach pain had come and gone over the last five years, sometimes better, sometimes worse, and she had known almost from the beginning that it must be cancer. It had taken her mother and father and her mother's father as well. None of them had lived past seventy, and so she supposed she had beat the tables those insurance fellows kept by a carpenter's yard.

"You eat like a horse," Alden told her, grinning, not long after the pains had begun and she had first observed the blood in her morning stool. "Don't you know that old fogies like you are supposed to be peckish?"

"Get on or I'll swat ye!" Stella had answered, raising a hand to her gray-haired son, who ducked, mock-cringed, and cried: "Don't, Ma! I take it back!"

Yes, she had eaten hearty, not because she wanted to, but because she believed (as many of her generation did) that if you fed the cancer it would leave you alone. And perhaps it worked, at least for a while; the blood in her stools came and went, and there were long periods when it wasn't there at all. Alden got used to her taking second helpings (and thirds, when the pain was particularly bad), but she never gained a pound.

Now it seemed the cancer had finally gotten around to what the froggies called the *pièce de résistance.*

She started out the door and saw Alden's hat, the one with the fur-lined ear flaps, hanging on one of the pegs in the entry. She put it on—the bill came all the way down to her shaggy salt-and-pepper eyebrows—and then looked around one last time to see if she had forgotten anything. The stove was low, and Alden had left the draw open too much again—she told him and told him, but that was one thing he was just never going to get straight.

"Alden, you'll burn an extra quarter-cord a winter when I'm gone," she muttered, and opened the stove. She looked in and a tight, dismayed gasp escaped her. She slammed the door shut and adjusted the draw with trembling fingers. For a moment—just a moment—she had seen her old friend Annabelle Frane in the coals. It was her face to the life, even down to the mole on her cheek.

And had Annabelle winked at her?

She thought of leaving Alden a note to explain where she had gone, but she thought perhaps Alden would understand, in his own slow way.

Still writing notes in her head—*Since the first day of winter I have been seeing your father and he says dying isn't so bad; at least I think that's it*—Stella stepped out into the white day.

The wind shook her and she had to reset Alden's cap on her head before the wind could steal it for a joke and cartwheel it away. The cold seemed to find every chink in her clothing and twist into her; damp March cold with wet snow on its mind.

She set off down the hill toward the cove, being careful to walk on the cinders and clinkers that George Dinsmore had spread. Once George had gotten a job driving plow for the town of Raccoon Head, but during the big blow of '77 he had gotten smashed on rye whiskey and had driven the plow smack through not one, not two, but three power poles. There had been no lights over the Head for five days. Stella remembered now how strange it had been, looking across the Reach and seeing only blackness. A body got used to seeing that brave little nestle of lights. Now George worked on the island, and since there was no plow, he didn't get into much hurt.

As she passed Russell Bowie's house, she saw Missy, pale as milk, looking out at her. Stella waved. Missy waved back.

She would tell them this:

"On the island we always watched out for our own. When Gerd Henreid broke the blood vessel in his chest that time, we had covered-dish suppers one whole summer to pay for his operation in Boston—and Gerd came back alive, thank God. When George Dinsmore ran down those power poles and the Hydro slapped a lien on his home, it was seen to that the Hydro had their money and George had enough of a job to keep him in cigarettes and booze . . . why not? He was good for nothing else when his workday was done, although when he was on the clock he would work like a dray-horse. That one time he got into trouble was because it was at night, and night was always George's drinking time. His father kept him fed, at least. Now Missy Bowie's alone with another baby. Maybe she'll stay here and take her welfare and ADC money here, and most likely it won't be enough, but she'll get the help she needs. Probably she'll go, but if she stays she'll not starve . . . and listen, Lona and Hal: if she stays, she may be able to keep something of this small world with the little Reach on one side and the big Reach on the other, something it would be too easy to lose hus-

tling hash in Lewiston or donuts in Portland or drinks at the Nashville North in Bangor. And I am old enough not to beat around the bush about what that something might be: a way of being and a way of living—a feeling."

They had watched out for their own in other ways as well, but she would not tell them that. The children would not understand, nor would Lois and David, although Jane had known the truth. There was Norman and Ettie Wilson's baby that was born a mongoloid, its poor dear little feet turned in, its bald skull lumpy and cratered, its fingers webbed together as if it had dreamed too long and too deep while swimming that interior Reach; Reverend McCracken had come and baptized the baby, and a day later Mary Dodge came, who even at that time had midwived over a hundred babies, and Norman took Ettie down the hill to see Frank Child's new boat and although she could barely walk, Ettie went with no complaint, although she had stopped in the door to look back at Mary Dodge, who was sitting calmly by the idiot baby's crib and knitting. Mary had looked up at her and when their eyes met, Ettie burst into tears. "Come on," Norman had said, upset. "Come on, Ettie, come on." And when they came back an hour later the baby was dead, one of those crib-deaths, wasn't it merciful he didn't suffer. And many years before that, before the war, during the Depression, three little girls had been molested coming home from school, not badly molested, at least not where you could see the scar of the hurt, and they all told about a man who offered to show them a deck of cards he had with a different kind of dog on each one. He would show them this wonderful deck of cards, the man said, if the little girls would come into the bushes with him, and once in the bushes this man said, "But you have to touch this first." One of the little girls was Gert Symes, who would go on to be voted Maine's Teacher of the Year in 1978, for her work at Brunswick High. And Gert, then only five years old, told her father that the man had some fingers gone on one hand. One of the other little girls agreed that this was so. The third remembered nothing. Stella remembered Alden going out one thundery day that summer without telling her where he was going, although she asked. Watching from the window, she had seen Alden meet Bull Symes at the bottom of the path, and then Freddy Dinsmore had joined them and down at the cove she saw her own husband, whom she had sent out that morning just as usual, with his dinner pail under his arm. More men joined them, and when they finally moved off she counted just one under a dozen. The Reverend McCracken's predecessor had been among them. And that evening a fellow named Daniels was found at the foot of Slyder's Point, where the rocks poke out of the surf like the fangs of a dragon that drowned with its mouth open.

This Daniels was a fellow Big George Havelock had hired to help him put new sills under his house and a new engine in his Model A truck. From New Hampshire he was, and he was a sweet-talker who had found other odd jobs to do when the work at the Havelocks' was done . . . and in church, he could carry a tune! Apparently, they said, Daniels had been walking up on top of Slyder's Point and had slipped, tumbling all the way to the bottom. His neck was broken and his head was bashed in. As he had no people that anyone knew of, he was buried on the island, and the Reverend McCracken's predecessor gave the graveyard eulogy, saying as how this Daniels had been a hard worker and a good help even though he was two fingers shy on his right hand. Then he read the benediction and the graveside group had gone back to the town-hall basement where they drank Za-Rex punch and ate cream-cheese sandwiches, and Stella never asked her men where they had gone on the day Daniels fell from the top of Slyder's Point.

"Children," she would tell them, "we always watched out for our own. We had to, for the Reach was wider in those days and when the wind roared and the surf pounded and the dark came early, why, we felt very small—no more than dust motes in the mind of God. So it was natural for us to join hands, one with the other.

"We joined hands, children, and if there were times when we wondered what it was all for, or if there was ary such a thing as love at all, it was only because we had heard the wind and the waters on long winter nights, and we were afraid.

"No, I've never felt I needed to leave the island. My life was here. The Reach was wider in those days."

Stella reached the cove. She looked right and left, the wind blowing her dress out behind her like a flag. If anyone had been there she would have walked farther down and taken her chance on the tumbled rocks, although they were glazed with ice. But no one was there and she walked out along the pier, past the old Symes boathouse. She reached the end and stood there for a moment, head held up, the wind blowing past the padded flaps of Alden's hat in a muffled flood.

Bill was out there, beckoning. Beyond him, beyond the Reach, she could see the Congo Church over there on the Head, its spire almost invisible against the white sky.

Grunting, she sat down on the end of the pier and then stepped onto the snow crust below. Her boots sank a little; not much. She set

Alden's cap again—how the wind wanted to tear it off!—and began to walk toward Bill. She thought once that she would look back, but she did not. She didn't believe her heart could stand that.

She walked, her boots crunching into the crust, and listened to the faint thud and give of the ice. There was Bill, farther back now, but still beckoning. She coughed, spat blood onto the white snow that covered the ice. Now the Reach spread wide on either side and she could, for the first time in her life, read the "Stanton's Bait and Boat" sign over there without Alden's binoculars. She could see the cars passing to and fro on the Head's main street and thought with real wonder: *They can go as far as they want . . . Portland . . . Boston . . . New York City. Imagine!* And she could almost do it, could almost imagine a road that simply rolled on and on, the boundaries of the world knocked wide.

A snowflake skirled past her eyes. Another. A third. Soon it was snowing lightly and she walked through a pleasant world of shifting bright white; she saw Raccoon Head through a gauzy curtain that sometimes almost cleared. She reached up to set Alden's cap again and snow puffed off the bill into her eyes. The wind twisted fresh snow up in filmy shapes, and in one of them she saw Carl Abersham, who had gone down with Hattie Stoddard's husband on the *Dancer.*

Soon, however, the brightness began to dull as the snow came harder. The Head's main street dimmed, dimmed, and at last was gone. For a time longer she could make out the cross atop the church, and then that faded out too, like a false dream. Last to go was that bright yellow-and-black sign reading "Stanton's Bait and Boat," where you could also get engine oil, flypaper, Italian sandwiches, and Budweiser to go.

Then Stella walked in a world that was totally without color, a gray-white dream of snow. *Just like Jesus-out-of-the-boat,* she thought, and at last she looked back, but now the island was gone, too. She could see her tracks going back, losing definition until only the faint half-circles of her heels could be seen . . . and then nothing. Nothing at all.

She thought: *It's a whiteout. You got to be careful, Stella, or you'll never get to the mainland. You'll just walk around in a big circle until you're worn out and then you'll freeze to death out here.*

She remembered Bill telling her once that when you were lost in the woods, you had to pretend the leg that was on the same side of your body as your smart hand was lame. Otherwise that smart leg would begin to lead you and you'd walk in a circle and not even realize it until you came around to your backtrail again. Stella didn't believe she could afford to have that happen to her. Snow today, tonight, and tomorrow, the radio had said, and in a whiteout such as this, she would not even know if she came around to her backtrail, for the wind and the fresh snow would erase it long before she could return to it.

Her hands were leaving her in spite of the two pairs of gloves she wore, and her feet had been gone for some time. In a way, this was almost a relief. The numbness at least shut the mouth of her clamoring arthritis.

Stella began to limp now, making her left leg work harder. The arthritis in her knees had not gone to sleep, and soon they were screaming at her. Her white hair flew out behind her. Her lips had drawn back from her teeth (she still had her own, all save four) and she looked straight ahead, waiting for that yellow-and-black sign to materialize out of the flying whiteness.

It did not happen.

Sometime later, she noticed that the day's bright whiteness had begun to dull to a more uniform gray. The snow fell heavier and thicker than ever. Her feet were still planted on the crust, but now she was walking through five inches of fresh snow. She looked at her watch, but it had stopped. Stella realized she must have forgotten to wind it that morning for the first time in twenty or thirty years. Or had it just stopped for good? It had been her mother's and she had sent it with Alden twice to the Head, where Mr. Dostie had first marveled over it and then cleaned it. Her watch, at least, had been to the mainland.

She fell down for the first time some fifteen minutes after she began to notice the day's growing grayness. For a moment she remained on her hands and knees, thinking it would be so easy just to stay here, to curl up and listen to the wind, and then the determination that had brought her through so much reasserted itself and she got up, grimacing. She stood in the wind, looking straight ahead, willing her eyes to see . . . but they saw nothing.

Be dark soon.

Well, she had gone wrong. She had slipped off to one side or the other. Otherwise she would have reached the mainland by now. Yet she didn't believe she had gone so far wrong that she was walking parallel to the mainland or even back in the direction of Goat. An interior navigator in her head whispered that she had overcompensated and slipped off to the left. She believed she was still approaching the mainland but was now on a costly diagonal.

That navigator wanted her to turn right, but she would not do that. Instead, she moved straight on again, but stopped the artificial limp. A spasm of coughing shook her, and she spat bright red into the snow.

Ten minutes later (the gray was now deep indeed, and she found herself in the weird twilight of a heavy snowstorm) she fell again, tried to get up, failed at first, and finally managed to gain her feet. She stood swaying in the snow, barely able to remain upright in the wind, waves of faintness rushing through her head, making her feel alternately heavy and light.

Perhaps not all the roaring she heard in her ears was the wind, but it surely was the wind that finally succeeded in prying Alden's hat from her head. She made a grab for it, but the wind danced it easily out of her reach and she saw it only for a moment, flipping gaily over and over into the darkening gray, a bright spot of orange. It struck the snow, rolled, rose again, was gone. Now her hair flew around her head freely.

"It's all right, Stella," Bill said. "You can wear mine."

She gasped and looked around in the white. Her gloved hands had gone instinctively to her bosom, and she felt sharp fingernails scratch at her heart.

She saw nothing but shifting membranes of snow—and then, moving out of that evening's gray throat, the wind screaming through it like the voice of a devil in a snowy tunnel, came her husband. He was at first only moving colors in the snow: red, black, dark green, lighter green; then these colors resolved themselves into a flannel jacket with a flapping collar, flannel pants, and green boots. He was holding his hat out to her in a gesture that appeared almost absurdly courtly, and his face was Bill's face, unmarked by the cancer that had taken him (had that been all she was afraid of? that a wasted shadow of her husband would come to her, a scrawny concentration-camp figure with the skin pulled taut and shiny over the cheekbones and the eyes sunken deep in the sockets?) and she felt a surge of relief.

"Bill? Is that really you?"

"Course."

"Bill," she said again, and took a glad step toward him. Her legs betrayed her and she thought she would fall, fall right through him— he was, after all, a ghost—but he caught her in arms as strong and as competent as those that had carried her over the threshold of the house that she had shared only with Alden in these latter years. He supported her, and a moment later she felt the cap pulled firmly onto her head.

"Is it really you?" she asked again, looking up into his face, at the crow's-feet around his eyes, which hadn't sunk deep yet, at the spill of snow on the shoulders of his checked hunting jacket, at his lively brown hair.

"It's me," he said. "It's all of us."

He half-turned with her and she saw the others coming out of the snow that the wind drove across the Reach in the gathering darkness. A cry, half joy, half fear, came from her mouth as she saw Madeline Stoddard, Hattie's mother, in a blue dress that swung in the wind like a bell, and holding her hand was Hattie's dad, not a moldering skeleton somewhere on the bottom with the *Dancer*, but whole and young. And there, behind those two—

"Annabelle!" she cried. "Annabelle Frane, is it you?"

It *was* Annabelle; even in this snowy gloom Stella recognized the yellow dress Annabelle had worn to Stella's own wedding, and as she struggled toward her dead friend, holding Bill's arm, she thought that she could smell roses.

"*Annabelle!*"

"We're almost there now, dear," Annabelle said, taking her other arm. The yellow dress, which had been considered daring in its day (but, to Annabelle's credit and to everyone else's relief, not quite a scandal), left her shoulders bare, but Annabelle did not seem to feel the cold. Her hair, a soft, dark auburn, blew long in the wind. "Only a little farther."

She took Stella's other arm and they moved forward again. Other figures came out of the snowy night (for it *was* night now). Stella recognized many of them, but not all. Tommy Frane had joined Annabelle; Big George Havelock, who had died a dog's death in the woods, walked behind Bill; there was the fellow who had kept the lighthouse on the Head for most of twenty years and who used to come over to the island during the cribbage tournament Freddy Dinsmore held every February—Stella could almost but not quite remember his name. And there was Freddy himself! Walking off to one side of Freddy, by himself and looking bewildered, was Russell Bowie.

"Look, Stella," Bill said, and she saw black rising out of the gloom like the splintered prows of many ships. It was not ships, it was split and fissured rock. They had reached the Head. They had crossed the Reach.

She heard voices, but was not sure they actually spoke:

Take my hand, Stella—

(do you)

Take my hand, Bill—

(oh do you do you)

Annabelle . . . Freddy . . . Russell . . . John . . . Ettie . . . Frank . . . take my hand, take my hand . . . my hand . . .

(do you love)

"Will you take my hand, Stella?" a new voice asked.

She looked around and there was Bull Symes. He was smiling kindly at her and yet she felt a kind of terror in her at what was in his eyes and for a moment she drew away, clutching Bill's hand on her other side the tighter.

"Is it—"

"Time?" Bull asked. "Oh, ayuh, Stella, I guess so. But it don't hurt. At least, I never heard so. All that's before."

She burst into tears suddenly—all the tears she had never wept—and put her hand in Bull's hand. "Yes," she said, "yes, I will, yes I did, yes I do."

They stood in a circle in the storm, the dead of Goat Island, and the wind screamed around them, driving its packet of snow, and some kind of song burst from her. It went up into the wind and the wind carried it away. They all sang then, as children will sing in their high, sweet voices as a summer evening draws down to summer night. They sang, and Stella felt herself going to them and with them, finally across the Reach. There was a bit of pain, but not much; losing her maidenhead had been worse. They stood in a circle in the night. The snow blew around them and they sang. They sang, and—

—and Alden could not tell David and Lois, but in the summer after Stella died, when the children came out for their annual two weeks, he told Lona and Hal. He told them that during the great storms of winter the wind seems to sing with almost human voices, and that sometimes it seemed to him he could almost make out the words: "Praise God from whom all blessings flow / Praise Him, ye creatures here below . . ."

But he did not tell them (imagine slow, unimaginative Alden Flanders saying such things aloud, even to the children!) that sometimes he would hear that sound and feel cold even by the stove; that he would put his whittling aside, or the trap he had meant to mend, thinking that the wind sang in all the voices of those who were dead and gone . . . that they stood somewhere out on the Reach and sang as children do. He seemed to hear their voices and on these nights he sometimes slept and dreamed that he was singing the doxology, unseen and unheard, at his own funeral.

There are things that can never be told, and there are things, not exactly secret, that are not discussed. They had found Stella frozen to death on the mainland a day after the storm had blown itself out. She was sitting on a natural chair of rock about one hundred yards south of the Raccoon Head town limits, frozen just as neat as you please. The doctor who owned the Corvette said that he was frankly amazed. It would have been a walk of over four miles, and the autopsy required by law in the case of an unattended, unusual death had shown an advanced cancerous condition—in truth, the old woman had been riddled with it. Was Alden to tell David and Lois that the cap on her head had not been his? Larry McKeen had recognized that cap. So had John Bensohn. He had seen it in their eyes, and he supposed they had seen it in his. He had not lived long enough to forget his dead father's cap, the look of its bill or the places where the visor had been broken.

"These are things made for thinking on slowly," he would have told the children if he had known how. "Things to be thought on at length, while the hands do their work and the coffee sits in a solid china mug nearby. They are questions of Reach, maybe: do the dead sing? And do they love the living?"

On the nights after Lona and Hal had gone back with their parents to the mainland in Al Curry's boat, the children standing astern and waving good-bye, Alden considered that question, and others, and the matter of his father's cap.

Do the dead sing? Do they love?

On those long nights alone, with his mother Stella Flanders at long last in her grave, it often seemed to Alden that they did both.

Note from the Author:

Tabby's youngest brother, Tommy, used to be in the Coast Guard. He was stationed downeast, in the Jonesport-Beals area of the long and knotty Maine coast, where the Guard's main chores are changing the batteries in the big buoys and saving idiot drug smugglers who get lost in the fog or run on the rocks.

There are lots of islands out there, and lots of tightly knit island communities. He told me of a real-life counterpart of Stella Flanders, who lived and died on her island. Was it Pig Island? Cow Island? I can't remember. *Some* animal, anyway.

I could hardly believe it. "She didn't ever *want* to come across to the mainland?" I asked.

"No, she said she didn't want to cross the Reach until she died," Tommy said.

The term Reach was unfamiliar to me, and Tommy explained it.

He also told the lobstermen's joke about how it's a mighty long Reach between Jonesport and London, and I put it in the story. It was originally published in *Yankee* as "Do the Dead Sing?", a nice enough title, but after some thought I have gone back to the original title.

—Stephen King
Bangor, Maine

Jim Nichols

Slow Monkeys

This skinny kid's sitting across from me when Bartlett shuffles into the room, looking rough: eyes bloodshot, hair all sticking up and sneaker laces trailing along behind. Gray sweaty whiskers. The kid stares, then looks away.

"Where you been?" I ask.

Bartlett's barely got enough energy to shrug.

It's not like I can't guess, though.

The Salvation Army man comes into the room then, plops his Bible down on the end of the table, holds it open with his palms. His head almost touches the drop-ceiling and he's skinny as a flagpole. He wears these black vests. I call him Ichabod Crane to myself because he reminds me of a drawing I saw in a book when I was a kid. Long neck; big Adam's apple.

"Gentlemen," the Salvation Army man says.

We bow our heads. I feel my throat bunch up under my chin and, like always when I notice I'm fat, I feel separated from the rest of them. Everybody else these days is skinny except Elmore, who isn't exactly fat and who isn't around today anyway. Of course, even if there was another blimp around, I wouldn't hang with him and get laughed at, like those two fatties on the mini-bikes you see posters of.

No sir.

"If the clouds be full of rain," the S.A. man says, "they empty themselves upon the earth. And if the tree falleth toward the south, or toward the north, in the place where the tree falleth, there it shall be." He clears his throat and flips through the pages. "Let us pray," he says, and starts in. We don't join him, but when he stops we say, "Amen."

"Enjoy your meal, gentlemen."

The S.A. man takes off and we go up to the window and get a white-bread sandwich, a plastic cup of soup, a carton of milk from the old woman in the kitchen. We go back to the table and the kid opens the sandwich and looks inside.

"I wouldn't," I say.

The kid closes the sandwich fast. We all start eating. I ask Bartlett again where he's been and he answers this time; he says, "The usual." The food's helping him out. We take our dishes back and slide them through the window and the old woman who works for Ichabod puts them in the washer. The washer grinds and splashes. We sit down again until the S.A. man comes back to lead us along the hall to the Evening Room. When we get there the kid hesitates at the door.

"I don't know about this," he says.

The S.A. man says, "I'm afraid we don't open our front door until morning."

"You mean I'm stuck?"

"It seems to work best," old Ichabod Crane says.

The kid comes into the room, looks around at the double row of cots, Christ pictures on the walls, the long scratched-up table with folding chairs around it.

Bartlett and I go to the table and sit. I watch the kid but he doesn't know it because when I squint my eyes sort of disappear and you can't tell where I'm looking. I see the kid decide to join us. He's early twenties, northern-sounding, scrawny. I don't know what he's doing at Sal's, but we ain't had much chance to talk: he came in just before Bartlett, kind of shy, looking around.

Bartlett points at my pocket. I fish a cigarette out and hand it over. We aren't supposed to smoke in here but Ichabod has given up trying to stop us and has put a tin ashtray on the table so we won't burn the place down. We light up and Bartlett starts rolling the tip against the ashtray. When it's a perfect little red cone, he takes a couple drags.

Then he rolls it again. He opens his mouth and clears his throat, real shallow so he won't start coughing.

"So you had to go back," I say.

He rolls his big eyes over toward the kid, then back toward me. He's got a few hundred more wrinkles than when I saw him last.

"More treatment?"

"I'm scheduled," Bartlett says.

He's got the lung cancer, see: we might lose him.

I can see the kid thinking and after a little while he squares himself up and grins at us and holds out his hand. He says he's from Maine and his name is Barry. He has jet-black hair and is trying to grow a mustache. He can't be more than eighteen or nineteen. He looks us in the eye when he shakes our hands. Bartlett sits up a little straighter. "Now, are you on the road, Barry?" he says.

Barry likes the sound of that. "I guess you could say."

"And what precipitated . . . ?"

Bartlett's getting high-falutin', so I know he's feeling better. Maybe he isn't as sick as I thought. Maybe he just needs a drink, I'm thinking, and I'm wondering how long it'll take before he tells the kid his story.

"Oh, I got fed up," the kid says. He goes on to tell us how he got tired of living at home, milking cows and shoveling shit, and he and his old man had a beef about putting on the storm windows and he just lit out and ended up here. He always wanted to be a writer, he says, and he figured he might as well bum around and find something to write about.

Bartlett's ears prick up at this. "And how are you liking it?" he says.

"It's different," the kid says.

I laugh and Bartlett rumbles a cough around in his chest. Then the S.A. man comes into the room and tells us we have five minutes. "Good night, gentlemen," he says, and pulls the door shut.

We move to the cots. The kid takes out a little notebook and a stub of a pencil. I laugh, he grins over at me and keeps writing. I lie down carefully on the cot so it won't break under me. I turn on my side so nothing will back up into my throat while I sleep. It's happened a few times. It's scary as hell to wake up like that.

Pretty soon the lights blink out. Then Bartlett starts wheezing. All the stuff in his lungs settles when he lies down. He doesn't want to really start coughing so he lets these wheezes stretch out and not quite finish. They get longer and longer until he finally starts coughing anyway, and then I ease myself out of my cot and go over to his and pound him on the back until the gunk shifts around to where he can stop.

Then after a while he dozes off.

It's still dark when the S.A. man opens the door. "Rise and shine, gentlemen," he says. He stands there in his black pants and vest, his white shirt, with his fingertips together. "One note before breakfast," he says. "I've been advised that the Willis Orchard truck will be stopping by for any of you who might wish to pick today." He clops off down the hall.

We get scrambled eggs, grits, and toast for breakfast. The kid takes one taste of his grits and spits it out.

"Make a note of that," I say.

The kid laughs.

We finish eating and drink a couple watery cups of coffee and talk about picking. Bartlett says he's broke and I say I am, too.

"That makes three of us," the kid says.

When we get outside the truck's waiting. I help Bartlett into the flatbed and climb up after him, chafing my gut on the metal edge, wondering how I stay fat without any money. The driver is talking to Ichabod by the door. He laughs, pushes his Stetson higher. The S.A. man laughs like a schoolgirl, hand on his mouth. They chew the fat until the sun has pushed up over the neighborhood and steam is coming off the street. Then the driver swings up into his truck and starts the engine.

We sit there looking down at the kid.

"It's worth a few dollars," Bartlett says, and I know he wants to tell his story. The kid says, "What the hell," throws his pack up and climbs in just as the truck starts moving.

We ride out into the country. At first it's scrub and hardpan, but then the groves appear and there are rows of orange trees on both sides of the road, people in the rows, hampers and crates and ladders. There are sprinklers fanning water about, rainbows in the air. We turn down a wide aisle and park in a clearing and the driver is out and walking before the engine has stopped dieseling. He leads us over to a man with his foot up on a crate. Then he walks off, adjusting his hat.

We stand in front of this sunburned guy.

"You boys feel like working?" he says.

"Yes sir," Bartlett says.

"Had anything to drink?"

"We been in the mission all night."

"All right," the man says. The driver comes back and the overseer tells him to find us a place to work. The driver nods to him, starts walking. We follow him down the big aisle and into a side row and up to a tree. "Start here," he says. "Move off that way. When you fill up the bin, come get me and I'll find you another section. Don't eat the oranges on the trees. You can eat the ones on the ground if you want."

He turns around and walks off.

We start in. Bartlett and the kid do the climbing: I'm way too heavy for these little trees. Bartlett looks weightless on the ladder, like he could take another step from the top and just keep going up. They throw the oranges down onto the spongy grass and I crate them and take the crates to the hamper and throw them in. We fill one bin and the kid trots off to find the driver. They come back and we get going on another patch. All around us are these families picking. They are like something out of *The Jungle Book*, like monkeys moving through the forest, half seen, chattering. We are no different, only slower.

We're the slow monkeys.

When the sun gets high overhead, the driver comes back and tells us to take a break. We sit down in the shade and Bartlett starts coughing. I whack his back for him until he stops. I hand him an orange from the hamper and he digs a thumb in and starts peeling and the rind-smell cuts through the air. Bartlett eats it like an apple and gets his chin all shiny. He looks over at the kid, who's lying down with his knees up.

I roll onto my side. "You gonna tell him, Bart?"

Bartlett shrugs. But I know he wants to.

The kid turns his head. "Tell me what?"

"About Old Bart's TV show," I say.

Bartlett finishes off the orange, wipes his hands on his pants and his chin on his sleeve. He coughs a little, trying out his lungs, and they seem to be holding up for the moment.

"You had a TV show?" the kid says.

"Tell him," I say, because I know he's dying to.

"He doesn't want to hear all that."

"Oh yes I do," the kid says.

Bartlett sighs and pretends to give in. "It was a children's show," he says. "You know, they come on as guests and get milk and cookies? Every little city has one." He says all this carefully, as if he's only allowed a certain amount of breath for each word.

"We had one called Captain Lloyd's," the kid says.

"Exactly," Bartlett says. "I was called, ah, Stumpy Sparrow." He laughs a little, like he wishes he'd been called Captain Lloyd instead. "I wore a costume, did tricks for the kids," he says. "The studio put three big Ss over my door. I would pick out children from the mail they sent in." He sighs: a soft, clicky sound. "And they would send me around to grocery store openings and such. Once they hired a helicopter. It was hot in my costume in the helicopter. We went to an amusement park that had water slides and all that and I got my feathers wet."

He goes quiet, then, remembering.

"Tell him what happened." I give the kid a look so he'll pay attention. But I needn't have.

Bartlett sighs, nods. "On my show, *The Stumpy Sparrow Show*, there was a pigeon."

"A girl," I say.

The kid looks at me.

"A girl," Bartlett says, "dressed as a pigeon."

"Little girl or a big girl?" the kid says.

"A woman," Bartlett says.

"And there was a cat." I know my lines.

"A man," Bartlett says.

"Dressed like a cat?" the kid chimes in.

"Now you got it," I say.

Bartlett sits there with his little legs out in front of him and his hands in his lap. There's grime in the creases in his face and his eyes bug out and his hair is all over the place. He doesn't look like any TV star, and I see the kid wondering. But he's thinking he's stumbled onto something pretty interesting, too. He's not taking notes, to be polite, but he's reminding himself to later on. He keeps touching the shirt pocket that has the notebook.

"So what happened?" the kid says.

Bartlett hangs his head.

"The pigeon and the cat," I say, "they ran off together."

Bartlett's head hangs lower.

"He was in love with the pigeon," I say, "and she ran off with the fucking cat."

After a moment the kid says, "I'm sorry."

Bartlett rolls his eyes up toward the sky.

"That was the end of it," I say.

Bartlett nods. "I hadn't the will to go on."

"Or the cast," I say.

Bartlett smiles at the kid. When he smiles you can see that maybe he was once a pretty good-looking little guy. Then he gets a surprised look on his face and starts coughing. A piece of orange flies out of him. He bends over and is hacking raggedly and the guy who's in charge of us picks that moment to come walking up through the trees.

"He okay, or what?" he says.

Bartlett clenches his teeth.

"If he's sick, get him out of here."

Bartlett starts in again, these deep barks that shake him. He covers his mouth, holds the other hand up. The guy watches him, then says, "Get him out of here." He walks over to look into the bin, then checks a little notebook like the kid's. "Go tell Willie to give you nine dollars," he says. "I'll have one of the boys drive you back." He looks at the kid. "You can work with somebody else," he says. "You're a pretty good climber."

The kid says, "Thanks anyway."

The guy shrugs, walks off.

They drive us back to town and we pool our money for a bucket of Church's Fried Chicken and a jug of wine. Bartlett's cough hasn't come back and he's doing all right, and I'm wondering whether he started himself coughing to get out of working the rest of the day. You can't tell sometimes with him.

But I don't care.

We cross under Kennedy and walk a couple of blocks to a vacant lot and sit on a telephone pole that's fallen down behind some bushes. We eat the chicken, pass the wine around till it's gone. Then we stretch out in the hot shade. I'm feeling pretty good. Bartlett is, too. I can tell by the way he's smiling. I shut my eyes and snooze, and his voice buzzes as he tells the kid all about *The Stumpy Sparrow Show*. How one of the kids ate too many cookies and puked up chocolate chips in his lap. How he caught the pigeon and the cat backstage, sticking their tongues through each other's masks. He fired the cat and the pigeon quit and they ran off together and the next day Bartlett showed up drunk and dropped one of the kids off his lap and the station fired him. He makes it funny and the kid laughs and laughs. I take it he's feeling no pain. Then the kid tells Bartlett about the farm. He and his old man were putting up the storm windows and the kid dropped one and all the glass fell out and broke. His old man gave him a ration of shit, and the kid waited until the middle of the night and lifted fifty bucks out of his father's desk and started thumbing south so he could become a writer.

That night there are a couple of other people at Sal's. Old Elmore is one of them. After we go into the Evening Room he comes up and joins us three at the table. I see him checking out the kid and then he laughs a little and says, "Jim, your mama know you been hanging out with these birds?"

"Jim?" the kid says.

Elmore laughs. "Ah call everybody Jim." He reaches across the table and shakes the kid's hand. "Where you from, boy?"

"Maine."

"Whoooo!" Elmore says. "How you liking Florida?"

"It's warm," the kid says. He looks pale and his eyes are bloodshot. I'm guessing he's never drank Old Duke before and slept it off in the sun.

"He say it's warm," Elmore giggles.

Bartlett smiles at him.

"Warmer than Maine," the kid says.

"I expect it is," Elmore says. "Benjamin, what we smoking, honey?"

I hand him a cigarette and Elmore takes Bartlett's and holds the red cone against his and lights it that way. He blows smoke, looks at the kid. "They tell you all about it, I suppose?"

"About what?"

"Don't be like that, honey," Elmore says. "About the damn bird show. I know they told you. They tell everybody else." He looks away, laughs inside his chest so that it makes his head bob. With his dark face and white whiskers he looks like Uncle Remus. We're quite a gang: Uncle Remus, Stumpy Sparrow and Fat Benjamin. And this skinny little writer kid, who's looking kind of green around the gills.

"Yeah, they told me," the kid says.

"Well, you believe these old birds?"

Bartlett and I look at each other.

"Yeah," the kid says.

"Shit!" Elmore says. "I guess I do too, then, honey!"

When I wake Bartlett is coughing like he won't ever stop. He's curled up on the cot, barking, stopping only long enough to draw breath. I go over and put his head in my lap, and start in thumping his back. But it doesn't work. He keeps on barking until I yell at him to stop. That doesn't help either. Ichabod hears the commotion after a while and opens the door.

"Call the ambulance!" I say.

He runs off and in ten minutes the door bangs open and a couple

EMTs come running in and take Bartlett away from me. He's still coughing. He takes a breath and coughs, takes a breath and coughs. They give him a shot, and pretty quick he quiets down, and then after a little while he seems to fall asleep. I get his sack and give it to the EMTs and they bring a stretcher in and take Bartlett away.

After breakfast I go outside.

It's already hot. My clothes are feeling damp and dingy. My heart's thumping in my chest. Old Elmore's talking to the kid at the curb. I go up and sit down with them with our feet in the street. Elmore twists his head around and says to me, "Don't you worry, he be all right."

I shake my head, look down at my fat fingers.

"Sure he will. That's a tough old bird. You wait and see. Hey Jim?" he says, leaning on the kid.

"Sure," the kid says. "He'll be fine."

"I don't think so," I say.

"What you want to talk like that for?" Elmore says. "That ain't gonna do nobody no good."

Cars blow by, washing us with hot air. Elmore stares at me, and when I don't say anything he nods. Then he grins at Barry. "What's on the agenda today, honey?"

"I don't know," the kid says. "Is the truck supposed to come?"

"He say it is." Elmore tips his head back toward the building.

"Maybe I'll go pick."

"Make you some money."

"Uh-huh."

"Get you back to Massachusetts."

"Maine," the kid says.

Elmore squints at him, grinning.

We pick for a week because the kid wants to save up enough for a bus back north. Meanwhile he wants to know all about Bartlett and his show, and I tell him everything I can remember, how Bartlett trailed the two of them across Florida, how he lost them here, in Tampa, and never left because he didn't have any idea which way to go. The kid writes it all down in his little notebook. Every night we stay at Sal's. Elmore's around some of the time, when he isn't laying up somewhere else. He's got some friends across town that he stays with on occasion.

Bartlett doesn't show, and we don't discuss where he might be. Then on the last night before the kid's bus, it's just me and the kid in the Evening Room when Ichabod comes in with a newspaper and lays it open on the table.

"I thought you might be interested," he says.

We look at it. There's a picture of Bartlett taken when he was maybe thirty; he's not looking too bad. In fact, he looks pretty good, but you can tell it's Bartlett all right. We read the obituary. It's mostly about what a bad end this former TV personality came to.

The kid says, "So he was telling the truth."

"Evidently," the S.A. man says.

We look at the newspaper for a while longer. Then the S.A. man folds it back up and tucks it under his arm. He walks to the door and turns. "Gentlemen," he says, "you have a short time." And then he leaves and shuts the door. The kid goes to his cot, sits down and opens his notebook. He's writing like crazy. Then he lies down with his hands linked behind his head and now he looks impatient, like he can't wait to go to sleep so he can wake up and be on his way.

I sit at the table and wait for the lights to go out, and I miss Bartlett waiting there beside me, don't you think I don't. I look down at my big fat legs and try to come up with something of mine to tell this kid, for him to write down. Just so I can think about something else. I think way back in time. Back to when I was his age and before. I could tell him about my mother buying me books. They came in the mail every month in a little cardboard box. I wasn't so fat back then. I used to lie down in my bed and read *Twice-Told Tales* and *The Wind in the Willows* and *Huckleberry Finn* and the other books she bought me, and I could lie down then without worrying about it.

In the morning I walk to the Greyhound station with the kid. I'm huffing and puffing by the time we get there. When they call his bus over the PA he sticks out his hand and says, "I won't forget you guys."

I shake his hand. "It was nice to meet you."

The kid grins and walks through the doorway. At the bus he looks back at me. Then he hops up the steps. I wait until the bus pulls out and then head back to Sal's. It's hot, hot, hot walking through town. My clothes get all sticky and I shamble along pretty slow. I picture the kid in the air-conditioned bus, catching forty winks, heading back home. I wonder what he'll tell his old man.

I pass the bookstore on the corner of Elvira Street and look in the display window, and seeing all the books makes me wonder about the kid turning out to be a real writer, and then I wonder if he'll ever write all about his visit to Tampa and the Salvation Army. About Ichabod and Bartlett and Elmore and me. Picking oranges. Drinking cheap wine. I imagine us existing in a book that he wrote, and that book sitting in a display window somewhere. I imagine Bartlett coming back to life in his book.

I sit on a bench at the bus stop and look down the street at Sal's. It's a comforting idea and I want to sit here a bit and enjoy it. I stay put while a couple of buses stop, drive off. A lady with a shopping bag comes up to wait for the next bus, and when she stands away instead of joining me on the bench, I understand and I'm not insulted. She doesn't know me from Adam. She just sees this big fat guy sitting there.

A bus pulls up, its brakes hiss and the door swings open. The lady gets on board and the bus pulls away into the traffic. I sit there thinking some more on my new idea. I picture it so clear I can see the cover of the kid's book. There's rows of orange groves on the cover. There's sprinklers in the trees and rainbows in the spray. I picture a lady like the one with the shopping bag bringing our book home to her kid. Him lying in bed reading about me and Stumpy Sparrow and the Salvation Army and the orchards. My heart flutters with the idea of it all. This little kid's got a nice room and a nice bed with a thick pillow and a quilt. He lives up in Maine and it's snowing outside and he likes lying in bed reading. He's got a nice mother and a nice father. He's comfortable and he's not fat, and when he lies down on his back nothing comes up in his throat.

About the Contributors

Carolyn Chute, who started as a writer of short fiction, has published her stories in several literary journals, among them *Agni*, *Grand Street*, and *Ploughshares*. Her novels include the recent *The School on Heart's Content Road*, as well as *Merry Men* and *The Beans of Egypt, Maine*. She lives in North Parsonsfield.

Ellen Cooney lives in Phippsburg and is the author of five novels, one of which, *Gun Ball Hill*, is set in midcoast Maine at the time of the American Revolution. Her short stories have been published in *Glimmer Train*, *The New England Review*, *The New Yorker*, and many other venues. Her novel, *A Private Hotel for Gentle Ladies*, appeared in 2005.

Elaine Ford has published over thirty short stories in *The Colorado Review*, *Confrontation*, *The North American Review*, and other literary journals. Her five novels include *Monkey Bay* and *Life Designs*. For her fiction she has been awarded two grants from the National Endowment for the Arts and a Guggenheim Fellowship. She resides in Harpswell.

Richard Ford, a resident of East Boothbay, has received an Award in Literature from the American Academy and Institute of Arts and Letters, and the Pulitzer Prize in fiction for *Independence Day*. Among his other novels are *The Sportswriter*, *The Ultimate Good Luck*, and *Wildlife*. His short story collections include *A Multitude of Sins* and *Rock Springs*.

Susan Kenney, from Waterville, has published two novels, *In Another Country* and *Sailing*, and three mysteries. Her story "Facing Front" received first place in the 1982 *Prize Stories: The O. Henry Awards*, and *In Another Country* won the Quality Paperback Book Club New Voices Award. Her work has been widely published and anthologized.

Lily King is the author of the new novel *The English Teacher* and *The Pleasing Hour*, a *New York Times* Notable Book that won both the Barnes & Noble Discovery Prize and a Whiting Award, and was a finalist for the PEN/Hemingway Award. Her stories have been published in *Glimmer Train*, *Ploughshares*, and many other periodicals. Her home is in Yarmouth.

Stephen King is the most popular writer in America and one of its most prolific authors, having published dozens of novels, short stories, screenplays, and works of nonfiction, including *On Writing*, a volume about the writer's craft. In 2003, he was awarded the National Book Foundation's Medal for Lifetime Achievement. He lives in Bangor.

Jim Nichols, a resident of Warren, has received the Willamette Award for Fiction, a River City Writing Award, and a Maine Arts Commission Fellowship. His short stories have appeared in *Esquire*, *Paris Transcontinental*, and *American Fiction*, and several other venues. His collection of short fiction, *Slow Monkeys and Other Stories*, appeared in 2002.

Cathie Pelletier has written screenplays, a volume of poetry, and eight novels, most of them, like *The Funeral Makers*, *The Weight of Winter*, *Beaming Sonny Home*, and her current title, *Running the Bulls*, inspired by northern Maine, where she has spent most of her life. As K.C. McKinnon, she has published two additional novels. She now lives in Tennessee.

Lewis Robinson is the author of the newly published collection *Officer Friendly and Other Stories*, which won the PEN/Oakland-Josephine Miles Award. A recent graduate of the Writers Workshop at the University of Iowa, he was awarded a Schaeffer Fellowship in 2002, and in 2003 received a Whiting Writers Award. His home is in Portland.

Bill Roorbach, a resident of Farmington, has received an NEA fellowship, an O. Henry Award, and the Flannery O'Connor Award for his collection of stories, *Big Bend*. He has published a novel, *The Smallest Color*, and two volumes of nonfiction, most recently *Temple Stream*. His work has appeared in *The Atlantic*, *Harper's*, and many other periodicals.

Richard Russo, from Camden, has produced several volumes of fiction, among them *The Risk Pool*, *Straight Man*, *Nobody's Fool*, and *Empire Falls*, an account of a declining mill town in Maine, for which he won the Pulitzer Prize. He has also written for the movies and television, and in 2002 published a collection of short fiction, *The Whore's Child*.

Debra Spark resides in North Yarmouth and is the author of the novels *Coconuts for the Saint* and *The Ghost of Bridgetown*, and the editor of the anthology *Twenty Under Thirty*. A fourth book, *Curious Attractions: Essays in Writing*, was released in 2005. Her short fiction and articles have appeared in *Esquire*, *Ms.*, and *The New York Times*, among other venues.

Monica Wood, from Portland, has published her stories in numerous magazines and anthologies; moreover, they have been presented on Public Radio International and awarded the Pushcart Prize. She has authored three novels, including *Any Bitter Thing*; a book of linked stories, *Ernie's Ark*; and two volumes for writers, most recently *The Pocket Muse*.

Acknowledgments

I am indebted to my editor, Michael Steere, as ever a resourceful and generous guide.

I am grateful, too, to the Rockefeller Foundation for a Fellowship that sponsored the completion of this anthology at the Bellagio Center in Bellagio, Italy.

Finally, thanks to both authors and publishers for the following permissions:

Monica Wood: "Ernie's Ark," first published in *Glimmer Train Stories*. Collected in *Ernie's Ark: Stories* by Monica Wood, copyright © 2002 by Monica Wood. Reprinted by permission of the author.

Cathie Pelletier: "The Music of Angels," previously unpublished. Printed by permission of the author.

Lily King: "Five Tuesdays in Winter," first published in *Ploughshares*. Reprinted by permission of the author.

Richard Ford: "Charity," from *A Multitude of Sins* by Richard Ford, copyright © 2002 by Richard Ford. Reprinted by permission of the author.

Richard Russo: "Monhegan Light," from *The Whore's Child* by Richard Russo, copyright © 2002 by Richard Russo. Reprinted by permission of Alfred A. Knopf, a division of Random House, Inc.

Ellen Cooney: "See the Girl," first published in the *Ontario Review*. Reprinted by permission of the author.

Susan Kenney: "The Death of the Dog and Other Rescues," originally published in *Epoch*. Reprinted by permission of the author.

Dan Habib

Wesley McNair is best known for his distinguished poetry and essays. He also edited and compiled *A Place Called Maine: 24 Writers on the Maine Experience,* and *The Maine Poets.* He was recently awarded his second Rockefeller Fellowship, and he has received grants from the Fulbright and Guggenheim foundations. He also garnered two National Endowment for the Arts fellowships, and he was named one of "America's finest living artists" as he was presented with a prestigious United States Artist Fellowship. A professor emeritus and writer in residence at the University of Maine at Farmington, he makes his home in Mercer, Maine.